IT'S SEPTEMBER 1939, and London is preparing for the Second World War. As blackout blinds are drawn and air-raid shelters hastily built, ten-year-old Shirley is woken early and told to pack her things. She doesn't know where she's going, or what will happen to her when she gets there. All she's told is that she's going on 'a little holiday'.

Shirley is evacuated to a quiet village that feels worlds away from home, along with two boys from the East End: wary, troubled Kevin and confident, mischievous Archie. Their experiences living in the strange, half-empty Red House, with mysterious and reclusive Mrs Waverley, will change their lives for ever.

Bestselling and beloved author Jacqueline Wilson turns to this period of history for the first time in a beautiful story of friendship, loss and bravery.

JACQUELINE WILSON wrote her first novel when she was nine years old, and she has been writing ever since. She is now one of Britain's bestselling and most beloved children's authors. She has written over 100 books and is the creator of characters such as Tracy Beaker and Hetty Feather. More than forty million copies of her books have been sold.

As well as winning many awards for her books, including the Children's Book of the Year, Jacqueline is a former Children's Laureate, and in 2008 she was appointed a Dame.

Jacqueline is also a great reader, and has amassed over twenty thousand books, along with her famous collection of silver rings.

Find out more about Jacqueline and her books at jacquelinewilson.co.uk

Jacqueline Wilson

Illustrated by Nick Sharratt

Wave Me Goodbye

DOUBLEDAY

DOUBLEDAY

UK | USA | Canada | Ireland | Australia
India | New Zealand | South Africa

Doubleday is part of the Penguin Random House group of companies
whose addresses can be found at global.penguinrandomhouse.com.

www.penguin.co.uk
www.puffin.co.uk
www.ladybird.co.uk

Penguin
Random House
UK

First published 2017

002

Text copyright © Jacqueline Wilson, 2017
Illustrations copyright © Nick Sharratt, 2017

The moral right of the author and illustrator has been asserted

Set in 11/16 pt New Century Schoolbook by Jouve (UK), Milton Keynes
Printed in Great Britain by Clay Ltd, St Ives plc

A CIP catalogue record for this book is available from the British Library

Hardback ISBN: 978–0–857–53515–3
International paperback ISBN: 978–0–857–53517–7

All correspondence to:
Doubleday
Penguin Random House Children's
80 Strand, London WC2R 0RL

For Joan and Barbara

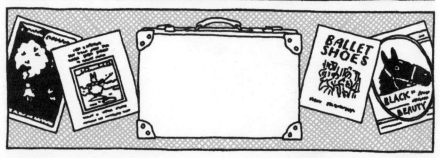

'**WOULD YOU LIKE TO** go on a little holiday?' asked Mum, the moment she'd shaken me awake.

I sat up in bed and stared at her.

'Don't wrinkle your nose like that!' she said. 'You look like a rabbit.'

'I like rabbits,' I said. I'd been begging her for a pet rabbit for months. I'd given up on the idea of a dog, because I was at school all day and Mum was planning to go back to work so there would be no one at home to look after it. I tried asking for a cat instead but Mum said they smelled. It was only Miss Jessop's ginger tom that ponged a bit, and that might not be his fault because Miss Jessop herself was a bit whiffy, so Mum was talking nonsense.

She was clearly talking nonsense now. A holiday? We never went on holidays. We'd been on a coach trip to Clacton once, and I'd paddled in the sea and had a cornet and a sixpenny ride on a donkey. I'd thought it was the best day ever, but the men in the coach drank a lot of bottled beer on the way home and had a rude sing-song. Dad sang too. I thought it was funny, but Mum said it was common and we never went on a coach trip again.

'Do you mean another coach trip, Mum?' I asked.

'No, you'll be going by train,' she said.

This was even more exciting. I'd never been on a train before. I loved standing under the railway bridge when they thundered overhead. You could scream all sorts of things and no one could hear a word you were saying.

'A train!'

'Yes, a train,' said Mum. 'We've to be at Victoria station to catch the ten o'clock so we'd better look sharp. What would you like for breakfast? Boiled egg or porridge? Or would you like both?'

I never had *both*. In fact, most days it was bread and dripping or bread and jam. Now I couldn't decide. Boiled eggs were good, especially with toast soldiers, but sometimes there was a weird little red thing in the yolk, which Mum said was a baby chick. I felt like a murderer eating a *baby*, especially when it hadn't even been born. Ever since, I'd eaten boiled eggs with my stomach clenched.

Porridge could be good too, but sometimes it was too sloppy and sometimes it was so stiff it had a slimy edge, and that turned my stomach too.

'Make your mind up, Shirley!' said Mum.

'I can't,' I said. 'Could I perhaps have bread with butter and sugar as a special treat instead?'

'There's no goodness in that,' Mum started. Then she sighed. 'But all right. You'd better have a glass of milk with it. I'll bring it up on a tray, shall I? I daresay you'd like breakfast in bed.' She went downstairs.

I fished Timmy Ted out from under the bedcovers and shook my head at him. 'Curiouser and curiouser,' I said, and made Timmy nod in agreement.

I was quoting from my Christmas present – *Alice's Adventures in Wonderland*. I'd read it three times in the last nine months, and I agreed with Alice that I only liked books with pictures and conversation. However, I didn't like all the riddles and the feeling that nothing made sense. It was especially odd when babies turned into pigs and royalty became playing cards.

Mum seemed different too. Why was she making such a fuss of me? And why, why, why were we going on holiday? Indeed, *how* were we going on holiday when we didn't have any money? It was the thing Mum and Dad rowed about most. And what about Dad? How could he come on holiday when he'd just gone away to be a soldier?

Mum came back with the wooden tray and my sugar sandwich and cup of milk carefully set out, along with a cup of tea and her pack of Craven A cigarettes and the matches.

I took a quick hungry mouthful of my sandwich while she was lighting up.

'Mum, what about Dad? Won't he feel sad if we're going on holiday while he's away being a soldier?' I asked.

'Don't talk with your mouth full,' said Mum, drawing deeply on her cigarette. 'There's no need to feel sorry for your dad. He couldn't wait to get away from us. Honestly, what does it look like, joining up before they've even started the bally war!'

'He's being brave,' I said, chewing. 'He wants to fight for Britain.'

'Your dad's not brave,' said Mum. 'He squeals every time he sees a spider. Him, fight? He couldn't fight his way out of a paper bag.'

The sandwich turned lumpy in my mouth but I couldn't swallow. I hated it when Mum talked about Dad like that. I suddenly missed him so much. I took a big gulp of milk and spluttered.

'Oh, Shirley, for goodness' sake! And look, you've spilled milk all over your sheets, you mucky pup. Here!' Mum put her hand under my chin and tipped up my face so she could have a good look at me. 'You're not crying, are you? Whatever for?'

'I miss Dad terribly,' I said.

'For heaven's sake, he's only been gone a couple of weeks!'

'Yes, but I miss him so. I'm scared someone might ambush him and shoot him.'

'You've seen too many cowboy films at the Saturday morning pictures! He's not fighting yet anyway, he's still at training camp. Now eat that sandwich quick, before I take it off you,' said Mum.

I ate. Mum watched me, her head on one side. Then she picked up a strand of my hair. 'Perhaps we'd better give your hair a good wash,' she said.

'But it's Friday,' I said, puzzled.

'I know, but I want to send you off clean as clean. I've put the immersion on, so you'd better have a bath and get your hair washed. You can use my Drene shampoo if you like.'

I suddenly felt alarmed. 'Mum, are you kidding me? I haven't got to go to no hospital for my tonsils, have I?'

I'd had my tonsils and adenoids out two years ago, and I'd been scrubbed from top to toe first. Hospital was really scary and my throat had hurt horribly, though they'd given me ice cream and jelly for dinner instead of meat and potatoes, which was an unexpected treat.

'I haven't got to go to *any* hospital,' said Mum. 'How many times do I have to tell you? I don't want you growing up talking common just because we live in this awful dump now. And of course you're not going to hospital to have your tonsils out. How can you, when they've already been taken out, you daft sausage?'

'You promise?' I said, still suspicious. 'You're acting all funny this morning.'

'Promise,' said Mum, but she suddenly sat on the edge of my bed and gave me a hug, almost tipping the tray over.

That seemed odder than ever, because Mum always said

she wasn't one for lovey-dovey stuff and hardly ever hugged. She hadn't even given Dad a hug when he went off to be a soldier, just a quick peck on the cheek.

I breathed in Mum's lovely smell of scent and powder. She rubbed her cheek on the top of my head and gave an odd little sniffle, but then pushed me away. 'Enough of that,' she said, as if I'd started it. 'Get into the bathroom spit-spot and start washing. Don't forget your neck now, and behind your ears.'

'*Spit-spot, spit-spot, spit-spot,*' I said, running to the bathroom. I sat on the toilet while the taps ran. Mary Poppins said *spit-spot*. I loved Mary Poppins. She could be a bit snappy like Mum, and she wasn't one for hugging, either, but she worked the most amazing magic. She knew some wonderful people too. I especially loved Maia, the youngest of the star sisters, who came down to Earth to do her Christmas shopping. I'd had her as an imaginary friend for a while, and sometimes she took my hand and flew me right up into the sky to meet Orion and the Great Bear and the Little Bear. Sometimes she walked to school with me and held my hand tight when Marilyn Henderson gave me a thump on the back and called me a la-di-da, toffee-nosed nitwit.

Maia still came visiting occasionally, but I didn't need her so much now because I was the fourth Fossil sister, and Pauline, Petrova and Posy looked out for me. *Ballet Shoes* was my absolutely favourite book.

I played a quick *Ballet Shoes* game now, muttering under my breath because Mum hated me playing imaginary games and said I was soft in the head. We discussed our auditions for Madame Fidolia's new production of *Sleeping Beauty*, and they all agreed I'd be picked for Princess Aurora, with Posy as a little Lilac Fairy. Pauline hoped she'd get to be the Prince, as there weren't any boys at our stage school. Petrova wanted to be the hundred-year-old bramble at the end, so all she had to do was sway in the breeze and try to scratch the Prince with prickly fingers. We all laughed at her.

'What are you giggling about?' Mum called. 'I can't hear any splashing. Get on with that bath!'

'Yes, Mum,' I said, and did as I was told.

It was a treat washing my hair with Drene when I usually just rubbed it with Lifebuoy soap. I had to keep dunking my head in the bath to get it squeaky clean. I pretended that each dunk was making my hair grow longer. It sprang out of my scalp inch by inch, right down to my shoulders. I could almost feel it swishing this way and that when I turned my head.

When I wiped the steam off the bathroom mirror and saw that my hair still only came down to the tip of my ears I felt disappointed. I hunched my shoulders up but I couldn't make it look any longer. While it was wet it *did* look a bit curly, but by the time I'd rubbed it with the towel it was poker-straight again.

'Clean vest and clean knickers and clean white socks,' Mum commanded when I went back to my bedroom. 'And your pleated skirt and your Fair Isle jumper.'

I quite liked my pleated skirt with its sewn-on white

bodice. I sometimes held out the pleats and pretended it was a ballet dress. I kept Dad's penknife in the pocket. I'd tried to give it back to him when he went to join the army, but he said I could keep it as a lucky mascot. But the Fair Isle jumper was another matter.

'It's too hot, Mum. And it itches. It's not winter yet,' I said. 'Can't I wear a dress?'

'Not for travelling. But I'll pack your smocked dress.'

My smocked dress was my best frock – tiny red and white checks with red gathers across the chest and a proper sash at the back. It was to wear to parties with my red patent shoes, though I didn't get asked to parties at my new school. I loved my red shoes, though they rubbed under the strap and were getting very small for me now; you could see the outline of my toes under the patent leather.

'Can I wear my red shoes, Mum?'

'Well, you're meant to wear stout shoes. Lord knows what they mean by that. I suppose they mean brown lace-ups, but I'm not putting any daughter of mine in clodhoppers – they're for boys. You haven't *got* any stout shoes apart from your Wellingtons, and you'd look a right banana in those, seeing as it's sunny. So yes, you can wear your red shoes. Now stand still while I do your parting and tie your hair ribbon,' said Mum.

I stood still, stretching out my toes before I had to cram them into their red cages.

'You're doing that nose-wiggling again. Stop it,' hissed Mum, a hairgrip in her mouth, ready to stab my damp hair into place.

8

I was thinking over what she'd just said. 'They?' I asked.

'What?' said Mum, tying my hair ribbon on one side and pulling it out carefully so the ends were even.

'Who are they?' I repeated. 'You said that *they* said I should wear stout shoes.'

'Oh, Shirley, stop your silly questions and hurry up! Did you clean your teeth? I thought not. Now, go and give them a good scrubbing, and then I want you to get your toothbrush and the toothpaste and your flannel – squeeze it out properly – and we'll put them in my sponge bag.'

'Shall I get your toothbrush and flannel too, Mum?'

'You leave me to organize myself,' she said. 'Now, let's get you packed.' She reached up to the top of my wardrobe and brought down my cardboard suitcase. She blew the dust off and looked at it critically. 'It's falling to bits! And what have you got inside?'

She opened it up and stared at my colouring pencils and notebooks and my conker doll's-house furniture and my old toy tea set and my poor plastic Jenny Wren dolly who had lost her eyes inside her head and now gave me the creeps.

'For heaven's sake!' Mum exclaimed. 'What's all this junk? And I thought you'd said your teacher had confiscated your dolly when you took her to school . . . What's she doing here? And what have you done to her eyes? That doll cost seven and six, miss!'

'I'm sorry, Mum. She had an accident and I was scared to

tell you,' I said. 'Her eyes fell in and now they rattle around inside her and won't come out again. It wasn't my fault – they just did it, honest.'

'Honest*ly*. And you're making it worse, lying like that. *You* did it, didn't you?'

Of course I'd done it, though I didn't mean to. I was playing with Jenny Wren, even though I knew I was too old for such games. After all, I'd turned ten this summer. Jenny Wren was more of an ornament than a doll, but that meant she was pointless. I'd been taken to Bertram Mills Circus at Olympia for a special Christmas treat, so I turned Jenny Wren into a tightrope walker, tying my dressing-gown cord between my wardrobe handle and a knob on my chest of drawers. She was balancing so splendidly in her little knitted socks that I let go for half a second.

She fell on her head and there was an awful *click*, and then she didn't have eyes any more, just awful dark blanks, and I had to shut her up in the suitcase quick. Quick*ly*.

'Well, it's your loss, because you're allowed to take one toy, and that doll was your best toy but you can't take her like that – she looks shocking,' said Mum, tipping everything out of the suitcase helter-skelter onto the floor.

'Timmy Ted's my best toy,' I said.

'But he looks awful too,' said Mum, holding him up by one paw and sniffing disdainfully. She had put him in the wash because he was getting so grubby and he'd never been the same since. He'd gone all droopy and his snout was lopsided, but I still loved him, unlike poor Jenny.

Luckily Mum had dropped him and started fussing about the state of the suitcase instead. 'Look at that handle! That's not going to last, is it? The stitches are already unravelling at one end. And it looks so shoddy. Oh dear Lord, it'll come to pieces before you get there,' she said.

'Get where?'

'The country,' said Mum, abandoning my suitcase and going into her bedroom.

'Where in the country?' I called. I was surprised. Mum had never been keen on the country. She always said there was nothing there but a load of fields and trees, so what was the point.

'Oh, do give over, Shirley,' said Mum. 'Clear up all that mess on the floor and stow it back in that old suitcase. You'll have to use this one.' She brandished the big, glossy brown samples suitcase.

'But that's Dad's!' I said, shocked.

Dad was a commercial traveller, a brush salesman. 'Any sort of brush, madam – nailbrush, toothbrush, hairbrush, clothes brush – every size and shape of high-quality brushes.' That was his patter. He sometimes pretended that I was one of his customers. Then he'd flip the lid open, and there were all the brushes lined up in neat rows and I'd take my pick.

'He's not needing it now, is he? He's in the army,' said Mum. .

'But it's not even *his* suitcase. It belongs to the Fine Bristle Company,' I said, pointing to the name inside the case.

'Yes, well, they won't be bothering about that now, not when war's going to be declared any minute. Help me unslot all these bally brushes,' said Mum, trying to wiggle each one out from under the tight bands keeping it in place.

'You're not meant to take out the brushes,' I said. 'Dad will get cross.'

'Dad's not here, is he? And he took the only decent suitcase with him, so we'll have to use this and he can jolly well lump it.'

It was very odd seeing Mum putting my washing things, clean nightie, another set of underwear and socks, my smocked dress, my hairbrush, a pack of three hairgrips and a spare ribbon into Dad's sample case.

'Now, this toy . . . Why don't you take that nice jigsaw puzzle of the map of the world? It'll keep you busy for ages and it's educational,' said Mum.

'I don't really like jigsaw puzzles. And you can't cuddle them,' I pointed out. '*Please* let me take Timmy Ted.'

'Oh, all right then,' said Mum, sighing. 'Put him in.'

I tried to make a little bed for him in amongst my clothes so he wouldn't be bumped around inside the suitcase.

'I just spent ages smoothing out that dress and now you're getting it all crumpled,' said Mum, elbowing me out of the way. 'Right. Nearly done. You can take one book too.'

'*One?*' I said.

'Yes, well, I know that's a bit limited, the way you rush through books. You'll have read it all on the train journey.

Perhaps you can slip in two. Choose. Quickly now.'

I knelt on my bed and looked at the row of books on my new shelf. It wasn't straight and the edges were rough and gave you splinters if you weren't careful. Dad wasn't very good at household jobs. I looked at all the books standing in neat alphabetical order. I'd decided I was going to be a librarian when I grew up and was practising. *Alice's Adventures in Wonderland*, *Ballet Shoes*, *Black Beauty*, *A Little Princess*, *Little Women*, *Mary Poppins*, *Peter and Wendy* and *The Squirrel, the Hare and the Little Grey Rabbit*. I also had *Orlando the Marmalade Cat*, but it was too big to fit on the shelf, so I'd laid it across the other books, with a little plaster cat made with my modelling kit on top.

I was so pleased with my book arrangement that I often sat up in bed and looked at it for sheer enjoyment. But now my eyes scanned each title anxiously. I loved them all, even *Alice*. How could I possibly choose?

'I want to take them all,' I said. 'Shame you've got to squash all your clothes into the case too, Mum, otherwise there might be room.'

Mum didn't say anything.

I turned round. I saw her face.

'Mum?'

'Hurry up now.'

'Mum, you *are* coming too, aren't you?' I asked. My voice was suddenly squeaky.

'Well, no, I'm not coming,' she said.

'But you said . . .' I went over everything in my head, trying to remember exactly what she *had* said. 'So is Dad taking me then?'

'Shirley, have you gone simple? Your dad's in the army, for pity's sake.'

'Yes, but I can't go on holiday on my own!'

'You're not going to be on your own. You're going to go with lots and lots of other children,' said Mum.

'Which other children?' I asked anxiously.

'All your school friends.'

I'd started going to Paradise Road Juniors three months ago. My class still called me the New Girl. I didn't seem to *have* any special friends, but I had a Deadly Enemy. Marilyn Henderson made my life a misery.

'I don't want to go on holiday with my school!' I said firmly.

'It's not just *your* school, Shirley. It's children from all over London. You're all going on this holiday. You're being evacuated. It's to keep you safe if those wicked Germans start dropping bombs.'

'Are they really going to drop bombs, Mum?'

'Don't you worry about it. You'll be safe in the country, having a whale of a time. Now, choose. Two books, if you must. I'd take *Alice in Wonderland* – it's not as tattered as the others, and it was your Christmas present.'

I ignored this idea. I chose *Ballet Shoes* because it was my favourite, and *Mary Poppins* because I felt in need of a nanny who could do magic. Then I saw Little Grey Rabbit in her soft grey dress looking at me imploringly, so I picked *The Squirrel, the Hare and the Little Grey Rabbit* too. I clutched all three to my chest.

'Can't you count? And why choose those three? They're all falling to bits. You've read that bally *Ballet Shoes* at least ten times, and *Mary Poppins* too. Look, the cover's all torn. And that rabbit book is far too babyish,' said Mum. 'You've had it since you were five! People will think you're backward, when in fact you're a really good little reader.'

'I want them. Please, Mum. Especially *Little Grey Rabbit*. She lives in the country and you said we were going to the country. Only now you're not coming. Oh, Mum, *why* aren't you coming?' I wailed.

'Because war's going to be declared any minute, and all the grown-ups have to stay behind and help. Everyone knows that. I've got to do my bit. I've applied for a job at Pendleton's,' said Mum, tucking my three books into the sample case and then snapping it shut.

'Pendleton's Metals, where Dad used to work?' I asked, astonished. Mum had always hated Dad working in a factory. She made him apply for a job in Grey's department store instead, but that hadn't worked out, and then he worked in the hat shop which closed down, so then he was a commercial traveller, but he couldn't sell many brushes no matter how hard he tried, so we'd had to move to Whitebird Street where the rents were cheaper, and I had to go to a new school where nobody liked me.

'It's not going to be Pendleton's Metals any more, it's going to be Pendleton's Munitions, making weapons for the army.

They're changing all the machinery over as part of the war effort,' said Mum.

'You're going to work in the factory?' I asked, trying to imagine her in overalls with her hair tied up in a scarf like the ladies I saw hurrying to work when I went to school.

'No, you noddle! You know perfectly well I was a trained secretary before I married your father. I'm going to be Mr Pendleton's private secretary,' said Mum.

'Why didn't you tell me about your job and my holiday and all this?' I demanded.

'Hey, hey, watch your tone, young lady. I didn't want to tell you before because I knew you'd simply get into a state, just the way you are now. And there's no time for it – we have to get you to that station, and the buses are a nightmare now. Come on. Put your coat on. Wait while I pin this daft label on you.'

'But I'm already boiling in this woolly jumper.'

'You do look a bit pink,' said Mum, sighing. 'Well, I'll pin it on your jumper. Keep still – I don't want to pull any of the threads.'

I peered down at my chest and read the label upside down. I said it aloud. '*Shirley Louise Smith, Paradise Road Junior School.*'

'I know. Why you have to have a label at your age I don't know. You're hardly likely to forget your own name,' said Mum. 'Now, put the coat in your case and then we'll get cracking. I'm going to put on my hat and jacket.'

She went into her bedroom. I undid the case, folded my coat inside, and then very quickly grabbed all the rest of my books and tumbled them on top of my clothes, even *Orlando*. I put my gas-mask case strap over my shoulder, then snapped the case shut and hauled it off the bed and down the stairs, *thump, thump, thump*. I could barely lift it, but I didn't care. I needed all my books with me. I was pretty sure I wasn't going to enjoy this holiday one little bit.

THE BUS DID TAKE ages. It crawled along, stuck in thick traffic, so when we got near the station Mum made us get out and walk.

'Come on now, Shirley, don't dawdle like that. We haven't got all day!' she said.

'I'm coming!' I stumbled along with the suitcase banging against my knees. My right arm felt as if it was stretching like plasticine. By the time I'd got to the end of the road it felt as if my burning hand were brushing the pavement.

'Dear goodness, don't be such a weakling,' said Mum. 'You've hardly got anything in that case. Here, give it me. But you'll have to manage it yourself when you get off the train.'

'No, I'm fine, Mum, really,' I panted.

Mum sniffed and seized the suitcase. 'Dear God, what

have you got in here? It weighs a blooming ton!'

'You told me to put my coat in,' I said.

'This feels as if it's got fifty coats inside.' Mum put the case down on the pavement and snapped it open. I wished I'd hidden all my books under my clothes. 'I can't believe it!' she exclaimed. 'You naughty, naughty girl! *Three* books, I said. And you're only meant to be taking one. Oh, Shirley, why do you always let me down?'

'I want them all,' I said. 'I *need* them, Mum.'

'Well, look, we haven't got time to stand here arguing.' Mum snapped the suitcase shut and picked it up again with a groan. 'You'll have to get one of the lady helpers to carry it for you when you get there.'

'Where's *there*?' I asked as we ran towards the station. I felt hemmed in by all the big grey buildings, and it was scary when we had to dodge the cars to cross the road.

'I don't exactly know where they're sending you,' said Mum. 'They won't say. Security, I suppose. So when you get wherever it is, you must write the address on a postcard and send it off to me. I've tucked one in your gas-mask case, already stamped – and a pencil. There's a half-crown too, just in case. But don't spend it on sweets, it's for emergencies only. Keep it safely hidden.' She patted the box hanging over my shoulder.

I hated my gas mask. We had to practise putting them on at school, and suddenly everyone turned into hideous monkey aliens, even me.

'Promise you'll send the postcard as soon as possible. I'll

be worrying about you,' said Mum. 'And make sure you go to a really good family. Keep nice and clean on the journey and tie your hair ribbon properly if it comes undone. I want them to see you come from a decent home. We're not cockney riff-raff.'

There was a whole stream of mothers and children making for Victoria station now. It was like a vast stone palace and so noisy, absolutely crammed with children. There were big kids, little kids, fat kids, thin kids, every kind of kid, some laughing and larking about, some bawling their eyes out. There were scruffy kids with grubby faces, girls in skimpy summer dresses with their vest sleeves showing, and boys in torn jerseys with scabby knees. There were posh girls in purple school uniforms with straw boaters standing two by two in a long line like Noah's Ark animals, chivvied into place by four nuns like flapping penguins.

An announcement suddenly boomed out on the station's loudspeaker. *'Hello, everyone! Listen carefully!'*

'Oh my Lord,' Mum murmured. 'It's like the Home Service on the wireless!'

The unseen speaker told us all to go and line up with our schools. Mothers were to say goodbye to their children and not try to go on the platforms.

'Stuff that for a game of soldiers,' said Mum, taking hold of my hand. 'I'm putting you on the train myself and making sure you get a good seat next to someone decent.'

'Which train will it be, Mum?' I asked, because there were big steam engines at each platform.

'See all those bossy-looking women in green uniforms holding lists? They'll know,' said Mum.

'Are they in the army like Dad?'

'No, you soppy date, they're Women's Voluntary Services, and they all think the world of themselves.' Mum elbowed her way through the great crowd, using my heavy case rather like a battering ram. I scuttled along in her wake.

'Excuse me – could you tell me where the Paradise Road schoolchildren are lining up?' she asked the nearest Green Uniform.

'Yes, Mother, over on platform eight,' the woman replied.

'Mother!' Mum hissed to me as we made for the right platform. 'I'm not her bally mother! Who do they think they are?'

We found platform eight, and I recognized a few of the children in the long straggling line. Oh no – there was Marilyn Henderson, tossing her ringlets and showing off. She was wearing a new yellow dress and a fluffy white bolero made of angora rabbit fur. I'd always ached to have a bolero like that.

'Are these Paradise Road children?' Mum asked me.

'I think so,' I muttered.

'Good Lord, what a rowdy bunch! Are you *sure*?'

'That's Marilyn Henderson over there,' I said. 'You know, I told you – the girl who pushed me over.'

'The one in yellow? Well, she looks a right little madam. Pretty hair though,' said Mum.

'I don't want to sit next to her!' I said.

'You're not going to, don't worry.'

There was another woman in green uniform standing at the entrance to platform eight, holding a clipboard with a great long list.

'This is Shirley Louise Smith,' Mum told her.

'Paradise Road?' said the woman, barely looking up. 'Yes, here we are. You'll be sitting in one of the carriages towards the end of the train, Shirley. I'm afraid you're all going to be packed like sardines. We're putting the St Agatha's Convent girls up at the front.' She glanced at the orderly parade of purple uniforms marching two by two to platform eight.

Mum looked at them too. Then she peered at the Paradise Road pupils. The children were haring about in all directions, some of the boys bashing each other with their suitcases. 'Can't my Shirley sit up at the front with the convent girls?' she asked.

'No, not if she's Paradise Road,' said the WVS woman, frowning. 'Now, say goodbye to Mother, Shirley, and go and join the others.' She looked at Mum. 'Best not to prolong things. You'll only upset her. Don't worry, she'll be fine.'

She turned away to deal with two children who were crying because they couldn't find the right platform.

'Don't worry!' said Mum. 'It's blooming chaos here. I'm not going till I see you're all right, pet.'

She only ever called me pet when she was really fond of me, like the time I came home from my old school with a gold star. I hung onto her.

'Turn round so she can't see,' Mum said.

I did as I was told. Quick as a wink, she tore the bottom

half off my label – the part that said *Paradise Road Junior School*.

'There now! You can join up with the convent girls – they look like little ladies,' said Mum. 'I'll come down the platform and make sure you get a good seat with them.'

'Will it be a long journey? What if I feel sick?' I asked. I'd nearly disgraced myself on the coach trip to the seaside.

'You won't feel sick on a train – though perhaps you shouldn't risk reading just to be on the safe side.' Mum approached the clipboard lady again. She had dispatched the weeping children elsewhere. She sighed when she saw that it was Mum and me again.

'Haven't you said your goodbyes yet?' she asked, though the answer was obvious.

'I know you're not allowed to say where the kiddies are going, but could you give me some idea of the length of the journey, please?'

'Oh Lordy – haven't a clue,' she said. 'I'm not going with them. I have to wait for the next batch at eleven.'

'But what about their dinner? Will they be served something to eat on the train?' Mum persisted.

'You're not expecting silver service in the first-class carriage, are you? You should have packed her some sandwiches and a flask,' said the WVS lady, and then turned away to deal with a bunch of children pretending to be trains, *choo-choo-chooing* up and down, barging into everyone.

'I'm not having you going hungry,' said Mum. 'Wait there, Shirley. Sit on your suitcase. I'll be back in two ticks.'

'No! Mum! Don't go!' I said, but she'd already started running in the other direction.

I started staggering after her, hauling my case.

'Hey, you. Shirley, is it? Wait there. You can't go with your mummy – you'll be getting on the train in a minute,' said the lady. She took the case from me. 'Good Lord, what have you got in here, bricks? It was supposed to be one light case with a change of clothing and a toothbrush. Now, sit on that case and be a good girl. How old are you?'

'Ten.'

'Well then, that's much too old to be a crybaby,' she said.

'I'm not crying. I've got a smut in my eye,' I muttered. I sat on the case and bent my head so that she couldn't see my wet cheeks. 'Mum! Oh, Mum, come back!' I whispered.

I sat there in a torment while children shrieked and adults shouted and trains hissed all around me. Any minute now we'd be herded together and put on board and I wouldn't even have a chance to say goodbye to Mum. At least I'd been able to hug Dad and tell him I loved him and beg him to keep safe. Afterwards he'd called me his little sweetheart and popped a chocolate toffee in my mouth, and although it was still desperately sad saying goodbye, at least we'd done it properly.

I wanted Timmy Ted badly but I didn't dare get him out in case the other children saw and laughed at me for being a baby. And if bossy Clipboard Lady spotted all my books, I wouldn't put it past her to chuck half of them in the nearest bin.

I waited with my chin on my chest so no one could see

25

the tears dripping down my cheeks and then dribbling inside the neck of my jumper.

Then the train let out three toots and a whole team of ladies sprang into action. Some wore the Women's Voluntary Services uniform. Some were vaguely familiar teachers from Paradise Road. I couldn't see my own teacher, Miss Grimes, a little woman with untidy grey hair and a whispery voice. I didn't really like her but I felt sorry for her because my classmates mucked around in her lessons.

'Come along, boys and girls, look nippy!' shouted the biggest, bustiest lady in green uniform. 'Say a quick goodbye to any mothers still here and then walk nicely along the platform. No pushing, no shoving, and no glum faces. Tell you what – let's have a little sing-song. Who knows "The Lambeth Walk"? *Any time you're Lambeth Way, any evening, any day, you'll find us all, doing the Lambeth Walk – Oi!*' She sang it loudly, marching along, and when she did the 'Oi' at the end she stuck her thumb in the air.

The children started singing the song, linking arms and strutting along, some even forgetting to say goodbye to their mothers as they headed down the platform. A couple of St Agatha's girls linked arms and started singing too, but the nuns frowned at them and pulled them apart, clearly thinking it too vulgar a song for convent girls.

'Come on, little girl on the big suitcase. Up you get!' someone shouted at me.

I sat where I was, going *Mum, Mum, Mum* inside my head.

'Shirley!'

My head jerked up. There she was, running wildly towards me, turning her ankles in her wedge shoes, a paper bag in one hand and a bottle in the other.

'Oh my Lord!' she gasped. 'The cafeteria was jam-packed. I had to barge to the front of the queue and I was practically lynched! But I wasn't having you going off hungry. Look, I've got you dandelion and burdock cordial. It's full of vitamins and ever so expensive, but I didn't want you drinking that fizzy pop – it's bad for you. The only sandwiches they had left were corned beef and I know you're not over-fond of it, but at least they'll fill a hole. I got you a Mars bar too, as a special treat, but mind you wipe round your mouth afterwards – you're ever such a mucky pup with chocolate.'

She went on gabbling instructions as we lumbered onto the platform, Mum helping haul the case.

'Come on, madam, get the kiddie on board – we're off in a tick,' said a guard standing in one of the doorways.

'Where are those convent girls?' Mum gasped. 'You're not sitting with that rabble.'

She pulled me onwards, right up towards the front of the train, and spotted a sea of purple through the window. 'Here! Come on, Shirley, heave-ho,' she said, pushing me and the suitcase up the steps.

There was a nun in the corridor guarding her girls. 'Your little girl can't sit here with us. This is specially reserved. There isn't a seat to spare anyway,' she said. She was obviously a lady, but she had a very neat moustache above her upper lip. I wondered if she actually shaved it into that shape.

'I'm sure there's plenty of room if your girls all budge up a bit,' said Mum, pushing me right into the compartment. 'Yes, just as I thought. And my Shirley's only a tiddler. She's been brought up nicely – quite the little lady. You girls with the plaits! She can sit with you, can't she?'

I got shoved between them before they could object. I clutched my bottle and paper bag dolefully while Mum tried to heave the suitcase onto the luggage rack. It defeated her.

'It'll have to stay on the floor,' she said. 'Right, come here, Shirley.'

She clasped me to her and whispered in my ear, 'Be a good girl now and don't take any notice of Charlie Chaplin with the moustache.'

We both giggled hysterically and then gasped when the train gave a little jerk.

'Oh Lordy, I'll have to make a dash for it!' said Mum, and ran out of the carriage without even kissing me goodbye.

I stared after her, thinking I should make a dash for it myself. I seized the suitcase, but it was so heavy I couldn't edge it past all the girls' knees.

'Watch out – you've just bashed me with that blessed suitcase!' one of them protested.

'Sorry, I just – I need to go!' I said frantically, but I was stuck. The train gathered speed.

I decided to abandon the suitcase, and Timmy Ted and all my precious books. I barged past them all and flew to the door in the passageway, but the train was already going too fast. I undid the leather strap, clawed at the window, got it open and leaned out.

I saw Mum far away down the platform, and I waved wildly

at her. She waved back and blew me kisses while I yelled, 'Love you, Mum!'

Then someone hoicked me away from the window, shut it fast and strapped it in place again. 'There now! Don't want you falling out, you silly billy!' She was another Women's Voluntary Services lady, but she was younger than the others, with short curly hair and a smiley face. 'Hey there. I'm Miss Haverford, but you can call me Annie. What's your name?'

'I'm Miss Smith, but you can call me Shirley,' I said. I was simply copying her to be polite but it made her chuckle.

'Thanks, Shirley. Now where have you sprung from?'

I jerked my head at the carriage of convent girls.

She raised her eyebrows. 'How come you're not in that purple get-up then?'

'My mum said I had to wear my best jumper and my pleated skirt,' I said truthfully.

'And very nice they look too. Well, better go back to your seat, there's a good girl,' she said.

I didn't have a seat. The two girls with plaits were sitting together again. Someone had put my sandwich in the corner. The bottle had rolled under the seat. I had to bend right down and burrow for it while the girls giggled. I hoped my knickers weren't showing. They were an embarrassing shade of pink with a lace frill, not plain white like proper knickers. I knew I was blushing when I stood up again.

The nun in the corner sighed at me. 'Here, you'd better come and sit with me,' she said.

I did my best to squash into the meagre space between her and a girl with gold-rimmed glasses and black hair in a long ponytail. She didn't say anything but she gave me a little smile.

She seemed to be the only friendly person in the carriage. The other girls all talked in swanky voices, laughing and joshing each other and making silly jokes. None of them seemed to have proper names. They were all Goofy and Munchkin and Snubby and Pinky.

I thought they were ridiculous, and wished Mum hadn't shoved me in with them. They clearly didn't think much of me, either, surreptitiously pulling faces at me when the nun wasn't looking. Then they started kicking my case, Dad's special shiny sample case. First the two girls with plaits kicked. One was Goofy, though her teeth didn't stick out particularly, and the other, smaller one was Munchkin. Then they all started joining in, except for the girl in glasses next to me. They weren't kicking hard, but their posh Start-rite sandals were making dusty marks on the leather. I couldn't bear it.

'Stop it! That's my dad's suitcase!' I said sharply.

They all giggled. Goofy kicked it again.

'*Stop it! That's my dad's suitcase!*' Munchkin said, in a funny common accent.

I realized she was mimicking me. She thought *I* was common. The children at my school mocked me because they thought I talked posh. I couldn't win. But I *could* stop them kicking the suitcase. I watched the nun, and when she started delving in her own suitcase for something, my foot shot out and I kicked the Munchkin girl sharply on the ankle.

'Ow! You beast! Sister Josephine, that girl just kicked me!'
she screamed.

The nun frowned.

'I'm so sorry, I didn't mean to! It's just so crowded in here.
I was trying to get up because I need the toilet and my foot
just went the wrong way,' I gabbled.

Charlie Chaplin was famous for his cane and this
nun could have one tucked up her long black sleeves for all I
knew.

The girls were giggling again, even the Munchkin one I'd
kicked. 'She needs the *toilet*!' she gasped.

'Oh, little Totty Toilet!' said Goofy, and they all shrieked
again.

'Girls! Stop this vulgar nonsense!' said Charlie Chaplin.

'She's the one that said it, Sister Josephine,' said Munchkin.

'That will be enough, Monica,' she said firmly. She looked
at me. 'You'd better go and find the double-you-see then.' She
whispered the weird word as if it was very bad.

Double-you-see? I'd never heard the toilet called that
before, but it was clearly what she meant. I didn't really *need*
to go, I'd just made the first excuse that came into my head,
but I was committed now. I stood up and squeezed past my
suitcase. Monica gave me a vicious poke as I went, but Sister
Charlie Chaplin was watching.

'Monica, I saw that! How dare you be so unkind! What
would Jesus say?' she snapped.

I didn't know what Jesus would say, but *I* said *Hurray!*
The short-haired smiley woman was still guarding the

door in the corridor, having a cigarette.

'Hello, Shirley. I hope you haven't come to fling yourself out of the window again,' she said cheerily, and then took a long drag.

'Is that a Craven A?' I asked.

'No, it's a Player's. I like my gaspers full strength,' she said.

'My mum smokes Craven As,' I said.

'Then your mum's a lady.'

I beamed at her. 'Please, Miss – er, Annie, do you know where the – the double-something is?'

'Double what?'

'I forget what she called it, that nun lady in there. I want the toilet.'

'Oh! I think she might have called it the W dot C dot. W.C. Short for water closet. Very refined people, nuns. The toilets are at either end of the train, but the one at the front is already out of order. Some kid's been sick in it. You'll have to shove your way right to the back. They've packed so many kids on this blooming train that some of them are sitting on their suitcases in the corridor. Mind how you go.'

It was a long and precarious trek down the train. There were children spilling out into the corridor. The younger kids from Paradise Road were singing 'Ten Green Bottles', holding up their hands and counting it out on their fingers. They looked as if they were having far more fun than the St Agatha's lot.

There were some older boys larking about further up, riding their cases, pretending to be cowboys.

'Hey, there's an old moo-cow – let's lasso her!' Kevin shouted. He was in my class, a gangly boy with jug ears, always in trouble.

I glared at him. He whirled his school tie at me. I dodged and the end of his tie flicked me hard.

'Oh, my eye! My eye!' I said, holding my head. It hadn't hurt my eye, it had caught my eyebrow, but it sounded more dramatic.

'Oh, Kev, what you done?'

'You've only gone and blinded her!'

'I didn't do nothing, I was just being Roy Rogers!'

I left them accusing and protesting and pushed my way onwards until I got to a queue of children waiting for the toilet. It wasn't a happy queue. One little boy had already wet himself – the front of his trousers was soaking. Even his socks were soggy. His big sister was giving him a telling-off, fussing like an old biddy though she was only about six herself. Another girl had been sick and it had dribbled down her blouse. She was plucking at it anxiously, her face screwed up. She was in my class too, a girl called Mary.

When I stood behind her she started to wail. 'I don't know what to doooo,' she said. 'That lady back there said I should go to the toilet, but how will that help? It's all down my best blouse and Mum will wallop me.'

'Your mum's not here though, is she? So she can't wallop you,' I said. My voice wobbled as I took in the fact that my mum wasn't here, either.

The train jerked and I very nearly fell against the poor girl. I backed away hurriedly because she smelled.

'You can take your blouse off in the toilet and dab the stained bits with water. It won't matter if it's a bit damp after – at least it will be clean,' I said.

'Dab it with water? What, from the *toilet*?' she asked, horrified.

'No, you banana. There'll be a basin, won't there? And soap so we can wash our hands. So *you* can wash your blouse. Here, I'll come in with you and help you if you like,' I said.

It made me feel a bit better, looking after her. I'd always quite liked Mary, though she was in Marilyn Henderson's gang. I went into the cubicle with her and got her blouse off and rinsed it under the tap. There wasn't any soap but I made a reasonable job cleaning it. It still smelled faintly, but she'd just have to put up with that.

We took turns using the toilet, turning our backs on each other politely, and then washed our hands and shook them dry, spraying each other and giggling. She was much nicer than those stuck-up convent girls. I wished I was sitting with her. Maybe we could make friends, and Marilyn Henderson would just have to lump it. I could lend her some of my books, even *Ballet Shoes*.

We walked back down the corridor together. I remembered to clutch my head and whimper when we passed the cowboys.

'I'm telling,' I said, just to torture them. I wasn't that fussed about being flicked in the face, but I hated Kevin calling me an old moo-cow.

I was about to explain all this to Mary, but she suddenly darted back into her own carriage. Marilyn Henderson greeted her warmly and sat her down and shared a drink with her. Mary didn't even turn her head to say goodbye or thank me.

I trailed back to the carriage with Charlie Chaplin and the purple pupils.

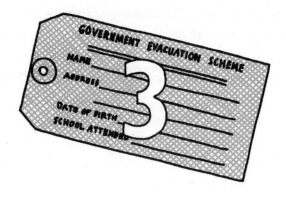

I SAT SQUASHED UP beside Sister Josephine while the train hurtled forward, carrying me miles and miles and miles away from my mum. I did my best to avoid catching any of the girls' eyes. I looked upwards instead. There was a large luggage rack stacked with all their suitcases. They were plain grey, all neatly bound with purple belts. I wondered how they could tell whose was whose. Perhaps it didn't matter. Their clothes were all identical.

Underneath the luggage rack there was a picture. It showed apple-green hills and a pale grey sky and a strange white horse. It seemed to be lying down but its legs weren't tucked up. It was very big, a giant horse, even bigger than the great Shire brewery horses that pulled their wagons around to all the public houses at home.

After reading *Black Beauty* I hadn't been able to bear

looking at horses pulling carts. I tried to imagine Black Beauty now, no longer working, galloping happily up and down that hill, saying hello to the giant horse. I made the softest little whinny, but it went wrong and I found myself snorting.

'Blow your nose, child,' Charlie Chaplin commanded.

I dug in my skirt pocket and found a crumpled hankie. I also found an old Merry Maid toffee and seized it joyously. I unwrapped it under cover of my hankie and stuck it in my mouth, but it was a bit of a disappointment. It was covered in grit and fluff and I had to swallow it down quick.

I was starting to feel really hungry. I spent the next half-hour longing to eat my corned-beef sandwich and my Mars bar and drink my dandelion and burdock, but I didn't like to tuck in with everyone staring at me. When I so much as rustled the paper bag, the nun frowned at me.

Perhaps eating was a sin in a convent. Maybe they were only allowed to eat in private, as if they were going to their silly double-you-see. They didn't even seem to need the toilet anyway. They just sat there, the girls whispering to each other, and Charlie Chaplin staring into space and occasionally muttering to herself. Perhaps she was saying her prayers.

Maybe she was asking God not to send a bomb down on us. Mum had gone on about the danger and I couldn't help worrying. The train made such a rattle and thump that it sounded as if bombs were exploding right now.

What if a bomb exploded on Mum back in London?

The idea got stuck in my head, though I kept shaking it violently.

'What's that girl doing? Is she having a fit?' Goofy whispered.

'She's just acting loony,' said Munchkin.

I thought I'd show them what loony looked like. I crossed my eyes and let my tongue poke out sideways, and they both squealed.

The nun glared. 'Stop being silly, girls,' she said.

'But we're bored, Sister Josephine,' Goofy whined.

She sighed. 'How about playing I-Spy?' she suggested. 'I spy with my little eye something beginning with . . . T.'

They guessed *train*, and *tunnel*, and *toes*, and *Theresa*, and then someone suggested *tummy*, which made them giggle.

'I know – *toilet*!' said Goofy, and that made them all laugh fit to bust.

I tried to look like I didn't care, but I knew I was blushing.

'*Tunic*,' said the girl next to me, the quiet one with the long black ponytail.

Her own tunic was too long for her, way past her knees, and a deeper purple. It made her face look very pale.

'Yes! Excellent, Jessica!' said the nun.

The other girls groaned. Jessica didn't seem to be very popular. She was the one I liked best.

'It's your go now, Jessica,' said Sister Josephine encouragingly.

'I spy with my little eye something beginning with . . . H,' she said.

I knew, straight away! But *they* didn't. They tried *handkerchief* and *hat*, and then went through a tedious list of *hair – hair ribbon, hairslide, hairgrip* and *hairband.*

'There aren't any more H words in the carriage,' said Munchkin.

'Yes there are,' said Jessica.

'You're just bluffing, Newbug,' said Goofy.

'No she's not,' I piped up. '*I* know what it is.'

'You're not playing. You're not one of us,' said a freckly, red-haired girl.

'Now, now,' said Charlie Chaplin. 'That's not very kind. Go on then, say what you think the word is, child.'

'*Horse!*'

'It's not *horse*, stupid! How ever could it be *horse*?' said Goofy.

'Maybe she's seen one out of the window, but that doesn't count,' said Munchkin.

'No, she's absolutely right. There *is* a horse in here,' said Jessica, and she pointed to the painting below the luggage rack.

They all peered up and then groaned.

'That's not a *real* horse,' chorused Goofy and Munchkin.

'Of course it's not,' said Jessica. 'It's a painting of a white horse. Nobody said a chosen object had to be real.'

'It's not even drawn right – it's all tipping over,' said the freckly girl.

'It's a chalk horse. They cut them out on grassy hillsides. I saw another one from a train once,' said Jessica.

'Oh, bully for you, Newbug,' said Goofy nastily. 'It's my turn now.'

'No, it's not, it's hers. She guessed H is for *horse*,' said Jessica, nodding at me.

'But she's not one of us. She just squashed in for somewhere to sit.'

'And somewhere to park her massive suitcase,' said Munchkin. She tried to lift it. 'What have you *got* in there?' She made to open one of the locks.

'Don't you dare!' I said.

'All right, all right, keep your hair on. Why are you getting so shirty?'

'Maybe it's a body!' said the freckly girl, and they all squealed stupidly.

'Girls, girls, stop it,' said Charlie Chaplin. 'I think that as we had such an early breakfast it might be time for lunch.' She heaved herself up and reached for two bulging carrier bags on the luggage rack.

They all started making an eager fuss, as if expecting a banquet. I thought of the glorious spreads I'd seen in the *Beano* comic: mounds of mashed potato with sausages sticking out at interesting angles; great jellies and blancmanges like quivering castles; enormous platters of cakes oozing jam and cream.

The food that emerged from the carrier bag was a huge disappointment. The nun handed each girl a small greaseproof-paper parcel containing four squares of meat-paste sandwich and a custard cream biscuit. Then they were given small bottles of milk with a straw.

I felt very superior tucking into my own corned-beef-and-pickle sandwich and swigging dandelion and burdock straight from the bottle. Then I produced my Mars bar. They all stared at it enviously, even Charlie Chaplin. I nibbled slowly, licking my lips.

'Lucky you,' Jessica said softly.

'Here, you have a bite,' I said, offering it to her.

'Really?'

'No, girls, don't share your food like that,' said the nun, but she was too late. Jessica had already taken a big chocolatey bite.

'Thanks ever so,' she said. 'I'm Jessica.'

'I know. I'm Shirley.'

'Like Shirley Temple.'

'Yes, only I'm not a bit like her. My hair's dead straight for a start, though my mum used to try to put it in ringlets. They didn't work though.'

'I think ringlets look silly,' said Jessica. 'And Shirley Temple's got a silly face too. She's like a Mabel Lucie Attwell drawing.' She puffed out her cheeks and pouted.

'Mabel Lucie Attwell did the pictures in my *Alice in Wonderland* book,' I said.

'Someone called Tenniel did the pictures in my *Alice*,' said Jessica.

I was tremendously excited. I'd never met anyone else who had an *Alice* book. 'Did you like the story?' I asked.

'Yes, it makes me laugh.'

'I've got my book in my suitcase,' I whispered. 'Lots of books.'

'Ah! So that's why it's heavy. You lucky thing. We were only allowed to take one book.'

'What did you choose?'

'It was so difficult. In the end I chose *The Blue Fairy Book*.'

This was a surprise. A fairy book? Jessica seemed very clever and serious. I'd have guessed she'd have some big fat grown-up book like a Charles Dickens.

'So what have you got with you?'

'All my books,' I said.

'*All?*' she said. 'You can't have!'

'Yes, I can. I've got *Ballet Shoes* and—'

'Oh, *Ballet Shoes* is my favourite!' she declared.

'Oh, that's amazing!' I said, and just then the train let out a loud hiss of steam as if it were exclaiming too.

We gazed at each other excitedly.

'Which sister is your favourite?' Jessica asked.

'I can never quite choose. I think Petrova is the nicest, but I wouldn't really want to be a car mechanic. Pauline's the prettiest, but I hate it when she gets big-headed. So I think I like Posy best. I'd give anything to be a wonderful ballet dancer, wouldn't you?' I gabbled.

'No, I'd hate it. My mother made me have ballet lessons and I was awful at it. I couldn't even get my feet to go in the right positions. They just stuck out sideways like Charlie Chaplin's,' said Jessica.

I glanced at the nun, who was still chewing on her meat-paste sandwich. Her moustache wobbled slightly at every bite.

I squashed up even closer to Jessica and whispered right in her ear. 'My mum said your Sister Josephine looked like Charlie Chaplin.'

Jessica's eyes opened wide behind her little gold glasses. Then she burst out laughing. I laughed too, long and hard.

'Girls! Girls, calm down now!' said the nun.

That made us laugh even harder. Jessica started coughing and spluttering.

'That stupid Newbug's choking,' Goofy announced.

'Thump her hard on the back, someone,' said Munchkin. 'Hey, you, Totty Toilet, hit your new friendy-wendy on the back!'

I tried rubbing Jessica's back tentatively, not wanting to hurt her. She was bright red in the face now.

'Oh, for goodness' sake, Jessica!' said the nun. 'Go and stand outside in the corridor and take a few deep breaths at the window.'

'Please, miss, I'd better go with her to make sure she's all right,' I said.

'You call me Sister, not miss. Very well. Off you go,' she said.

Jessica and I sidled out past my suitcase and escaped into the corridor. The short-haired lady was still standing by the window, smoking another cigarette.

'Choke up, chicken,' she said to Jessica. 'You girls! Forever getting the giggles. Still, at least you're having fun. All the little ones back there have started howling for their mums. I'd better go and see if my friend has managed to calm them down.'

I was still weak with laughter, but I felt as if someone had flung a bucket of water over me at the mention of mums. I wanted my mum too. I felt two tears spurt out of my eyes, and hoped Jessica would think I was just crying with laughter.

I sniffed hard. Jessica was sniffing too.

'Are you missing your mum too?' I asked.

'No!' she said. 'Not in the slightest. I can't stand her.'

I stared at her. I'd never heard anyone say they couldn't stand their own mother before.

'Why?' I said. 'Is she horrid to you? Does she smack you a lot?'

My mum smacked me sometimes – she said it was for my own good. I had to learn. Though all I learned was to run fast and bolt myself in my bedroom when she raised her arm.

'No, she doesn't smack me. She's hardly ever there,' said Jessica.

'What do you mean? Mums are always there, getting you up, putting you to bed, doing the washing and the ironing and the cleaning and the cooking.'

'My mother doesn't do any of that. She works,' said Jessica. She said it as if she were ashamed.

'Heaps of mums work, especially now,' I said reassuringly. '*My* mum's going to work now there's going to be a war. She's going to be a personal secretary.' I wasn't quite sure what that entailed, but I said it grandly because Mum sounded proud of her new position.

Jessica simply shrugged.

'What sort of work does your mum do then?' I asked.

She hesitated. She was very posh, even though she was proving extraordinarily nice. Her mother couldn't do anything

45

too lowly, surely? I ran through all the occupations that would make my mum turn up her nose. Factory hand? Bus conductress? Bar lady? Lavatory attendant?

'She's an actress,' Jessica blurted out.

This took me by surprise. 'Crikey! Really? What, a film actress?'

'Sometimes. And she's also on the stage.'

'Would I have heard of her?' I asked. I'd try to remember the name and see if Mum had ever seen her. She liked to go to the Odeon once a week as a treat.

'She's Imogen Starlight,' said Jessica flatly.

My mouth fell open. Imogen Starlight was the most famous British actress ever. Mum was always reading about her in *Picturegoer*. I'd never seen any of her films because Mum said they were too grown up for me, but I'd pored over the photos of her. I'd seen her in chic dresses and high heels, in sweaters and slacks, in sparkly evening dresses, even in her swimming costume. She was beautiful – very slender, with fair hair, a kittenish face, and the most amazing, enormous violet-blue eyes.

I looked at Jessica doubtfully – her long dark plait, her pale round face, her little gold glasses. She didn't look remotely like Imogen Starlight. She had to be telling fibs. If so, I understood. I'd sometimes told stories to the other children in my class, though I took pains to make them convincing.

Besides, I'd never heard of Imogen Starlight having a daughter. I remembered a husband, maybe several, but Mum would have shown me if there had been a photo of Imogen with her child. Film stars always dressed their daughters in frilly mini versions of their own clothes, and sometimes they carried dolls in minute matching outfits too. Mum always cooed over these pictures. She had knitted matching mother-and-daughter jumpers for us, and I'd always felt hot and self-conscious when people remarked on them.

'I take it you've heard of Imogen Starlight,' said Jessica.

'Of course I have,' I said. I didn't know what to say next. I couldn't accuse her of downright lying. 'So, is your name Jessica Starlight then?'

'Don't be silly. I'm Jessica Lipman. My father's Michael Lipman. He's a film producer but you probably won't have heard of him. And Imogen Starlight isn't my mother's real name anyway. She was born Agnes Potts, but that doesn't sound very glamorous, does it?' said Jessica. 'But she's Imogen Starlight now all right, twinkling away, smiling her famous smile with all those pretty white teeth. Half of them are false, actually. Like her.' She spoke with such vehemence that I changed my mind. She had to be telling the truth after all, unlikely as it seemed.

'What about your dad then? Is he all right? I love my dad. He's joined up already. He's very brave,' I said. Dad was actually quite timid – when we found a rat in the kitchen, he'd squealed and run away, and Mum had had to deal with it. Still, I was sure he'd be a wonderful soldier and come home with medals on his chest.

'I don't see my father much. He lives in Hollywood. I had a

stepfather who was OK, but I can't stand my mother's new boyfriend,' said Jessica. 'It was his idea to send me to this awful convent.'

'Those girls aren't very friendly,' I said.

'You're telling me. And Charlie Chaplin is positively foul,' said Jessica.

We both giggled weakly again.

'Still, maybe living at the convent is better than living at home with your mother and this stepfather if you don't like them?' I suggested.

'No, because I didn't see them much. I had Nanny. She's looked after me since I was a baby. I love, love, love Nanny,' said Jessica fiercely.

'I had a nanny too, Nanny Margot. She was my dad's mum and she was ever so nice. I did jigsaw puzzles with her,' I said. 'But she's dead now.'

'Nanny isn't my grandma. She's my actual nanny. You know, like a nurse,' said Jessica.

'What, like Mary Poppins?' I asked, very impressed.

Jessica nodded. 'Only she doesn't have a parrot-head umbrella or a carpet bag and she doesn't do magic, but she's just lovely, even so. She's not thin like Mary Poppins, she's small and very plump and she's got arthritis so her hands don't work very well now and she can't walk very fast. She's the person I love most in the world, but now my mother's sent her away. She says I don't need a nanny any more. And it's awful because Nanny's too old to get another job and she's hasn't got a proper home of her own and she's had to go and live with her sister. I miss her so much.' Jessica was crying now, tears pooling inside her glasses. She took them off to wipe them. She looked much younger without them. They'd left little pink marks on either side of her nose.

'Oh, Jessica,' I said.

'Sorry. I don't usually drip on like this,' she told me.

'You drip all you want.' I swallowed hard, wondering if I dared say it. 'Jessica, could we be friends?'

'I would love to be friends, Shirley. You're the only girl I've ever been able to talk to properly,' said Jessica, and she took my hand and squeezed it.

'And we'll stay friends when we get to wherever we're going? And play together? Or will they keep you shut up in school?' I asked.

'I'll creep out if they do. We'll meet up heaps, I promise.'

'And you can borrow my books if you like,' I said. 'Any of them. Especially *Ballet Shoes*.'

'You're the nicest girl ever,' said Jessica.

I swallowed, overcome.

Then the door of our carriage slid open and Sister Josephine came lumbering into the corridor.

'What on earth are you two girls up to? Surely you've calmed down by now, Jessica?' she demanded.

'Shirley was being very comforting.' Jessica couldn't quite look at Sister Josephine, and I didn't dare, either. We knew that her moustache would set us off laughing all over again.

'Well, come and sit down properly. We've started a game of

Famous People. You can both join in,' she said.

It was a rather lame game where one girl had to think of a famous person and the other girls could ask twenty questions to see if they could guess who it was. It was the red-haired girl with freckles. They'd discovered that she was thinking of an actress who had been in lots of films.

'What if it's your mum!' I whispered in Jessica's ear. 'Do they know?'

'I'm not telling this lot,' she whispered back.

'Now then, girls. Don't whisper secrets in company, it's very rude,' said Charlie Chaplin. 'Join in the game.'

The famous person wasn't Imogen Starlight, it was Ginger Rogers. Then it was Munchkin's turn. Jessica and I sat silently while the others asked silly questions.

'Come on, Jessica, make an effort,' said Charlie Chaplin. 'Try to guess the famous person.'

'I don't know any famous persons,' said Jessica.

I caught her eye and we both started giggling again.

'You're a pair of silly billies,' the nun said disapprovingly.

'Let's start our own private club,' Jessica murmured to me. 'We'll call ourselves the Silly Billies.'

'Goofy and Munchkin got there before us!' I whispered.

'Girls! What did I just tell you? No whispering! At all!'

So we sat in silence while the others played their silly game. Jessica pulled a little red-leather diary out of her blazer pocket. I gazed at it in awe. I hadn't realized how easily you could tell the difference between real leather and plastic. I itched to own a beautiful little diary like that, but of course it would cost a fortune. Jessica unsheathed the tiny pencil from its spine and started busily scribbling something on the page. She held the diary very close to her chest, her head bent. I decided she must be very short-sighted in spite of her glasses.

I couldn't see what she was writing even though I was right next to her. I wondered if it was about me! What might she put?

She suddenly held the open diary in front of me. She hadn't been writing at all – she'd been drawing. She'd done a brilliant little cartoon likeness of Sister Josephine – though she was wearing a bowler hat on top of her wimple and holding a cane, and her black lace-ups were sticking out sideways. Jessica had drawn in every hair of her toothbrush moustache. Sister Josephine was Charlie Chaplin to a T.

I struggled desperately not to laugh. I bit down on the insides of my cheeks but I couldn't stop myself shaking.

Sister Josephine could feel me vibrating. 'Jessica Lipman, let me see what you've written in that diary,' she demanded.

'I haven't written anything, Sister Josephine,' Jessica said truthfully.

'Hand it over immediately!'

'But I can't let you look in my diary! It's private,' Jessica insisted.

'I've just seen you show it to the little girl beside you,' said the nun.

'That's different. Shirley's my friend.'

'Ooh, Newbug's palled up with Totty Toilet!' said Goofy.

'What a perfect pair!' said Munchkin, holding her nose as if we smelled. 'How pathetic.'

'Gertrude! Monica! Stop being so unkind,' said Sister Josephine. 'I won't have silly name-calling, no matter what the circumstances. And, Jessica, give me that diary immediately!'

But all at once the train tooted, jolted, and then started braking.

'Oh crumbs, we're here!' Goofy cried.

'I do believe you're right!' said Sister Josephine, leaping up in a panic and brushing meat-paste-sandwich crumbs off her black habit. 'Start getting your cases down from the rack, and tidy yourselves up a little. I want you to look as smart as possible. Lady Amersham may very well be meeting us. She's kindly allowing us to set up school in her magnificent country house. We're all very privileged.'

Jessica slid her diary into her pocket, flaring her nostrils with relief.

'I wonder if my school's going to live in a posh country house too?' I asked. 'Do you think it's big enough for two schools?'

'I hope so!' said Jessica.

I thought how thrilled Mum would be if she knew I was living with a real lady. I didn't like Sister Josephine, I hated all the other convent girls, but I liked Jessica enormously. Perhaps we could share a desk and sleep next to each other at night. She might help me with my lessons – she seemed much cleverer than me. We could read all my books together. We'd wander around arm in arm and whisper secrets to each other.

My heart started thumping hard under my itchy Fair Isle. It would be glorious!

MEADOW RIDGE

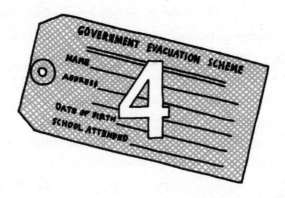

THE TRAIN PUFFED INTO the small station and ground to a halt. I saw a sign suspended from two chains: MEADOW RIDGE. There was a murmur as everyone read it.

'Right, girls! Out you get, and woe betide anyone who leaves her suitcase behind!' Charlie Chaplin commanded, springing into action.

I struggled with mine, scarcely able to lift it.

'Here, you pull and I'll push,' said Jessica.

She helped me edge it out into the corridor, and then she jumped down the steps and helped steer it as I pushed it slowly down to the platform. We were both panting when we got it there.

'It feels like you've got not just Pauline, Petrova and Posy, but all Madame Fidolia's stage school in there!' Jessica declared.

'What?' said Munchkin.

'Totally batty, the pair of them!' said Goofy, making a skewering gesture into her head.

'Talking total loony-babble!' said Freckle Face.

'Girls, come *along*. It's so crowded – we must all stick together,' Charlie Chaplin shouted.

Three other nuns were waving and gesturing like giant bats, herding their own purple charges into a long line. Paradise Road pupils were dashing all over the place. Half the boys were already tearing along the platform to look at the engine, though we were supposed to be going out through a wicket gate at the other end.

I saw my own class wandering about, Marilyn Henderson showing off as always. Mary hovered nearby. She seemed so mousy and boring. I wondered how I could ever have wanted her as a friend. I had Jessica now, the most interesting girl I'd ever met. And she liked me. She didn't give two hoots if I said *toilet* instead of *double-you-see*.

Charlie Chaplin didn't need to command me to stick close. I scuttled along beside Jessica, hauling my case, my arm feeling as if it was being pulled right out of its socket. We passed through the wicket gate two at a time, and were then herded down a dusty path with hedges on either side.

I caught sight of Annie, the friendly, short-haired WVS lady.

'Please, miss, where are we going?' I puffed.

'To the village hall. Someone said it's down this lane. Who knows?' she said cheerfully. 'All I *do* know is that we're at

Meadow Ridge and we seem to be in the depths of the country. Breathe in and smell that lovely fresh country air!'

We were all wrinkling our noses and trying not to breathe because there was the most disgusting smell wafting on the breeze.

'Who's farted?' a boy yelled, and a teacher swatted him on the back of the head for being rude.

'I don't know, but it must be a giant to make that pong!' Annie jumped up and peered through the top of the hedge where the branches straggled. 'Ah, I thought so! Wait till we get to the gate up there! You're going to see a sight for sore eyes.'

Everyone started pushing and shoving to get there first, and even Sister Josephine hurried along in her stout black shoes, lifting her long skirts because the lane was getting very mucky. And there, through the gate, we saw a herd of black-and-white creatures peacefully munching grass, ignoring us. One lifted up its tail and a brown shower cascaded out onto the ground. There was a great shriek of hilarity and disgust.

Some of the little ones were trying to run away, clearly scared. Sister Josephine caught hold of a small boy with a shaven head who started pelting back towards the railway station.

'No, no, you mustn't run away, you naughty boy!' she said, hanging onto his arm.

'Got to, missus! There're monsters in that field!' he protested.

'Don't be silly. They're only cows,' she said.

'Cows?' he repeated.

'Yes – surely you know what a cow is? It's how you get your milk!'

'You what, missus?'

'The cows give you your lovely creamy milk,' said Sister Josephine.

She had a little gang of children staring at her now, while the St Agatha's girls nudged each other in a superior way.

'How do they do that, Sister Josephine?' Munchkin asked innocently.

'Yes, exactly how, Sister Josephine?' Goofy repeated.

'Don't be silly, girls, you know perfectly well,' she said, going pink.

'Yeah, but we don't, missus,' said the little boy.

'This isn't the time or the place for a nature lesson,' said Sister Josephine. 'Now come along! We have to find the village hall. Quick sharp!'

The children stayed put, staring at the cows in puzzlement.

'You must all be soft,' said an older boy. 'I've had a holiday on a farm. I've seen all the cows being milked. The farmer squeezes those pink dangly things between their legs – udders, they're called.'

All the children shrieked again. I wasn't simple – I knew all about milking cows from storybooks, but it was the first time I'd seen udders close up, and the whole process did seem hilariously revolting.

'I don't think I'm ever going to drink milk again,' I told Jessica.

'I've always hated it anyway,' she said. 'What was that strange drink you had on the train?'

'Dandelion and burdock,' I said.

'Does it taste good?'

'It's lovely. I should have given you a sip. I'll get my mum to buy you a bottle if you like,' I said, without thinking.

But when was I going to see Mum? How long was this little holiday going to last? What if I was stuck here for weeks? Months? For ever? I suddenly felt sick and dizzy. My hand was so slippery with sweat that I lost my grip on the suitcase and it fell onto the road with a thud.

'Here, I'll help you,' said Jessica.

I nodded my thanks, not daring to open my mouth in case I threw up. It would be terrible if I were sick down my best Fair Isle jumper. I didn't want to end up stinking like Mary.

'You look all wobbly,' said Jessica. 'Sit down on your suitcase for a minute.'

She gently pushed me down and sat beside me. 'Is it the cow smell?' she asked.

I shrugged my shoulders and then fidgeted with the straps on my shoes. They were really rubbing me now, and the patent was getting horribly dusty.

'I love your shoes,' said Jessica. 'Look at my disgusting clodhoppers! And this vile uniform. My tunic's much too big for me – it's practically trailing on the ground. Nanny said she'd turn up the hem for me, and take it in a bit at the side seams so it wouldn't be so bunchy, but my mother sent her packing before she had a chance.'

'I could sew it for you,' I said.

'Can you really sew?' she asked.

'Of course I can,' I said airily. 'I've sewn dresses and nighties and all sorts.' I hadn't really sewn any proper clothes, but I'd made several outfits for my doll, Jenny Wren.

'That would be ever so kind of you,' said Jessica.

'Hey, you, Newbug!' It was horrible Goofy again. 'Sister Josephine's looking for you. We've all got to keep together. Come *on*!' She tugged at Jessica's blazer.

'Oh, get lost,' said Jessica. 'And why do you keep calling me Newbug? It's pathetic.'

'*You're* the one who's pathetic,' said Goofy, tossing her plaits over her shoulder. 'You're obviously Newbug because you're new to our school and you're so lowly you're like a little loathsome creepy-crawly bug. Anyway, are you coming or not?'

'Not,' said Jessica.

'Well, don't blame me if you get the hairbrush tonight.'

'The hairbrush?'

'Sister Josephine has an especially hard hairbrush, and anyone who's been really naughty gets whacked with it after supper. It really hurts. I bet you'll boo your eyes out.' Goofy flounced off to join the others.

'I can't stand her, or that Munchkin,' said Jessica.

'Neither can I,' I said.

'Are you feeling better now?' she asked.

'A bit.'

'Then I suppose we'd better get going,' she said.

I stood up and struggled to lift my suitcase again.

'I'll take a turn,' said Jessica. 'You can carry mine.'

'That's not fair on you though,' I protested.

'I don't mind. I'm quite strong, you know. Once I tried to lift Nanny up for a laugh, and I got her feet right off the ground.'

'Goodness!'

Jessica flexed her muscles comically like Popeye the Sailor Man. 'Give it here,' she said.

So we swapped suitcases and joined the jostling troupe of children. The lane got wider, the hedges smaller, and we started to see houses – small houses with tangled gardens and people peering at us as if we were a circus parade. One old lady smiled and waved, and another came hobbling to her gate and offered us all jelly babies from a big paper bag.

Mum had always warned me about taking sweets from strangers so I hesitated and then shook my head politely, but Jessica took two.

'Don't you like jelly babies? I absolutely love them, especially the black ones,' she said, happily decapitating one.

'Yes, but I didn't like to,' I mumbled.

'Silly sausage.' Jessica had already chewed up her first sweet and was licking the second with her pink pointed tongue.

I breathed in the sweet jelly smell.

'Here, have this one,' said Jessica, handing it over. 'You don't mind that I licked it, do you? I haven't got any bugs, even though that's what those stupid girls call me.'

'I don't mind a bit,' I said.

I felt a soaring happiness that we were close enough friends to share licked sweets. But then an old man with a very neat garden, all red, white and blue in regimental order, came out of his gate and started shouting at us.

'Get back where you belong, you bunch of young hooligans!' he hollered. 'What you doing here? We don't want you! Nasty little thieving cockneys!'

'I'm not a cockney!' said Jessica. 'I was born in America and my father's originally from Lithuania and my mother's of Irish origin.'

'As if I care, you snippy little miss,' he said. 'You can't kid me. You're all from London, and that makes you all bleeding cockneys.'

Jessica raised her eyebrows at me. 'Hello, bleeding cockney,' she said to me the minute we were past him.

'Watcher, snippy little miss,' I said, and we both cracked up laughing.

The houses were clustered together now, and when we peered around we saw much larger homes on the lower slopes of a hill.

'I wonder if one of them belongs to this Lady Amersham who's letting St Agatha's set up school in her house?' said Jessica.

'I wish I went to your school. I don't think any lady would

really let Paradise Road pupils near her house,' I said.

'Look, everything's muddled now. Most of the nuns don't have a clue who I am. Why don't we pretend you're new to the convent too?' Jessica suggested.

'Yes, but I haven't got the uniform,' I said.

She put my suitcase down and wriggled out of her blazer. 'You have now,' she said, holding it out for me.

'I can't take your blazer!'

'Yes you can. I'll say I lost mine. And I'll write to my mother and ask her to get me a new one. She's used to me losing stuff,' said Jessica.

'But I haven't got a blouse or a tie or the right tunic,' I said.

'Well, who cares?'

'And Sister Josephine knows I'm not one of you lot.'

'Well, you can go in one of the other classes and kid them you're a new girl. Only then they'll call you Newbug too, and you'll find that very annoying,' said Jessica.

'Better than Totty Toilet!' I said.

'Anyway, put the blazer on!'

'You're so good to me. Look, let's share all my books. And you can have *Ballet Shoes* for yourself, honest.' I felt a bit dizzy as I said it, and knew I might regret it. Still, I didn't need Pauline, Petrova and Posy as friends now, not when I had Jessica.

'Let's share it,' she said.

'Let's share everything, you and me. Because we're best friends, right?'

'Definitely. Look, there's another even bigger place up on that hill over there. A real mansion. *That* will be our new school, I bet.'

I stared up at it. It was very large and white and elegant, terrifyingly grand. I felt my throat drying, and wished I still had some dandelion and burdock.

'Will this lady still be living there too?' I asked anxiously.

'Oh yes, I think so.'

'So will she have servants?'

'Well, obviously. You can't imagine a titled lady down on her knees scrubbing all the floors in that huge house, can you?'

'I don't like the idea of servants,' I said.

'Why on earth not?' Jessica asked.

I was frightened they'd be just as snobby as the St Agatha's girls and sniff at my accent and my pink knickers and raise their eyebrows if I forgot that I mustn't say the word *toilet* any more. But I didn't want to admit this to Jessica because it made me sound so wet.

'I don't think it's right, one set of people having to do all the dirty work for another set,' I said, adopting as lofty a manner as I could manage. 'It's mean and unfair, just because they weren't born posh.'

'I suppose you could say that. But servants seem to have a much better time than the people they work for. Our servants were always having secret parties, though they let me come too because they knew I'd never tell my mother. And Nancy, my mother's maid, often used to dress up in her clothes.

Sometimes she wore them when she was going out with her sweetheart, just to impress him. She looked fantastic too – though of course it would be hard not to look impressive in Schiaparelli and Vionnet.'

I nodded, though I didn't have a clue who these strange, foreign-sounding people were, and the sort of clothes they designed.

'And Nanny was technically a servant, but she *liked* looking after me, I know she did,' said Jessica.

'Yes, I'm sure she did. It was silly of me to say that,' I said apologetically.

'No, no, you still have a point,' said Jessica, also wanting us to agree. She paused, nibbling at her lip. 'Shirley, have I put my foot in it?'

I blinked at her. 'In what way?'

'Well, I just wondered – is your mother actually a servant?' she asked, going pink.

Mum would be outraged to hear that! 'No, she's a managing director's personal secretary,' I said, elaborating each syllable carefully. 'Well, she's going to be now. She didn't work at all before, apart from when she left school, when she was a typist in a solicitor's office.'

'Oh, sorry, sorry! So *now* I've put my foot in it!' said Jessica.

'Not at all,' I told her. 'Here, do let me take my suitcase back, you've been carrying it for ages. It must be hurting you terribly.'

'I tell you, I can carry things heaps heavier than this suitcase,' Jessica insisted.

But when I forced her to let me take a turn, I saw that her palm was bright red with weals across it, as if she'd been given the cane.

I felt terrible, but knew she'd be upset if I commented. I took the handle and hauled the case along myself. I wondered how heavy it had been for Dad when it was full of brushes. What must it have been like calling on house after house after house, mostly being turned away at the door? Even when he was invited in to display and demonstrate each brush, when he got out his order book out the housewife would often sigh and say she wasn't sure, she'd better consult her husband – she was sorry but she couldn't possibly commit to any purchase without his say-so.

Dad would act it all out for Mum and me, trying to make it funny, mimicking the lady, his voice all high-pitched and silly, but I could see that it was actually sad. Mum wasn't a bit sympathetic. She'd tell Dad he must be a useless salesman if he could never make a sale, especially with brushes, when any fool knew that every housewife needed a handful, and the bristles wore out soon enough.

Sometimes Dad got angry and told her to stop nagging. And sometimes he didn't even bother replying – just sat there on the sofa with his arms dangling between his knees and his head bowed. No wonder he'd been in such a hurry to join up and be a soldier.

Everything was happening in a hurry. Year after year we'd been jogging along together as a family, and yet now Dad was away in the army and Mum was going to work and I was in a place called Meadow Ridge which I'd never even heard of until fifteen minutes ago.

I'd thought Mum and Dad and I all fitted together tightly like three pieces of a jigsaw puzzle. Now we'd been abruptly broken up. It was a disaster, wasn't it? Though Dad might like being a soldier. Mum might like being a personal secretary. I knew I wouldn't like it at St Agatha's with all those strict Sisters and snobby girls, but I liked Jessica enormously and, as long as we stuck together, then everything would be all right.

We were now trailing at the end of the long line of children, because I was so slow dragging my case. I was so hot, my vest was sticking to my back inside my jumper. Jessica's blazer felt like a fur coat but I couldn't take it off because I had to pass as a St Agatha's pupil.

Then the line gradually got smaller, and when I squinted up ahead I saw that the children were all being guided into a red-brick building by the crossroads.

'That must be the village hall!' I said.

'Stick with me, kid,' Jessica muttered out of the side of her mouth, like an American gangster in a film.

'You bet I will,' I said. I tried to do an American accent too, but I was no good at it.

Annie and another WVS lady with a big clipboard were standing at the door. The little boy with the shaven head was leaning against Annie's hip, his fists clasping the stiff material of her skirt.

'Here we are again!' she said cheerily. 'Now, I need to tick off your names and schools.'

67

'I'm Jessica Lipman,' Jessica said. 'I'm at St Agatha's. And this is my friend Shirley and she's at St Agatha's too.'

Annie ticked Jessica off, but then looked at me, her head on one side. 'Aren't you a Paradise Road pupil, Shirley?'

'I've joined the convent now,' I said, flapping my big purple blazer.

'Are you sure?'

'Yes, she's a new girl like me. We're going to stick together,' said Jessica.

Annie raised her eyebrows, but gave me a tick and added my name to the St Agatha's column.

Her colleague stared. 'Annie!' she said sharply.

'As if it matters,' said Annie. 'If they want to be together, why can't they? Go and wait inside, girls.'

I wanted to fling my arms around her neck. 'Thank you,' I breathed.

'Yes, thank you ever so, ever so much,' said Jessica, and we went inside hand in hand.

The hall was already crowded with children. Village ladies were handing out cups of milk and a currant bun to each child.

Our lady barely glanced at us, just taking in our purple blazers. 'The St Agatha's pupils are right over at the back of the hall, waiting for Lady Amersham's cart to collect all the suitcases. Then you're to walk up to the White House in a crocodile,' she said.

'*Tick-tock, tick-tock*,' said Jessica.

I giggled, so happy that I'd read *Peter and Wendy* and knew all about the crocodile who swallowed a clock.

We pushed our way through the heaving mass of children over to the large purple group at the end.

'Keep away from Sister Josephine!' I said.

'We won't go anywhere near old Charlie Chaplin. We'll stick with the form below. We're both quite small,' said Jessica.

'Yes, but they'll soon twig I'm not really a St Agatha's girl,' I said anxiously.

'It'll be OK once we're there, at this White House. You won't have anywhere else to go, will you? So they'll have to keep you,' Jessica told me.

'They'll think I'm not posh enough,' I said.

'Oh, that's total rubbish! *Do* stop fussing. It'll work out, I promise you.' She helped me lug my suitcase right to the back, near all the girls in purple, pushing some little Paradise Road boys off a bench so we could sit down and drink our milk and eat our buns in peace.

'Watch it!' one said angrily. 'Who do you think you are, shoving like that?'

'I'm sorry, but these benches are for St Agatha's girls,' I said.

'Stupid snooty-pants!' he said, but then sloped off.

'There, *he* thinks you're posh,' said Jessica.

It was so noisy in the room I could hardly hear her. You couldn't move for children, and yet now a whole load of adults were squeezing in too, peering intently at everyone. Several women already had hold of little girls – pretty ones with curly hair and clean faces.

A big lady in a tweed suit and an odd purple hat with a little feather stood on a chair and blew a whistle. 'Ladies, ladies!' she shouted. 'I'm Mrs Henshaw, Chairman of the Women's Institute. I've been put in charge of the billeting. I allocate the children to their new homes. I'm afraid this is turning into a bear garden! Let's have a little order. Please be patient and don't attempt to choose any children just yet. We must let all the St Agatha's pupils go first. Apparently Lady Amersham's gardener has arrived with his cart. You can go now, girls, and deposit your suitcases in it.'

Jessica squeezed my hand. I squeezed it back. We took our suitcases and stood at the back of the purple line. I kept my head down in case any Paradise Road children saw me. I practically bent double when I saw Marilyn Henderson nearby, but I managed to get to the door without anyone calling after me.

St Agatha's girls were handing their suitcases to a strange man who looked like Worzel Gummidge, with long mad hair and ragged clothes. The four nuns were flapping around, gathering up girls. Sister Josephine was right at the front, well away from us.

Jessica turned to me, smiling. 'See! We'll just tag along at the end of the crocodile. Simple!'

We waited with our suitcases. Jessica offered hers to Worzel Gummidge, who was wedging the cases into neat stacks. He swung it up easily onto the back of the cart. Then it was my turn. I tried to lift Dad's case, but I was so tired I could only raise it a couple of inches off the ground. Jessica seized hold of the handle to help.

Worzel Gummidge shook his head at us pityingly. He swatted our hands out of the way and picked up the case – and was taken by surprise. The weight bowed his arm, he lost his grip, and it fell to the ground with such a crash that the locks burst open. My belongings scattered everywhere – all my books, Timmy Ted, my smocked dress, Viyella nightie, sponge bag, hair ribbon, socks, vest and a pair of pink knickers with frills.

I sank to my knees and desperately started gathering them all up, Jessica helping. The other girls were all craning round, giggling, remarking on my embarrassing underwear. Sister Josephine came flapping over to see what was going on.

'What on earth is it now?' she demanded. She looked at my suitcase. Then she looked at me. 'What are you doing here? Take your wretched suitcase and all your belongings and go back into the village hall at once.'

'But she's coming to our school, Sister Josephine. Look, she's wearing a St Agatha's blazer,' said Jessica.

'Nonsense! She's the Paradise Road child you were so pally with on the train. Now do come along. Apparently it's a good half-hour walk to Lady Amersham's, so look sharp.'

'No, you don't understand, Sister Josephine. Shirley's left Paradise Road now. She's coming to our convent. Her mother's going to fix it. She's writing to you!' Jessica gabbled.

'I very much doubt that, Jessica. Please stop these pointless fibs and say goodbye to this little girl,' said Sister Josephine firmly.

'I can't bear to say goodbye! Shirley's my best friend in all the world,' Jessica declared, and she threw her arms round me.

'For goodness' sake, stop acting so hysterically! You've only known the child five minutes. Come along at once or you will be severely punished.' Sister Josephine shook her hard. 'And you, Shirley!' She said my name as if it made a bad taste in her mouth. 'Take that blazer off immediately and give it back to Jessica.'

'I gave it to her!' Jessica protested.

'You have no right to do such a thing. That blazer is the finest quality from Harrods. Whatever would your mother say?'

'She wouldn't mind in the slightest,' said Jessica. 'Don't take the blazer off, Shirley! You keep it. I don't want the wretched thing.'

But Sister Josephine took hold of me and pulled it off. She snapped my suitcase shut and tugged it upright. 'Now, take your ridiculous case and get back inside the village hall this instant. Jessica, you will walk with me at the front, in disgrace. Come along, Sisters, come along, girls.'

She marched off so determinedly that her habit swung round, exposing her thick ankles and stout shoes. She dragged Jessica along, struggling and wailing and crying out to me.

I stared after them, crying too.

'Hey, hey, cheer up, chicken,' said Annie, hurrying over to me. 'Oh dear, I didn't really think you'd get away with it. I'm so sorry! Come inside with me and we'll try to find you a lovely new billet – hopefully with another girl just like your friend.'

'I don't want any other girl. I want Jessica,' I sobbed.

She put her arm round my shoulders, picked up my case

and led me back inside. 'You sit on that bench at the front. I'll make the other children squash up so there's room for you. I'm sure you'll get picked soon,' she said cheerily.

I sat precariously on the very end of the bench, still snivelling. I waited. And waited and waited and waited.

PARADISE ROAD DIDN'T HAVE a Lady Someone offering them private accommodation for the entire school. We all had to be housed separately, even the teachers. There were far more of us than there were village people. The large lady with the feathered hat stood on a chair and counted, frowning. Then she blew her whistle again.

'It's me again – Mrs Henshaw, Chairman of the Women's Institute,' she announced unnecessarily. 'I'm afraid they've sent far more children than we were expecting. We're only a small village, after all. But we must all do our bit for the war effort.'

'War hasn't even been declared yet, missus!' someone shouted.

'I think we're all agreed that it's inevitable,' Mrs Henshaw said firmly. 'And whether it's declared next day, next week or next month, it doesn't alter the fact that we have at least a hundred children here who need a proper supper, a bath and a bed for the night. If you can all offer a home for two children, we should just about manage to accommodate them all. Thank you so much. Please start picking out your children now.'

The villagers came crowding around us. They were mostly women. Some were young and gossipy, with babies on their hips. Others were older like my mum, but not as smart. Then there were really old ladies, thin and withered or built like tanks. There were a few men, mostly old too. One looked very like the scary man who had shouted at us. I hoped he wouldn't pick me.

I wanted one of the young mothers because they looked more fun. I liked the idea of a baby too. I could help feed it and bath it and take it for walks in its pram, like a special big sister. I decided on the mother I liked best – a woman with long curly dark hair holding a chubby baby boy in a bright blue knitted jersey. He was clutching a small toy dog, waving it around in the air and going 'Woof, woof!' It would have got on most people's nerves, but his mum just laughed at him and said it back to him just as many times. If I couldn't be with Jessica at St Agatha's I wanted to be with that young mother because she looked so happy and seemed so patient.

I tried smiling at her hopefully, though it was a bit of a struggle because I was still sniffly from crying. I kept thinking about Jessica. What if Sister Josephine really did punish her? Did nuns give girls the cane? At Paradise Road only the boys got the cane, thank goodness, but it still made me feel sick when one had to go up to the front of the class to get whacked. Especially when Mr Bentley, the headmaster, did it, because he made the boys pull their trousers down too. I always shut my eyes, but you could still hear the cane whistling through the air – and the cries.

I shut my eyes now to try to stop howling, and when I opened them again I saw that the dark-haired mother had walked straight past me and chosen two little boys with straight partings in their hair and nicely knitted red jumpers with a black Scottie dog pattern across their chests.

If she liked knitted jumpers, why hadn't she picked me? Mum said Fair Isle was the best you could buy! But I could see that the little boys matched the baby, though I was sure they wouldn't help feed and bath him.

I knuckled my eyes and sat up straight, peering at the other young mothers, but none seemed to be taking any notice of me. They were going for the really little cute children or the much older ones who looked neat and sensible.

'Come along, ladies, simply take the nearest two children. I'm sure they're all lovely kiddies,' Mrs Henshaw advised.

They took no notice, marching up and down the benches. One of the old men even made two of the boys open their mouths so he could examine their teeth. All the children sat still now, brothers and sisters or best friends in tight little huddles. I wished, wished, wished I could be with Jessica. It felt so lonely by myself.

Two rows back there was another girl who was also sitting on her own. She was smaller than me, probably in the class below. She had ringlets like Marilyn Henderson's and a red coat. She was quite a bit prettier than me – I'd have much more chance of being picked if I could pair up with her. I stood up and tried to haul my case over, but another Women's Institute lady frowned at me and told me to stay put.

'We don't want little girls dashing about all over the place. Sit quietly, dear,' she said.

We were all sitting quietly now, even the rowdiest of the boys. It was so awful being looked at and then rejected. I did my best to look attractive, but I suspected that my nose needed blowing, and I'd somehow lost my ribbon, so my hair flopped over my forehead and got in my eyes. I kept tossing it back until I heard one woman mutter to another that I had a nervous tic.

I held my head rigid and clasped my thumbs tight because I'd read that it brought you luck. It didn't seem to be working. People went straight past me – or, worse, had a long look and then walked on, not quite meeting my eyes. I turned round to see who they'd pick instead. Sometimes it was the pretty girls and the handsome boys, the bright-eyed, rosy-cheeked ones with ready smiles and frank glances. But sometimes it was the sad, pale little ones with patched jumpers and Wellington boots that made the women shake their heads and sweep them up in their arms.

I looked down at my Fair Isle jumper and my smart red patent shoes and felt despairing. What would Mum think if she could see me? There weren't as many villagers now. The same ones kept going up and down the benches as if they were hoping that a row of fresher, cuter children would suddenly be sitting there, as if by magic.

'Come along now, Meadow Ridgers,' Mrs Henshaw called. 'Please take any two children. War is imminent and we have to do our best to protect these little ones if there's bombing. It isn't a lifetime commitment! Everyone's saying this will be a short, sharp war, over by Christmas. The children will only be with you for a few weeks. You're literally saving their lives. So come along, pick two!'

The villagers looked irritated, and several muttered about 'old Bossy-boots'. But it hurried them up a little. The girl with the ringlets and the red coat was chosen, along with a small boy with fair hair. Marilyn Henderson was chosen too, along with Mary. If only my own hair were long and wound into ringlets I'd have a much better chance! Two brothers were chosen, even though the smaller one had a squinty eye. Two fat sisters were chosen, though they were bursting out of their cardie buttons, and a villager joked they'd eat her out of house and home.

Off they went, two by two, two by two, two by two, like Noah's Ark animals. I was left there, along with a big girl with spots, a girl wearing thick glasses, the frame mended with sticking plaster, a small girl who kept her head on her chest and wouldn't look at anyone, the little kid with the shaven head who was scared of cows, and awful Kevin, the gangly boy with jug ears who had tried to lasso me with his tie.

The villagers had all gone home with their chosen children. Even the horrid-looking old man had picked two boys who didn't look happy about it. I stared at the door, wondering if any more villagers might come. We seemed to be stuck here with Mrs Henshaw and the Women's Institute ladies, Annie and the other WVS ladies, and our headmaster, Mr Bentley, who was yawning and consulting his watch. Some of the Paradise

Road teachers were staying in a hostel together. Mr Bentley was going there too, but he was checking to see that we were all successfully billeted. We waited. Nobody came.

I clenched my fists until my thumbs nearly snapped off. I was out of luck. Not a single soul wanted me. What was going to happen now? Were the WVS ladies going to the train station to make the long journey back to London? Would the Women's Institute snap the lights off in the village hall and leave the six of us sitting here in the dark?

I started shivering. The spotty girl turned her back on everyone. The girl with the mended specs wiped them with her hem. Her eyes went all peepy without them. The small girl bent so low her head was almost on her knees. Kevin bit his nails. The shaven-headed boy scowled.

I went over to Annie. 'What's going to happen to us now?' I asked.

'Don't worry, sweetie. We'll find you a good home,' she said brightly, but she looked worried too.

She went to confer with Mrs Henshaw and the other women. They whispered together, glancing at us every now and then. Finally Mrs Henshaw came over, her sensible brogues squeaking on the polished floor.

'Gather together, children. Don't look so down-hearted!'

'Of course we're down-hearted, miss. No one bleeding wants us!' said Kevin.

'Now, now, language!' Mr Bentley intervened briskly. 'You need to wash your mouth out with soap, lad.'

'Don't be silly, dear, of course you're wanted,' said Mrs Henshaw.

'No we're not, or we wouldn't be sitting here, would we?' Kevin muttered, biting his nails again.

'Don't do that! Goodness me, you won't have any fingers left. Now, I daresay we could all do with a nice cup of tea. My colleague's gone to seek out a kettle, and there are lots of buns left, so we can all tuck in to a jolly feast. And then, when we're all refreshed and in better spirits, we're going to find you a lovely new home.'

'Just him, miss? Or me too?' asked the little shaven-haired boy.

'All of you,' she said. 'Three homes. We'll pair you up.'

I didn't want to be in a pair with any of them. The spotty girl was too old and the glasses girl was too young, and they were nothing like Jessica. I certainly didn't want to be paired with either of the boys. They both spoke with broad cockney accents, their clothes didn't fit and they didn't look very clean. The little one probably had a shaven head because he had nits. Mum always had a horror of my catching nits and made me kneel with my head on a towel in her lap once a week so she could comb it through carefully, checking.

I decided that the little girl with the bent head would be my best hope. She was so small she could be my little sister. She wouldn't be as sweet as a baby but I could still look after her and teach her how to do things and read to her at night. I was a little put off because she smelled of wee, but she was very small, after all, and anyone could have an accident.

I tried putting my arm round her. I hoped she'd cuddle into me but she went rigid.

'It's all right. I just want to look after you,' I whispered. 'Like a big sister.'

'I ain't got a big sister,' she said, and pushed me away.

The other children sniggered. I kept my chin up, pretending I didn't care.

We sat silently together, although we felt horribly separate. The small boy started sniffing loudly. He wiped his nose with the back of his hand and it smeared all over his cheek, making me feel sick.

I hoped I didn't have snot on *my* face too after all the crying. I felt it gingerly but couldn't tell. I peered around, wondering if there was a cloakroom with a basin.

'Are you all right, pet?' asked Annie, coming over.

'Please could I wash my hands and face?' I whispered it, but the boys heard me.

'*Oh, please could I wash my stupid hands and face?*' Kevin imitated, in a high, silly voice, while the little boy snorted.

'Now, now, boys, don't be silly. I think you could all do with a wash and brush-up. There's a little room at the back. You pop in and spruce yourselves up,' Annie suggested.

I started lugging my case.

'No, you don't need to take that with you, do you? I'll keep an eye on it,' said Annie.

'Please, I need my sponge bag,' I said.

'*My sponge bag!*' Kevin mimicked.

But I couldn't find it! All my things were higgledy-piggledy in my case because I'd had to scoop them back in such a hurry. I rummaged amongst them fruitlessly. I even took everything out and put each item back, but there was still no sponge bag.

'What you got all them books for?' asked Kevin.

'Look, she's got a teddy,' said the little boy.

'And pink knickers!' added Kevin, smirking.

'Hello, Mr Teddy,' said the little boy, picking him up.

'Put him down!' I commanded.

I tried to snatch Timmy Ted back but the little boy darted away, holding my bear aloft.

'He wants to come with me, he says. He's my bear now, aren't you, Mr Teddy?' he said, and he made Timmy Ted nod his head.

It was too much. I was exhausted, I was missing Mum, my best friend had been dragged away, none of the villagers had picked me, none of these children left here liked me, I'd lost my sponge bag so I'd end up with grey skin and green teeth, and now this horrible little boy had stolen my teddy.

'Give him back, you hateful pig!' I yelled. I dashed after him and rugby-tackled him to the floor.

'Hey, hey, that's enough now!' Mr Bentley dashed up and hauled me off him. 'Dear me, what a temper! And he's only half your size. What are you thinking of? You need to be taught a lesson!'

'He stole my bear!' I cried, though I knew I sounded ridiculous.

'Poor Shirley's had a very hard time,' Annie said quickly.

'And this little soul didn't steal – he just wanted to look at the teddy, didn't you, dear?' said Mrs Henshaw. 'But you're going to give it back to the little girl, aren't you?'

The small boy sat up, sniffing, and silently handed my bear back. His eyes looked very big in his pale face. There were purple shadows underneath them. He seemed smaller than ever, and very pathetic.

I'd actually knocked him over. I felt dreadful.

'I'm thoroughly ashamed of you, Sally,' said Mr Bentley. He didn't even remember my name! 'I won't have bullying from anyone at Paradise Road! You deserve a good smacking.'

He was bullying *me* now, but I was too scared to point this out.

'I'm sure she's very sorry,' said Mrs Henshaw. 'Aren't you, dear?'

'Yes, I'm sorry. I hope I haven't hurt you,' I mumbled.

''S all right,' the boy said. 'Didn't hurt anyway. My mum says I've got a bonce like a bleeding cannon ball.'

'*Language!*' Mr Bentley said, but gave up and retreated to a bench at the back of the hall.

The big woman was feeling the little boy's boiled-egg head carefully. 'No lumps or bumps, thank goodness. Right, off you go, all of you, and have a wash. Especially you, young man – you've got a very dirty face.'

'I can't wash, Mrs Henshaw. I've lost my sponge bag with my flannel and toothbrush and everything. Mum even let me have her special Coty L'Aimant soap that she got for Christmas,' I said wretchedly.

'Oh dear, dear, what a tragedy,' she said, but it didn't sound as if she were taking me seriously.

But lovely Annie was listening. 'Let me have a look in your suitcase. I'm sure it'll be there somewhere,' she said. She knelt down. 'Goodness, what a jumble!'

'It *was* packed ever so neatly, but then it burst open when that man with the cart took hold of it,' I said.

'Yes, you nearly got away with it, tagging along with the convent girls! You might have regretted it though. I went to a convent and the nuns were unbelievably strict. What a lot of books you've got!' she said, sorting through them.

'They were all told the rules. Just *one* book,' said Mrs Henshaw. 'The silly child can barely lift her suitcase now.'

'Still, nothing beats a good read. Oh, *Black Beauty*! I wept buckets over that when I was a kid.' Annie put my books back and snapped the case shut again. 'You're right, no sponge bag. But if your case fell open outside, maybe your sponge bag spilled into the gutter somehow. Shall we go and look?'

She held out her hand and I took it gratefully. I trotted along beside her as if I was a really little kid. I seemed to have lost three or four years in the course of the train journey. I wanted to rub my nose against Timmy Ted's furry snout. I hoped the little boy wouldn't try to get him out of my suitcase again. I wanted to find my sponge bag, but I'd have been far more upset if my bear went missing.

It turned out my sponge bag wasn't missing at all. It was lying in the gutter, just as Annie had suggested. I peered inside and everything was there – my toothbrush, my tin of Gibbs Dentifrice, my pink flannel, even Mum's cake of Coty L'Aimant soap, still in its red packet.

'There we go,' said Annie, patting my shoulder. 'Now, have your wash and brush-up, and then we'll have a nice cup of tea, if old Broody Henshaw has managed to rustle up that kettle.'

'Broody Henshaw!' I giggled delightedly.

'Shh, now!' she said, giggling too.

The boys had already had their wash, though they still looked pretty grubby. The three girls were in the cloakroom now. The spotty one was dabbing cream all over her spots. I thought she was making them look worse, but obviously I didn't say so. The girl with the broken glasses was copying her, pretending to dab invisible cream on her own face. The littlest girl made no attempt to wash and yelled when the spotty girl tried to help her.

I waited until I had the cloakroom to myself. I could use the toilet – the double-you-see – without fear of them listening, and then I could clean my teeth without them seeing me spitting. There was a cake of Wrights Coal Tar beside the basin, so I didn't need to break open my packet of soap.

I washed thoroughly and repositioned my hairgrip so that it anchored my hair out of my eyes. There wasn't a mirror, but I hoped I looked better. Perhaps the next village lady through the door would look straight at me and say, 'Oh, I want that clean little girl with the tidy hair!'

I had a sudden dizzying thought. What if Mum wasn't my mum, and was one of these village women? Would *she* have picked me? Or would she have picked a little girl with curls and dimples, just like the film-star Shirley? Or would she have picked one of the boys?

Everything seemed to have gone topsy-turvy in the space of a day. Where was I again? For a moment I couldn't even remember the name of the village. Then the station sign flashed into my mind. Meadow Ridge. So where *was* Meadow Ridge?

I thought of the map of Great Britain on my jigsaw-puzzle box. I didn't know whether Meadow Ridge was north or south, east or west. For all I knew the train could have gone through a tunnel and burst out into a new land altogether, a place where you didn't have your mum to tell you what to do, and you met scores of strange people, and the only one you really liked was snatched away from you.

My eyes felt watery again.

You are not to cry again, baby! I told myself fiercely. I was ten, for goodness' sake.

I put both my thumbs under my chin and pushed upwards. *Chin up, Shirley*, I commanded, and marched myself back into the hall. Mr Bentley was still sitting by himself at the back, irritably puffing on his pipe. The WVS and WI ladies were all mixed up together, chatting and drinking tea. Annie and Mrs Henshaw were sitting at either end of a bench, clutching cups of tea too. Annie decorously kept her knees together but Mrs Henshaw had planted her large legs wide apart, so I could glimpse her knickers. They were pink directoire, the legs gathered tightly with elastic just above her knees. I was really annoyed to see that my knickers were the same colour as hers.

The spotty girl and the speccy girl were sitting together, sipping milk and eating white iced buns. The spotty girl ate hers by nibbling the icing off first. The speccy girl copied her. The tiny girl didn't seem interested in her milk or her bun. She put them on the floor in front of her and sat grimly still and silent. Kevin sat astride the bench, riding it like a cowboy, holding a bun in each hand. The bald boy sat cross-legged, absent-mindedly picking at the scabs on his knees. He had so much bun in his mouth that he looked like a chipmunk. There was a plate of further buns on the bench between them.

'Come over here, dear,' said Mrs Henshaw, beckoning to me. 'What's your name?'

'Shirley Louise Smith,' I said, saying it in a clear sing-song, the way Mum had taught me.

The two boys snorted and did silly imitations, spluttering crumbs.

'Boys, stop it! You'll choke if you talk with your mouths full. Do you want me to take the buns away?' Mrs Henshaw asked.

They shook their heads and carried on stuffing themselves.

'We're all getting to know each other, Shirley,' said Mrs Henshaw. 'This is Kathleen and Vera, and we think this little one is Irene, according to our list, but she's lost her label so we can't check.'

'*Not* Irene,' the small girl muttered fiercely. 'Renee.'

'Ah! Renee, of course. And these boys are Kevin' – she nodded to him – 'and Archie. There, we all know each other now. Sit down and grab a bun before these little gannets devour them all.'

The bun was starting to harden, and stuck in my mouth. I wondered why Kevin and Archie were wolfing them down. Then I looked at the boys properly. Kevin was so skinny his wrists looked as if they'd snap, and his prominent ears were emphasized by the pinched thinness of his face. Archie looked peaky too, his eyes too big, his neck tiny, his little hunched shoulders very narrow.

Were the boys actually starving? I thought of Sara Crewe from *A Little Princess* in her black dress, begging for stale bread. Did Kevin and Archie live in garrets back in London? And did they have a pet rat like Sara? I shuddered. I'd always identified with Sara Crewe, but I was so scared of rats I knew that sharing a room with one would drive me crazy.

'It's all right, Shirley,' Annie said gently, seeing me shiver. 'We're going to get you sorted out. When you've had your tea, Mrs Henshaw's going to take you on a little trip around the village.'

'Mrs Henshaw's taking me?' I asked. I wasn't sure I liked the idea. She fussed so. She seemed posh, which would please Mum. She might wear dreadful granny knickers but her heather-fleck tweed suit was clearly high quality, and her purple hat with a feather was stylish in a country sort of way.

She didn't look very mumsy though. She wasn't the slightest bit cuddly – large but not at all soft. Nothing jiggled when she walked. She looked as if she was made of cast iron underneath the tweed suit.

'Is she taking me as well?' Kevin asked, nibbling at his nails.

'And me?' Archie whispered.

The girls all looked at her too, even Renee.

'Oh no, dears, I'm afraid I can't take any of you,' said Mrs Henshaw, going pink. 'I'm expecting my own little granddaughters any day now, all three of them, so that's my spare bedrooms spoken for. But there are several people in the village who I happen to know have *many* spare bedrooms. I think they need a little gentle persuading, don't you?'

I listened in alarm. I thought of the old man in the cottage at the edge of the village, the one who had called us nasty thieving cockneys. What if a man like that had a spare bedroom? I would sooner sleep under a hedge.

'But what if they don't want us?' I said.

'Of course they'll want you, chickie,' said Annie, and Mrs Henshaw nodded so determinedly the feather in her hat wagged.

I wasn't so sure. The others all drooped too. It was obvious we weren't the pick of the bunch.

The other WVS ladies were gathering up cups and saucers and putting them on a tray. One of them came over to Annie.

'The train back to London goes in twenty minutes. Come on, we'd better get back to the station,' she told her.

I found myself clinging to Annie. 'Don't go,' I begged. 'Can't you stay? I want *you* to find me a home.'

'Oh, lovey, I wish I could.' She looked at her wristwatch. 'Maybe I could get a later train,' she suggested to her colleagues.

'Don't be daft, Annie, this is the last train back. We're out in the sticks, remember. Come on!' said her friend.

'Don't worry, dear, the children will be fine with me,' said Mrs Henshaw.

'Oh well,' said Annie. 'I don't suppose I have any choice. Be good kids, now. I'll be thinking of you.'

She gave everyone a hug and a kiss, even Archie, who was unpleasantly sticky. When she put her arms round me I pulled her closer. 'Can't I come back to London with you?' I whispered in her ear.

'Well, that would defeat the whole object of this caper,' said Annie. 'London's not going to be safe for little sprogs like you. You're going to love it here. All the fields to play in, and trees to climb! You'll have a whale of a time. Now give us a smile!'

I did my best.

'Toodle-oo,' she said, giving us all a wave.

She went off with her cronies. The Women's Institute ladies disappeared into the kitchen, and we were left with Mrs Henshaw and Mr Bentley. They didn't look as if they appreciated each other's company.

'We'd better be off too, children,' said Mrs Henshaw. 'Would any of you like to visit the W.C. before we leave?'

'You what?' said Archie.

'The toilet,' I said, raising my eyebrows. 'Don't you know anything?'

'**C**OME ON NOW, KEEP** together,' said Mr Bentley. 'Quick march! Left, right, left, right, left, right!'

We stared at each other. Was he serious?

'We're not a bleeding army,' Kevin muttered.

'I heard that!' said Mr Bentley sharply. 'Any more swearing and I'll pick you up by those remarkable ears and give you a good shaking, young man.'

Kevin mouthed a whole series of bad words the moment his back was turned, but took care not to say them out loud. He did an approximation of marching, and the others copied, except for the spotty girl, Kathleen. She swayed her hips, tossing her hair and walking her own way. She looked quite pretty from behind. It was such a shame about her spots. I hoped they wouldn't start sprouting from my own face when I was older.

Vera did her best to sway her hips too, but she looked ridiculous, a total waggle-bottom. Kevin nudged little Archie and they stuck their own scrawny bottoms out and wiggled them around, snorting with laughter at their silly antics. They even raised a smile from Renee.

Mrs Henshaw tutted disapprovingly, and pointed warningly at Mr Bentley at the front, but it was clear that she was on our side. She carried Renee's suitcase because she was so little, but I was left struggling with mine. It pulled on my arms terribly and made the palms of my hands sore. I was sure I was getting blisters. I couldn't march – I could barely walk. I thought of the valiant way Jessica had helped me with it, doing much more than her fair share.

She would be at the White House by now. Was she missing me the way I was missing her? Or was she already chatting to one of the other girls, doing her best to find a new friend? Not ghastly Goofy or Munchkin, but one of the quieter ones. Maybe when they unpacked they'd compare books, and promise to do a swap. Maybe this other girl liked *Ballet Shoes* too, and they were having a wonderful discussion about their favourite Fossil sister, Pauline or Petrova or Posy.

I tried to distract myself by imagining the three Fossils struggling along beside me, evacuated too. Pauline would complain that Nana had sent her in her velvet audition frock, and now it was so tight under the arms she was scared the seams might tear. Petrova would linger by the little village garage we were passing in real life, and hope to make friends with one of the mechanics there. Posy would be fuss-fuss-fussing about her dancing, wondering who would teach her ballet now, and whether they could possibly be good enough.

I became a little too distracted by my imaginary book friends and didn't look where I was going. One of the paving stones was loose. I tripped over the raised edge, and was so lopsided with my heavy suitcase that I couldn't recover my footing. I fell flat on my face.

'Whoops-a-daisy!' said Mrs Henshaw.

I lay there stunned, unable to move.

'She's dropped down dead!' Archie rasped.

'Dear Lord, now what? Who was horsing around?' Mr Bentley demanded.

'This little girl's simply fallen over. I'm sure she's all right,' said Mrs Henshaw, but she sounded scared.

I heard a rustle as she squatted down beside me.

'Shirley, is it? Are you all right, dear?' she asked, giving me a tentative shake.

I didn't want to open my eyes because I felt so foolish. I wanted to stay lying there, throbbing, until they eventually got fed up and wandered off, as the Fossil sisters seemed to have done.

'Shirley, Sally – whatever your name is! Come on, sit up,' Mr Bentley commanded. 'I need to see if you've really hurt yourself.'

'I'm all right,' I mumbled, horrified by all the fuss. I sat up to prove it. I was heartbroken to see that I'd scuffed the toes of my beautiful red patent shoes. I barely noticed that I'd scuffed my knees too, and both were bleeding.

'Oh dear, oh dear,' said Mrs Henshaw, wincing, dabbing at them with her lace hankie. Her face was very close to mine. I could even see the little smudge of dark red lipstick on her front tooth. Her fancy hat was now a little skew-whiff, at an unsuitably jaunty angle.

I felt uncomfortable being so near her and tried to wriggle away.

'That's it, check all your limbs, though I'm pretty certain you haven't broken anything. What made you fall over? Did you suddenly feel dizzy or did you trip over something?' she asked.

'No, I – I just fell,' I mumbled, but I couldn't stop myself from glancing at my case.

Mrs Henshaw took hold of my suitcase handle and tried to lift it. 'Oh my goodness! Well, it's perfectly obvious why you fell over, Shirley. This is much too heavy for a little girl.'

'Didn't your mother get the correct list?' Mr Bentley demanded, opening my case without so much as a by-your-leave. 'The silly woman's packed everything but the kitchen sink. And what on earth are all these books?'

I felt as if I would scream if anyone else questioned me about them. I saw all my favourite fictional friends, human and animal, wincing at his voice.

'I'll take them with me. We'll start a little library for everyone,' said Mr Bentley.

'Oh!' I said. 'Oh, no! You mustn't do that!'

'I beg your pardon,' he said. 'Don't you use that tone with me, young lady!'

'I think it's just the shock,' said Mrs Henshaw quickly, patting my back.

Mr Bentley snorted and started gathering up my books, looking at them rather disapprovingly. 'I can't see any of the boys wanting to borrow these, but I suppose the girls will like some of the stories,' he muttered.

I couldn't bear the sight of his big hands holding them – hair grew right down to his knuckles, as if he were a gorilla inside a big grey suit. I thought of all those other hands grasping my books, opening them clumsily, breaking the spines, turning down the corners of the pages. I thought of Marilyn Henderson scribbling all over my favourite drawings of Pauline, Petrova and Posy and printing *This is stupid rubbish* in the margins.

'I'm very sorry, Mr Bentley, please don't be cross, but I simply have to keep these books myself,' I said.

He had all my precious books gathered in his arms now. He shook his head at me. 'Well, you're a very selfish little girl, aren't you?' he said. 'It will do you good to learn how to share.'

'You don't understand, sir,' I said desperately. 'They're not *my* books. They're my mum's. They were all her favourites when she was a girl.' I knew some of them hadn't even been published when Mum was little, but I hoped Mr Bentley wouldn't know that.

'Well, when you go home again I daresay you can return them all to her. I'm sure *she'd* like to share her childhood favourites with the rest of the school,' said Mr Bentley pointedly.

He must be mad to think Mum would want to lend so much as a torn comic to any of the children at Paradise Road Juniors.

I thought hard, my brain whirling at top speed like a little top. 'I know, but . . . but Mum's not here now. She died. We've only just had the funeral.' I felt so wicked saying it, as if I were tempting fate. Perhaps Mum really *would* die now. I felt the tears welling in my eyes at the thought.

'Oh, you poor little pet,' said Mrs Henshaw, putting her arm round me.

'And Dad's away in the army on this special secret mission to do with the coming war, and I'll have to go and live with my auntie when I'm back, and these books are the only things of my mum's she's letting me keep, and I need them so,' I wept, almost believing it.

'There now, there now,' said Mrs Henshaw, pressing me to her large tweed bosom. 'Of course you can keep all your mother's precious books. Don't worry, I'll mention it when we find your billet and make sure you can have them all by your bedside, dear. Isn't that right, Mr Bentley?'

Mr Bentley didn't look as if he agreed at all, but he didn't argue any further. He put them all back in my suitcase, tossing them in as if they were quoits, and when he saw Mrs Henshaw looking at him he gave the top of my head a dog-pat. 'Now, now,' he said.

'Your mum's *died*?' Vera asked, peering at me through her thick glasses. She clearly wasn't very quick on the uptake.

I nodded solemnly.

'I think my mum's died,' Archie said matter-of-factly.

'I'm sure that's not true,' said Mrs Henshaw said.

'But you don't *know*,' said Kathleen. 'When the war starts and all the bombs come, all our mums could get blown up.'

'*My* mum?' said Vera, looking as if she were going to start crying too.

Mr Bentley flashed me a look that said, *Now see what you've started!* 'Come along, children, let's stop all this morbid nonsense.'

'You're going to need a bandage, Shirley,' said Mrs Henshaw. 'Anyone got another spare hankie?'

Archie didn't have one. Nor did Vera or Renee. Kathleen might have, but she was keeping it to herself. Kevin offered one, but it was grey and in a disgusting state. Mrs Henshaw reeled back at the sight of it and shook her head. Then she looked up at Mr Bentley.

'Aha! I can see a lovely clean white hankie peeping out of your top pocket, Mr Bentley,' she said.

He sighed and handed it over. Mrs Henshaw bound it tightly around the worst knee.

'There now, that should staunch the flow. Now let's see if you can walk on those poorly legs.' She helped me up and I walked gingerly.

'There, right as rain!' said Mr Bentley. 'Come along then, troops. It'll be getting dark soon. This good lady needs to find you all a decent roof over your heads.'

I struggled to lift my suitcase. Mrs Henshaw looked pointedly at Mr Bentley. 'We don't want her tripping all over again,' she said.

He sighed and seized the handle from me. 'Good Lord

above,' he murmured, but he carried it for me.

'And you, lad – Kevin, is it? Take Shirley's arm,' said Mrs Henshaw.

I don't know which of us looked more appalled, Kevin or me.

'I'm not taking her arm, miss. She's not my sweetheart or sister or nothing,' said Kevin.

'I simply need you to help her along, you fathead. I'm not suggesting you become betrothed,' said Mrs Henshaw, laughing heartily.

'I don't need any help,' I insisted, but she took hold of my arm and forced my hand to grip Kevin's bony elbow.

'There now,' she said.

So we straggled on around the village. I had to stay hooked onto Kevin, smelling his musty unwashed clothes. We couldn't walk properly together because we were such different sizes. He took great strides, while I was reduced to hobbling. I felt the blood soaking through Mr Bentley's handkerchief. It started trickling down into my sock. If it got stained red it would match my patent shoes. My toes were so sore and cramped. Perhaps they were bleeding too. I wondered how long it would be before every drop of blood drained out of me and I collapsed like an empty paper bag.

Mrs Henshaw knocked on various doors. Her message was the same at each one: 'Hello there, so sorry to trouble you. I'm Mrs Henshaw from The Hall, Chairman of the Women's Institute. I'm sure you've seen me around the village. I've been appointed Chief Billeting Officer. According to my list, you haven't yet volunteered to be a foster-parent. I'm sure you'd like to take two of these children. Two girls? Two boys? One of each?' She edged forward as she spoke, getting a foot in the door in an intimidating fashion.

But it didn't work. The villagers shook their heads and muttered excuses. One simply slammed the door in her face.

'We don't want any London kiddies, thanks very much. And you can plead till you're blue in the face, but we don't have to, not if we don't want,' they retorted. 'There's no law says we've got to.'

'I wish there *was* a law,' Mrs Henshaw muttered. 'Really, I'm ashamed of some of these Meadow Ridgers.'

'Could we not try the next village?' Mr Bentley suggested.

'That's a good five miles away. It's much too far for the children to walk, and it would be a nightmare trying to find transportation. I have a car but my husband is using it on business,' she said. 'No, we must keep pressing on. *Nil desperandum.*'

'Nil indeed,' said Mr Bentley uncertainly.

But it seemed a hopeless task. Mrs Henshaw kept consulting her lists and trying all the homes that didn't yet have their two allocated evacuees, but people shook their heads determinedly, and one fierce couple even threatened to set the dogs on us if we didn't leave immediately. They were two barking Alsatians straining at their leashes, and even Mr Bentley looked frightened and backed away rapidly.

Then, at last, one woman softened when she opened the

door of her tiny cottage and saw us all standing on her garden path. 'I've got five kiddies of my own, three boys and two girls, all in one room. Still, I daresay I might squeeze in just one more. I'll take a small girl if you've got one,' she said cheerily.

I hunched up, trying to look extremely small, but it didn't work. Renee was much smaller than Kathleen or Vera or me. She got taken in, and the rest of us were left.

Mrs Henshaw tried the houses at the end of the village. She crossed her fingers as she marched up the overgrown path of the very last house, a large square one like a child's drawing. She knocked loudly on the door and waited. Then she knocked again. And still waited.

'It's obvious nobody's in,' said Mr Bentley, looking at his watch.

'I'll try once more,' said Mrs Henshaw, doing so. 'It might take them a little time, and I suspect they're hard of hearing.'

As she spoke, a very elderly lady in a lavender frock opened the door, and we glimpsed another similar lady standing a few paces behind her.

'Ah, Miss Robinson. And, er . . . Miss Robinson. Hello there, so sorry to trouble you. I'm Mrs Henshaw from—'

'Oh, we know who you are, dear,' said the Miss Robinson at the door. She peered at us curiously. 'Oh, my! Are these the poor little children from London?'

We drooped uneasily.

'Stand up straight!' Mr Bentley hissed.

The first Miss Robinson looked at him. 'Are you their father?' she asked.

He looked appalled. 'No, no, madam, I am their headmaster,' he said, enunciating the word with exaggerated care. 'I am trying to find a billet for the last of my pupils.'

'We wondered if you and your sister would care to take two of them?' Mrs Henshaw asked.

Miss Robinson blinked in surprise. 'Oh, goodness me! We couldn't possibly. We're far too old to look after little children. We can barely manage to look after ourselves nowadays. Besides, we're maiden ladies. We have no experience.'

'Perhaps the two boys might be a help to you, fetching and carrying and doing a little gardening?' Mrs Henshaw suggested.

'Oh, definitely not. We couldn't cope with noisy boys,' said Miss Robinson. 'I'm sorry, Mrs Henshaw, but it simply wouldn't do.'

She made to close the door, but her sister came forward and stood shoulder to shoulder with her. 'Perhaps one of the girls, sister?' she said timidly.

The first Miss Robinson looked astonished.

'I'm sure a girl wouldn't be too noisy,' the second sister said. 'Look at them, poor little mites. They look exhausted. I think we could take a girl. Perhaps two at a pinch?'

'Well, sister, if you really think so,' said the first Miss Robinson. 'I suppose we could train them up a little.'

Kathleen, Vera and I looked at them hopefully. I didn't particularly want to go and live with two ancient old ladies, especially as it seemed likely they'd want to turn us into housemaids. But neither did I want to spend the rest of the night traipsing to the next village, and then the next and the next.

I knew my hair looked too plain without its ribbon and I had two bloody knees and scraped shoes – but Kathleen had a bad complexion and a sulky expression and Vera's broken glasses didn't help her looks.

But the second sister shuffled towards Vera, smiling at her. 'What about this little one?' she said.

'Excellent!' said Mrs Henshaw. 'And I'm sure you'll want to take her friend too as company. You'd like that, wouldn't you, Vera?'

'Oh yes!' said Vera huskily, and held out her hand to Kathleen. 'She's my friend.'

My heart sank. Mrs Henshaw put her arm round my shoulders. 'Perhaps all three girls?' she tried.

'We can only manage two at the most,' the first Miss Robinson said decidedly. 'And that's going to be a pinch.'

'There will be an allowance, though the paperwork is going to be a massive task,' said Mrs Henshaw. 'And doubtless it will all have to be organized by Yours Truly. Still, we must all do our duty. Thank you very much, ladies. Bye-bye, Vera and Kathleen.'

We left them standing uncertainly on the doorstep. So I was the last girl. I prickled with the humiliation.

'So what about us, miss?' Archie said, tugging at Mrs Henshaw's tweed skirt. 'Why ain't we got nowhere to stay?'

'Because nobody wants us, you daft little beggar,' said Kevin, shrugging. I think he meant to sound as if he couldn't care less, but his voice wobbled.

'Nonsense,' said Mrs Henshaw. 'Two fine lads, and a lovely little girl – of course people will want you. We just have to find the *right* people. Now let me put my thinking cap on.'

She looked back down the main village street. Then she looked up at the hill. I saw the long white gleam of Lady Amersham's manor house.

'I know!' I said. 'I know where we can go! Up there, with St Agatha's. I know for a fact they'll have spare beds because Jessica said several of the girls didn't turn up at the station.'

'I'm not going with no girls!' said Kevin.

'Me neither,' agreed Archie. 'Well, not them posh ones.'

'I could go though,' I said. 'Jessica's my best friend. And I know the others too. And Sister Josephine. Oh, please, Mrs Henshaw, can't I go and live at Lady Amersham's?'

'No dear, you can't go there, you're not a bona fide pupil,' she said, barely listening. She'd turned her back on me and looked up in the other direction.

'Bona fidee?' I asked.

'It's Latin, dear,' she murmured, staring up at the other hill.

I still didn't have a clue what *bona fide* meant. I knew Latin was an old language that was only taught in posh schools. If you knew Latin, you were very clever.

'I come top of my class, Mrs Henshaw,' I said quickly, to

show her I might be able to learn it too. 'And I was top at my old school too.'

Mr Bentley tutted at me. 'Now, now, no one likes a show-off,' he said sharply. I had a feeling he didn't know Latin, either.

Mrs Henshaw wasn't listening to us. 'I think I know where you can go!' she said, tossing her head so that her feather waved in the air.

'Just her, miss? Or us too?' Archie asked.

'I don't see why you can't *all* stay there. I'm sure you could have a room each!' said Mrs Henshaw. 'Do you see that big house up there – it's called the Red House?'

A Red House on one hill, a White House on the other. It sounded like a scene in *Alice*.

'I reckon there's at least six bedrooms, but only one lady lives there. Well, two ladies, actually,' she said.

'Old ladies like them Miss Robinsons?' asked Kevin.

'No, the house is owned by Mrs Waverley, a lady about my age,' said Mrs Henshaw.

We thought Mrs Henshaw must be very old so that wasn't reassuring. Mr Bentley didn't look happy, either.

'For goodness' sake, do we really have to go traipsing all the way back through the village and halfway up that hill? It'll be getting dark soon. Why didn't we try there first?' he demanded.

'I suppose you have a point, Mr Bentley. Mrs Waverley entirely slipped my mind. She's rather a recluse – she doesn't come down to the village very often.'

'A recluse?' he asked. 'Do you mean she's not quite the ticket?'

'Oh no, she's entirely *compos mentis*,' said Mrs Henshaw, spouting her precious Latin again and leaving us all in the dark. She smiled at Kevin and Archie and me. 'Come along then, chaps and chapesses! Best foot forward.'

'She's bonkers,' Kevin muttered to me. 'I don't know what she's on about half the time.'

I didn't, either, but I was too tired and sore to care. Archie seemed past it too. He clung to Mrs Henshaw, sniffing continuously. And Mr Bentley was making heavy work of carrying my suitcase, putting it down every tenth step and groaning.

'Oh dear, poor Mr Bentley,' said Mrs Henshaw. 'Perhaps I'd better take a turn with that wretched suitcase.'

'I have serious problems with my back,' he said huffily. 'But I'll manage. I'll have to. Though it's a shame some people weren't more considerate.' He looked balefully in my direction.

'Why don't you stay down in the village, go to your digs at the hostel. I'll sort the children out,' Mrs Henshaw offered.

'Certainly not. I am the headmaster and all Paradise Road pupils are my responsibility,' said Mr Bentley. 'Besides, I can't leave a lady unescorted.'

Mrs Henshaw thawed a little and gave a girlish giggle.

So we laboured on, dragging back through the village. Archie heard distant mooing and panicked. Mrs Henshaw ended up carrying him and his cardboard case of tattered belongings. He probably weighed more than my suitcase, but Mrs Henshaw didn't complain.

When we started climbing the narrow chalk path that led to the Red House, Mr Bentley gestured to Kevin. 'Here, lad, you're almost as big as me. Perhaps you could take a turn with this bally case!'

It was more an order than a request. Kevin was so spindly I thought he'd buckle at the knees, but he proved surprisingly strong and lugged the case with scarcely a grunt.

'There! You should have offered sooner!' said Mr Bentley, with an astonishing lack of gratitude.

I peered up at the house in the gathering twilight. I hadn't realized just how big it was. It had a special driveway with beautiful gates with hearts cut out of the wood. I ran my finger along inside the shapes.

'Hearts!' I said. 'Aren't they lovely! I've never seen gates like these before.'

'Mrs Waverley had them specially made,' Mrs Henshaw told me.

Mrs Waverley came alive in my imagination: a beautiful, romantic, particular woman who floated around her lovely house in lace dresses. I hoped with all my heart that Mrs Waverley would let me live with her.

The driveway was long and unlit. The trees rustled overhead, a thick, dark canopy. Huge plants sprang out along the side, their great umbrella leaves brushing my cheeks.

'It's like a bleeding jungle!' Kevin panted.

'Language!' said Mr Bentley. 'Though I'm inclined to agree

with you. It seems very overgrown. Are you sure this Mrs Waverley is still living here, Mrs Henshaw?'

'Oh yes, I'd have heard otherwise. It's been a bit of a wilderness ever since . . . well, for a long time. The gunneras have certainly run wild,' she said.

'Gunners?' Archie piped up, suddenly interested.

'Gunneras, dear. These big plants. They grow near water. There's a big pond somewhere.'

'Can we fish in it?' Kevin asked. 'I go fishing with my dad down Hammer Ponds. Well, I did once.'

'You'll have to wait and ask Mrs Waverley. Or Chubby,' said Mrs Henshaw.

'Chubby? Is that Mr Waverley?' I asked, seeing him as a fat, cheery man with a brocade waistcoat bursting its buttons.

'Oh no, dear. Chubby is . . . I suppose she's Mrs Waverley's maid,' Mrs Henshaw told me.

Inside my head Chubby turned into an old lady in a pinny brandishing a mop. I hoped more than ever that Mrs Waverley would take me. Mum would be so impressed if she knew I was living in a house where there was a maid.

I silently practised what I was going to say. I'd better sound as grand and grown up as I could: *How do you do, Mrs Waverley. What a pleasant evening! I am Shirley Louise Smith. I would love to come and live with you.*

As the driveway twisted I'd lost sight of the Red House, but then we turned a corner, the trees thinned a little, and suddenly there it was, the tiled roof sloping up and down, the windows wide and patterned with glass lozenges, the door painted green, the wooden knocker shaped like a picture-book tree. It was a beautiful house, but the surrounding flower beds were thick with weeds. Everything had grown immensely tall, and ivy was creeping up the brick walls, trying to smother them.

'I don't like it here – it's scary!' Archie whispered, clinging to Mrs Henshaw.

'Nonsense, dear,' she said, but she looked worried as she rapped on the door with the tree-shaped knocker.

The house was so dark and still and silent it seemed deserted. I jumped when the door opened suddenly.

'How do you do,' I quavered, but then my voice tailed away. I didn't know who it was standing there. It wasn't a grand lady in a beautiful gown. It wasn't a maid in a white cap and apron. It couldn't be Mrs Waverley. This woman wore a turban that emphasized her sharp cheekbones, a crumpled check dress with a tear under the arm, bare legs and pom-pom slippers.

'What do you lot want, eh?' she said, crossing her arms and peering at us, eyes narrowed.

She wasn't a lady so she had to be the maid. She was skin and bones, her little body as thin and flat as a child's, her wrists and ankles so sticklike they looked ready to snap. Chubby? She was the exact opposite.

'Good evening, Miss Chubb,' said Mrs Henshaw. 'I'm Mrs Henshaw from the village and—'

'I know who you are! For heaven's sake, we grew up in the same village!' the tiny woman said irritably.

'Well, if you know who I am, you'll know what I'm doing here with these children.'

'They're the evacuees,' Miss Chubb said scornfully. 'I suppose you've dragged them all the way up the hill as a last resort because no one else will take them. Well, you're wasting your time, Margaret Henshaw. We can't take any kiddies here.'

'Please will you call Mrs Waverley, Chubby?' Mrs Henshaw asked. 'She is the householder, not you.'

'Do you think she's going to say any different?' asked this Chubby.

'Madeleine!' Mrs Henshaw called loudly, ignoring her. 'Madeleine, please come to the door, it's urgent!'

'She won't come. She'll hide in her room. She always does,' said Chubby, shaking her head.

'Then I shall have to go and find her.' Mrs Henshaw pushed past into the hallway, hauling Archie with her. 'Come along, follow me!' she commanded the rest of us.

Kevin and I exchanged doubtful looks. Even Mr Bentley seemed hesitant. We edged inside, keeping close to the walls. They were patterned with dark green paper with swirly leaves and tangled honeysuckle, as if the overgrown garden had crept indoors.

'Come back here, Margaret Henshaw!' Chubby shouted, but Mrs Henshaw had already rounded a corner and opened a door.

We heard a little gasp from someone inside.

'Would you credit it!' said Chubby, clenching her fists, and darted after her.

We followed, finding ourselves in a dark red room with one entire wall covered in bookshelves. In the dim light of the single rose-coloured oil lamp I peered at all the amazing books. The lamp stood on a table beside a chaise longue. On it lay a lady, propped up with embroidered cushions. She was wearing a long blue velvet robe, perhaps a dressing gown, and her hair was long too, waving past her shoulders, gleaming palely in the dark room. It was pure white, and her skin was milky pale too, almost ghostly. She was too old to be pretty, but she was certainly striking.

'Hello, Madeleine!' said Mrs Henshaw, still cradling Archie in her arms. 'I haven't seen you for such a long time. How are you? You do know who I am, don't you?'

'Of course I know who you are, Margaret,' said Mrs Waverley, sounding dazed. 'What are you doing here?' She looked at Chubby.

'*I* didn't let her in!' said Chubby. 'She barged in without so much as a by-your-leave, bringing half a dozen little brats with her, and this stray bloke into the bargain. The cheek of it!'

'I am Mr Bentley, the children's headmaster,' said Mr Bentley indignantly.

'And there are only three children, Madeleine – the last three of our little evacuees from London. I've managed to find billets for all the others, and I'm very much hoping you will welcome these three into your lovely home,' said Mrs Henshaw.

'Then you can think again!' said Chubby. 'We can't possibly act as nursemaids for all these London brats!'

'They won't be any trouble. They'll be at school most of the time,' said Mrs Henshaw. 'You're to send them this coming Monday, please.'

'I should coco!' said Chubby. 'We never put our name down on that stupid form you sent round. It said it was voluntary. Well, we're not volunteering. We can't cope with kiddies here.'

'Circumstances have changed now that we're on the brink of war,' said Mrs Henshaw. 'It's compulsory now. The law's changed. Every householder with spare rooms is compelled to take evacuated children under their roof. I'm certain you have several spare rooms.'

I stared at her. She was telling a lie! I hadn't realized that adults could fib as fluently as children.

'We might have spare rooms but they're not . . . not adequately furnished,' said Mrs Waverley.

'Oh, don't give me that, Madeleine! Your house is furnished sumptuously.' Mrs Henshaw gestured around the room with her spare hand. Archie stopped lolling against her chest and peered about sleepily. He looked like a strange little alien with his bald head and huge eyes. He blinked, a tear running down his cheek.

Chubby's face softened as she stared at him. 'Let's take the baby,' she said to Mrs Waverley. 'He doesn't look too much trouble. I daresay I'll cope.'

'Very well,' said Mrs Waverley. 'There you are, Margaret. Mission accomplished.'

'Couldn't you possibly take this little girl too?' said Mr

Bentley. 'I can't carry her suitcase another step. It weighs a ton!'

'It's full of books, Madeleine,' said Mrs Henshaw. 'She couldn't bear to leave them behind.'

Mrs Waverley peered at me. 'Do you like reading, child?'

'It's my best thing ever, Mrs Waverley,' I said.

She seemed surprised, maybe even a little amused. 'It's my best thing ever too.' She looked at Chubby. 'Perhaps we ought to take this little girl too?'

Chubby shrugged. 'Well, you'll have to amuse her then. I'll have my hands full with the baby.'

'That's excellent!' said Mrs Henshaw. 'And you'll take the big boy as well?'

'I like books and all,' said Kevin quickly. He went to the bookshelves and grabbed one of the leather volumes. 'See, I can read.' He started slowly spelling out a sentence from the book, stumbling over the long words. He tried turning the page, licking his finger and crumpling it slightly.

Mrs Waverley winced. 'Please put that book back on the shelf!' she said. She turned to Mrs Henshaw. 'I'm sorry, Margaret. I'm sure it's not compulsory to take *three* evacuees. I think the older boy would be happier somewhere else.'

'But there isn't anywhere else,' said Mrs Henshaw. 'Please couldn't you just take Kevin tonight, and then perhaps I'll find a place for him at one of the farms. But we can't go on traipsing around all night. We're exhausted.'

I looked at Kevin. His hands were trembling as he slotted the book back on the shelf. He started nibbling a nail again. His face screwed up and I knew he was trying not to cry. I couldn't bear it.

I went to Mrs Waverley and knelt beside her, going down with a thump on my sore knees. It hurt so much it was easy to start crying myself.

'Please let Kevin stay too!' I sobbed imploringly.

Mrs Waverley sighed. 'Oh, very well,' she murmured.

MRS HENSHAW AND MR BENTLEY left immediately, quickly saying goodbye to Kevin, Archie and me. I think they were scared Mrs Waverley might change her mind if they dithered. We stood there uncertainly in the large, dark, book-lined room, not knowing what to say or do. I looked at Mrs Waverley hopefully. She seemed to have taken a shine to me. She'd said I could stay because I liked reading, as she obviously did. She'd let Kevin stay too because I had begged her. I expected her to sit up properly and start a conversation about books. But she gazed at me helplessly, not saying a word.

Then she turned to Chubby.

'Now look what you've got us into,' Chubby declared. 'What do you propose we do with them?'

Mrs Waverley clasped her hands together, frowning. 'Why, we'll give them some supper and then we'll give them a bath, and then we'll put them to bed,' she said.

'Oh, *we* will, will *we*?' said Chubby. 'And what exactly are we giving them for supper, and how will we get hot water at this time and, even more to the point, how are we going to put them to bed, Mrs Mad?'

We blinked at her. She wasn't like any of the servants I'd read about in books. They wore uniforms and said 'madam' a lot and did as they were told. They didn't argue or ask questions in a rude tone of voice or call their mistress cheeky nicknames to her face. *Mrs Mad!*

Perhaps Mrs Waverley *was* a little mad. She *acted* a little mad, lying on her Victorian sofa in that dressing-gown garment, her hair floating past her shoulders. She didn't seem physically ill: she was tall and imposing with a biggish chest. She could have made two small, skinny Chubbys. But as she seemed like an invalid, perhaps she was mentally ill.

I stared at her fearfully. I'd seen mad people on the streets, shuffling along talking to themselves. Once a madman had started shouting at me; another had opened up his coat and done something so astonishingly rude I couldn't possibly have told my mother. I'd never *known* any mad people though. I hadn't read about any in a book, though I knew about the madwoman in *Jane Eyre* because I'd glanced at a scary comic-strip version. That madwoman had long hair and a long dress too, but her face was purple and bloated, with rolling eyes. Thank goodness Mrs Waverley's face was pale pink and her eyes were lovely, big and very blue. She was peering pleadingly at Chubby.

'Yes, well might you look at me. You were the one who insisted on taking the girl, and then this great string bean of a boy. *I* just wanted the baby,' said Chubby.

She picked up Archie, who was tottering with exhaustion. 'There now, little man. Come with Chubby,' she said, marching across the room in her pom-pom slippers. They were worn down at the back so they made a contemptuous little flapping sound as she moved.

I stood there. Kevin did too, his head bent. Chubby and Archie disappeared through the door. Mrs Waverley sat where she was on the chaise longue, fidgeting with her hands. I realized she was wringing them. I'd read this phrase in books but had never quite understood it. I'd seen Mum wringing wet clothes, but she did it so fiercely that the water streamed out. If she'd wrung her own hands like that she'd have broken all her fingers. Mrs Waverley's wringing was soft and ineffectual.

'Chubby?' she called.

The slippers stopped slapping. 'Come on, you two big ones. Follow me,' Chubby shouted impatiently.

I bobbed my head at Mrs Waverley and hurried out of the door, Kevin following me. Our suitcases stood in a row in the hall, my big one, Kevin's medium bashed one and Archie's tiny cardboard one.

'They look as if they belong to the Three Bears,' I said.

Kevin didn't answer. His head was turned away from me. We went down a long corridor with bare floorboards, scurrying after Chubby.

I saw that Kevin was knuckling his eyes now. 'Don't cry,' I said. 'I'm sure they'll let you stay here.'

He glared at me. 'I ain't crying,' he said. 'And I don't *want* to stay here with them two daft old women. So shut your face.'

I was appalled. How could he be so rude to me when I'd tried so hard to help him? He was a stupid, horrible, ungrateful boy and I would never try to be kind to him again.

The door at the end of the corridor was ajar. I hesitated. Kevin did too.

'Come on then, you gormless kids,' Chubby called.

We went into a large kitchen with a flagged stone floor and a big wooden table and a wooden dresser with drawer handles in the shape of hearts.

'Oh, I love those hearts,' I said. 'I wish our dresser at home was like that.'

'She had it specially made,' said Chubby, sitting Archie on a corner of the kitchen table. 'Don't fall off now,' she commanded him.

She filled a kettle and put it on the hob. Then she opened the larder door. I expected it to be full of jams and jellies and pies and pastries because this was such a grand house, but it looked almost as bare as Old Mother Hubbard's. She opened a bread bin and lifted a plate covering two slices of greyish meat, tutting dubiously.

'It's hers and mine – and it looks like it's on the turn anyway,' she muttered to herself. 'Better give them bread and milk. Best get them clean first.'

She poured the nearly boiling water into the enamel washing-up bowl and found a rag and a sliver of red Lifebuoy soap. She attacked Archie first, scrubbing his face and his hands and his blackened knees. He wriggled, protesting bitterly.

'Keep still, you silly little baby,' said Chubby.

'Not a bleeding baby!' Archie protested, and then shrieked as soap went in his eyes.

'Jeepers, what a fuss! Anyone would think I was trying to murder you! All right, you're not a baby. You're a squirmy little skinned rabbit,' said Chubby, laughing at him.

I remembered Mum saying *I* looked like a rabbit. It seemed at least six weeks ago, not that very morning. My stomach felt hollow and achy. I missed Mum so. I missed Dad too. I wanted everything to be normal again, back at our old house before we had to move. I'd be in the sitting room, sitting on the pouffe reading my library book, and Dad would be back from work, flicking through the *Evening Standard* and sharing the comic strip with me. There'd be a lovely rich savoury smell of pork chops or macaroni cheese or shepherd's pie, because Mum was in the kitchen making supper, whistling if she was in a good mood.

'What you rubbing your front for?' Chubby asked me, wiping Archie dry with an inadequate tea towel. 'Got a belly ache?'

I blushed. Mum would never let me say the word *belly*, not even *belly button*. I shook my head. 'My tummy feels . . . funny,' I mumbled.

'You're probably hungry. I'll get cracking with your suppers in half a tick. Just got to get you all washed. You next.' Chubby dipped the rag in Archie's now murky water and rubbed it with soap. 'Come on!'

I stared at her, appalled. 'I can wash myself!' I protested. 'And can't I have clean water?'

'No you can't. I'm not faffing about boiling another kettle. What's the matter with this?' She dipped her elbow in the bowl. 'It's still nice and hot.'

'But it's dirty from Archie!'

'Yes, and it'll get even dirtier from you.' She handed me the soaped rag. 'You do it then. And be quick about it.'

'I've got a proper flannel in my suitcase. I'll go and get it,' I suggested.

Chubby sighed irritably. 'Look, Lady Muck, you're in my kitchen and you'll do as I say. Get your face and hands washed now – and you'd better give those sore knees a proper soaking too.'

'Lady Muck,' Kevin sniggered. He attempted an imitation: *'I've got a proper flannel!'*

'None of your cheek now,' said Chubby, but she was smirking too. 'There were eight of us when I was a kid, and we was lucky if we had a bath once a week, and that was *after* our mum and dad. You should have seen the colour of the water when our Jimmy, the youngest, got in it. Like Brown Windsor soup, yet *he* never complained.'

I took the hateful rag and got on with washing myself, my lips pressed together. It was awful having to wash in front of them all. Would we have to bath in front of each other too? If I had to strip off in front of Kevin I'd die.

My knees stung horribly when I dabbed at them. When I was finished and Kevin was giving himself a lick-and-a-promise, Chubby came at me with an evil-looking bottle.

'What's that?' I asked fearfully.

'It's just gentian violet. I'll put a spot on both them knees and they'll heal up in no time.' She poured a little on a piece of cotton wool and set to.

It was dark purple and stung terribly but I was too proud to make a fuss. I was worried the purple might stain the hem of my good pleated skirt and hitched it up cautiously when, at last, we sat down at the kitchen table to have supper.

Bread and milk. I was interested to see what it tasted like. Children in books were often given it when they were tired or sick. It was simply warm milk with lumps of bread mashed up in it, but Chubby had sprinkled it with sugar too. It slipped down easily and was very comforting, reminding me of the sugar sandwich and glass of milk I'd had for breakfast so long ago.

'There,' said Chubby when she saw my empty bowl. 'I bet your belly feels better now. You was just hungry.'

Kevin and Archie had wolfed theirs down too. Archie even picked his bowl up and licked all round it. I thought Chubby would tell him off but she just laughed.

'Now, let's take you to the toilet,' she said.

It was like being back in the nursery class. Still, at least she didn't insist we call it the double-you-see. Chubby went in with Archie, but thank goodness she let Kevin and then me manage by ourselves. There was a nice solid wooden toilet seat and it was mercifully clean. In our new flat we had to share a toilet with the lady downstairs and Mum was always having rows with her because she didn't use the toilet brush or any disinfectant.

'There now,' said Chubby. Archie rubbed his eyes and gave an enormous yawn. 'Well, I suppose we ought to put you to bed. Somehow. Get them suitcases and bring them upstairs.'

She saw that I was struggling and Kevin didn't seem inclined to help, so she set Archie on his feet and sent him tottering off while she hauled my suitcase up the stairs for me. Then she stood on the landing, panting, her hand on her flat chest.

'That was knackering,' she said, setting it down. She looked up and down the landing as if she was suddenly lost and didn't know which way to go. Then she sighed and led us along to the right and opened a door halfway down. We peered inside and then did a double take. It was empty. Not just sparsely furnished, but completely empty, though there were curtains at the window. But there was no carpet, no dressing table, no chairs, no washstand, no beds whatsoever.

Chubby flip-flopped over the bare floorboards and set my case down with a thump. 'You'd best sleep in here,' she said.

We stared at her.

'There's no beds, missus,' said Kevin.

'I ain't a missus, I'm a miss, but you can call me Chubby like everyone else. I know there's no beds. I don't know what Mrs Mad wants me to do. Work a bally miracle? Hang on a sec.' She left us standing there, utterly baffled.

Archie walked all around the room as if expecting to bump into an invisible bed any second. Kevin and I looked at each other.

'She's gone off her head,' he said.

'Why has she dumped us in here when it's empty?' I said. 'Why can't we sleep in a proper bedroom?'

'Search me,' said Kevin. 'Let's find one.' He went out of the room.

'Kevin! I don't think we're allowed!' I whispered.

'That Chubby's right down the end – I can hear her rummaging,' he said. 'Come on.' He walked a few steps to the next door and opened it cautiously. It was another completely empty room.

'Oi!' Chubby called from along the corridor. 'Stay put, you lot. I'm just coming.'

We went back to the first room and stood there awkwardly, shuffling from foot to foot, completely unnerved.

Chubby came back carrying an unwieldy pile of bedding. 'Here we are. They're old sheets, all sides to middle, but they're still decent quality. I can't rustle up no blankets, but it's still summer so you should be all right. And there's no spare mattress – but look, I'm giving you the eiderdown off of my own bed, and it's lovely and soft and fluffy. So come on, girl, help me get it all ship-shape,' she said, nodding at me.

'But where's the bed?' I asked helplessly.

'For Gawd's sake, can't you see – there aren't any beds. Just two in the whole house. One for Mrs Mad and one for me. She's not going to share with you lot, and I'm certainly not, either. So you can kip here, the three of you,' she said.

'The three of us?' I said. 'You don't mean I've got to sleep with the boys?'

'What's wrong with that? I slept with all my brothers and sisters when we was little. We topped and tailed so it wasn't too much of a squash,' said Chubby. 'Lucky job we was all on the skinny side.'

'But these boys aren't my brothers! I'd never met them before today,' I said, thinking she simply hadn't understood.

'Well, it's up to you, Little Miss Fussy. You can sleep next door, all by yourself, if that's what you want, but I haven't got any more spare bedding, so you're going to be pretty chilly and uncomfy. Or you can huddle up here. Suit yourself. Night-night now,' said Chubby.

Archie started crying as she went to the door.

'Come on, don't start that boo-hooing, little man,' she said, but she went back and gave him an awkward hug. 'Settle down. Stands to reason you feel a bit humpty being dumped here with us, but you'll feel better in the morning. And then you can run about in the garden and climb trees and paddle in the lake. You'll have such a lovely time, and you'll see lots of rabbits and squirrels and heaps of other animals.'

'I don't want to see them cows,' said Archie, but he let Chubby take his tight jumper and shorts off and settle him in the middle of the makeshift bed, still wearing his tatty vest and pants and socks.

'There, you two big ones hop in either side of him,' said Chubby. 'Night-night. Again.'

We were still too dumbfounded to reply. I knew one thing: I wasn't going to strip off in front of Kevin – not for all the tea in China. I took my suitcase and dragged it next door. This room was even bleaker than the one Chubby had chosen for us. It seemed darker too. I kept looking around, wondering if there was anyone standing very still in a corner, waiting to get me.

I unsnapped my suitcase and it sounded incredibly loud in the still room. I fumbled around for my nightdress, then quickly pulled my jumper over my head and dived into my nightie so that I would be decent if the boys came barging in. I took the rest of my clothes off underneath. It felt chilly in the empty room, but I knew Mum would hate it if I went to bed in my underwear. Though of course I didn't have a bed. I so, so, so didn't want to have to curl up with Kevin and Archie.

I decided I'd simply sleep where I was and show them all. I lay down on the floor but the bare boards were incredibly cold and hard. They felt dusty too and I was wearing a clean nightie. I had no covers to pull over me and, worst of all, I didn't have a pillow. My neck was already hurting after hauling my heavy case around. I thought of my soft pillow at home and longed to nestle into it, with the crook of my neck properly cradled.

It was a mistake to think of home. I pictured Mum, all alone, then being blown up by a German bomb the moment war was declared. I thought of Dad fighting all the Germans, and them shooting him – *bang, bang, bang!* like in a cowboy film. Even though my tummy was full of bread and milk, I had an empty feeling. My eyes were watery and my nose prickled. I rubbed my eyes and pinched my nose.

It was so weirdly quiet in the country. I wished I could hear cars going past, footsteps, chatter. I couldn't start crying again now. The boys next door would hear.

Even Chubby might hear if her bedroom was just along the corridor. She might be cross or poke fun at me. She didn't mind Archie crying – he was only little, after all, but she'd think me too old. She didn't seem to like me anyway. I could just hear her chanting 'Crybaby'.

I am not, not, not going to cry! I said it to myself over and over again, and whenever a tear dripped down my cheek I knuckled my eye hard to punish it. I wanted to distract myself by reading, but it was too dark to see the pages and I didn't have a nightlight or a torch. Of course there was a proper light switch by the door. I fidgeted, wondering whether I dared put it on. Mum didn't allow me to switch the light on again after she'd kissed me goodnight. She was always fussing about electricity bills. But Mrs Waverley must be very rich to live in such an enormous house. Perhaps she wouldn't mind if I read just for ten minutes?

I jumped up and switched on the light, hoping it wouldn't show through the makeshift blackout curtain. I took *Ballet Shoes* out of my case and sat cross-legged with it under the light. The bare bulb must have been a very low watt because I could still barely see. I had to hold my book uncomfortably close to my face. I could just about read the first page, partly because I practically knew it by heart, but I couldn't seem to lose myself in the story. I wanted to walk along the Cromwell Road with Pauline, Petrova and Posy, but I stayed shivering on the bare floor of a strange house in the middle of nowhere.

I flicked through the book, looking at the illustrations – pictures that had become like a family photo album to me. That worked better. I even stood up, bunched up my nightie into a ballet-dress shape, and tried twirling around the room, and for a few seconds I was dancing a magical duet with Posy. Then I stumbled and subsided in embarrassment.

I raided my suitcase to try to put together a makeshift bed. I ended up lying on *Orlando the Marmalade Cat* with tomorrow's clean knickers and socks tucked inside my jumper as a pillow. I put out the light, and in the dark room arranged my best smocked dress on top of me, hoping I wouldn't roll over in the night and crease it.

I was sure I wouldn't be able to sleep a wink, and so I started making up a story about Pauline, Petrova and Posy and me and all the other pupils of Madame Fidolia's stage school being evacuated to the country. We were to share facilities with St Agatha's Convent, so I could be best friends with Jessica.

Then Pauline, Petrova and Posy faded away, and Jessica and I were being told off by Sister Josephine, her moustache bristling, and suddenly she wasn't like Charlie Chaplin any more. She was the spitting image of Hitler with his toothbrush moustache. She actually became Hitler – though still wearing her nun's wimple and habit. She shouted and ranted at us, and we clutched hands and ran, and she charged after us, her hobnail boots suddenly huge, marching left, right, left, right . . . and then I woke up, stiff all over.

It was light, which made the empty room look even odder. I stretched out, trying to get more comfortable, but I kept sliding off *Orlando*, and anyway I didn't want to lie on top of him any more. I knew it was ridiculous, but the picture of Orlando on the front of the book looked very flat. I didn't want to squash him altogether.

I stood up, yawning and rubbing all my worst aching bits. I needed to go to the toilet. I needed to go so badly that I couldn't possibly wait until breakfast – if there was any. I couldn't even wait until I'd washed and dressed. I pulled on yesterday's knickers to stop feeling quite so bare and vulnerable, stuck my feet into my red shoes, and hobbled off in search of a double-you-see.

I knew not to try next door, because that only contained Kevin and Archie. I timidly peeped into the rooms on either side of the corridor, but they were empty too. The situation was getting urgent. I knew there was a toilet downstairs, so I made a rush for it, my shoes biting now. They made a loud clatter on the bare wooden stairs and I looked about me fearfully, worried that I might be disturbing Chubby or Mrs Waverley, but no one came. I found the right door at last and sat on the toilet, mightily relieved. I shook my head sadly at the state of my red shoes. I wasn't at all sure Chubby would have the right sort of polish and be able to get them to shine properly again.

When I came out into the corridor I heard faint scuffling sounds coming from the kitchen. Perhaps Chubby was starting to make the breakfast. I wondered what it would be. Maybe more bread and milk. Perhaps if I offered to help her lay the table she would start to like me a little.

I walked into the kitchen. Chubby wasn't there. It was

Kevin and Archie, fully dressed, with a sugar packet and a slab of butter between them on the table.

'We're having sugar fingers!' Archie crowed. 'Look, you do it like this.' He dug his finger into the butter, then wiggled it around in the sugar packet. 'It tastes lovely, it does,' he said, sucking his finger appreciatively.

'You'll cop it if Chubby catches you,' I said, though my mouth was watering.

'It's her fault. We're starving. Fancy only giving us bread and milk! My dad said I'd be fed royally in the country – bacon and sausages and great big steaks. He'd do his nut if he knew they were just giving us bread and milk,' said Kevin. 'What about your dad, Archie?'

Archie shrugged. 'Don't see him no more.'

'Maybe Archie's dad is d-e-a-d,' I said, pretty sure Archie wouldn't be able to spell yet.

'Here, Archie, Shirley here says your dad's dead,' said Kevin.

'No I didn't!' I protested.

'He's not, he's in the nick,' said Archie, dabbing his finger in the butter and sugar again.

'In the where?' I said, looking at Kevin.

'The nick,' he repeated. 'You know. Prison.'

I looked at Archie, horrified. 'Oh, you poor thing. What did your dad *do*?'

He shrugged again. 'I don't know. Stuff. Robbery and that. He went down for a long stretch because he had a shooter.'

I blinked at him. He seemed to have jumped out of a

gangster movie, and yet he was still only little Archie. I pictured his dad like a big Archie, bald in a blue pinstripe suit with a fedora hat and a gun in each hand.

'Were you scared of your dad, Archie?' I asked.

'Didn't see him much.'

'I'd hate not having a dad,' said Kevin. 'Me and my dad are real pals.'

'Who looks after you if you haven't got a mum and your dad's in prison?' I asked gently.

'Got an auntie,' said Archie.

'Is she nice to you?'

'Don't really know this latest. Keep getting new ones.'

'Oh, Archie, you poor thing,' I said, putting my arm round his bony shoulders, but he shrugged me away.

'Get off of me,' he said, wriggling.

'Archie, one more thing,' said Kevin. 'What's happened to your hair?'

'Kevin!' I tutted at his lack of tact.

'This new auntie shaved it off because I had nits,' said Archie.

I edged away from him, glad I hadn't slept with him last night.

'Thanks, mate!' said Kevin, starting to scratch his own mop head.

Archie had yet another helping of butter and sugar.

'You'd better stop that, you'll be sick,' I said. 'Chubby will give you what for when she sees all those poky marks in the butter. You don't want her to send you away, do you?'

He looked worried. 'I won't let her catch me,' he said.

He jumped up and ran to the door at the back of the kitchen. It opened into a scullery with a big stone sink and various buckets. There was another door beyond it. It had a big bolt. He struggled with it, his small fingers surprisingly skilled and strong. He had it open in a couple of seconds and then he was out.

Kevin and I looked at each other, and then followed him.

WE WERE IN A little courtyard with logs piled up under a makeshift shelter.

Archie ran down some steps to a brick path with weeds pushing through every crack.

'Careful, Archie!' I called.

He took no notice and charged onwards, following the path round. We followed, of course. There was a flower bed of sorts, and a big vegetable patch – mostly cabbages. I wrinkled my nose. I hated cabbages. They even smelled bad simply growing in the earth. But when we were past them, running round to the front of the house, the smell was better, much, much better: I smelled fresh grass and faraway roses.

The sounds were magical too – birds singing their heads off, some high, some low, some soft and cooing. I hardly ever heard the birds at home because there weren't any trees in our street. In the sooty park I saw sparrows and sad pigeons hopping along on twisted claws, and very occasionally flocks of starlings flying high in the sky at twilight. These country birds all seemed so different. If the village had a library I might take out a bird book and learn some of their names.

'Aren't the birds lovely?' I said, but Kevin looked at me as if I were daft.

'They're just birds,' he said.

'Wait till you see these birds here – they're whoppers!' Archie shouted.

When we went round the side of the house we found a cluster of hens coming out of a small hut, bobbing their heads and looking expectant.

'Ah, they've got their own little house, these birdies!' said Archie, clapping his hands.

The hens clucked, flapping their wings, scurrying along. Archie chuckled and made little rushes at them, and they parted in alarm.

'Don't, Archie! You're frightening them,' I said, taking hold of his small wrist.

He wriggled it away. 'You can't tell me off. And I'm not frightening them – I'm only playing, aren't I, you great big sparrows.'

'They're not sparrows, silly, they're hens,' I said.

'Hens?' said Archie, looking blank.

'You know. They lay eggs. I wonder if they've laid any eggs overnight? Chubby might let us have them for breakfast,' I said hopefully.

'What do you mean, lay eggs?' Archie asked.

'You know what eggs are. You fry them and have them with chips. Well, hens make them. They squeeze them out their bums,' said Kevin.

'*What?*' Archie squealed. 'That's disgusting. You're kidding me, right?'

Kevin mimed cutting his throat and hoping to die if he told a lie.

'I don't like all them country animals,' said Archie. 'They're dirty. Cows squirting milk out of them pink dangly bits and hens doing a big toilet. It's all mucky!'

'You're the mucky pup,' said Kevin.

'I'm not! I didn't do it. I'm sure it was you,' Archie protested.

'What? What did you do?' I asked, but they both looked coy and wouldn't tell me. 'As if I care,' I said. 'Come on, we'd better go back now.'

'I'm not going back,' said Archie. 'I'm running away. I'm going back to Auntie. I don't like it here.'

'Don't be daft. How are you going to get back? You haven't got any money for the train,' said Kevin.

'Babies go free. I'll scrunch up really small.'

'As if that would work!'

'That Chubby thinks I'm a baby,' said Archie. 'But I won't bother with no train. I'll just run and run all the way back to London. I'm a good runner, see.'

He set off to show us, charging round to the front of the house again, then down the driveway. He did run fast, fists clenched, his matchstick arms pumping, his knees lifting high at each stride.

'Silly little tyke,' said Kevin. 'We'd better go after him.'

So we chased him. He was half our size but it was hard work trying to catch up. When he heard us coming closer he veered left off the drive and started running through the grass, zigzagging round bushes and dodging under the big umbrella plants.

'Archie! Come back! You'll get lost,' I called.

He was out of sight now. Kevin and I ran in the direction he'd taken. The grounds were so overgrown it was as if we were in an enchanted wood in a fairy tale. There were so many trees the sky was blotted out and it was as dark as night. The trees were old, with long, twisting roots tunnelling in and out of the earth. There were nettles everywhere – I could feel them stinging my legs as my nightie caught on brambles.

'Archie, come *back*!' I called.

Then we heard him yell.

'Oh, flip, what's he done now?' said Kevin.

We ran harder. The trees thinned and we came to a clearing – and there was Archie, capering on the grass beside a vast stretch of water.

'It's the sea!' he screamed excitedly. 'I've run away to the sea!'

'The sea!' said Kevin. 'Crikey, look at it!'

I looked and saw a glittering green oval, with rushes growing all around. 'It's not the sea, it's a lake,' I said.

'It is so the sea. Lakes are little, not massive like this. My dad took me to a boating lake and it was only big enough for toy boats, not real ones. This is definitely the sea,' said Kevin.

I knew perfectly well it wasn't the sea. I'd been to the real sea on that coach trip with Mum and Dad. I'd seen the sands at Clacton, and the vast expanse of sea glittering in the sunshine, white-topped in the wind.

'It's not the sea,' I repeated, but Kevin and Archie weren't listening to me.

'I'm going swimming!' said Archie, and he went charging into the water fully clothed, splashing and shouting.

'*Can* you swim?' Kevin called.

Archie threw himself forward, head lowered, arms outstretched. He went right under, bobbed up again with his little bald head dripping and his mouth a great O of astonishment, and then disappeared.

'He can't swim!' I said.

I tucked my nightie into my knickers, Kevin stepped out of his shorts, then we both tugged off our shoes and socks and ran in. Archie hadn't gone in very far, thank goodness. I grabbed one of his spindly arms, Kevin the other, and we hauled him out.

He was coughing and gasping, water streaming off him, shivering with shock, but as soon as he had breath to talk he yelled triumphantly, 'Did you see me swimming? Shall I have another go?'

'No, you daft banana! You nearly drowned! You scared us silly,' I said, scraping little strands of water weed off him.

'I bet *you* can't swim!' said Archie, shaking himself like a dog.

'*I* can swim – my dad took me down Hornsey Road baths. I'm a brilliant swimmer, me, but you mustn't try again, nipper – you're too small. You really could drown,' said Kevin.

'I don't mind. I could drown and float about like a ghost and scare everyone and they'd all run away, and then I'd come alive again and go *Ha ha ha*,' said Archie. His teeth were chattering now.

'We'd better get him back to the house and find him a towel,' I said.

'Perhaps he ought to run about first and get a bit less wet,' said Kevin. 'Let's all play chase up and down the driveway. I bet I win.'

'Of course you'll win – you've got much longer legs than Archie and me,' I said.

We raced for a few minutes and of course Kevin kept winning. Archie came second in spite of being soaking wet. I came a poor last, and the boys laughed at me because I ran in a funny way, my legs kicking out sideways, mostly because my feet were cramped in my red shoes. Archie seemed happy enough, but he was still shivering.

'He'll catch cold,' I said anxiously. 'Come on, let's take him back.'

'That Chubby will go mental when she sees him. She'll blame us,' said Kevin.

'She'll still be in bed. And Mrs Waverley. I think it's ever so early,' I said. 'Then we can towel him dry and maybe iron his clothes so they get dry too, and no one will ever know.'

'I'll know,' said Archie, his eyes shining. 'I did swimming!'

I took one of his hands and Kevin the other and we walked him back to the house. The sun came out, and it suddenly felt warmer.

'There, he's getting much drier already,' said Kevin.

I squinted up at the sun and the white clouds and vast blue sky. 'It's funny here – there's so much more sky than at home,' I said. 'And the sun seems hotter too. And look, look – oh, look!' I pointed to the grass where a small rabbit was running away from us, white tail bobbing. 'A rabbit! Oh, do you think we can catch it? I'd absolutely love a pet rabbit!'

'There's another. And another,' said Kevin.

'I want that first one, the little one.' I ran after it but the rabbit scuttled out of sight. 'Oh, I've frightened him away! I'm sorry, little rabbit. Don't be scared of me.'

'Don't act soft,' said Kevin, but he tried to catch me another one. He didn't have any luck, either.

'I suppose it's for the best,' I said. 'That little rabbit might miss his mother if I took him away with me.' I wasn't really thinking what I was saying. Then a great wave of wanting Mum washed over me. I screwed my face up.

'I'll get you a rabbit,' said Kevin.

'No, it's not the rabbit. It's just I'm missing my mum. Aren't you missing yours?'

'Nah,' said Kevin. 'I'm missing my dad though.'

'I'm not missing my auntie,' said Archie. 'I've changed my mind. I'm not running away no more. I'm staying here. I like it.' His big eyes were shining. He started skipping, still holding our hands. '*Happy days are here again, the skies above are clear again, so let's sing a song of cheer again, happy days are here again!*' Archie sang in his high little voice, word perfect.

We hoped that we'd be able to creep in and get Archie dried off without anyone finding out, but the moment we opened the back door Chubby came flying up to us, fully dressed.

'*There* you are! I've been looking all over. So you've been out then, you little monkeys!' Then she took in the state of Archie and gave a little shriek. 'Oh Gawd, he's wringing wet! Did he fall in the lake?'

'I didn't fall! I did swimming! I went right down to the bottom, I did, I did!' he insisted.

'I'll get right down to *your* bottom, young man, and give it a good whacking,' said Chubby, but she picked him up and cradled him. 'Let's get these wet clothes off of you and warm you up.' She glared at Kevin and me. 'How could you let him go in? Haven't you got any sense? He's not much more than a baby. He could have drowned!'

'We did try to stop him, truly,' I said.

'He was off like a shot,' said Kevin.

'You're a useless pair.' Chubby sniffed. 'You'd better start breakfast while I sort the baby out. Get that kettle boiling and the kitchen table set. And if you want more than bread and milk, go and see if the chickens have laid any eggs.'

'Hurray!' I said.

'I don't want no eggs!' Archie protested.

'Of course you do – a nice boiled egg with soldiers,' Chubby coaxed him, taking him by the hand and leading him away.

I stood in the kitchen staring anxiously at the kettle. I couldn't see how you lit the stove. I looked at Kevin imploringly. He was looking worried too, biting his nails as he listened to Chubby and Archie going upstairs.

'Kevin, could *you* light the gas?' I asked. 'I don't know how.'

'Baby!' he said. 'It's not gas. This is an Aga, see?' He put the kettle on the hob, shaking his head at me.

'And can you reach the plates and stuff down from the dresser – you're taller than me,' I said.

He reached up, but he was clumsy, and when he picked up one plate he sent another one toppling. I caught hold of it just in time.

'Phew! You'd better do it – I'm a bit clumsy like,' he said.

So I stood on a kitchen chair and carefully took willow-pattern cups and saucers and plates and egg cups down from the big dresser – five of each, for Mrs Waverley, Chubby, Kevin, Archie and me. I set them out on the table while Kevin fetched the cutlery from the drawer.

He put the knives on the wrong side of the plates and didn't fetch enough teaspoons, while I did my best to smooth the crock of butter so the finger marks weren't too obvious.

'Come on, fusspot, that'll do. Let's go and get the eggs,' said Kevin.

I wasn't too sure about this, either. The hens had beady little eyes and pointed beaks that looked very sharp. They gathered around us, clucking determinedly.

'They look like they're going to peck us,' I said.

'They're only silly old birds,' said Kevin, but he was skirting them warily too.

As we approached their little house the hens became more insistent. We opened the door cautiously. There were more hens inside, perched on shelves, and they started clucking at us too.

'Hey, look,' said Kevin, seizing a big white enamel pot with a word printed on it in blue – CORN. 'I bet this is *their* breakfast!'

He took off the lid and started scattering the corn on the ground, and the hens hurried over in a frenzy and started pecking it all up.

'See!' he said triumphantly. 'They were just hungry. I said so, didn't I? Go and get them eggs then, while I keep them busy.'

'Clever dick,' I said, but I was grateful.

The henhouse smelled a bit and there were several hens still sitting inside, clucking indignantly because I was disturbing them.

'I'm sorry, hens. I just want some eggs for breakfast,' I said, trying not to be frightened of them.

It was very dark inside, and even with the door wide open it was hard to see what I was doing. I had to feel for the eggs in the straw. I was so cautious at first I just poked the tips of my fingers in, terrified a mouse or rat might be nesting there too, ready to bite me. I couldn't find any eggs at all until I got bolder. Then I found one, and another, and of course I didn't know what to do with them because I hadn't thought to bring a bowl with me.

I couldn't be bothered to trail all the way back to the kitchen. Instead I looped my nightie up and made it into an egg pouch. I found two more eggs, and then nothing more until one of the hens started making funny noises and I realized what she was doing. I thought she'd get up when she'd finished laying but she sat there complacently.

Mrs Waverley, Chubby, Kevin, Archie and me. I *needed* that egg. I reached out uncertainly and lightly stroked the hen's feathers with one finger. She felt surprisingly soft and reassuring, rather like Timmy Ted.

'Have you laid an egg for me, little hen?' I asked, and felt underneath her.

There was the egg, still warm. It made me feel a bit weird, but it was just an egg, no matter where it came from, and I very much fancied a boiled egg for breakfast.

I walked carefully back to the kitchen, clutching my nightie at either side so the eggs wouldn't roll out. I felt a bit like a kangaroo with five babies in her pouch.

'Eggs for breakfast!' I said triumphantly as I went through the kitchen door.

Archie was back, scrubbed pink and wearing a bizarre pink and purple striped jumper to match his new complexion. It came down to his scabby little knees.

'What on earth have you got on, Archie?' I asked.

'It's that Chubby,' he said darkly. 'She took my stuff away to be washed and made me put her own blooming sissy jumper on because I don't have no other clothes.' He started trying to wriggle out of it.

'No, don't do that, Archie. It looks all right, honest,' I lied.

'Yeah, it looks ever so pretty. All you need to do is grow some curls and you'll be a lovely little girly,' said Kevin.

Archie flew at him and started pummelling him with his fists, while Kevin dodged about, laughing at him.

'You boys! Stop that!' Chubby shouted. They'd been making so much noise we hadn't heard her come back. She looked furious.

'We're just playing,' said Kevin.

'Never mind playing! You naughty, dirty little beggars – I've just been clearing up in your room. You've weed all over my lovely pink eiderdown and you didn't even have the guts to tell me!' She was looking at me too.

'It wasn't me!' I said quickly. 'I slept in the room next door, by myself.'

'It was Archie,' said Kevin. 'But don't be cross with him, miss, he's only little.'

'I'm not little, I'm a big boy now, and I didn't pee the bed, I'm sure I didn't,' Archie protested, and burst into tears.

It was the most sensible thing he could have done. Chubby's face screwed up too. 'Sorry, little chap. I suppose it's only to be expected at your age, and you must be feeling pretty dicky, shoved here among strangers. Don't you take no notice of old Chubby. I have my little rants – just ask Mrs Mad – but then I get over them. I was upset about my lovely eiderdown. Gawd knows how I'm going to wash it,' she said.

'I've got a whole shilling at the bottom of my gas-mask case. My auntie give it me. You can have it for a new eiderdown,' said Archie.

'Oh, the pet!' Chubby gave him a hug. 'I'm not taking your shilling, darling. I expect I'll be able to get the silky cover off and give it a good wash, and then I'll hang the insides on the washing line and give them feathers a good beating. You can give me a hand,' she said, nodding at me. 'What's that you've got in your nightie? Did you find any eggs?'

'Five!' I said jubilantly.

'Good girl,' said Chubby, as if I'd managed to lay them myself. My heart thudded pleasantly, because up till now she'd treated me as if I were useless. I gave her the eggs, shuffling up to her awkwardly and trying to be discreet, because I knew

Kevin would never stop teasing me if he saw my frilly pink knickers.

Chubby washed the eggs and then boiled them in a pan and toasted what was left of the loaf. She frowned when she looked at the butter dish. I'd made a good job of smoothing it over, but it was obvious it had shrunk a little. Even a lot.

'*Some* people have already had their butter so will have to make do with dry toast,' she said.

She only gave me dry toast too, which wasn't fair as I hadn't joined in the butter-and-sugar feast, but I kept quiet. The breakfast was still delicious. I hadn't realized eggs could be so tasty. I had tea to drink too, which made me feel grown up, even though I didn't like the taste much.

Mrs Waverley didn't join us for breakfast.

'You can take her a tray when you've had yours,' said Chubby, putting an egg cosy on Mrs Waverley's egg, and wrapping her toast up in a clean tea towel. 'Turn left at the top of the stairs. It's the bedroom right at the end.'

I fidgeted. I quite wanted to see if Mrs Waverley's bedroom had proper furniture, but I felt shy of her now. And what if she were really mad? She hadn't seemed very mad last night, but perhaps the madness came on in fits and starts. I dawdled over my final mouthful of egg and chewed my toast twenty times to make it last longer.

'Go on, take the tray up, and don't spill!' said Chubby, pouring Mrs Waverley a cup of tea. It was a very special cup and saucer, fine china with a rose pattern and a gold rim.

'Oh, that looks lovely,' I said.

'She likes things to look pretty, does Mrs Mad,' Chubby said fondly.

'Doesn't she mind you calling her that?' I dared ask.

'What?'

'Well, she isn't really mad . . . is she?'

Chubby stared at me, and then suddenly shook with laughter. 'You mean like mad loony? Of course not, you daft ha'p'orth. It's her name. Madeleine. I just shorten it, as it's a bit of a mouthful. What's your full name?'

'Shirley Louise Smith,' I said, and Kevin chorused it with me, sniggering.

'Well, if you was a grown-up rich lady and I was unfortunate enough to be your companion and general servant, I'd likely call you Miss Shirl. And you, lad, would be Mr Kev – but you'd stay Master Archie, little 'un, because you're my favourite and you'd always stay little to me,' said Chubby, fondly wiping toast crumbs from Archie's mouth.

'You're not supposed to have favourites,' I said.

'Who says? As if I'd pick a snippy little girl like you or a great string-bean scarecrow like you, Kevin. Now get going with that tray. You help me clear the dishes, Archie, and you get the broom out of that cupboard and get sweeping, Kevin.'

'I'm a boy. We don't do housework,' Kevin protested. 'My dad never does housework. He says it's women's work.'

'I don't give a stuff what your dad says!' said Chubby. 'You'll do as I say here. This is my house, my rules.'

'It isn't really her house, it's Mrs Waverley's,' I muttered to Kevin.

Chubby had sharp ears. 'Mrs Mad might own the deeds, but she'd be in a right old pickle without me,' she said. 'Now scoot with that tray before I give you what for.'

I seized the tray and carried it carefully all the way down the passage and up the stairs, wondering what Chubby's 'what for' would be like. Would she smack me on the backs of my legs like the teachers at school? Would she slap my face like Mum did when I was extra cheeky? Would she whack me with one of her wooden spoons? Might she even beat me with that broom?

It didn't really seem likely, but I was in this strange new place where all the rules seemed to have been changed. I hesitated at the top of the stairs and then turned left along the corridor. Chubby had said that Mrs Waverley's bedroom was right at the end, but I was very curious to see what was in the other rooms. I put the tray down carefully on the bare floorboards and turned the handle of the first door.

The room was empty! And the next one too! I tried all the rooms right down to the end, tiptoeing cautiously and opening each door very slowly so that it wouldn't creak. Empty, empty, empty, empty, empty. Then I found a bathroom – a beautiful bathroom with a sunken cream bath and an elegant pedestal basin and a low toilet that was definitely a posh double-you-see, with a spotless cream seat that would be a joy to sit on. There were cream towels too, a little faded and worn thin now, with entwined embroidered initials. W and M and W. It was obvious the M and W stood for Madeleine Waverley, but I wondered about the other W. She was Mrs, so W had to be her husband, Mr Waverley, but there was no sign of him in the house.

I peeped into the bathroom cabinet. There were no razors or shaving brushes or the peppermint medicine Dad took when he had a dicky tummy. There was a pot of face cream, a tub of powder and a lipstick. I ached to try the powder and lipstick but didn't dare.

I tried the next room but the handle wouldn't turn, though I jiggled it back and forth. It was locked.

'Who's that?' someone called sharply from the end room. 'What are you doing?'

I jumped violently. 'It's only me, Mrs Waverley.'

'Who are you?'

'Shirley! You know, the little girl who's billeted with you. I've brought your breakfast tray. I – I was just trying to find your bedroom,' I stammered. I charged back along the corridor, picked up the tray and hurried back. 'Please may I come in?'

'You may,' she said.

I had to set the tray down yet again to get the door open. Then I went in. It was like walking into a different house. The room was a beautiful pink, so full of furniture that only scraps of rose carpet showed. There was a huge bed with a satin coverlet and a pink padded headboard, a dressing table with a curved looking glass, a huge pale wood wardrobe that covered most of one wall, two raspberry-velvet easy chairs, and a number of little tables scattered around the room holding pink glass and patterned pillboxes and paperweights. The walls were covered with pictures, large and small. There was a lady on a swing wearing a flouncy pink dress; little cherubs with very pink cheeks and plump bottoms; a couple holding hands at the top of a hill watching a red sunset; another couple walking in a rose garden; and an old church with happy newly-weds standing outside in a swirl of pink and yellow confetti.

Mrs Waverley looked very pale propped against her pillows in her white nightdress, her white hair tangled about her shoulders. She was looking at me anxiously. 'Shirley?' she said uncertainly, as if she had a whole class of girls billeted in her house.

'Yes, Mrs Waverley. I've brought you your breakfast,' I repeated.

Maybe she wasn't mad, but she seemed very dazed and woolly. Perhaps she was what Mum called 'a bit simple'.

'Thank you, dear,' she said politely. 'I wonder, would you fetch my dressing gown from the peg over there?' She pointed to another door where a strange silky garment hung. It was predominantly pink of course, but it had an interesting pattern of blossom and delicate white birds with long legs.

I tried to help her put it on. The sleeves were very wide and an odd shape.

'It's a Japanese kimono,' she explained.

'It's lovely,' I said politely, putting the tray on her lap.

'An egg!' she said.

'I found it,' I said. 'I found five. I went into the henhouse. I've never seen real hens before, only in picture books.'

'My goodness. Yes, I suppose the countryside is very different if you're a London child,' said Mrs Waverley, taking the cloth off her toast.

'Archie's terrified of cows,' I said.

'Archie?'

'He's the little one with no hair.' I didn't like to mention Kevin in case she said he couldn't stay. I didn't like him but I seemed to be stuck with him now.

'Chubby's looking after all of you?' she asked.

'Well, yes,' I said.

'You can run about in the fields and the woods,' said Mrs Waverley. 'Do you have a garden at home?'

'We used to have a little garden at the old house. Dad let me have my own daisy patch on the lawn and I used to make necklaces. But where I live now we've only got a yard, and we have to share it with the other people in the house,' I explained.

'Well, you have plenty of space here,' said Mrs Waverley, gesturing towards the window, showing me the view all the way down to the village and then up to the opposite hill with the White House.

'Yes, there's a lot of space,' I said uncertainly. I wondered whether to remind her that most of her rooms were empty and there were no beds for us to sleep in, but it might sound rude. I hovered by her bed while she started eating her egg and toast and sipping her tea.

'I hope it hasn't got too cold,' I said.

'Well, I wouldn't say it was piping hot, but it's very tasty,' she said. 'Could you ask Chubby to come and run me a bath in five minutes or so?'

I stared at her. She wanted Chubby to trail all the way up here just to run her a bath? Why on earth couldn't she do it herself? Perhaps she was an invalid. I'd only ever seen her reclining. Maybe her legs didn't work.

'Yes, of course,' I said, looking at her pityingly.

But after her last mouthful of egg and toast she set the tray to one side, swung her legs easily out of bed and padded across to her dressing table on her long white feet. She sat on the velvet stool and started brushing her hair with a silver hairbrush.

'You can take the tray away now, dear,' she said dismissively.

I did as I was told and carried it along the corridor of empty rooms. I tried to make up my mind what I felt about Mrs Waverley. I wasn't sure whether I liked her or not. It was much easier in storybooks. Grown-ups were generally very nice or very nasty. If a lady had lovely clothes and long hair she was always young and beautiful, not old. If she lived in a huge house with so many rooms they would all be fully furnished, even if it was only with old chairs and sagging sofas and grandfather clocks that didn't tick any more.

I tried to have a conversation with Pauline, Petrova and Posy but they seemed shadowy this morning and barely talked back. Perhaps they found the house disconcerting too.

I looked back longingly at the door of the lovely bathroom. I wondered if I'd be allowed to have a bath in that beautiful tub. Perhaps Mrs Waverley had a bottle of bath foam so I could have bubbles just like they did in the pictures. I could lie back and pretend my hair was growing into long waves – and maybe my body would grow too, and I'd be a glamorous lady, lifting my glistening legs and pointing my toes, while outside a man kept knocking at my door and telling me he loved me.

Then I looked down at myself – my Viyella nightie and my poor scuffed shoes – and felt silly. I put down the tray and went into the room where I'd slept and quickly got dressed, though it was hard deciding what to put on. My smocked dress was for special visits and parties, not running around overgrown gardens with two rough boys, but I couldn't bear the thought of wearing that hot, itchy jumper again all day. In the end I simply wore my skirt. It had a white sleeveless bodice sewn onto the waistband so I was all covered up. It looked a bit odd, but Chubby and the boys wouldn't notice, and I couldn't possibly look stranger than Archie in his woolly stripes.

I wished I had my plimsolls with me so that I could run about easily, but Mum said they looked common with proper clothes and would only let me wear them for PT at school. After I'd pulled on clean socks I had to put my red shoes back on. I tried to rub them up a bit with my dirty socks but I couldn't see much of an improvement.

Then I retrieved the tray and went down to the kitchen.

'There you are!' said Chubby, splashing at the sink. 'I thought you'd got lost. I was about to send out a search party. Now, I'm cold-washing my poor eiderdown cover, and tackling his little lordship's wet clothes at the same time. Have you got anything you want me to wash through for you?'

I shook my head. I couldn't bear the thought of my socks and knickers swimming about in the murky suds with a wee-stained eiderdown and Archie's grubby clothes.

'Well, run along then. Don't stand there gawping at me, it gets on my nerves,' said Chubby.

'Run along . . . where?' I asked.

'Out in the fresh air, you gormless girl! Go and find the boys – they're out there somewhere.'

'Can I fetch a book?' I asked.

Chubby screwed up her face. 'You don't want to bury your face in a book, not on a lovely sunny day like this! Now, be off with you.'

So I had to trail out of the kitchen door.

I **WANDERED ABOUT, FEELING** lost and lonely by myself. It was so quiet, unnervingly so. The noise of my footsteps crunching on the path made me feel jumpy. I tried to creep about on tiptoe but my red shoes pinched so much that I couldn't do it for long.

I kept hearing little rustles in the vegetation to one side. I wondered if the boys were creeping up on me, ready to leap out and go *boo*. I swivelled my head from side to side but couldn't spot Archie's borrowed stripes or Kevin's lank hair and jug ears.

They wouldn't be able to keep quiet this long. It was probably just animals. I hoped it was more rabbits. I pictured myself sitting on a tussock surrounded by little grey rabbits, with maybe a hare and a squirrel too, like in my storybook. I'd tame them by stroking them softly and feeding them titbits, and then I'd make little clothes for them: a grey dress for Little Grey Rabbit, a blue coat for Hare and a pinky-mauve dress for Squirrel.

But what if the animals stalking me were stoats or weasels or rats – a multitude of rats with whiskery faces and long, bare, pink tails? I squeaked and started running. The rustling continued. It seemed to be at shoulder height. *Giant* rats? What other animals did you get in woods?

I thought of Little Red Riding Hood and ran faster. I wasn't sure whether wolves were real or storybook creatures but my heart was thudding and I kept thinking of big teeth, all the better to eat me up.

I veered to one side of the path and the animal burst out in front of me. I gasped. It was a deer! A small deer, probably a very young one, but unmistakably a deer, with a heart-shaped face and big eyes and a soft brown body and fragile legs that skittered past me before it disappeared into the undergrowth on the other side of the path.

I stood still, my heart banging inside my skimpy bodice. I'd seen a real deer! Wait till I told the boys! They'd be so envious. I was pretty sure they'd have gone back to the lake. I hoped Kevin would have the sense to stop Archie going in again. I didn't like him much, but I didn't want him to drown.

It took me a while to find the lake. I wasn't even sure I remembered which side of the path it was. I blundered backwards and forwards, reluctant to stray from the path because the undergrowth came right up to my calves and I hated not being able to see what I was treading on. I wished I was still wearing my long nightie. I kept brushing past stinging nettles and my short skirt offered no protection.

I didn't have a watch and wasn't very good at judging time. I seemed to have been searching for the lake for hours, but perhaps it was only ten minutes. However, at long last I found the clearing, and there was the lake, glittering in the strong sunlight.

'Kevin? Archie? Hey, you'll never guess what I've just seen!' I called.

They didn't reply. I shaded my eyes and peered across the water. I couldn't see them anywhere.

I looked at the water. In the water. What if they'd both gone swimming and sunk to the bottom of the lake? I tore off my shoes and socks, clutched my skirt up round my waist and paddled in past my knees.

I called and called until my voice was hoarse but there wasn't a ripple of response from the water. Perhaps it would take days for them to rise to the surface. Then they'd float there, pale and bloated, and stay floating in my nightmares for the rest of my life.

Stop it, stop it, stop it, stop it, stop it!

I muttered it again and again as I waded out of the lake and tried to dry my legs on dock leaves. It was what I always did whenever something got stuck in my brain and frightened me. I said it when, at night, I heard Mum and Dad arguing on the other side of the wall and wondered if they were going to split up. I said it in the girls' toilets when Marilyn Henderson told me that everyone in our class at Paradise Road thought I was a stuck-up little swot. I said it when I had to sit an important test and suddenly all the words wiggled on the page and wouldn't stay still. I said it when a teacher at my old school saw me sucking a gobstopper in the playground and said my teeth would all fall out: every morning for weeks I'd woken with a thumping heart, my tongue checking that my teeth were still attached.

Mum always said I was a silly old worryguts. I wished she were here now to give me a talking to and tell me I was daft. If only she could have been evacuated too. What if the Germans started chucking bombs on London the minute war was declared? What if one of those bombs had Mum's name on it?

Stop it, stop it, stop it, stop it, stop it!

I tried to distract myself by looking around. I gazed at the blue sky, the white clouds, at the grey water, the green reeds, the turquoise bird flying past me ... Was it a kingfisher? I didn't know a sparrow from a starling, but I'd often seen the cover of *The Observer's Book of British Birds* in the children's corner of W H Smith's. I was sure it was an actual kingfisher!

This huge overgrown garden seemed like a nature-lover's paradise. In the space of half an hour I'd seen a deer and a kingfisher! Perhaps I could find a notebook and a pen and keep a proper nature diary. Maybe I could turn it into a proper book. *Nature Jottings* by Shirley Louise Smith, aged ten. Then I'd appear in the newspaper as a child genius and

Mum and Dad would be so proud of me. I'd have my very own book in Smith's. Maybe they'd shelve it beside *Ballet Shoes* because my surname began with S and so did Noel Streatfeild's.

I wandered off, keeping my eyes peeled for more Nature with a capital N. Irritatingly, I couldn't even spot any rabbits now. I looked up into the trees for squirrels but had no luck there, either. I heard lots of birds and peered upwards until my eyes watered but I couldn't see any of them.

I realized that I wasn't really sure where I was going. I tried going left, I tried going right, but I couldn't find the path again, and without the path I didn't know how to get back to the house.

'I'm not lost,' I said out loud, trying to convince myself. I couldn't possibly be lost. I was simply in a great big garden, halfway up a hill. I'd reach the end of the garden, and then I could go through the gates with the little hearts. I needn't go back to Mrs Waverley's half-empty house. I could head down the hill to the village, walk right through it, and then up the other hill to find Jessica.

She'd be so pleased and surprised to see me. She'd dodge past Sister Josephine and we'd clasp hands and run away, and then we'd take shelter in some woods, and it wouldn't be a bit scary because we'd be together, and I knew perfectly well there weren't any real wolves roaming wild nowadays. We'd build a little hut, a play home like the one in *Peter and Wendy*, and we'd keep house together, and in the middle of the night I'd sneak back to Mrs Waverley's to retrieve my books, and then we'd have our own library. We'd take it in turns reading our favourite passages aloud to each other, and if any strangers ever came near we'd frighten them away.

'Go away! We'll shoot! *Bang, bang, bang!*'

I jumped violently, whirling round. I couldn't see anyone. The voice was unmistakably Archie's but where on earth was he? Then I looked up and saw a grubby foot dangling. He was up a tree, and there was Kevin with him, both of them perching precariously on a branch.

'Seen you!' I yelled.

'You can't see us. You're dead. I killed you with my gun,' Archie insisted, pointing a twig rifle at me. 'I'll kill you again – *bang, bang, bang*!'

'Stop being silly,' I said. 'I'm not the slightest bit dead, see?'

'Go away, hateful Indian squaw,' Archie hissed, 'or we'll scalp you.'

'You've got that the wrong way round. It's Indians who scalp cowboys. So I'm going to scalp *you*!' I said. 'Watch out, I'm coming!'

'No, no! *Bang, bang!* Go *dead*!' Archie insisted.

'She can't come up. Girls can't climb trees,' said Kevin, reassuring him.

'I can too,' I said, though I'd never so much as climbed a ladder before.

I seized the tree trunk, grabbed a branch and tried to swing a leg up. My red shoes were slippery and I couldn't get a proper grip.

'See? She's useless,' said Kevin, peering down at me.

That made me all the more determined. I hauled myself upwards grimly, panting with effort. I grazed my front on the rough bark and felt my bodice tear, but decided to worry about that later. I dug my shoe into the crook of a branch, scraping my sore knees all over again, but I still hung on. I went higher, and then there I was, up on the branch with the boys. I'd done it! I'd climbed a tree!

'Budge over a bit,' I said.

'No! *Bang, bang, bang!*' Archie yelled right in my face, poking his stick in my chest.

I snatched it and broke it in two.

'My gun!' he wailed. 'She's broke my gun!' He sounded heartbroken.

I felt guilty – after all, he was only little. 'It's two guns now,' I said. 'Not a boring old rifle. It's two six-shooters, so you can have one in either hand and shoot people much quicker.'

'Then I'll shoot *you*. This is *our* tree and we've captured it,' said Archie. 'And we're two cowboys and we ain't afraid of nobody.'

'Maybe we'll let her stay,' said Kevin. 'We can play we've captured *her*, and now she has to be our slave and do all our cooking and stuff.'

'No, you *think* you've captured me, but I'm a very clever Indian princess and this is actually an ambush. I have a deadly knife in my pocket, and when you two cowboys are asleep I shall slit your throats and then all your territory will be mine,' I said.

'You ain't got no knife,' said Archie.

'I have so,' I said.

'She'll just have a twig, like us,' said Kevin.

'Oh yeah?' I drew my penknife out of my skirt pocket triumphantly.

'Gawd love us!' exclaimed Archie.

Even Kevin looked impressed. 'Let's see the blade then,' he said.

I pressed the little button and the knife sprang out.

'That's fantastic,' said Archie. 'Where did you get a knife like that?'

'My dad gave it me,' I said proudly.

'He never!' said Kevin. 'My dad's got a knife like that but he won't let me borrow it. He says he'll give me a walloping if I so much as touch it.'

'Well, *my* dad never, ever wallops me,' I said truthfully. 'And this was just his second-best knife. His *best* knife is a huge great cutlass – you know, those curved thingies, like pirates hold in their teeth – the blade's so sharp it can cut a whole hand off, *whump*, with just one blow, but he even lets me hold that. He says I can share it.' I was telling downright lies now, but I thought it sounded impressive.

'Where is it then?' asked Kevin. 'I never saw no cutlass when all your stuff spilled out your suitcase.'

'Oh, I haven't got it. My dad's in the army and he needs it for fighting the Germans,' I said.

'The Germans have got bombs, not knives,' said Kevin.

'Yes, but this is for man-to-man combat,' I explained. 'Then you creep up on the enemy and slit their throat.'

'Or you kill them *bang, bang* with your gun,' said Archie. 'Let's play killing the Germans.'

'All right, though I'll be the captain, because I'm oldest and tallest, and I'll have the knife, and you can be my second-in-command, Archie, and you can shoot people with your guns,' said Kevin.

'It's *my* knife,' I said. 'I'm having the knife.'

'You can't, because then you might win, and you can't do that because you'll have to be the German,' said Kevin.

'No fear!' I protested.

'Well, someone's got to be the German, else how can we play killing them?' said Kevin. He added pompously, just like a teacher, 'Be reasonable, Shirley.'

I was furious. '*You* be blooming reasonable,' I said.

Mum would have fainted dead away if she'd heard me say that word, but I needed to shock the boys with the worst I could think of.

'And my dad made me swear I must never let anyone else have this knife, especially boys, because it's so sharp and dangerous, and boys can't be trusted to be sensible,' I said.

'I bet it's not really sharp,' said Kevin. 'It's probably just a silly old knife used for sharpening pencils.'

He was spot-on. Dad had given me his knife to put points on my set of twenty-four Derwent Lakeland colouring pencils.

'It's the sharpest ever knife,' I said. 'Watch!'

I jabbed at the bark. The knife slipped and nicked my finger.

'You idiot!' Kevin yelled, and Archie burst into tears.

I was a bit startled too. I gazed at my finger. 'It's only a little scratch,' I said.

But as we all peered, a bead of red appeared and grew bigger and bigger.

'She's bleeding to death!' Archie sobbed.

I started to be scared that I actually was. I bit hard on my lip, trying not to cry too.

'You need to bandage it,' said Kevin. 'Quick!'

'Oh well, ha ha, I don't happen to have a bandage on me,' I mumbled.

'Do you want to use my vest?' he offered, unbuttoning his shirt.

I caught a glimpse of it. 'I can't, it's too dirty. I'll get germs in the wound.'

'Suit yourself,' said Kevin huffily. He thought for a few seconds. 'What about that hankie thing you had tied round your knee? Mrs Fusspot gave it you when you went bonk on the ground.'

I felt in my other skirt pocket – and there it was, already stiff with knee blood, but otherwise bright white and very clean.

'Brilliant!' I fumbled with the hankie, blotting up the blood, and then wrapped it round my finger. I still had hold of the knife.

'Here . . .' Kevin took the knife, put it in his pocket and then tied the hankie tight. 'Better hold your arm above your head too – that stops the blood a bit, I think,' he advised.

'Thanks. Give me my knife back now,' I said.

'No, I'm keeping it safe so you don't do anything daft again,' said Kevin.

'You thief! It's my knife! Give it back!' I tried to get it from him, making us both wobble and nearly fall out of the tree.

'Watch out, you nutcase,' he said.

'Don't call me names!'

'Well, you just called me a thief and I'm not. I've never nicked anything in my life. But you *are* a total nutter. Isn't she, Archie?' he asked.

Archie was still snivelling, his nose running unattractively. 'Yes, she is,' he snuffled.

'I'm *not*! Now give me back my knife or I'll tell,' I threatened, though I'd never told on anyone before.

'Who are you going to tell? Them daft ladies in the house aren't going to care,' said Kevin.

I thought that was probably true. 'I'll tell Mr Bentley,' I said.

'We've not started at school yet. And old Mr Bentley wouldn't give a stuff anyway. Everything's gone haywire now,' said Kevin. 'Come on, Archie. Shall we go and find the lake again – if you promise not to drown yourself.' He started climbing down the tree. Archie followed, but his woolly jumper got caught on a jutting branch. When Kevin jerked him free, the jumper tore and started unravelling.

'Oh heck,' said Kevin.

'I don't care. I'm not wearing that stupid sissy thing no

more!' said Archie, pulling it over his head. He left the woolly on the ground and started running off in just his baggy pants.

Kevin and I looked at each other and giggled, even though we were still in the middle of an argument.

'It's true,' I said. 'It *has* all gone haywire. It's weird, isn't it?'

Kevin nodded. We looked each other in the eye. I could see he was scared too. Maybe even a little bit scared of me.

'I'm honestly not a nutter,' I said earnestly. 'I don't know how I managed to cut myself like that. I think I was just showing off.'

'I'm not a thief, either,' said Kevin, and he took the knife out of his pocket and handed it to me.

'Thanks.' I put it back in my own pocket. If Kevin had been a girl I'd have suggested we link little fingers and say, *Make friends, make friends, never ever break friends, 'cos if you do you'll get the cane!* But I'd feel shy holding his hand and I knew he would too.

He jumped down from the tree and then waited for me to clamber down.

'Come on, we'd better go after him, just in case he does something silly too,' said Kevin. 'He's a funny little chap, isn't he?'

'Especially in his pants!' I said.

We both laughed as we watched him. He'd hung onto his twigs and was practising shooting with alternate hands as he ran.

Then a gunshot rang out, startling loud and unmistakably real. Birds flew high out of the trees, crying in alarm. Archie dropped to the ground in his grubby pants and lay very still.

‘RUN!’ SAID KEVIN.

For a moment we both dithered. Run away? Or run to Archie? We could be shot too – but how could we leave him lying there?

We started running towards him. It was difficult to focus when we were moving so fast, but I thought I saw him move his little stick arms. As we got nearer I saw that he had his hands clasped over his head.

‘Oh, Archie, where are you hurt?’ I gasped, kneeling down beside him.

‘Any blood?’ Kevin asked, patting him all over gingerly. ‘Can you turn over, little pal?’

‘You’re tickling!’ Archie said, wriggling away.

‘Hey, hold still! We need to see where you’re hurt!’

‘I ain’t hurt,’ he said, scrambling to his feet. ‘See!’ He held his arms out and turned round, waving them as if he were a windmill.

'But you fell!' I said.

'Yes, that's what you do, don't you, Kev? Someone takes a pot shot at you, you go down *whump* and lie still. I did it right, didn't I?' Archie asked eagerly.

'But that was in our game, you little clot. This was real. A real gun. Some nutter's shooting at us,' said Kevin. 'Come on, we'd all better make a run for it, back to the house.'

'A real gun?' said Archie in awe. 'First a real knife and then a real gun!' His eyes shone.

'Do you think it's a German?' I asked, squinting into the sunlight, expecting a terrifying army to come goose-stepping out of the woods, Hitler at the front, his moustache bristling.

'I never thought! Maybe the war's started!' said Kevin, seizing Archie. 'Come *on*! Grab his other hand.'

We started running, Archie leaping along between us. Sometimes he lifted his feet and tried to swing himself, like a very little kid.

'Stop that!' said Kevin. 'They could be after us.'

'It was a real shot, wasn't it? We didn't imagine it? It wasn't just something banging?' I gasped.

I knew just how easily I could get carried away and believe anything. But the sound of the gun echoed in my head and the birds were still circling high above us.

'It was blimming real,' said Kevin, sweat glistening on his forehead. 'Keep on running, or we could all be goners.'

He was talking out of the side of his mouth like an American gangster, which made me want to laugh, but the situation seemed too serious. I wasn't even sure how to get back to the house and I couldn't see the chimneys through the trees, but luckily Kevin had a better sense of direction than me. He steered us back to the path and then we ran even faster.

Archie's tight grip on the hand I'd just cut hurt horribly, but it was my own fault, after all. The grazes on my knees hurt too, but I was determined not to lag behind.

'There's the house!' Kevin panted.

We charged up to the back door and fell inside.

'Chubby! Chubby! Chubby!' We all three yelled for her, but the kitchen was empty, though there was a big lump of pastry and some carrots and onions chopped up on the kitchen table, showing she must surely be around somewhere.

'Chubby!'

We looked in the pantry, the toilet, then further empty rooms and finally the big hallway.

'*Chubby!*'

We listened. The house was silent.

'Oh, you don't think the Germans came here first and killed Chubby and Mrs Waverley?' I gabbled.

I wanted Kevin to tell me I was being soft, but he looked as if he might believe it too. Then we heard footsteps. It wasn't Chubby in her flapping slippers. It was Mrs Waverley, looking almost like a normal lady, fully dressed in a pink silk blouse and grey slacks, her long hair tied up neatly.

'Good morning, children,' she said. 'Why all the shouting?'

'Oh, Mrs Waverley, we have to run down to the village!' I said. 'We think the Germans are here!'

'I don't think that's very likely,' she said calmly. 'I listened to the news on the radio and war hasn't been declared yet.'

'But we heard a gunshot, miss!' said Kevin.

'They was shooting at me!' added Archie, eyes round.

'Really?' said Mrs Waverley. 'It was probably just the farmer who owns the nearby fields scaring the birds away. Young man, why aren't you wearing any clothes? I should run and put a jersey and trousers on before you catch a chill.'

'Ain't got none,' said Archie cheerily. 'That Chubby took them away and give me her jumper but I took it off because it was sissy.'

'Did you now,' said Mrs Waverley. She looked at Kevin and me. 'Have you two brought any other clothes with you?'

'I got my jacket and another pair of pants and some socks, miss, only they're a bit holey,' said Kevin.

'I've got a proper Fair Isle jumper but it itches me. I've got my coat. And my smocked dress for best,' I said, wanting her to know that Mum clothed me properly.

Mrs Waverley didn't seem particularly impressed. She was looking at my shoes. 'Do you have any walking shoes?' she asked gently.

'Well, I walk in these,' I said. 'I know they need a proper polish.'

'I think they need a bit more than that,' said Mrs Waverley. 'Now run along, children.'

'But we can't go back outside, not with someone firing guns,' I said reasonably.

'Then you can stay indoors and read one of your books,' she said.

I thought this a very sensible suggestion, but Kevin and Archie groaned.

'We haven't got any books, Archie and me,' said Kevin.

'Perhaps Shirley will be a kind girl and lend you one of hers. She seems to have a little library tucked in her suitcase,' said Mrs Waverley. 'Off you go now.'

'I want Chubby,' said Archie.

'Yes, do you think she's all right? She's not in the kitchen – she's not anywhere,' I said.

Mrs Waverley didn't seem at all worried. 'I expect she's out pulling up vegetables for our lunch or busy doing the housework,' she said briskly.

She'd already got carrots and onions and it would be difficult doing housework in a series of totally empty rooms, but Mrs Waverley seemed so calm that I decided not to worry about Chubby or her whereabouts.

'Come on,' I said to Kevin and Archie. 'You can each choose a book.'

'Have you got any comics?' Kevin asked hopefully as they trailed upstairs after me.

'Mum won't let me have comics, apart from the *Chicks' Own* when I was little,' I said regretfully.

Kevin snorted. He seemed even less impressed when I got every book out of my suitcase. 'I'm not reading them,' he said, not even bothering to look at them properly. 'They're all girly books.'

'I'm not reading them, either,' said Archie. It was obvious he couldn't actually read at all, because he held *Orlando* upside down when I gave it to him.

'This way up,' I said. 'See, it's a story about a lovely big ginger cat. He's called Orlando.'

'Orlando!' Kevin mocked. 'That's a stupid name for a cat. You call them Moggy or Tiddles or Sooty, not blimming Orlando!'

'Well, *this* cat's called Orlando. And he has a wife called Grace. And they have three little kittens, Blanche, Pansy and Tinkle.' I said it slowly like a teacher, trying to interest Archie, but he simply sniggered at the last name, and so did Kevin.

'This is a stupid story.' Archie rudely delved into my suitcase and found Timmy Ted tucked into a corner, where I'd hidden him. 'I want the story about *him*,' he said, making Timmy dance about on his soft little paws.

'Well, hard luck, because there isn't one,' I said.

'Tell me it out of your own head. That's what my auntie does.'

'All right,' I said, rather flattered. 'Sit down properly then.'

Archie sat down and made Timmy jump up and down on his knee. 'Look, he's excited! He wants to hear the story too,' he said. 'And me. And Kevin.'

'Count me out. I don't want to hear a stupid baby story

about a teddy,' Kevin said, but he sat down too, biting his nails.

'Once upon a time—' I started.

'What?' Archie interrupted. 'What does that mean?'

'It's just the way you start a story. Now shush and listen,' I said. 'Once upon a time there was a little bear called Timmy and he lived in a bear cave in London with his auntie.'

'Did he really? Is this true?' Archie asked excitedly.

'Of course it's not true, you twerp,' said Kevin. 'Bears don't live in London. How many bears have you seen prowling the pavements?'

'It is *so* true,' I said. 'Timmy and his auntie lived in London Zoo, so there – in a special cave in some rocks. Lots of children came to see them every day. Timmy liked the children because sometimes they threw him buns. His auntie said he shouldn't eat them because they might make him sick, but Timmy didn't listen. He ate buns all day long, all different kinds. He liked to lick the sugary bit off the top first, and then he went *gobble, gobble, gobble* at the bun part.'

'*Gobble, gobble, gobble*,' Archie repeated, giggling, making Timmy gobble one of Kevin's protruding ears.

'Get off,' said Kevin, swatting at him.

'Timmy was a very happy little bear, though he was sometimes naughty and his auntie had to smack him,' I continued. '*Smack, smack, smack.*'

'*Smack, smack, smack*,' said Archie, and he made Timmy bend over to get his bottom royally smacked.

'But then one day the zoo was surprisingly quiet. Timmy looked out of the bear cave in surprise. All the animals were in their cages as usual but there were no visitors, not even a single child. The zookeeper came along and said the zoo was shut because there was going to be a war.'

'Uh-oh!' said Kevin.

'So what happens? Does he get bombed and shot – is he dead now?' Archie asked, clutching Timmy.

'No, no, of course not. Because Timmy and all the other young animals were evacuated,' I said.

'On a train?'

'Yes, just like us, on a train.'

'Animals on a *train*?' Archie asked.

'Yes – it was quite a struggle getting them all on. The great big elephant had to have a carriage all to himself.'

'He didn't squash Timmy, did he?'

'No, I *said*, the elephant sat by himself. Timmy sat with three other animals.'

'Who were they?'

'Well, there was a little baby monkey called Archie.'

'Me! That's like me! I'm a baby monkey!' Archie said, capering around the room, scratching under his arms. 'And was there a Kevin monkey and a Shirley monkey?'

'No, but there was a Kevin giraffe with a long, long neck. He had to stick his head out of the window because it wouldn't fit inside.'

'I don't want to be a giraffe. I'll be a lion,' Kevin insisted.

'You can't. It's *my* story and *I* get to say who people are.'

'Well, who are you? You'd be rubbish as a lion – you're not a bit scary,' said Kevin.

I tried hard to think what I could be. I fancied being a deer like the one I'd seen this morning, but I wasn't sure they kept deer in the zoo. What was the name of that African animal like a deer that was meant to be very graceful?

'I'm Shirley gazelle,' I announced, and ran around the room in a ballet version of a gazelle, whirling and leaping and holding my imaginary horns high.

I was furious when Kevin and Archie roared with laughter. 'Stop it! Stop laughing at me!' I shouted.

'Well, stop acting so daft,' said Kevin. 'Prancing about like a twerp!'

'It was a ballet dance! I can't help it if you're both too stupid to like ballet. Now clear off, both of you. Get out of my room. Go on, go away!'

'No, go on with the story. Timmy wants to know what happens next,' Archie begged.

I snatched Timmy away from him. 'He's *my* Timmy. Now, push off, I say!'

I was trembling with humiliation and anger. I didn't want them to see so I thrust my hands in my pockets.

'Watch out, she's got a knife,' Kevin said, and he grabbed Archie by the wrist and pulled him quickly out of the room, slamming the door behind them.

I hadn't meant to threaten them, but was rather glad they had come to that conclusion. I sat down beside my suitcase, wrapping my arms around myself. I was still trembling. I wanted Mum.

I remembered the stamped postcard at the bottom of my

Mrs Waverley's Red House,
Halfway up Hill, Meadow Ridge.
Dear Mum, This is a horrid place
and I want to come home. There are
two boys living here too and you
wouldn't like them one bit as they're
very silly and rough and call me names.
There isn't any furniture in my room,
not even a bed, so I have to sleep on
the floor. There are two ladies who
live here too but they're a bit odd. One's
little and very bossy and the other one's
dreamy and may be not all there.
We don't have proper meals, just bread
and milk and an egg. PLEASE can I
come home? This isn't a safe place
because the Germans are here already and shoot at us. Love from Shirley
xxx

Mrs D. Smith
9b Whitebird Street,
London
E 1

gas-mask case. I fished it out, along with the pencil. I wrote in tiny letters so as to fit as much on the card as possible, next to Mum's address.

I tucked it back in my gas-mask case, ready to post. Then I rolled over onto my tummy on the hard wooden floor and read *Ballet Shoes*. When my eyes eventually got blurry, I shut them and pretended that Pauline and I were acting out a story, and Petrova and I were attacking Germans with our knives, and Posy and I were dancing up and down the long landing in our red shoes. Then someone came running after us, *clatter, clatter*, and banged hard on all the doors and started yelling at us.

'Shirley!' Archie came rushing into my room in his pants and his lace-up shoes. 'Shirley, it's dinner time. Chubby's been calling us. Hurry, or she says she'll put it in the pig bin.'

'She hasn't got a pig,' I murmured.

I wasn't that bothered about dinner, especially if it was only bread and milk. But when I followed Archie out of my room I sniffed the most wonderful savoury smell wafting up from the kitchen. 'Mmm. What is it?'

'Chubby says it's a pie,' said Archie, rubbing his tummy. 'Let's hurry.'

I thought we would be eating in the kitchen again, but Chubby had set the table in the dining room that led off Mrs Waverley's sitting room. It didn't have much furniture, only a long table with an embroidered cloth, and six chairs, but there were paintings on the wall.

They were landscapes – some pale watercolours, others bolder oil paintings. I stared at the green hill that featured in all of them. Sometimes it was bright and sunny, sometimes grey and cold. There was a sunrise, and also a very dark, night-time one with a crescent moon. It was always the same hill, whatever the time of day or season, and I was pretty sure it was the very hill we were on, painted from several different angles. I looked carefully but I couldn't see Mrs Waverley's house in any of them.

'Don't just stand there gawping,' said Chubby, bustling in with one dish of potatoes and another of carrots. 'I need you to polish the water glasses and bring them in sharpish. And you, young Archie, stop bobbing about in your nothings. What you done with my jumper? Never mind – go and wrap a towel round yourself, your own clothes aren't dry yet.'

I found the glasses in the kitchen and gave them a rub over with the tea towel, peering at the big golden pie on its serving plate. The pastry was elaborately fluted and carefully pricked, so that little bursts of aromatic steam rose out of its depths.

Kevin was hovering beside it, running his finger round the rim where a little gravy had leaked. 'It tastes so yummy,' he said.

'Watch out, Chubby will have your guts for garters if she sees you licking at her precious pie,' I said, though I itched to do the same. 'Why are we eating in that dining room? It's such a bother carrying all this stuff in there.'

'Mrs Waverley's having dinner with us. We have to mind our p's and q's, whatever they are. Stuff like not talking with your mouth full. I'm not doing any talking at all. She doesn't like me. She looks at me like a bad smell,' said Kevin.

'No she doesn't,' I said, although she did, actually.

'She's going to send me packing, I know it.'

'No, she's not.' I tried to sound convincing.

'She only let me stay last night because you begged her . . .' Kevin paused. 'Could you beg her again, Shirl?'

'Shirley. All right, I will if she says anything about you going. But she won't. Here, help me polish these glasses.'

'No fear! I'll only drop one – I'm that clumsy,' he said.

I saw what he meant. He went to the kitchen to fetch the salt and pepper pots, and somehow managed to let one slide so that it fell on the tiled floor with an alarming bang. The bung came out of the bottom and salt erupted all over the place, but luckily the silver pot wasn't even dented.

Kevin tried to scoop the salt back inside with his fingertips.

'Don't! The floor will be covered in dust and germs!' I squealed. 'Let's find some fresh salt.'

I delved inside the pantry. The shelves were very sparsely occupied and it was easy enough to find the packet of Saxa. I shook it carefully into the pot and then popped the bung back in.

'There! Good as new!' I said proudly.

'Here, thanks, Shirley,' said Kevin. 'You're OK, you are. For a girl.'

I wriggled, weirdly pleased. I still didn't really like Kevin, but I couldn't help being pleased that he seemed to like me now.

'Come on, you two! What are you doing – making cow's eyes at each other?' said Chubby, bustling in. 'Scoot! I'm about to serve up the pie.'

We were all given extraordinarily large slices. 'Country portions,' Chubby called them proudly.

We had to help ourselves to carrots and potato, which was an ordeal for Kevin, and totally beyond Archie. Mrs Waverley sat at one end of the table and attempted light conversation, though we'd all sooner have concentrated on the pie. It was the most delicious thing I'd ever tasted. The pastry was crisp and golden on top and yet soft and yielding underneath. The gravy was thick and savoury and silky on the tongue.

The carrots and onions added interest and colour to each mouthful – but it was the meat that made the pie so superb.

I'd never eaten such tender, delicious meat in all my life. I couldn't work out what it was. Mum and Dad and I sometimes had a roast dinner on Sundays, but this meat wasn't dark and strong enough for beef. Was it pork? I knew you could get pork pies, but I was sure they were little humpy pies with pink minced meat, eaten cold.

I ate up every scrap on my plate and laid my knife and fork down neatly together, the way Mum had taught me. Mrs Waverley nodded at me approvingly.

I had the courage to smile at her, and at Chubby too. 'That was the most wonderful pie,' I gushed. 'What was the meat? I've never had it before but it was soooo lovely.'

'It was just rabbit,' she said.

My smile tensed. I gave a silly little giggle, thinking she was joking. 'Not rabbit!' I said.

'Course it was! Didn't you hear me go out and shoot it with my shotgun this morning? I'm a crack shot, even though I say so myself. We always have rabbit pie on Saturday. It's the one meal we don't have to bother the butcher for. We've got hundreds of the little beasts running wild,' said Chubby.

'Not – not the little grey rabbits with the fluffy white tails?' I stammered.

'What other kind are there? I've kept the tail I chopped off. Do you want it for a pom-pom on your hat?' Chubby asked.

I stared at her, my heart beating. I thought of the rabbit I'd seen. It might be the very rabbit inside me now, chopped into little bits and drowned in gravy. My stomach heaved. It felt as if it was scrabbling inside me.

'Murderer!' I gasped, and then I was sick all over my empty plate.

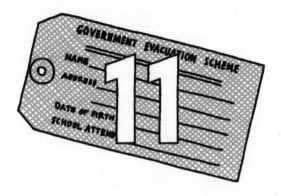

CHUBBY WHISKED ME OUT of the dining room so fast that I stumbled and nearly fell flat. She jerked me upright and dragged me down the corridor and into the toilet. I was sick again, several times.

'What a waste of my lovely pie!' she lamented.

'I – can't – help – it!' I gasped.

'Stop talking and concentrate on the job in hand,' Chubby said sternly.

When I'd stopped heaving at last she fetched an old rag, mopped my face and the bodice of my skirt, then fetched me a glass of water.

'Don't drink it! Just swill your mouth out,' she said. 'I ought to scrub it out with a stick of soap. Fancy calling me a murderer!'

'Well, you are! Shooting a poor little rabbit! How could you?' I said tearfully.

'We're living off the land, as nature intended. What else are we going to put in our pies?'

'You could have steak pies. Or mutton pies,' I murmured defiantly.

'Oh yes? Where do you get steak and mutton from then, Miss Clever Dick? Do you go and pick a big juicy steak off a bush and pluck a side of mutton from the vegetable patch? No, you kill a blooming great cow or a sheep. That's how you get meat, you silly little townie.'

'I know. I'm not stupid. But rabbits are different. They're little and fluffy and you have them as pets,' I said, blowing my nose as best I could on prickly Izal toilet paper.

'So it's all right to eat an animal if it's an ugly old cow or a daft-looking sheep, but wrong to eat a cuddly-wuddly, pretty bunny?' Chubby asked scornfully.

'Yes, because cattle and sheep live on farms,' I said, realizing this was an inadequate answer. 'They don't get shot anyway. That must be a simply horrible way to die. They get to die . . . peacefully.'

'I don't think any animal being herded into a slaughterhouse would agree with you,' said Chubby. 'Now come on upstairs, quick. I've got to go and clear up that nasty mess you made in the dining room. You'd better have a lie-down until you feel better.'

'What exactly is a slaughterhouse?' I asked fearfully.

'It's where they slit all the animals' throats,' said Chubby.

I shuddered, imagining brutal men and wild-eyed, screaming animals. 'I didn't realize they did that. I thought the animals just got old and died in their sleep,' I said.

'And that made it all right to eat them. That's what my mum said.'

'Then your mum must have given you some very tough plates of meat!' said Chubby. 'Townies! They talk a load of nonsense.'

She pulled me upstairs and along to my room. 'Lie down now.'

'I haven't got anything to lie on,' I said.

'That's true enough . . .' Chubby hesitated. 'Come with me.'

She took me along to the end of the corridor and opened the door. 'You can have a lie-down here, on my bed, just so long as you don't wet it like little Archie.'

'I never wet the bed! I'm ten!' I said indignantly.

'Well, start acting like it! Now lie down on top of the bed and have a little nap. Don't blame me if you're starving hungry when you wake up. There won't be no more to eat till teatime,' said Chubby, and hurried out of the room.

Chubby's bed wasn't much more comfortable than the floor. It was very narrow, with a thin mattress, and her pillow was hard. Her blankets were old and faded. I understood why she was so upset about her pretty eiderdown. I hoped Archie hadn't made too much of a stain.

My stomach gurgled. I tried rubbing it but that didn't seem to help. I hoped I wouldn't be sick again. My mouth still tasted horrid, and although Chubby had wiped my bodice with a damp cloth I worried that it might smell. Chubby had warned me about being starving hungry but I decided I didn't want to eat anything ever again.

I closed my eyes but I couldn't get to sleep. The rabbit-squirming-in-my-stomach thought kept coming back so, to distract myself, I got up and wandered around the room. It was nowhere near as nice as Mrs Waverley's. Chubby just had an old rug on the bare floorboards, a rickety chair, a rail of clothes behind a curtain, a washstand with a chipped jug and basin, and a small chest of drawers with a mirror propped on top as a makeshift dressing table.

I peered in the mirror. I was an unattractive pale green. I pulled a face at myself and the mirror-face grimaced back at me. I looked back at the door, listening hard. Silence. No flop-flop of slippers.

I dared to edge the top drawer open. I'd hoped for powder and make-up, but I only found a pink brush and comb and a little tube of salve for chapped lips. There was a neatly ironed pile of handkerchiefs, a pair of rolled-up stockings and an old chocolate box. I peeped inside. It served as a jewellery box but it only held a watch with a broken strap, an old-fashioned jet necklace and a small string of pearls.

The second drawer contained a neat pile of hand-knitted jerseys, a chiffon scarf, a pair of knickers and a suspender belt. I tried the last drawer, having to go down on my knees to get it open. This was much more interesting. It had things from Chubby's childhood: a finger-sized doll dressed as a fairy and a red storybook called *The Odd Little Girl*. I looked inside and found a label stuck on the first page: *Awarded to Maureen Alice Chubb for regular attendance at St John's Sunday School, Meadow Ridge*. Perhaps she was still pious now, because she also had a Bible. I flicked through the flimsy pages. Every now and then I came across a dried flower – a rose or a few sprigs of lavender, pressed as thin as the paper. Then, two thirds of the way through, between the testaments, there was a photograph.

I saw a young couple on a village green, slightly blurred because they were dancing. The man was much taller than the girl, and clearly stronger too because he was whirling her around so that her feet barely skimmed the grass. He wore a white shirt and white trousers – perhaps he'd been playing in a cricket match. The girl wore white too, with a flower in her hair. He was laughing, so handsome in the sunlight. She was looking coyly away from him, but she was smiling. There was something familiar about her sharp little face and her bright eyes. It was Chubby.

So who was the man? One of her brothers? No, he had to be her sweetheart! It was so strange to see fierce little Chubby in the arms of this handsome young man, looking so happy. So where was he now? She was *Miss* Chubb. Had he gone off with someone else – or been killed in the war?

I heard a faint flip-flop beyond the door. I stuffed the photo inside the Bible again, shoved it back in the bottom drawer and leaped onto the bed.

Chubby came in. 'Did you have a little nap?' she demanded.

'Well . . . not really,' I said.

'How are you feeling now?'

I wriggled. 'I'm not sure.'

'Do you feel dicky? Mrs Mad has got it into her head to take the car and drive you down to the village. It's a daft idea, if you ask me – she needs to keep that tank of petrol for emergencies, especially as it seems we'll be at war any day now. It's only a fifteen-minute walk, for Gawd's sake, but Mrs Mad will insist on wearing flimsy shoes – she'll likely turn her ankle if she attempts it. But if you throw up in her car, I'm the poor muggins who will have to clear it up. Just because she treats me like a skivvy doesn't mean I find it any easier doing the messy, smelly jobs. I'm human, just the same as she is. More so, in fact.'

Chubby chuntered on while my head reeled. I watched her thin face flush pink as she became indignant. It looked as if she were wearing rouge. I pictured her with mascara on her pale eyelashes and red lipstick turning her thin mouth into a cupid's bow. I curled her limp hair and puffed it out. I took off her bobbled jersey and tired skirt and ancient slippers and gave her a white dress and nylons and suede heels. Yes, it was definitely Chubby with the man in the photograph, but many years ago.

'Chubby, do you have a sweetheart?' I asked, before I could stop myself.

She stared at me. 'What's this nonsense? A sweetheart? What chance have I got to get a sweetheart, stuck here working all hours for Mrs Mad?'

I felt ashamed at my tactlessness. 'Yes, but maybe when you were younger . . . ?'

Chubby pinched her nose with two fingers and waggled it at me, to tell me not to be so nosy. But her eyes sparkled. 'I was quite popular in my day, even though I say so myself,' she said. Then she snapped back to the present. 'Right, up you get then. Is that bodice OK now? Oh, and look, you've torn it! You'll have to put your jersey on for decency, even though it's a scorcher.'

'What are we doing in the village?'

'Ah, it's a surprise. And it's a surprise for me too, I don't mind telling you. Mrs Mad doesn't often go on little jaunts,' said Chubby.

I thought carefully about it as I went to the room where I'd left my case and belongings. A surprise? That sounded as if it might be a treat. Where would we be going for a treat in the afternoon? If I'd been very good, Mum would some-times take me out for an iced bun in Peggy's Tea Rooms. Oh, I hoped Mrs Waverley might be taking us out for tea! My tummy was still churning, but I was sure a bun would slip down easily.

I felt I had to smarten myself up. My skirt bodice still smelled a bit and I couldn't bear the prospect of putting my Fair Isle jumper on top. I started itching at the very thought. Going out to tea with a grand lady was surely such a special occasion that I ought to wear my best frock!

I tore my skirt off and shook out my special dress. It was rather creased but it couldn't be helped. It was still a slithery treat sliding it over my head and shoulders, pushing my hands through each puff sleeve, smoothing it down and twirling round so that the skirt flared out. I wished I had a mirror.

I did a Posy dance around the room, pointing my toes in my painful red shoes and then sweeping a graceful curtsy to myself.

'Shirley? Are you coming or not? Mrs Waverley's getting the car out of the garage,' Chubby called.

I pulled my postcard home out of my gas-mask case. I didn't have any pockets in my party dress, but I folded it carefully in half and slid it up one of my tight puff sleeves. Then I rushed out of the room, sliding along the landing in my patent shoes, and clattered down the stairs doing a little Hollywood dance, tapping my toes and heels.

'What a noise! You're like a herd of elephants,' said Chubby. She was still wearing her pinny and slippers.

'Aren't you coming too?' I asked her.

She tossed her head. 'Some poor fool's got to stay at home and get on with the work,' she said.

It seemed desperately unfair. If you were a servant you got left out of everything nice. I thought of Mrs Waverley's beautiful bedroom and Chubby's sparse one. It had been kind of her to let me lie on her bed, especially after I'd called her a murderer.

I felt myself blushing. 'Chubby, I'm very sorry I called you a murderer,' I said earnestly. 'I still think it's wicked to kill rabbits and eat them, but I expect you were just following orders.'

Chubby looked amused rather than touched. 'Oh well, I've been called worse,' she said.

'Worse than *murderer*?'

'Oh yes,' said Chubby. 'As if I care. *Sticks and stones may break my bones, but words can never hurt me.*'

'I wish I didn't let words hurt me,' I said. I hated it when

194

Marilyn Henderson called me a posh-nob. I'd hated it when those St Agatha's girls whispered nasty things about me too.

'Oh, I daresay you'll toughen up in time,' said Chubby. 'Off you pop now. Out the front door. Mrs Mad will be waiting. And hang on tight – she's not that great a driver!'

Mrs Waverley looked surprisingly small hunched up behind the wheel of a very big black car. Kevin and Archie were bouncing around in the back ecstatically.

'It's a Bentley, an actual Bentley! We're going for a ride in a Bentley!' Kevin gabbled.

'It's like we're rich folk!' Archie crowed. 'I wish Auntie could see me now!'

He was dressed in his own washed shirt and short trousers, though they still looked damp. Someone had put a folded towel underneath him so he wouldn't stain the cream leather seat.

I looked in the back with the boys. I looked at the empty seat in the front beside Mrs Waverley.

'Could I possibly sit beside you, Mrs Waverley?' I asked politely.

She looked amused and opened the front passenger door for me.

'That's not fair!' said Kevin. 'You wouldn't let *us* sit in the front.'

'You're not wearing a pretty frock,' said Mrs Waverley, helping me in.

'Well, hers won't be pretty much longer, not when she's sick all down it,' Kevin muttered.

'You're not going to be sick again, are you, Shirley?' Mrs Waverley asked.

'No, I'm not,' I said firmly.

I felt triumphant sitting in the front, but the feeling didn't last long. Mrs Waverley was true to her name. She wavered first to one side then the other as she drove us down the long, steep, winding driveway. First it seemed likely she'd crash directly into a tree, then that she'd topple us right over the edge.

I clung to the slippery leather seat and pressed my lips together to stop screaming. The boys weren't so restrained, and whooped loudly as they slid about in the back.

'Pipe down, gentlemen,' Mrs Waverley muttered through gritted teeth. She peered ahead intently, her knuckles white because she was gripping the steering wheel so hard. I had never, ever had a ride in a car before but I knew Chubby was right. Mrs Waverley was a terrible driver.

Turning out of the driveway onto the road at the bottom of the hill was a nightmare. Mrs Waverley waited and waited, though the road was absolutely clear in both directions, and then ignored an approaching cyclist altogether and made a sudden bolt for it. He wobbled in fright and yelled at her, but she took no notice whatsoever, and drove fast into the village.

It was a huge relief when she parked the car, though it was a good foot away from the kerb. Across the road I saw a tea shop called The Inglenook. It looked very promising, with pretty curtains tied with ribbon and crinolined-lady ornaments on the sill. I ran over and peered in through the window. I could see plates of cakes by the counter: a Victoria sponge, fruit tarts and little rock cakes. I couldn't spot any iced buns, but a slice of sponge would be just as nice, especially if it had masses of jam and cream.

'Shirley! Come along, dear, we haven't time to peer in all the windows,' Mrs Waverley called.

'Aren't we going into The Inglenook?'

'No, of course not! We're here to do some shopping,' she said briskly.

I felt tremendously disappointed but trudged back over the road obediently. I wondered if there might be a bookshop in the village. We went into a tobacconist-and-sweetshop, and I saw a dusty shelf of books behind the counter with a sign saying: PENNY LENDING LIBRARY. I got excited, but I could see that the books were all silly romances, not at all the sort of stories I wanted to read.

'My goodness!' said the lady behind the counter. 'It's Mrs Waverley, isn't it? We don't often see you down in the village. And you've brought some kiddies from London too!'

The boys were eyeing up the sweets in the jars hopefully, squabbling over which were best, toffees, humbugs or liquorice.

'I like them all,' said Archie. 'Can I have some, miss?' he asked, tugging at Mrs Waverley's trouser leg.

'Please *may* I?' she corrected.

Archie misunderstood. 'Yes, you can have lots and lots so long as I can too,' he said.

The sweetshop lady chuckled. 'Bless him! Doesn't he

speak funny? What's happened to his hair?'

'Ain't got none now.' Archie rubbed the top of his shiny head. 'It hurts!' he wailed.

'Poor little mite!' said the sweetshop lady. 'Would you like a sugar mouse? He can, can't he, madam?'

'*Artful* little mite,' said Mrs Waverley. 'Very well, he can have the mouse. Say thank you, Archie. And you may weigh out four ounces of boiled sweets for the children to share.'

Kevin and I exchanged looks. It wasn't fair. We'd have liked a sugar mouse too. Boiled sweets were pretty boring, though better than nothing. When we got outside the shop we were allowed to have one each. I chose green, lime-flavoured, while Kevin had strawberry red. Two minutes later we'd crunched them up while Archie was still sucking away at his sugar mouse. He was soon sticky all round his mouth and halfway up his arm.

Next we came to a chemist's. Mrs Waverley went in but told us to wait outside.

'Jammy little devil,' Kevin said to Archie.

Archie nodded happily, slurping away.

Down the road I saw a red postbox. I darted off and posted my card.

'What were you doing?' Kevin asked.

'Sending a postcard to my mum,' I said. 'Aren't you going to send one to yours?'

'What for?'

'To tell her about your billet.' I lowered my voice. 'You know – that it's a bit weird.'

'She won't care one way or the other,' said Kevin. 'She's not my *real* mum.'

'So send one to *her*,' I said.

'Haven't got a clue where she is.'

I was so shocked I didn't know what to say. Both Kevin and Archie seemed to come from strange families where mums and dads disappeared as easily as hankies.

'I'd send a card to my new auntie but I can't write yet,' said Archie. 'I can print my name, though sometimes it comes out backwards.'

'*You're* the one who's backwards,' said Kevin gruffly, giving him a little shove. 'You get to be Chubby's favourite because you're little. And *you* get to be Lady Muck's favourite because you're a girl and suck up to her,' he added, nodding at me.

I knew this was true. I felt myself going red. 'I'm not her favourite,' I said, even so.

'Yes you are. When you chucked up all over the table I thought she'd go mental, but she just said, "Poor Shirley. She's very sensitive."'

'Did she really?' I liked the idea of being sensitive. It made me sound interesting and intelligent and special. I looked at the lovely big purple and red and green bottles glinting in the sunshine in the chemist's window. I saw three coloured Shirleys staring back, each small and shyly smiling and extra sensitive.

'Stop grinning at yourself like a nutcase,' said Kevin irritably. 'What's she buying in there? She's been an age.'

'It'll be special ladies' stuff,' I said.

'What's that?'

I wasn't sure. Mum always said she was needing ladies' stuff when she went into Boots. 'Oh, you'll find out soon enough,' I said, because that was what Mum said to me when I asked her.

It turned out Mrs Waverley wasn't buying anything special or mysterious. It was three tins of Gibbs Dentifrice and a large bar of Pears soap. She'd also bought three toothbrushes, three flannels and three small hairbrushes. She presented them to us as if they were the best Christmas toys in the world.

'Well, you could at least say thank you,' she said, upset by our lack of response.

'Thank you very much, Mrs Waverley, but actually I've already got my own toothbrush and flannel and hairbrush,' I said. I didn't want to sound ungrateful but I was insulted on Mum's behalf. She would have died if she'd known that Mrs Waverley thought her the sort of mother who didn't provide her child with washing things.

'My dad doesn't hold with toothbrushes. He says they just spread the germs around and rot your teeth. And he's got a fine set of choppers – hardly any missing,' said Kevin stiffly.

'I *like* them little brushes and cloths,' said Archie. 'I want them!'

'Yeah, well, a hairbrush is wasted on you, matey,' said Kevin.

Mrs Waverley frowned. 'Don't be unkind, Kevin. I didn't

want Archie to feel left out,' she said. 'Well, come along, we haven't finished yet.'

She shepherded us along the street towards a large shop at the end of the row. A group of village women stood there gossiping. They all stared at Mrs Waverley, and when I looked back they were all in a huddle, heads together, clearly talking about her.

I felt a pang. It was exactly the way the other girls at Paradise Road treated me. I peered up at Mrs Waverley, wondering if she minded.

'Even though I've got my own brushes and flannel, it will be lovely to have new ones,' I said to her. 'And I love the smell of Pears soap. It's very kind of you to get them for us when you didn't even really want us in the first place. That Mrs Henshaw tricked you into it, didn't she?'

She smiled at me uncertainly. 'It looks as if Mrs Henshaw has been very persuasive,' she said, because many of the village women had children with them, though some were clearly their own, rosy-cheeked and sturdy.

The evacuees looked as if they came from a different planet. They were nearly all small and skinny and pale by comparison, with dark circles under their eyes. Except for Marilyn Henderson. I winced at the sight of her. She had managed her own haircare because her ringlets were glossier and more gorgeous than ever. She was wearing a pink summer frock with the white angora bolero. Mary looked very mingy and sour beside her, in a grubby white Aertex blouse and a skirt with an uneven hem. Their foster-mother was smiling at Marilyn dotingly. Mary didn't get a look-in.

'Look, it's Marilyn and Mary!' said Kevin, as if he hadn't seen them for months. He waved to them but they ignored him. 'Stuck-up snot-noses,' he muttered.

'Yes, they are,' I said.

Then we saw Kathleen and Vera. They were rushing out of the chemist's and then leaning panting against the wall further up the road. Kathleen was looking furtive, showing Vera something with her hand cupped. Then she fiddled with it and quickly outlined her mouth.

'It's a lipstick!' I hissed.

'I bet she nicked it,' Kevin whispered.

'Fancy nicking a silly old lipstick!' Archie gobbled the remaining haunch of his sugar mouse and seized one of the blue hairbrushes out of the chemist's big paper bag. He started brushing his bald head.

'Don't, Archie, you'll hurt yourself,' I said.

'I'm just brushing my hair like a good boy,' he said.

'Don't be silly,' I said, but when I peered closely I saw a few prickles. 'Hey, you're right, it's starting to grow.'

'I know – I can feel it. Goody, goody, I hate being a baldy-bonce,' said Archie. 'Here, miss, how long will it take for my hair to grow back proper?' He clutched Mrs Waverley by the trouser leg again. His hand was appallingly sticky and she winced.

'I don't expect it will take very long,' she said, dabbing at her trousers with a hankie. She spat in a ladylike way, and then did her best to wipe Archie's hands and face. He wriggled and squirmed as if she were attacking him.

'Hold still, silly billy,' she said, trying to hang onto him by the collar.

'I'm *Archie*!' he insisted. 'And stop scrubbing at me. Chubby's already given me a good going-over.'

'I should think so too. But we need you to be clean. We're going to buy you some new clothes,' Mrs Waverley said.

'That's not fair,' said Kevin. 'He mucks up his clothes and he doesn't get a hiding, he simply gets a new lot.'

'*You're* going to get new clothes too,' said Mrs Waverley, and she steered us along the road.

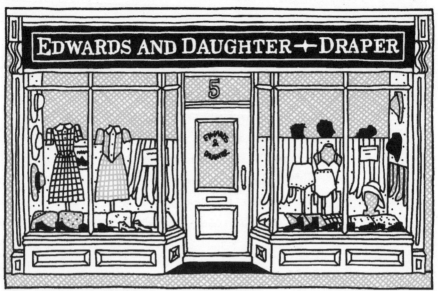

THE DRAPER'S WAS LARGER than the other shops, with a double front. The sign said EDWARDS AND DAUGHTER in gold writing. I liked the novelty of the DAUGHTER instead of SON. I imagined Dad coming back from the army and starting up his own brush shop. I'd help him on Saturdays, and when I left school I'd work with him full-time. We'd have a sign on our shop, SMITH AND DAUGHTER, and folk would come from far and wide to buy our range of superior brushes.

Ladies with long hair like Mrs Waverley would insist on our fine bristle hairbrushes. Men as bald as Archie would still want a set of our tortoiseshell brushes to take pride of place on their bathroom shelves. Our fame would spread far and wide. Maybe the Queen would want one of our curling brushes for her shiny brown hair, and Princess Elizabeth and Princess Margaret Rose would squabble over who got our one and only real silver brush-and-mirror set . . .

'Shirley? What's taken your eye in the window? You've gone all dreamy,' said Mrs Waverley.

I blinked. The window display was particularly dreary: limp check dresses draped on headless plaster models, rows of thick lisle stockings and depressing salmon-pink underwear, floppy sunhats and sou'westers, and ugly lace-up shoes marching two by two in a random pattern.

Mrs Waverley was going to buy clothes for the boys *here*? I had a vision of Kevin with a sunhat crammed over his jug ears, wearing a pink corset and brown clodhoppers, and shook with silent laughter. We trooped into the shop and lolled against the wooden counter while a middle-aged lady with a tape measure round her shoulders (*daughter?*) bustled round trying to please Mrs Waverley, clearly surprised she'd come into the shop.

I wondered if she bought her underwear at Edwards. She certainly didn't buy her silk blouses or stylish trousers or long gowns there. She'd go to Harrods or Selfridges for them, I was sure. Mum and I went to both grand department stores every December when we went to the West End to see the Christmas lights. We never *bought* anything there as it was all very expensive. 'But it doesn't cost so much as a farthing to have a look,' said Mum.

'I'd like two plain white cotton shirts for each of the boys, and one pair of short trousers. And a jersey each too, as it will be getting cold soon. Boys, go into the dressing room and Miss Edwards will bring you the clothes to try on,' said Mrs Waverley.

It was strange. She seemed so odd in her own house on the hill, but now she acted like any posh lady giving orders, and

Miss Edwards jumped to it, scurrying backwards and forwards, plucking shirts and jumpers and shorts out of drawers in wooden cabinets. She didn't need to measure Kevin and Archie with her tape. She just gave them one quick glance and sized them in her head, though she frowned at Kevin's long arms and legs.

There was a lot of scuffling and muttering behind the curtain as Kevin and Archie got changed.

'Ready, boys?' Miss Edwards asked, and then opened the curtain with a flourish, like a magician.

Archie was transformed. I'd seen him look waif-like in dirty, ragged clothes, ridiculous in a lady's woolly jumper, and comical in his pants. But apart from his lack of hair, in his shirt and short trousers he looked like an ordinary little boy. They fitted him perfectly. Poor Kevin wasn't so lucky. Miss Edwards had given him the biggest size of boys' shirt: the sleeves barely reached his wrists, but the shoulders were baggy. His short trousers were particularly disastrous – they came halfway up his thighs. His pale spindly legs seemed to go on for ever.

'Oh dear,' said Mrs Waverley.

'It's the biggest size of boys' short trousers, madam, but he's so *tall*,' said Miss Edwards. She looked at Kevin reproachfully as if he'd grown that big on purpose.

Mrs Waverley and Miss Edwards sighed together. Kevin flushed. Even his ears went bright red. I couldn't bear it.

'Couldn't he have some *long* trousers?' I asked. '*Men's* ones.'

'But he's only a boy,' said Mrs Waverley. 'How old are you, Kevin?'

'Ten. Going on eleven.' Kevin's voice was hoarse with emotion. '*Could* I have some long trousers, miss?'

'Well, I'm not sure what your headmaster will say when you start school next week. Try a pair and we'll see what they look like on you,' she said.

Miss Edwards provided him with a pair of men's trousers, looking doubtful. 'They'll be much too big around the waist,' she said. 'He's as slender as a girl.'

Archie snorted and Kevin glared. He drew the curtain and struggled into the long trousers, taking a long time about it.

'Kevin?' Mrs Waverley called. 'Come along, we haven't got all day. Do those ones fit you?'

'Yes!' Kevin gasped. 'Yes, they do fit, honest. I'll take them off now and—'

'Don't take them off! We want to see what they look like,' said Mrs Waverley, and she pulled the curtain open.

Kevin stood there, clutching the trousers by the waist. Miss Edwards was right. They were much too big. If he let go they'd drop to his knees. But even so the long trousers suited him. The cuffs came right down to his plimsolls. He looked different without his knobbly knees and bony ankles on display – nowhere near as gawky. He looked almost like a man.

'I told you they'd be too big,' said Miss Edwards. 'And that's the smallest waist size we stock in men's trousers.'

'I don't care. I can hold them up. They look tremendous,' Kevin said hoarsely.

'Perhaps a belt might help?' Mrs Waverley suggested.

Miss Edwards found him a striped elasticated belt with a snake clasp. The trousers still bunched at the waist but the belt helped enormously.

'Oh, please can I have them, miss?' he begged.

'Yes, of course you must have them,' said Mrs Waverley. 'They look very smart.' She was peering at his plimsolls. His big toes had poked holes in them. 'We'd better buy you a proper pair of shoes to go with the trousers.'

'Leather brogues would be just the ticket,' said Miss Edwards.

'*I* want leather brogues! And I specially want a snake belt! I want one just like Kev's!' Archie cried.

Miss Edwards frowned disapprovingly. 'Haven't you been taught that "I want" gets nothing? You should say "Please may I have" first,' she said.

'Please may I have I want one of them belts and them brogue things,' Archie gabbled.

'Please fetch them for him, Miss Edwards. Let's not be too hard on him, he's not much more than a baby,' said Mrs Waverley.

'He's a greedy little boy, if you ask me,' said Miss Edwards, but she provided Archie with a snake belt and a miniature pair of shoes.

'Dear me, this shopping trip is costing me a fortune,' said Mrs Waverley, but she didn't seem particularly fussed. There was a tinge of colour on her high cheekbones and she seemed much livelier.

I wondered if she'd ever had children when she was married to Mr Waverley. Was she still married to him, even though there was no sign of him in the house? Or had he died? But weren't widows supposed to wear black? Mrs Waverley's silk blouse was peach and her trousers grey and she had maroon suede wedge sandals, very fancy.

Mrs Waverley saw me looking her up and down. 'I expect you're feeling a bit left out, Shirley,' she said. 'Shall we see if we can find you some new clothes too?'

'Oh, no thank you, Mrs Waverley. This dress is practically brand new and it fits perfectly,' I said, a little ruffled.

Mum had bought it for me in the July sales at Derry & Toms. I'd only worn it once, when Dad took Mum and me out for Sunday lunch at The Griffin the day before he left to join the army. We'd had roast beef and Yorkshire pudding and roast potatoes and carrots and peas, and then trifle for pudding, a special treat. It had cost five shillings each, an absolute fortune, Mum said. But somehow it didn't taste right. We all left a lot on our plates, even the trifle.

We hadn't felt like *us* sitting there. We didn't know how to talk to each other. It was as if we were in a play. Mum and Dad were barely on speaking terms anyway, because she was so irritated with him for joining up so soon. Dad kept licking his lips nervously and running his fingers through his very short hair. I just sat looking at them, wishing I could turn them into the happy, joking mums and dads you found in storybooks.

I wrapped my arms round myself.

'I know it's a lovely party dress, Shirley, but I think you should keep it for best. You don't want to spoil it running through the woods, do you?' said Mrs Waverley. 'And you can't possibly wear it to school.'

I *wanted* to wear it to school! I looked almost pretty in my magical dress. I wanted Marilyn Henderson to see me wearing it. Well, she'd already seen it just fifteen minutes ago but perhaps she hadn't really taken it in.

'I think the little girl needs something more everyday and practical,' Mrs Waverley told Miss Edwards. 'A couple of plain white blouses and a tunic.'

I felt as if she'd kicked me in the stomach. I *hated* the idea of anything plain, and the thought of a tunic was beyond terrible. They were so boxy and bunchy and had that silly girdle thing. The St Agatha's girls all looked a nightmare in their huge tunics.

'Please, please could I not have a blouse and tunic? My mum thinks they're hideous,' I said, truthfully enough. 'Perhaps I could have another dress, just a cheap one – maybe pink?'

'There's not much point buying you a dress when summer's nearly over,' said Mrs Waverley.

'Maybe I could have a little bolero to wear over it – one of those fluffy angora ones,' I said hopefully.

'We don't stock anything like that, miss,' said Miss Edwards. 'But we've got white blouses your size, and tunics in a choice of three colours.'

I sighed. 'Do you have purple?' I asked.

'There's no call for purple. We have navy, brown or bottle green,' she said.

I couldn't believe she could think that any girl would be happy wearing such hideous colours. I ended up with bottle green. The tunic looked even worse than I'd imagined. And the blouse was a horrible cut with a silly collar. I felt a total fool standing in front of everyone.

'Perhaps she needs a tie to set off the blouse?' Miss Edwards suggested, and produced one – bottle green with navy stripes!

I felt like throttling myself with it. And that wasn't even the worst thing.

Mrs Waverley was looking at my shoes. 'She needs some new shoes too,' she said.

'But these are my best! I know they look scruffy now but they'll come up lovely with a bit of polish,' I said.

'I think they're a bit too small for you,' said Miss Edwards, bending down and prodding my toes through the soft leather. 'My goodness, yes. Take that shoe off, child.'

When I didn't immediately unbuckle it, she did it herself, pulling my foot out and then peeling off my sock as if I were a toddler. I curled my toes over quickly, but she saw all the sore red bits.

'For goodness' sake! What was your mother thinking of, letting you hobble around in shoes like this!' she said.

'My shoes fitted perfectly back home. My feet must have grown suddenly,' I declared ridiculously. I'd obviously known for weeks that my shoes were pinching, but hadn't said a word because I loved them so.

'Never mind, Shirley, we'll get you some nice new shoes and you'll be able to skip around without a care in the world,' said Mrs Waverley.

Miss Edwards checked my size and then went to look for a pair, climbing up a ladder to peer at the labels on the stacked shoeboxes.

'Could they be red patent again?' I called.

'We don't stock red patent.' Miss Edwards's mouth puckered as she said the words.

'Well, black then?' I asked. 'Black patent with a strap round the ankle?'

'We don't go in for anything fancy, miss.' Miss Edwards seized a box. 'Ah! These are a lovely leather.'

They were brown lace-ups – the most hideous shoes in all the world. I had to struggle not to burst into tears. I lied frantically when they made me try them on, insisting they rubbed and were desperately uncomfortable, but Miss Edwards said they'd soften after a couple of wears.

'I don't know why you're making such a fuss, Shirley. They look very smart and sensible,' said Mrs Waverley.

I looked down at her maroon suede wedge sandals reproachfully. 'Your shoes aren't sensible,' I pointed out.

Miss Edwards gasped. 'The cheek of it! Don't you dare take that tone with Mrs Waverley, especially as she's been kind enough to buy you these lovely new things.'

'I didn't ask for them,' I retorted, though I knew I was being very rude.

'I don't know why you bother, madam, I really don't. It's a real shame you've had these slum children foisted upon you. I don't know how the village is going to cope. That Mrs Henshaw tried to get me to take a pair, would you believe, when I've got Father in his wheelchair in the back of the shop forever needing attention and the business to run five and a half days a week. She said the evacuees could help in the shop! As if I'd let any of them near the till!'

Archie wasn't paying attention, too busy snapping his snake belt and marching around in his baby brogues, but Kevin was standing up straight, glaring. 'We're not thieves,' he said.

'And we're not slum children,' I said. I rather thought that Kevin and Archie *were*, but I felt that solidarity was called for.

Miss Edwards sniffed, clearly disagreeing.

'Perhaps you could wrap the children's old clothes and give me the bill, Miss Edwards?' Mrs Waverley said coolly. Her tone was wonderfully dismissive.

Miss Edwards bustled off, sniffing again.

'The poor lady has an invalid father who's a difficult man. Her nerves are frazzled. Take no notice,' Mrs Waverley murmured.

'Please can't I wear my own clothes home?' I begged, worrying dreadfully about going back through the town. If Marilyn Henderson and Mary were still lurking they'd laugh themselves silly at the sight of me.

'These *are* your own clothes,' Mrs Waverley said gently. 'I think you look very smart, Shirley, truly. I wore a practically identical outfit when I was a little girl.'

That was the point. I looked terribly frumpy and old-fashioned in my long droopy tunic and awful sturdy shoes. If Mum could see me now she'd be appalled. I wished I could fish my postcard out of the letter box and add a postscript: *They've stolen my party dress and best red patent shoes and given me hideous new clothes!*

I couldn't possibly wear these clothes to school. I'd wear my pleated skirt and my jumper, and I'd just have to put up with the itching. And maybe I could borrow a sharp pair of scissors and cut along the fronts of my red shoes to give them peep toes – then they'd fit perfectly.

I felt a little comforted as we went out of Edwards and Horrible Daughter and started trailing back down the street towards the car. I looked around anxiously for anyone from my school. All the Paradise Road pupils seemed to have gone now, but there was a purple crocodile processing down the pavement instead.

'Oh!' I said, peering at all the St Agatha's girls. There, right at the end, was a girl with a plait by herself, hopscotching down the gutter and twirling her straw boater by the elastic. 'Jessica!'

She looked up in my direction and then gave a great whoop. She came running over and gave me a huge hug. 'Shirley! Oh, Shirley, how wonderful! I thought I'd never see you again! What on earth are you wearing? Have they stuck you in a convent too?' she gabbled.

'Who's she, Shirl?' Kevin asked.

'She don't half talk posh,' said Archie, giggling.

'Oh, Jessica!' I said, hanging onto her. It was wonderful that she was so pleased to see me. I turned my back on the boys. Luckily Mrs Waverley had been waylaid by a lady with a string bag full of onions asking her if she'd turn part of her grounds into a public allotment for the war effort.

'How are you?' Jessica asked urgently. 'Are you with *them*?' she said, nodding at Kevin and Archie.

They had snatched an old tin from someone's dustbin and started a game of Kick-the-Can.

'Yes, worst luck,' I whispered disloyally.

'And her?' said Jessica, glancing at Mrs Waverley. 'What's she like?'

I wrinkled my nose. 'She's . . .' I couldn't find the right words. 'I suppose she's quite kind but she's a bit odd sometimes. She's got a very funny house, ever so big – the red one on the opposite hill to you. Some of it's very grand but most of it's *empty*. We haven't even got beds!'

'Neither do we! We have to make do with the most awful camp beds, and they're all so old and rickety that they collapse when you turn over. We're all squashed together – one whole form of girls to each room. It's quite ghastly. And you know what Goofy and Munchkin are like. They're being so childish and irritating,' Jessica complained. She was looking at my bottle-green tunic, holding out the pleats and playing with the girdle. 'If you don't mind my saying, your tunic is even worse than mine!'

'I know, I know,' I said miserably.

'Still, take heart. The *Ballet Shoes* sisters were always fussing over their clothes, weren't they? Now quick, Shirley – how are we going to meet up again? Can you come down to the village next Saturday? We're allowed to spend our pocket money here in the afternoon, though we're stuck with dreadful Sister Josephine.'

I stuck my finger sideways under my nose like a moustache and Jessica giggled.

'I expect I could ask Mrs Waverley,' I said.

'Can't you come by yourself, not with her? And don't bring those boys, either,' Jessica whispered in my ear. She took my elbow and steered me several feet away from them.

'I'll try not to,' I promised, though I didn't really know how.

'We could sneak off somewhere, just the two of us,' said Jessica.

'Yes!'

'And maybe run away together.'

'Yes, definitely,' I said. It was as if we were storybook girls starting an adventure.

'Do you have any money?' Jessica asked.

'I've got half a crown hidden in the bottom of my gas-mask case,' I said proudly. I'd never had so much money in my life. I got sixpence a week, but I always spent it on a comic and a Sherbet Fountain and a penny chocolate bar. My half-crown wasn't proper pocket money. Mum said it was for emergencies – but surely running away counted as that?

Jessica looked disappointed. 'Half a crown isn't going to get us very far,' she said. 'Nanny lives in Wales now, and a train ticket there costs at least a pound, probably more – and there's two of us.'

I was a little startled. I hadn't realized Jessica wanted to run away somewhere specific. I didn't want to run away to this Nanny person. I wanted to run back to London and my mum.

'Don't you have any money yourself?' I asked.

'No, my horrid mother wouldn't give me a farthing!' Jessica said bitterly.

'But I thought she'd be rich – she's a famous actress.'

'She *is* rich, stinking rich, but she's too mean to give me any money. She says she can't trust me, and I'd only use it to try to run away,' said Jessica.

'But that *is* what you want to do!'

'Yes, but it's still mean of her. All the other girls have pocket money. They're all scoffing sweets now. I shall probably starve to death! We hardly get any food at Lady Amersham's. We had the tiniest sliver of tongue and pickled beetroot and a wizened potato for lunch today, would you believe! I've got stomach pains from sheer hunger,' Jessica said dramatically.

I murmured sympathetically.

'What's the grub at your place like then?' she asked.

'Well, last night we just had bread and milk,' I told her.

'Goodness, that's baby food!'

'And we had the most disgusting dinner today – rabbit pie! I was sick,' I said.

'Rabbit pie's actually quite tasty,' said Jessica.

'But it's awful, eating *rabbits*. This woman, Chubby – she's a sort of servant – she went out with a gun and *shot* one. Can you imagine? Maybe we'll be having *squirrel* pie for our Sunday dinner tomorrow!'

'Or badger pie. Weasel pie. *Rat* pie!' said Jessica.

We both fell about laughing.

Mrs Waverley came over, having finally shaken off the allotment lady. 'Do you two know one another?' she asked.

'Oh yes, we're best friends,' said Jessica. 'How do you do, Mrs Waverley. I'm Jessica Lipman. I'm at St Agatha's. It's so fantastic that Shirley and I have been evacuated to the same village. It's such a shame we can't see more of each other! I wish I could invite Shirley to tea tomorrow, but the nuns are so *inhospitable*!' She emphasized the grown-up word, hissing it a little. 'We aren't allowed to invite anyone to the convent, even though it's not really a convent any more, it's just a lot of girls and a few nuns squashed into Lady Amersham's house. I wonder if you know Lady Amersham, Mrs Waverley . . .'

'I do, as a matter of fact.'

'We've only met her very briefly. She's this little old lady who has to walk with a stick, though she doesn't seem at all frail. She's very strict and bossy, rather like a nun herself,' said Jessica.

'I think that's a very accurate description, Jessica. My sister is formidable,' said Mrs Waverley.

'Your *sister*! Oh crikey! I didn't mean to be rude. I'm so sorry.'

'I didn't take offence. My sister and I are estranged.'

I was astonished. I wondered what on earth had made them quarrel. But Jessica took it in her stride.

'Oh goodness, how I wish *I* could be estranged from my relatives,' she said. 'Well, I'm glad I haven't totally put my foot in it, because I was rather angling for you to invite me to tea with Shirley tomorrow, seeing as I can't have her to tea with me. Would that be all right, do you think?' Jessica looked at Mrs Waverley pleadingly while I held my breath.

Mrs Waverley looked amused, but she shook her head. 'I'm afraid I'm going to have to be inhospitable too. We're rather at full stretch as it is. We only have Kevin, the older boy, on a temporary basis.'

I glanced round, but Kevin was still kicking the can with Archie, too far away to hear. His ears looked especially prominent from the back. I felt painfully sorry for him.

'Oh dear, I would so have loved to come to tea,' said Jessica, not giving up.

'I'm sorry,' said Mrs Waverley briskly. 'Now, I think you'd better go, Jessica. That nun over there is gesticulating in your direction.'

Jessica looked over her shoulder. 'Oh Lordy, Sister Josephine is clearly on the warpath. I'd better hop it.' She gave me a hug and breathed in my ear, *'See you next Saturday!'*

'Come along then, Shirley. Let's get back to the car before I find half the evacuees inviting themselves to tea,' said Mrs Waverley. 'Still, your friend Jessica is rather sweet – quite a little card.'

She called to the boys. Kevin kicked the can high over Archie's head and it clattered alarmingly against a drainpipe.

'Kevin! For goodness' sake, you'll break a window in a minute!' said Mrs Waverley. 'You can't play games like that in the village high street!'

'I play in our street all the time. We all do,' he said. 'Where else are we going to play?' He'd got her there.

'Well, it's considered very rude and uncouth to kick filthy old cans about the street here. Look, you've got baked-bean juice all over the toe of your new brogues. You're going to have to learn to behave. Come on, all of you, back to the car.' She took Archie's hand and pulled him along. He swung on her arm, stamping happily in his new shoes.

'It was Archie who rootled about in that dustbin,' Kevin muttered resentfully. 'Why doesn't she give him a telling-off too?'

'Because he's little, I suppose,' I said.

'Yeah, right little twerp,' said Kevin. 'I don't see why I always get lumbered with him, just because we're both boys. It's you and me who should be pals because we're the same age.'

I was startled. 'You want to be my *friend*?'

Kevin's ears went red. 'Not like a *girl*friend, stupid. Like mates.'

'Oh. I see. Well, I suppose we are. But Jessica's my actual friend. *Best* friend,' I said proudly.

'That stuck-up purple pain?' Kevin sneered.

'Don't you dare call her that! And she's not a bit stuck-up, she's ever so friendly,' I insisted.

'She's even worse than you. Toffee-nosed snobs, both of you,' said Kevin.

I blinked at him. 'Make your mind up. First you want to be pals and then you start insulting me and my best friend,' I said.

'Best friend! You didn't even know her before you got on that train yesterday!' said Kevin. 'And you'll probably never even see her again.'

'Yes I will so. Next Saturday, in the village. It's all arranged,' I said.

'So I've got to mess about with Archie while you two girls yack on, la-di-da, blah-blah-blah,' Kevin moaned.

I wondered if he was jealous and felt a bit guilty, but he was so irritating in the car on the way back, leaning forward and untying my hair ribbon and tickling the back of my neck that I decided not to care. It didn't look as if he would be staying long anyway.

Chubby gave us a plain tea of bread and butter in the kitchen. I was starving and bolted my two slices too quickly. I eyed the half-loaf of bread on the kitchen counter.

'You wouldn't be so hungry if you'd eaten my lovely rabbit pie properly,' said Chubby, but she cut me another slice.

'Did you really shoot it with your gun, Chubby?' Archie asked.

'Well, how else am I going to kill it? It's not going to wander in here and jump into a pie all by itself, is it?'

'Please don't,' I begged.

'Where do you keep your gun, Chubby? Can we look at it? Hey, can I have a go with it?' Kevin asked eagerly.

'Do you think I'm daft?' she said.

'Can I have another slice of bread?' asked Archie. '*She's got one!*'

'You can't have another slice till you eat all them crusts up,' said Chubby. 'Don't think I can't see you've hidden them all under your plate, you daft little mite.'

'They hurts my teeth,' Archie whined, angling his head artfully.

'Oh, teeth hurting, are they? Well, there's a very fierce dentist down the village – he'll fix you up good and proper.'

'No! No, they're fine, really.' Archie tried stuffing all his discarded crusts into his mouth in one go, and then choked and coughed, spraying them everywhere.

'You mucky little monster,' said Chubby, but she cleaned him up, wiped the kitchen table and then cut him another slice of bread after all.

Kevin opened his mouth.

'Yes, you can have one too,' she said, cutting it. 'And me. Got to build myself up, acting as nursemaid to you three when it's a full-time job looking after Mrs Mad and her house as it is.'

'Still, you don't have to do much housework,' said Kevin, sniggering.

Chubby's eyes opened wide. She stared at him so ferociously he hunched his gawky frame into a question mark.

'What? What have I done now? I ain't done nothing,' he mumbled.

'I'll thank you not to make snide remarks about the state of this house, you little guttersnipe,' said Chubby. 'That goes for you two and all.' Her eyes swivelled to include Archie and me. 'There's things you don't understand. Reasons. Only they're none of your business. Nobody's business. So when you go to school on Monday you're to keep your mouths shut about everything that happens in this house. Folk have big noses. They'll try to wheedle things out of you. But you're to keep your lips buttoned up tight. Understand? You're part of this household now, like it or not. So you don't give away no secrets.'

The three of us nodded solemnly and promised we wouldn't do any such thing.

I **SLEPT BY MYSELF** in the empty room again. Chubby purloined a couple of chair seats from the sitting room and spread a threadbare sheet over them. It was almost like a proper bed, so long as I kept my legs tucked up.

'This is just temporary. If we really go to war and you lot are stuck here, Mrs Mad's going to order camp beds from the Army and Navy Stores,' she said.

'How many camp beds?' I asked.

'That's up to her,' said Chubby, knowing what I was getting at.

'She can't get rid of Kevin. He hasn't got anywhere else to go.'

'Well, we'll just have to wait and see.'

'She did buy him those new trousers and shoes and stuff. She wouldn't have done that if she wasn't going to keep him,' I said hopefully.

'Wouldn't she?' said Chubby, refusing to give an opinion.

But as she was going out of the door she looked back over her shoulder. 'She can take in all kinds of waifs and strays when she feels like it,' she said.

I didn't know what she meant, but I felt comforted. Chubby could be quite kind sometimes – though she was anything but kind the next morning.

I was woken by shrieks and slaps from the boys' bedroom.

'Soaking! And yet you've got a potty in the room, you lazy little tyke! I can't be doing with this. Didn't you promise me this wouldn't happen again?' Chubby shouted.

'I didn't mean to!' Archie sobbed. 'I didn't even know I'd done it!'

'So I've got to start washing and scrubbing on a Sunday, when I've the blooming roast to cook and a dozen other things to attend to. You're the flipping limit, you are!' she said, obviously giving him another whack, because there were further yells.

At breakfast poor Archie was very subdued. Kevin kept telling him silly jokes to cheer him up, but Archie drooped until his chin was almost on the table. When Chubby had her back turned Kevin even dug his finger into the butter and sugar and offered it to Archie, but he shook his head.

I was sent to Mrs Waverley's bedroom with her breakfast tray. She frowned when she saw I'd put on my pleated skirt again. The bodice seemed spoiled now so I'd pulled on my Fair Isle jersey too, though I was roasting. I had also defiantly crammed my feet into my red patent shoes.

'Why aren't you wearing your nice new blouse and tunic?' Mrs Waverley asked.

'I wanted to keep them looking clean and fresh for school,' I lied.

Mrs Waverley looked down at my feet.

'I'll wear my new shoes tomorrow, I promise. I just wanted to wear my red shoes one last time,' I said quickly, adding, for pathos, 'My mum bought them for me.'

'Are you missing your mother, dear?'

I nodded. Suddenly I wasn't just putting it on. I felt a great ache inside me. 'I'm missing her terribly,' I said, sniffing.

I was being truthful – but it also stopped her nagging on about my new clothes.

'Now, you can go and play with the boys for a while, but you must all come to my sitting room at eleven o'clock,' said Mrs Waverley, nibbling her toast.

I wondered if we might be going to church. I was quite curious. Mum said she didn't hold with religion and Dad didn't seem bothered, either, so I'd never actually been to a Sunday service. I'd peeped into the church down the end of our new road and liked the high ceiling and the coloured-glass windows and the strange smell. I enjoyed hymns at school too, singing about glassy seas and green hills and all things bright and beautiful.

But Mrs Waverley and Chubby didn't seem to be church-goers, either, though Chubby took off her pinny and even discarded her old slippers in favour of black buttoned shoes. Mrs Waverley was wearing a smart suit and had done her hair up in an elaborate bun. At eleven she turned on her big wireless, tuning it carefully. Were they all dressed up just to listen to dance music? I wondered.

'Sit down, children,' said Chubby solemnly.

We sat down obediently on the floor, cross-legged like we did at school.

The announcer on the radio told us we were about to listen to Mr Chamberlain.

'Who?' said Archie.

'Shh!' said Chubby, nudging him. 'The Prime Minister!'

Archie didn't look any the wiser and opened his mouth again, but Chubby shook her head and put her finger to her lips. Mrs Waverley had her ear to the mesh of her wireless.

We listened.

'This morning the British Ambassador in Berlin handed the German Government a final note stating that unless we heard from them by eleven o'clock that they were prepared at once to withdraw their troops from Poland, a state of war would exist between us. I have to tell you now that no such undertaking has been received, and that consequently this country is at war with Germany.'

'Oh Gawd,' said Chubby.

Mrs Waverley sat back in her armchair. She didn't say anything. Her face was expressionless, yet tears started sliding down her cheeks. The Prime Minister went on talking but none of us were listening now.

'So we're really at war!' said Kevin excitedly. 'Get your gun, Chubby! You're going to have to give us lessons now. Don't worry, we'll shoot all those Germans – *bang, bang*!'

'Bang, bang, bang!' Archie echoed, killing everything in sight with two fingers.

'Hold your tongues, you silly boys,' said Chubby. She went over to Mrs Waverley. 'There, Mad. Don't take on.' She gently wiped her tears away with the back of her hand.

Mrs Waverley still didn't say anything, but she took Chubby's hand and squeezed it tight. They didn't look like mistress and servant now. They seemed more like best friends.

'I'll go and make us both a cup of tea,' said Chubby. 'Run away and play, you kids.'

It was hopeless trying to play with Kevin and Archie now. They both charged around shooting, bombing and flying with their arms stretched out. I went back to my room. I thought about Dad. He had a real fight on his hands now. Would he have to kill someone? Dad was so soft-hearted he couldn't even step on an insect, and when a cat-mauled bird flew in through our window and beat itself silly against our walls, wings all mangled, it was Mum who had to finish it off.

Mum was in London. She'd sent me away because there might be bombing. It could have already started. I imagined the boom of a bomb, and Mum torn apart like that long-ago bird.

I sat down on the floorboards with my back against the wall and read *The Squirrel, the Hare and the Little Grey Rabbit* for comfort. They lived safely and snugly in the country. I wished I lived in their cosy little cottage with the soft sofa and the spotted curtains instead of this huge, empty house.

I felt too restless to read a proper book. I took off my red shoes and rubbed my poor sore toes and then wandered soundlessly up and down the corridor. I peeped into the boys' room, stripped of its bedding again, though it still smelled faintly of wee. I was so glad I hadn't decided to sleep in there with them.

I peeped into Chubby's room once more. I even dared to look at the photograph inside the Bible again. The man and girl in white were still dancing in the sunlight. I shut them back inside the book and wondered if they were still whirling round and round, or whether they were motionless, pressed flat until someone opened the Bible again. I looked around for another photo, maybe even an old love letter, but I couldn't find anything.

I wandered towards the other end of the house. I admired Mrs Waverley's bathroom again. I tried the next door but it was still locked, so I went into her bedroom. She hadn't bothered to make her bed and her clothes were tossed here and there. Her suede sandals were lying sole up on the carpet.

I couldn't stop myself. I stuffed my stockinged feet into the sandals and staggered across the room to her looking glass. They looked a bit odd with my short socks, but they were still glorious. I struck attitudes, sticking one leg out to the side, hoping I looked like a film star. Why couldn't she have bought me a pair of shoes like these divine sandals?

I strutted about, and then my ankle suddenly twisted right over and I nearly fell. I froze, not worrying about the pain in my ankle, only concerned that I'd made a noise and they might have heard me downstairs in the sitting room. I unstrapped the shoes and tried to remember exactly where they'd been left. I started making up a panicky excuse about wanting to fetch Mrs Waverley's breakfast tray, even though I knew Chubby had collected it when she ran her bath.

I couldn't hear anyone coming, thank goodness. I put my ear to the rose carpet and heard the soft murmur of voices beneath me. I was safe! It was so magical being by myself in that beautiful bedroom. I slowly eased the wardrobe door open and gazed at all the clothes. There were lots of dresses pressed together – silks and chiffons in pink and peach and sky blue. Right at the back I found a black evening frock, stiff with silver beading.

I stroked the tiny bobbles as if it were an exotic animal, picturing a young Mrs Waverley going to a ball. The clothes smelled musty though, for all they were so beautiful, so I shut them back in the wardrobe and padded over to the dressing table.

I sat on the pale pink stool and picked up a silver-backed hairbrush. I tried it out, eyes shut, pretending the brush was magic and could make my hair spring out of my scalp, way down to my waist, but when I opened my eyes I saw my own boring short bob.

I put the hairbrush down again, sniffed Mrs Waverley's box of violet talcum powder, and then opened a blue leather box. It was a jewellery case. I'd hoped for diamonds and rubies and emeralds, but there was just a string of pearls, a pair of matching gold bangles, a few rings. And a key. A silver door key. A key to the locked room next door?

I knelt down on the floor again and listened for voices. Then I snatched up the key and hurtled out of Mrs Waverley's bedroom. My hands shook as I pushed the key into the lock.

For a moment I thought I'd made a mistake because it didn't turn, but then I jiggled it a fraction and something clicked. The door opened.

I saw a house. A red-tiled house with chimneys and gables and leaded windows and two doors, one at the front and one at the side. A perfect house in every detail. A house I already knew, because I'd been living in it since Friday.

The house was standing on a big table in the middle of the room so I could circle it. I'd seen big doll's houses in Selfridges and Harrods toy departments, but they were all obviously toys, with pretend windows and front doors that didn't open.

This house looked astonishingly real, a scaled-down replica of Mrs Waverley's home. I felt dizzy staring at it. I imagined a girl inside peering at an even smaller house, and then a flea-sized girl peering into a bead-sized house. I'd always been fascinated by the label on the Gale's honey jar. I'd stare at it all through breakfast, looking at the bear hugging a jar of honey, on which there was a label showing a tiny bear hugging his own honey jar. I'd peer until my eyes watered, trying to see how many bears and jars I could make out.

The miniature house on the table had two gold clasps in the middle. I undid them and pulled gently. The front of the house opened up.

I'd expected to see lots of empty rooms, just like the real house, but it was all fully and beautifully furnished. The walls were hung with tiny paintings, the floors carpeted, and every mantelpiece and table had minute china ornaments. There was a music room with a grand piano and a library with wall-to-wall miniature books the size of my thumbnail. There was even a nursery with a cot and a rocking horse and a tiny teddy bear.

There were people too – proper little models rather than the usual doll's-house dolls with woollen hair and pipe-cleaner limbs. I looked into the kitchen and into Chubby's bedroom, but she wasn't there. But stretched out on a small chaise longue in the sitting room, reading a book, I saw Mrs Waverley, her hair curling past her shoulders. It was blonde, not white, and she wasn't leaning on a couple of cushions. She was leaning on a man instead, a dark man who had his arm round her shoulders. He was looking at her fondly. His lips were slightly open and so were hers. It looked as if they were having a conversation.

I leaned forward, straining to hear, though of course I knew they were only small wax dolls, incapable of speech. I ached to play with them. I wanted to make the Mrs Waverley doll walk upstairs and brush her hair. I thought the gentleman doll might like to go to the music room and play a tune on the piano.

I knelt on the floor and listened for voices but I couldn't hear them properly from here. Unless they'd stopped talking . . . Perhaps Mrs Waverley was walking upstairs right this minute.

I pushed the front of the doll's house back into place, snapped the clasps shut, darted out of the room, locked the door, dashed into the bedroom and put the key back in the jewellery box. I took a breath then, and tried listening on the floor. There was a few seconds of silence, and I heard my blood pulsing in my head, but then murmurs again. It was all right. They were still downstairs.

I didn't dare go back to the doll's-house room though. I went into my bedroom and squatted beside my suitcase, trying to make sense of everything. That doll's house – made to scale and furnished so elaborately – must have cost an absolute fortune. I had longed for a simple, ordinary doll's house, but the cheapest on sale at the local toyshop cost 27/6, which was much too much even for a combined Christmas and birthday present.

I had saved my pocket money for months to buy a set of doll's-house furniture, even though we couldn't afford the house itself. I'd chosen a little plywood table and two chairs, and two small white china plates and two tiny metal forks and knives. I especially loved those spidery little pieces of cutlery, gently digging them into the flesh on my arm and marvelling at the pinpricks they made on my skin.

I'd lay the table obsessively, arrange portions of red and yellow and green plasticine carefully on the miniature plates, and sit Timmy Ted and myself down to a slap-up dinner of meat and potatoes and runner beans. After we'd cleared our plates we'd have a five-minute break and then feel peckish all over again.

I was too old for such babyish games now, but I still wished I'd thrust the doll's-house furniture and plasticine into my suitcase along with my books. All my old doll's-house longings came surging back.

I glanced at the shoebox containing my hideous new lace-ups. I tipped out the shoes and peered at the box. Could

I turn it into a little doll's house?

I picked up Timmy Ted and put him in the box. He was a small teddy but he took up a lot of the space. It wouldn't be a proper house with an upstairs and a downstairs, more a cramped bungalow, but it was better than nothing. I tried to fashion a window and a little door with my penknife, but it made too jagged a cut. I really needed scissors.

I remembered seeing a pair glinting in the kitchen, hanging on a hook on the dresser.

'Wait there,' I said to Timmy.

I crept downstairs and padded towards the kitchen, and then I heard clattering noises. Chubby was making dinner! I started tiptoeing away but she came to the door.

'What are you up to, creeping about? Were you going to help yourself to some of my precious butter and sugar? Don't try that Little Miss Innocent look with me, I've seen them fingermarks!' she said, flouncing back into the kitchen.

'Well, they're not mine,' I said, following her. 'And I wasn't coming for something to eat, I wanted to borrow some scissors.'

'Scissors!' said Chubby. 'What's the matter with you kids? First you want to see my gun so you can shoot yourselves and now you're after blooming scissors. Do you want to stab yourself or cut off all your hair?'

'Of course not,' I said. 'If you must know, I wanted to make a door and some windows.'

'You wanted to . . . what?' Chubby asked. 'Oh yes, of course! Silly me. Doors and windows. I'd forgotten you was in the building trade.'

'Why do you always have to make fun of me?' I asked.

'Because you're such a silly little sausage.' Chubby was beating away at some yellow mixture in a big bowl.

Mum sometimes called me that. I blinked fiercely.

'Hey, you're not crying, are you? Can't you take a ragging?' said Chubby.

'Yes, I can,' I said, though I didn't even know what she meant. 'It's just – it's just . . . I want my mum!' I couldn't stop the tears dribbling down my cheeks.

'Oh, I'm sorry, lovey. I wasn't thinking. Of course you miss your mum.' Chubby sat me down at the kitchen table and mopped at my face with the dishcloth. 'There now. No more tears. I've done enough mopping for one day already.'

'Who else has been crying? Archie?'

'No, he's charging around the grounds with Kevin, happy as Larry, bless him. Those silly boys just think war is exciting. They can't help it, they haven't been through one before. But Mrs Mad is heartbroken, and even I got a bit teary, truth to tell,' said Chubby.

'Why is she heartbroken?' I asked.

'Because it brings it all back.'

'Brings what back?'

'Questions, questions. Ask me no questions and I'll tell you no lies. Here, you have a go at beating this batter – my arm's about to fall off,' Chubby said.

'Is it for pancakes?' I asked hopefully, starting to beat.

'Careful now, don't let it slop over the edges. It's not pancakes, it's for a Yorkshire pudding. You wait till you try

236

one of my Yorkshires. They're a golden joy, even though I say so myself.'

'What's it to go with?' I asked cautiously, looking at the oven. 'You haven't shot another rabbit, have you?'

'You don't have rabbit with Yorkshire pudding! No, it's a nice bit of beef,' said Chubby. 'Here, let me do that – you're a bit heavy-handed, though I can see you're trying hard.'

'Beef?' I said. 'You went and shot a *cow*?'

Chubby roared with laughter. 'Who do you think I am, bleeding Annie Oakley? Of course I didn't! How does your mum get her beef?'

'She goes to the butcher's shop,' I said, shuddering because I hated the smell and the blood on the sawdust and the great sides of dead animal swinging from hooks.

'Well, that's how I get my beef too – though actually the butcher's boy brings it up the hill to me, bless him.' Chubby stopped beating and looked at me. 'What did you really want them scissors for? And don't tell me it was for doors and windows this time!'

'But it was. I wanted to turn a shoebox into a doll's house.'

'Well, why didn't you *say*? You'll be careful, won't you?'

'Of course I will. So can I?' I jumped up and reached for the scissors hanging from the dresser hook.

'Not them ones, they're too big and too sharp,' said Chubby. She rummaged in a drawer and found me a smaller pair. 'Here, these will do. But don't let them boys borrow them. That Kevin's hopelessly clumsy and young Archie's only a baby, bless him. Though too old to be wetting the bed. I don't know what I'm going to do with him. I can't keep up with the washing. Surely he should be dry already. Are London kids a bit backward?'

'I've never wet the bed in my life,' I said indignantly.

'All right, calm down, I was only asking,' said Chubby. 'My, you're a prickly little thing.'

I pictured myself covered in prickles like a ball-of-holly Christmas decoration. I felt rather proud. I used to be so shy and soft I couldn't say boo to a goose. But when we moved to Whitebird Street I'd had to toughen up. Now I had to stick up for myself – I didn't have anyone else to fight my corner. Well, now I had Jessica. She seemed just as keen as me to be best friends.

I wondered what she'd think about us being at war now. Would her father or stepfather go and fight? I felt proud of my dad being a soldier, but worry gnawed at me. I went back to my room and decided to pray for him. It wasn't something I usually did. I generally gabbled a quick *Please don't let Mum be cross with me because I've torn my dress/lost my hair ribbon/ dropped the sixpence she gave me down the drain.* But now I knelt down properly and put my hands together.

'Dear God, please let my dad be all right and not be killed in the war. And if you could possibly fix it, don't let him have to kill anyone, either, because I know he'd hate it. Just let him stay safe and happy and come back to us quick. If you could let the war be over by Christmas we'd all be very grateful. And please don't let my mum be blown up by a bomb. Keep her safe too. And I know it's not as important as the war, but could you stop Marilyn Henderson picking on me and make

238

sure Jessica and I stay friends for ever? And make Archie's hair grow back properly and let Kevin stay with us even though he's so annoying because he hasn't anywhere else to go. Amen.'

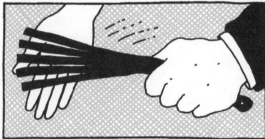

THE NEXT MORNING, WHEN we were all sitting at the kitchen table in our new clothes, ready to go to school, I peered at Archie's head. It had a promising dark shadow now. I rubbed my hand across it to see if it felt prickly.

'Leave off,' he said irritably, swatting my hand away.

'What's up with you, Mr Grumpy?' Chubby asked.

'I don't want to go to school, do I?' Archie growled. 'It's not fair. In London I hardly ever had to go. My last auntie said I could stay home if I felt poorly. And I feel poorly now. Look.' He lolled in his chair and stuck his tongue out of one side of his mouth. It had porridge all over it and looked horribly unattractive.

'Put that tongue back in at once and stop playacting,' said Chubby. 'You're going to school and that's that.'

'I don't mind school,' said Kevin. 'Me and the other lads have a laugh. I'm looking forward to it. I'm fed up of sticking around with girls and babies.' He pointed at Archie and me with his spoon and spilled porridge down his new tie.

'For pity's sake,' said Chubby. 'What is it with you kids? Can't you keep clean for five minutes? Clean and *dry*.' She glared at Archie, who had disgraced himself again in the night.

I didn't want to go to school, either. I wasn't even sure where it was. Chubby had told us but it seemed such a long walk down the hill and through the village. I'd hoped Mrs Waverley would take us in her car, but she wasn't even up yet.

Chubby packed us off at eight o'clock. She took us all the way down the drive, holding Archie's hand and chivvying Kevin and me along.

'I'm not having you darting off into the woods and playing hooky,' she said.

'I don't know how to play hooky,' Archie objected. 'Is it that game with sticks?'

'That's hockey, Goofy,' said Kevin, laughing at him.

'How's he to know that – he's only little,' said Chubby. 'You hold your tongue, Mr Know-All.'

Kevin stuck his tongue out at her. It was only the tip, hardly noticeable, but her hand whipped out and cuffed him on the back of the head.

'Don't you cheek me, mister!' she said. 'Come on, stop messing about. Quick march!'

'My shoes hurt,' I said. They really did – almost as much as my red ones. These new clodhoppers were big enough, but the leather was so hard it was like wearing iron boots. It dug right through my socks. I was sure my feet were starting to blister already. I started limping ostentatiously but Chubby sniffed at me so fiercely that I stopped, scared I might get a clump on the back of the head too.

I caught up with Kevin and smiled at him. 'Kev, do you think I could have the shoebox your shoes came in?' I asked. 'And Archie's too?'

'What for?' he said, rubbing his head. His hair was already sticking up and he was making it worse.

'I'm making doll's-house stuff,' I explained.

Kevin rolled his eyes. 'Baby,' he muttered.

'No I'm not. It's not just kids that play with doll's houses, you know,' I said. I was bursting to tell him about Mrs Waverley's extraordinary secret, but I didn't trust him to keep quiet about it. I'd have to wait till Saturday afternoon and then I could tell Jessica.

How I wished Jessica went to our school! Then I'd be rushing along to meet her and share everything and school wouldn't be scary at all. If she were in my class we'd sit together and copy off each other. In the playground we'd wander around arm in arm, and we'd both laugh in a superior fashion and roll our eyes if Marilyn Henderson started saying horrible things.

Archie was straining to be let loose. 'Can't I go and see that lovely sea again, just for a minute?' he begged. 'I promise I won't go *in*, I just want to look.'

'Now listen to me, Sunshine. You're not going to the lake because you're going to school. In fact, you're not going to the lake full stop, because it's dangerous and I'm not having you drowning yourself. If you go anywhere near it I'll hunt you down with my gun and shoot you,' Chubby threatened.

There seemed a lack of logic there, with Archie ending up dead in both scenarios, but she was in such a mood that I didn't dare point this out. We got to the end of the driveway and Chubby shooed us through the large wooden gates and then bolted them. She stayed on the other side, peering at us fiercely through the heart-shaped cut-outs.

'There! I'm not having you sneaking back in! I know what you kids are like. Now off you go to school,' she said.

'What if we get lost?' I asked anxiously.

'For heaven's sake, it couldn't be more simple. Go down to the street where all the shops are and then turn right down School Lane. *School* Lane, see. Meadow Ridge Primary. And mind you behave yourselves,' Chubby ordered us.

'But how are we going to get back in?' I asked.

'I'll come down and unbolt the gate at four o'clock,' she said. 'Go on now, scoot.'

So we scooted, though our footsteps got slower and slower as we neared the village. We couldn't get lost because we simply had to follow the road. Kevin put his hands in the pockets of his new trousers and whistled as if he hadn't a care in the world, but his face was white.

Archie tried to copy him, but couldn't get the knack of whistling and kept dribbling down his chin instead. He gave up and suddenly grabbed my hand. 'I don't want to go to no school,' he said.

'I know. I don't, either,' I said.

Kevin stopped whistling. 'Then we won't. We'll scarper. Bet you no one will even notice.'

I bent to ease my horrible shoes, considering. 'They'll have a register. They might send a policeman after us if we don't turn up,' I said.

'I'm not scared of no policeman,' said Kevin, swaggering.

'I am,' said Archie. 'They took away my dad. Don't let them take me away too!' He was gripping me so hard my fingers hurt.

'It's OK, Archie. Maybe there aren't any policemen here. Or if there are, they might have gone to join the army now that we're at war.' I stuck my chin out proudly. 'My dad's in the army, ready to fight for us.'

'My dad says joining the army is a mug's game,' said Kevin.

We bickered about it as we walked. There were other children on the road now. Some were running and skipping. Some were scuffling along, heads down. Even if we'd been wearing the school uniform, it would have been easy to tell who was a village child and who came from London. The village kids were suntanned, with rosy cheeks, and their clothes were ever so old-fashioned. Some of the girls were even wearing pinafores and they nearly all wore boots – ugly, sturdy brown boots. My clodhoppers looked almost dainty by comparison.

Kevin was eyeing up the boys. He was the tallest, but the Meadow Ridge boys had broad faces and thick necks and big shoulders. They seemed very tough. They were staring back at Kevin. They didn't look friendly.

'They've just got short trousers. You've got long ones,' I said quickly.

'Let's do a runner,' he muttered. 'Let's go up the other hill. We could go and spy on your stuck-up friend and all her purple mates.'

It was a clever suggestion. I'd probably have said yes, and Archie would have followed us happily enough, but suddenly that bossy-boots Mrs Henshaw darted out of nowhere. She was holding a clipboard and register, just as I'd predicted.

'Hello, you three! You're Mrs Waverley's little tribe, aren't you? How are you getting on?'

We shrugged our shoulders.

'It's . . . all right, thank you,' I said.

'I see Mrs Waverley's been kind enough to kit you out with smart new clothes,' said Mrs Henshaw.

'I like that Chubby best. She's got a gun!' said Archie enthusiastically.

'A gun?' said Mrs Henshaw, looking startled.

'And I went for a swim in the sea.'

'Did you, dear?' Mrs Henshaw obviously thought that Archie was making it all up.

She gave Archie and me a tick in her register. She paused when she came to Kevin. 'Now, I know you're only with Mrs Waverley on a temporary basis, Keith. No, sorry, Kevin. And I think I've found the perfect billet for you. They're opening up a big boys' training camp over in Hailsham. They're a bit short of equipment and you might have to share a bed, but that'll doubtless add to the fun. It'll be like camping with the Scouts.'

Kevin swayed on his feet. 'I'm not a Scout, miss,' he said hoarsely. 'I'd sooner stay where I am. With her and him.' He nodded his head at Archie and me.

'Yes, but there are three of you, and Mrs Waverley and Miss Chubb made it plain that they couldn't cope.'

'She's changed her mind now,' I said. 'Honest. Honest*ly*.'

'Oh well, that will save a bit of admin,' said Mrs Henshaw, and she gave Kevin a tick on her register too. 'Right, off you go now. Into school. Enjoy your first day.'

Meadow Ridge Primary was nothing like Paradise Road. That had been a large, bleak, modern building with high railings all round and a bare asphalt yard. It had looked like a prison. This school was like a sprawling house, very tumbledown, with broken tiles on the roof and weeds sprouting out of the chimneys. The playground was mostly uneven, mossy paving stones. Archie tripped immediately and had to be hauled upright and his knees mopped while he cried noisily, his mouth square.

'Don't cry, Archie. All the other kids are staring at you,' I hissed. 'You've only got a little scratch. *My* knees are much worse from when I fell over on Friday.' This was true. They had started to bleed again, but this might have been because I couldn't stop picking at the scabs in the night. At least my hideous tunic was long enough to hide them.

There were two grown-ups standing at the main door. One was a very round lady with a bun scraped up on top of her head. She looked like a wooden Noah's Ark toy. The other was Mr Bentley. I didn't like him at all, but it was somehow a relief to see a familiar face.

'Ah, you're the three waifs and strays who took so long to find a billet,' he said, as if it had been our fault. 'This is Miss Appleby, the headmistress of Meadow Ridge. She is generously sharing her school facilities with us refugees from Paradise Road. You two older ones, go to the classroom on the right. The little boy will be in the Infants class on the left. Wipe your nose, child!'

Archie wiped it with the back of his hand. 'I'm not going in no Infants. I'm going with them,' he said, nudging up to Kevin and me.

'It's lovely in the Infants, dear. We've got big packets of wax crayons and plasticine!' said Miss Appleby. 'Come along, I'll show you.' She dragged him away.

I stared after them longingly. I'd have loved spending a day drawing pictures and making plasticine jewellery. I'd have much sooner been an Infant.

The Juniors was horrible. It was a terrible squash for a start. The Meadow Ridge children had bagged all the wooden desks. All the Paradise Road pupils had to sit cross-legged on the floor at the front. I couldn't find a space next to any of the nicer girls. I didn't want to be anywhere near Marilyn Henderson. She had noticed my terrible tunic and was whispering to Mary. They were both sniggering. In the end I sat down beside Kevin.

Our own teacher, Miss Grimes, hadn't been evacuated with us, so we had to share the Meadow Ridge one. I hoped for a kind round lady like Miss Appleby, but we had an ancient, stooped little man with thick glasses called Mr Mitford. He looked very weak and weedy, but he soon made bossy Mr Bentley seem like Santa Claus.

He handed out pencils and thin exercise books with rough paper and told us all to write a composition: 'What I Did in the Summer Holidays'.

'I want you to write at least two sides in your best handwriting, and I don't want to see a single spelling mistake,' he said. 'Are you listening, Arthur and George?'

They were two of the big Meadow Ridge boys at the back who were duelling with their pencils.

'We're all ears, sir,' said one.

It wasn't an especially cheeky remark but Mr Mitford quivered in outrage. 'I will not have you using that insolent tone to me, Arthur Briggs. Come up to the front of the class,' he said.

I thought he was just going to get a telling-off, but Mr Mitford went over to a cupboard and brought out a leather strap with a sinister fringe at the end. All the Paradise Road children gasped. The Meadow Ridge pupils sat as still as waxworks.

'I am using you as an example, Arthur Briggs. This is what happens when pupils misbehave in my class,' said Mr Mitford. 'Hold out your hand.'

I thought he must be bluffing, simply wanting to give this Arthur a fright. But then he raised his arm and the strap snapped in the air and the leather fringes struck Arthur's hand so hard he was nearly knocked off his feet. He went scarlet, and tears streamed down his cheeks, though he struggled not to make a sound.

I thought I might be sick into my lap there and then. I could feel Kevin shivering beside me.

'Return to your seat, Arthur,' Mr Mitford said calmly. He stood in front of us, holding the hateful strap in both hands. 'Now, does any other member of this class feel like being insolent?'

249

Silence!

'I'm pleased about that. It should save me a lot of effort. Still, I won't put my strap away just yet. I'll keep it here on my desk as a little reminder to you.'

We didn't need reminding. The snap of that strap echoed in our ears.

'Now get on with your compositions,' Mr Mitford commanded. He sat down at his desk, took a newspaper out of his briefcase and started reading. I could see the headline in big bold print: BRITAIN AT WAR WITH GERMANY.

It was clear that Mr Mitford was AT WAR with the entire class. My hand trembled as I started writing my composition. It was very uncomfortable without a desk. I tried balancing my exercise book on my knee but it made my writing go wobbly and I was certain Mr Mitford would be a stickler for even lettering and straight lines. I had to put the book on the floor and then hunch over.

Kevin was hunched too, grasping his pencil with one hand and biting the fingernails of the other.

'Take that finger out of your mouth, boy!' Mr Mitford shouted suddenly, though he didn't seem to have raised his eyes from his newspaper.

Kevin jumped and his hand shot down to his lap. I held my breath. Surely Mr Mitford couldn't strap him, not just for nibbling a nail! But, thank goodness, he simply shook his head sternly and turned the page of his paper.

I started writing again. I had lots of things to talk about: Dad had left to join the army. The house had seemed so strange without him. Mum went out a lot. I realized now that she'd probably been looking for work. I did some of the shopping. Mr Keith the grocer said I was a handy little housewife because I could add up the cost of half a pound of streaky bacon and four ounces of marge and a packet of custard creams in my head and give him the right money. I sometimes walked all the way to the park, though there weren't any swings. I went to the library nearly every day. Miss Smith, the library lady, let me help her tidy the card index and rub out the silly scribbles in the storybooks. I read a lot. I could list all the books I'd read and give each story a little review.

I wrote and wrote, and my hand started to ache. Kevin was sitting still, looking agonized. His page was still blank.

'Write something!' I whispered.

'I don't know what to put,' he muttered. 'I didn't do nothing in the holidays. I just mucked about.'

'Well, make something up then,' I suggested.

Kevin nibbled at his lip instead of his nails, but eventually started writing. Then he stopped. 'Have you got a rubber?' he mouthed.

I shook my head. His face screwed up. Then he licked his finger and tried to rub out his sentence like that. It just made a huge grubby smear on the page. Kevin looked horrified. 'He'll strap me!' he whispered.

I ducked down low behind the girl in front and seized his exercise book. Very slowly and carefully I tore out the smeared front page and the page at the back too. I was an expert at doing this. I was forever starting to write stories in notebooks from Woolworths and then wanting to change the beginning.

I handed the good-as-new blank exercise book back to Kevin and he looked at me so gratefully it made me feel funny inside. Perhaps he wasn't so bad after all. I didn't know what to do with the two torn-out pages. In the end I folded them up very small and stuck them in my tunic pocket.

Kevin tried again. We were all trying, breathing heavily. Suddenly a girl put up her hand. A girl with long fair ringlets, wearing a fluffy bolero. Marilyn Henderson.

One of the Meadow Ridgers shook her head and gestured, but Marilyn persisted, waving her arm about until she caught Mr Mitford's eye.

He glared at her. 'Get on with your work, child,' he snapped.

'I'm sorry, Mr Mitford, sir, but I can't,' she said.

Every child in the room stared at her. Mr Mitford stared too, shaking his head as if he wasn't sure he'd heard her. I'd seen the film of *Oliver Twist. Please, sir, can I have some more?*

Mr Mitford folded his newspaper and leaned across his desk, linking his fingers. They brushed the end of the strap coiled there. 'You can't get on with your work?' he asked. His voice was very quiet, but ominous.

I prayed that he wouldn't strap her. I detested Marilyn but I couldn't bear the thought of her being hurt like that.

'I'm afraid I've broken my pencil, and I don't have a sharpener with me,' said Marilyn, seeming not the slightest bit scared.

I couldn't help admiring her. She was smiling pleasantly at Mr Mitford as if he were an old friend. He blinked at her. Then he picked out a pencil from the jar on his desk and beckoned to her.

Marilyn stood up, head on one side, hair streaming past her shoulders, as fluffy and adorable as her bolero.

'Don't press so hard this time!' said Mr Mitford, almost jovially.

'I'll take extra care,' said Marilyn, taking the pencil and skipping back to her space.

Kevin and I rolled our eyes at each other. It was so, so, so unfair. Marilyn could get away with murder. Mr Chamberlain should send her over to Germany. All she'd have to do was toss her ringlets and say, 'I'm sorry, Mr Hitler, sir, but could you please stop this silly war,' and then we'd all be able to go home.

Perhaps Mr Mitford wasn't so fierce with girls, I thought. But when Mary put up her hand and said she'd broken her pencil too, he was furious. He didn't strap her but he shouted at her, calling her a copycat.

'I'm not wasting another pencil on you. Now get on with your work!' he bellowed.

'But I can't – my pencil's broken,' Mary gabbled, nearly in tears.

'You should have been more careful. Now hold your tongue!'

So Mary simply had to sit there, unable to finish her composition. She still didn't have a pencil for Arithmetic and couldn't copy out any of the sums. I couldn't believe Mr Mitford could be so unfair. I wished I was brave enough to stand up and confront him, but knew this would be suicide.

At break time there was a great hubbub in the grassy playground. All the Paradise Road children huddled together, calling Mr Mitford all the names under the sun – all except Marilyn Henderson.

'He's very strict, but I suppose he has to be, with all them big tough country boys,' she said. 'He's OK as long as you keep on the right side of him and don't look frightened.'

Mary was such a fool that she actually nodded in agreement. One of the boys took pity on her and chewed on the end of her broken pencil until the lead was exposed again.

Archie came skipping up to us, beaming brightly, talking nineteen to the dozen about sailing a toy boat in a water trough. His new shirt was soaking but he didn't care. He said he loved Miss Appleby.

'Trust us to get a total nutter for a teacher,' said Kevin. 'I just know I'll end up getting strapped.'

'No you won't, not if you don't cheek him,' I said.

'I'll break my own blooming pencil or knock something over or spill something. You know what I'm like,' said Kevin. 'And I just wrote a whole load of rubbish for my composition thingy. You're all right, you wrote pages. You're a real clever-clogs, Shirley.'

'No I'm not,' I said modestly, though I hoped he was right.

After break we had a PT lesson. It was terribly embarrassing because us girls had to take off our frocks and skirts and tunics and the boys had to remove their shirts and shorts. So there we were, all in our vests and pants. I had to show my pink frills to an entire class of sniggering children. Even Mr Mitford raised his eyebrows. I wanted to die.

I was in trouble at dinnertime too. We were each served a plate of brown stew. I asked Kevin if he thought it was rabbit. He said it wasn't, but I couldn't be sure. I asked all the children on my table and they just shrugged. One said it was mutton, another said it was beef, but a third said it *could* be rabbit.

I decided not to risk it. I nibbled at my potatoes and carrots but didn't touch the brown meat, not even the gravy.

'You'll get into trouble,' said one of the village children. 'Mr Mitford always inspects our plates when he's on dinner duty. You have to eat everything, even the fat and gristle.'

I had a vision of Mr Mitford prising open my mouth so he could shovel the brown stew down my gullet. I retched in anticipation.

'I'll eat it for you,' Kevin said quickly, and swapped plates with me. He wolfed my stew down in seconds.

'Thank you! Thank you so much, Kev,' I said.

''S nothing. I was still hungry. Anyways, us two are pals, right? You help me out, I help you out,' he said.

He couldn't help me out in the girls' toilets. They were unbelievably horrible. It wasn't simply that they smelled dreadful. There were no doors, just two rows of wide wooden benches with bottom-sized holes cut in the top! I'd never even imagined such a terrible and embarrassing thing.

The Meadow Ridge girls didn't seem to mind. They sauntered in, tore off a sheet or two of lavatory paper, and then hitched themselves over a hole, idly chatting. I stared, horrified, deciding I could never, ever do that. I would simply have to hang on until I got back to the Red House.

My bladder was aching. What if I couldn't hang on? What if I wet myself in class? What would Mr Mitford say?

I waited until I heard the bell ringing for afternoon school. The other girls ran off. I jumped onto a hole and used it as quickly as I could and then tore off to the classroom, making it back a split second before Mr Mitford himself.

We had an Art lesson next, but there wasn't enough sugar paper to go round so half of us had to make do with lined sheets. There were no powder paints, just a few wax crayons. The Meadow Ridge children grabbed these quickly, so the Paradise Road pupils had to make do with their lead pencils.

'The subject is "The Countryside",' said Mr Mitford.

Kevin and I exchanged despairing glances. How could we possibly draw the countryside with a pencil, a scrappy sheet of paper, and nowhere to rest our page?

'Does he mean draw all them hills and trees and cows and everything?' Kevin whispered.

'Search me. I think we'd better draw just one thing,' I said.

I drew a kingfisher flying through the trees. With no blue or orange crayon it looked like any old bird but I couldn't help it. I drew me looking up at it, pointing, a smile on my face.

'That's good,' said Kevin.

I peered at his page. He'd drawn Chubby, a stick lady with a shotgun. He'd printed *BANG BANG BANG* coming out of the gun. Chubby was standing on a line to indicate the ground. At the other end of the line lay a rabbit, identifiable because it had long floppy ears. It was on its back with its paws in the air. It had a little arrow pointing to its head with a stark message: *DEAD!*

'What do you think of mine then?' Kevin asked. 'Do you get it? That's Chubby and—'

'Yes, I get it, but maybe you shouldn't have made it like a comic. He said do a picture,' I said, worried.

'It *is* a picture,' said Kevin.

I hoped Mr Mitford would think it was, though I doubted it. He chose Marilyn to be class monitor and asked her to collect up all the pictures. He didn't even glance at them when she put them on his desk in a tidy pile.

Then we had the last lesson. School seemed to have been going on for six days already, so it was a slight comfort to think that there were only forty minutes of torture to go. It was a lesson called Vocabulary. I looked around at the village children at their desks. They were all pulling faces. They didn't look as if they liked Vocabulary one little bit.

Mr Mitford stood at the blackboard and wrote a sentence in a clear, looping hand. The chalk tapped again and again on the board. His sentence was surprisingly autobiographical.

Mr Mitford went to immense pains to a . . . . the new children in his classroom, but there weren't enough chairs to go round.

When he'd finished he made us read it aloud in unison. Some of the children from both schools read very slowly, stumbling and spelling words out under their breath. He made us read it again, with more expression, giving a little nod when we came to the missing word.

'Now, children. Who can fill in the missing word for me?' he asked.

There was a long silence. I thought I knew the answer but didn't dare put up my hand. He might strap me if I got it wrong.

He started picking on children one by one. 'You, Peter Howard!'

'Don't know, sir.'

'Well, make a guess, boy.'

'Is it . . . *ask*?'

'*Ask?* How could that possibly make sense, you stupid boy? *Mr Mitford went to immense pains to* ask *the new children in his classroom*? That's not grammatical, it's not a proper sentence, and it's ridiculous anyway. Stand up with your hands on your head, you little dunce.'

He selected another child. 'You, Beth Morgan. What is the missing word? Come along, I've given you a clue. It begins with A. Think!'

'A is for *apple*,' she blurted, frightened back to Infant school.

Several children tittered nervously. Poor Beth stood up too, her hands clasped over her parting, another dunce.

Mr Mitford looked around at the Paradise Road children, sitting cross-legged at the front. We all hunched down, but poor Kevin couldn't help being the most conspicuous.

'You, boy! The great gawky one. What's your name?'

'Kevin Moffat.'

'Kevin Moffat, *sir*. Now can you fill in the missing word for me, Kevin Moffat?'

I tried to mouth it to him but he wasn't looking at me. He was staring helplessly at Mr Mitford. 'No, sir,' he mumbled.

'Well, stand up, you great lummox. My goodness, exactly how tall are you?'

'Don't know, sir,' said Kevin.

'"Too tall" is the correct answer. Now, girl next to the giant ignoramus, you were intent on whispering something to him. Could it possibly be the missing word?'

'I – I – It might be, Mr Mitford, sir,' I stammered, my throat so dry I could scarcely speak.

'And what might it be?'

'Is it – is it *accommodate*, sir?' I mumbled.

'Yes! At last. What is your name?'

'Shirley Louise Smith, sir.'

'And would you care to spell *accommodate* for the benefit of the class?'

I was less certain now. I shut my eyes, trying to visualize the word. There was a double *c*, wasn't there? Or was it a double *m*? Or both?

I took a deep breath. 'A-c-c-o-m-m-o-d-a-t-e?'

'Excellent! Well done, Shirley Louise Smith! You can remain seated.'

He wrote the next sentence on the board. *The children were very b. . . . . and unruly but Mr Mitford soon had them under control.*

Marilyn put up her hand and suggested the word *bad*.

'A good try,' Mr Mitford conceded. 'But look how many dots there are. The word couldn't possibly be *bad*, now could it? So stand up, Marilyn. Hands on head. That's the way.'

Marilyn's face was as pink as her dress. Mr Mitford had been relatively gentle with her, but she still obviously hated having to stand up in disgrace.

Mr Mitford asked several other children and then turned to me. 'Well, Shirley Louise Smith, do you think you could supply us with the correct answer again?'

I struggled. I wasn't daft. I knew all the other children would hate me if I answered correctly. But I couldn't bear not to give the right answer. 'I think it might be *boisterous*, sir,' I said.

Mr Mitford clasped his hands to his chest in a pantomime gesture of glee. 'At last! I have a child in my class who has an excellent vocabulary! Well done, little Miss Smith.'

'Little Miss Suck-up Snotty-nose Swot,' someone behind me muttered.

I'd done it now. At the end of the lesson I wanted to get away quick in case they all rounded on me. As soon as the bell went, Kevin and I struggled to our feet and rushed for the classroom door.

'Not so fast! Walk slowly and sensibly, if you please. And Shirley Louise Smith, stay behind. I want a word with you.'

My heart started pounding. Perhaps he thought I was being insolent by answering every question. He seemed so terrifyingly unpredictable that anything might be possible. The strap was still on his table.

He stared at me, looking me up and down. I started trembling. 'So how do you account for your excellent vocabulary, Shirley?' he asked.

'I – I don't know, sir,' I mumbled.

'Do you have professional parents? What does your father do?'

'He's in the army now, sir, but he's a brush salesman by profession.'

'And your mother?'

'She didn't work, but now she's got a job in a factory.'

'Mmm. Do you do many crossword puzzles?'

'No, sir.'

'Then perhaps you read a lot?'

'Oh yes, sir, I love reading,' I said.

This seemed to be the right answer. Mr Mitford beamed. 'Excellent! So what is your favourite book?'

'*Ballet Shoes*, sir,' I said eagerly.

I seemed to have got it wrong this time. Mr Mitford shook his head. 'Girls' slop,' he said dismissively. 'George Alfred Henty – he was my favourite. Wonderful adventure stories. *Under Drake's Flag* and *With Clive in India*. Look out for them!'

'Yes, I will, sir. Thank you, sir,' I said, though they didn't sound my cup of tea at all.

'Off you go then,' he said. He put the strap back in the cupboard. At the door I looked round and saw that he was casually tossing all our pictures into the wastepaper basket.

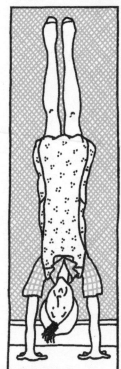

CHUBBY WAS WAITING FOR us, swinging on the gate like a little girl. She had her head cocked, one eyebrow raised.

'Well, how did you lot get on?' she asked.

'We're not going back there again, ever, ever, ever,' said Kevin. 'Are we?'

'Never,' I said, though I was still glowing with the thought that I was better than anyone else at Vocabulary. I was better than Marilyn Henderson. Mr Mitford might smile at her and make her monitor, but he recommended his favourite books to *me*. Not that I wanted to read old-fashioned boys' books. And not that I liked Mr Mitford.

'Our teacher's a total saddist,' I said.

'He's sad?' Chubby looked puzzled.

'No, saddist – when you like being horribly mean and cruel to people for no reason,' I said.

'I think you mean *sadist*,' said Chubby, laughing.

Kevin laughed too. 'There, thought you were so good at Vocabulary,' he said.

Archie laughed as well, though he didn't have a clue why. He jumped up beside Chubby and swung too.

'How about you, little man? How did you get on? Have you got a mean, scary teacher like Mr Mitford?' she asked, rubbing her hand lightly over the tiny prickles on his head.

'How did you know ours was called Mr Mitford?' I asked. 'We didn't tell you his name, did we?'

'There's only one Mr Mitford. Give you the strap soon as look at you!' said Chubby. 'I was that scared of him I nearly wet meself every time he looked at me.'

'He once taught *you*?' It was difficult to take it in. Of course I knew Chubby must have been a child once, but it was hard imagining her little, though she still wasn't much bigger than a child.

'*My* teacher's nice,' said Archie complacently. 'She read us a story, and any girl or boy who's extra good gets a sweetie at the end of the week. She showed us the tin. I'm going to get one on Friday, I bet you.'

'That's right, my lovely,' said Chubby, jumping off the gate and swinging him off too. 'Come on then, I expect you're hungry. I've got a treat waiting for you.'

She'd made us a cake – a yellow slab cake with cherries. She cut us each a big slice. Mrs Waverley came and joined us in the kitchen. She was dressed in a shirt and slacks and her beautiful suede shoes, but her hair was loose around her shoulders and she wasn't wearing any make-up.

It made her face look vaguer than ever, just a mist of pale features.

She asked us how we'd got on but she didn't really seem to be listening to our answers.

'Did you have Mr Mitford as your teacher when *you* were a little girl, Mrs Waverley?' I asked.

She blinked at me.

'Mrs Mad didn't go to the village school, silly,' said Chubby.

'I didn't really go to school when I was your age,' Mrs Waverley said, making an effort.

'You never went to school? You lucky beggar,' said Kevin, wolfing down another slice of cake.

'I had a governess though. She was very strict, especially with me. Then my parents sent me away to boarding school,' she said, sipping her tea.

'Oh, you lucky thing,' I said. I'd borrowed a whole series of boarding-school books from the library and the girls always played tricks on each other and had midnight feasts and tuck boxes.

'I hated it,' said Mrs Waverley. 'It was a convent and I'm sure the nuns were even stricter than your Mr Mitford.'

'Sister Josephine is certainly strict,' I said. 'She's my friend Jessica's teacher. Mrs Waverley, *couldn't* Jessica come to tea?'

'I don't think it would be allowed, not if her nuns are anything like my nuns,' she said.

'Couldn't you ask Lady Amersham though? You said she was your sister,' I persisted.

Chubby looked astonished. 'Someone's been chatting to the kiddies!' she remarked.

'You've got a *lady* for a sister?' Kevin asked with his mouth full. 'So you must be swanky posh and ever so rich.'

I glared at his tactlessness.

Mrs Waverley shook her head. 'I'm not at all posh, Kevin, not nowadays,' she said.

She couldn't be rich, either, I thought – she didn't have enough money to furnish all her rooms. Perhaps she'd spent it all on the miniature furniture for the doll's house. Yet she'd kitted us out in new clothes from head to toe. I didn't *like* my tunic and clodhoppers but I could see that it was very generous of her in the circumstances. I felt rude persisting, but I wanted to see Jessica so badly. Saturday seemed so far away.

'Perhaps if you asked Lady Amersham if Jessica could come to tea as a special favour, then she would tell all those bossy nuns to let her come. They'd have to do as she suggested, seeing as she's accommodating the entire convent,' I said.

'*Accommodate!* That's that fancy word you said in Vocabulary!' said Kevin. 'She got them all right, Mrs Waverley! She's a real brainbox!'

I blushed. I hadn't liked to tell Mrs Waverley or Chubby myself because it sounded like boasting, but I was grateful to Kevin for letting them know. It might even make Mrs Waverley give in.

But she was smiling wistfully. 'Well done, Shirley. But I'm afraid Lady Amersham wouldn't want your friend to come to tea. And I don't entertain any more,' she told me.

'No visitors, unless they're foisted upon us like you three,' said Chubby. 'And I suppose now we're at war we've got to do our bit, haven't we?'

When Mrs Waverley drifted away to her sitting room Chubby looked at us meaningfully. 'Stop pestering her! And don't mention Lady Amersham again. Mrs Mad and her ladyship don't speak no more,' she said.

'They've had a row?' I asked with interest. 'What was it about?'

'Nosy parker!' said Chubby, waggling her own nose impressively.

Archie tried to copy her but failed. Kevin and I couldn't manage it, either.

'How do you *do* that?' he asked.

'It's one of my magic tricks,' said Chubby.

'I know who you remind me of! It's Mary Poppins!' I said.

'So who's she when she's at home?' said Chubby.

'She's this nanny lady in books. She looks after some children and she does all these magic tricks and takes them to meet magic people. I love it when they eat their tea upside down,' I said.

'Well, I'll turn *you* upside down if you like and you can eat the rest of your cake with your head on the floor and your feet waggling in the air, but don't blame me if you choke,' said Chubby.

'No one could eat standing on their heads!' said Archie, giggling.

'Oh yes they could.' Chubby stepped out of her sloppy slippers, tucked her skirt and pinny into the legs of her long, elasticated knickers as if she were going paddling, and then did a perfect handstand.

'Feed me a bit of cake – go on,' she said.

Archie posted a cherry in her mouth and she ate it, grinning.

'You're *exactly* like her!' I said. 'She sounds all snippy but she's actually very kind. And she does surprising things and so do you.'

'I don't do anything surprising.' Chubby swung herself neatly upright again and slotted her slippers back on her feet. 'But maybe I am a little bit magic.'

'Then magic it so we don't have to go back to that awful school no more,' said Kevin.

'There's a limit to my powers, Sunshine,' said Chubby.

'Well, I'm not going back, no matter what,' Kevin whispered to me.

Maybe Chubby heard too, because the next morning she didn't just take us to the wooden gates, she insisted on marching with us all the way to the school. We were forced into school that day. And the next and the next and the next.

Mr Mitford stayed just as frightening. He strapped two more Meadow Ridge boys, rapped many knuckles with his ruler, threw the blackboard eraser at several heads, and bellowed at us all every day. But when he returned the compositions about our holidays he'd given me nine out of ten, with a little red-ink star and a message: *Well done, Shirley. A very good effort.* When everyone compared notes at break time I found out by eavesdropping that Marilyn had only got six, and had to write out all her spelling mistakes five times. It turned out six was a good mark by Mitford standards. Poor Kevin got one out of ten, and a much curter message: *Disgraceful.*

Mr Mitford picked on Kevin almost as much as on the Meadow Ridge boys. He didn't strap him, but once he leaned forward across the first row of cross-legged Paradise Road children and slapped him about the head, simply because he'd made a silly mistake in Mental Arithmetic.

Kevin struggled desperately not to cry.

'Cheer up, lad, I'm doing you a favour,' said Mr Mitford. 'Simply trying to flatten out those dreadful ears of yours.' He leered at the class, clearly requiring a response. Most of the children tittered in a hysterical fashion.

I kept my face poker-still but didn't dare show my feelings any further. I hated myself for my cowardice, especially when Mr Mitford smiled at me and called me 'dear'.

'You're definitely Teacher's Pet,' said Kevin as we toiled up the hill on Friday, Archie zigzagging in front of us, arms stretched out because he was being an aeroplane.

'No I'm not,' I said.

Kevin rolled his eyes. 'It's bleeding obvious, and you know it.'

'Do you think I should ask him not to keep picking on you?' My tummy turned over at the very thought, but I felt I had to offer.

'As if that's going to do any good,' said Kevin. 'He'll just start picking on you too if he thinks you're siding with me.'

'Well, if you're sure,' I said, breathing out heavily.

'Anyway, don't let's talk about old Bully Mitford and that bally school. We're free now for two whole days!' said Kevin, and he raised his arms and chased after Archie in a game of bomber pilots.

It was wonderful to wake up on Saturday knowing I'd be seeing Jessica that afternoon. I didn't even have to wear my awful tunic, as Chubby wanted to get my blouses washed over the weekend. She'd already washed and mended my pleated skirt. She'd got it looking as good as new, Persil white, but hadn't been able to press the pleats of the skirt back into shape. They stuck out in a sort of frill now.

She'd apologized gruffly, but I didn't mind particularly. In fact, when I slipped the bodice over my head, I was thrilled. I didn't have a looking glass but it *felt* as if I were wearing a proper tutu. I spent ten minutes dancing around my room barefoot, attempting all the movements Pauline, Petrova and Posy learned at Madame Fidolia's stage school.

It was actually an advantage having a room without any furniture. I could whirl about, flinging out my arms and attempting pirouettes. I didn't overbalance once. I decided to practise every morning. I knew I needed a proper ballet teacher if I were ever going to become a serious dancer, but if I practised my exercises and built up my stamina and read those ballet-class passages over and over again, maybe I'd be able to attend a proper ballet school when I went home. I'd learned vocabulary from book reading, so maybe I could learn dancing too.

When I went down to breakfast I had to wear the horrible clodhoppers because my red shoes hurt so badly now. The heels of my new shoes went *clackety-clack*. Perhaps I could try tap dancing. I shuffle-tapped my way down the stairs, feeling just like Ginger Rogers.

'Here, missy, was it you making that racket on the stairs? Don't clump about like that, you'll scuff all the woodwork, and I'm the poor soul who has to polish it,' Chubby said, but I didn't let her lower my spirits.

'Don't nag, Chubby,' I said, and I gave her waist a quick squeeze. She felt astonishingly little and bony underneath her baggy pinafore.

'Cheeky monkey! Still, it's nice to see you all perky. Go and see if them hens have been obliging, ducks,' she said.

I could only find four eggs.

'Well done – one for all of us,' said Chubby.

'But what about Mrs Waverley?'

'She's having her breakfast in bed so she won't see it's an egg day,' she said.

'She can have mine,' I offered.

'But you're only a skinny little girl and she's a great big woman. You need the nourishment,' said Chubby. 'Dear Lord, you haven't decided you won't eat eggs as well as rabbit?'

'No, I just want to give Mrs Waverley my egg. And can I take her tray up to her?' I asked.

'All right, Funny Face,' said Chubby.

'So you're sucking up to *her* as well as Mr Mitford,' said Kevin sourly.

'So what?' I said, refusing to be riled.

I ran out through the kitchen door, remembering the straggling roses near the henhouse. I didn't have the kitchen scissors with me, but I managed to break off a little pink rose without getting too scratched. Then, while Chubby was making Mrs Waverley's toast and pouring her tea, I found a little blue vase and put the rose in it.

'Pretty,' said Chubby approvingly. 'Mind you don't knock it over going up the stairs.'

I was very careful. I walked slowly along the corridor, pausing outside the locked door. I peered hard at it, as if I thought the wood might turn into a window so I could have one more look at the magical house.

I'd made reasonable progress with my own cardboard effort. I'd got Kevin's and Archie's shoeboxes and stuck them one on top of the other so the house had three storeys, and I'd attempted some furniture. Chubby's packets of Player's Weights cigarettes became a three-piece suite, and I'd turned Mr Bentley's hankie into cushions and pillows and a bedspread. The bed itself was a cracked, oblong pin tray I'd found in a kitchen cupboard, but the slice-of-bread mattress had to be renewed every other day. I hadn't managed a bathroom yet, but I discovered that an egg cup was the right shape for a double-you-see.

The chief resident of my house was much too big for it. Timmy Ted squashed the furniture and bumped his head on the ceilings whenever he stood up. Chubby said she'd show me how to make a little doll out of a clothes peg but she hadn't got around to it yet. I didn't think a peg doll would look very realistic.

I thought of the two beautifully modelled dolls in Mrs Waverley's house, and ached.

She didn't answer when I knocked on her door. After three goes I opened it cautiously. Mrs Waverley was still asleep, lying on her back with her hair spread over the pillow. I said her name softly but she didn't stir. I wondered if I dared scrabble for the key in her jewellery box and tiptoe next door with it so I could have another look at the doll's house.

I bent right over her, checking she was deeply asleep, when she suddenly opened her blue eyes. We both jumped violently. I sprang backwards and she sat up.

'My goodness, Shirley, you startled me,' she said. She rubbed her eyes. 'And I was having such a lovely dream. We were sitting watching the sunset under the cedar tree and—'

'*We* were?' I said, puzzled.

'No, silly, it was—' Then she shook her head. 'Sorry, I'm still half asleep. Why are you in my bedroom, Shirley?'

'I've brought you your breakfast tray,' I said. 'Shall I plump up your pillows so you can sit up properly?'

I fussed around her and then carefully laid the tray on her knees.

'A rose! How sweet of Chubby. And I see it's an egg day.'

'I went and fetched them. There were only four, actually,' I said.

Mrs Waverley didn't seem to take in the significance of my statement. She ate, daintily but greedily.

'Are you enjoying your egg, Mrs Waverley? I didn't have one,' I said.

'Don't you like eggs, Shirley?'

'Yes, but I wanted you to have mine,' I said. 'And the rose was my idea.'

'That was very sweet of you. Why are you being so nice to me?' Mrs Waverley asked, peering at me from behind her curtain of hair.

I decided to come straight out with it. 'So you will be in a very good mood and drive us to the village this afternoon.'

'I'm not sure about that, dear. I don't think we're supposed to make unnecessary car journeys now there's a war on,' she said.

'Oh! Well, we could walk, couldn't we? You wouldn't even need to come with us. Kevin and Archie and I walk to school every day, don't we? So we can go down to the village, can't we? You promise?' I said eagerly.

'Are you wanting sweets by any chance?' she asked.

'Well, sweets would be lovely, though I think I'm going to start saving any money I get,' I said hopefully. 'But most of all I want to see my friend Jessica.'

'I see.'

'You know what it's like when you have a very best friend and you just can't wait to see them,' I said.

'Yes, I do,' said Mrs Waverley, smiling at me. 'Very well, you can all three go into the village, so long as you behave yourselves. Can you bring me my handbag?'

'We'll be as good as gold,' I said, fetching it from the dressing table.

Mrs Waverley took three yellow threepenny bits from her purse.

'Pocket money for the three of you,' she said, handing them over. 'So what are you saving for, Shirley?'

'I'd like a little doll's-house doll,' I said.

She stared at me. 'Why do you want a doll's-house doll?' she asked softly. 'You haven't got a doll's house.' Her blue eyes looked suspicious.

I forced myself to keep looking back at her, thinking of ice and polar bears so that I wouldn't blush. 'I'm making one,' I said. 'Out of shoeboxes.'

Mrs Waverley relaxed. 'That's a lovely idea.'

'The only trouble is, I really need more shoeboxes,' I said. 'I'd love to make some extra rooms. I haven't even managed a kitchen yet.'

'Ah, you're taking this project seriously,' said Mrs Waverley. 'Go and look in my wardrobe.'

I blinked at her. I hadn't been hinting, I'd only been thinking aloud. I opened the wardrobe, trying to feign surprise and admiration for her dresses even though I'd already peeped at them. There on the floor at the front were her suede wedges – but behind them were three shoeboxes.

'Take out the shoes. I keep them in the boxes to be tidy, but I don't really need them. You build your extensions, dear,' said Mrs Waverley.

'Are you sure? You're so kind!' I removed some smart court shoes, a pair of conker-coloured walking shoes, and two sparkly silver dancing shoes with peep toes.

Mrs Waverley sighed when she saw them, screwing up her face.

'Are you all right?' I asked.

'Yes, yes. Those shoes bring back memories, that's all,' she murmured. 'But take the boxes.'

'If you're absolutely sure. They'll be so useful for my doll's house.'

'You must show it to me sometime. But run along now. I think I might have a little nap. I'll see if I can go back to my dream.'

I skipped off, clutching the boxes. Kevin and Archie wanted me to go out in the woods with them, but I didn't fancy playing silly boys' games. I borrowed glue and the scissors from Chubby and turned my house into a six-roomed palace. I still had the three shoebox lids so I made a white stove and a sink.

Chubby brought me a glass of milk and a biscuit for elevenses and admired my efforts. 'You're making a neat little job of that house, Shirley,' she said.

'I wish I could figure out how to make saucepans for the stove and taps for the sink. If I had a bar of chocolate I could use the silver paper, but I haven't got any,' I said.

I really *was* hinting this time, wondering if Chubby had a Fry's Chocolate Cream or a Kit-Kat hidden away in the kitchen cupboard.

'Wait a minute,' she said, and shuffled off.

She didn't bring back a bar of chocolate, but she gave me a large ball of crumpled silver paper.

'I used to save it for Christmas but we don't bother with decorations nowadays. You use it, Shirley,' she said.

'Thank you, thank you, thank you!' I said, thrilled – though of course I'd have liked a chocolate bar too.

I spent most of the morning making kitchen equipment. It was fiddly work, especially the taps, but very satisfying. Timmy Ted came to watch – though he didn't seem particularly impressed that I was working so hard to make him a beautiful home. I tried to prop him up but he kept falling on his back and staring vacantly up at the ceiling. He wouldn't chat to me any more. He stayed a shabby little toy with a sewn-on mouth.

I conjured up my *Ballet Shoes* girls instead, though they all had very different ideas. Pauline wanted me to turn one of the shoeboxes into a glamorous movie-star apartment with cream carpets and furniture and a grand piano in the corner. She said I should turn my vest into a carpet and upholstery, which seemed possible, but I didn't have a clue how to fashion a piece of cardboard into a piano, complete with movable lid and black and white keys.

Petrova wanted me to construct a garage, with several cars inside. I rolled my eyes at the idea of making cardboard cars but she said I could buy a Dinky car at a toyshop this afternoon. I didn't think I had enough money for a Dinky car and I hadn't seen a toyshop in the village, but I *did* like the idea of miniature cars in a garage. It would help my house look much more real.

Posy thought that these were both silly ideas – I absolutely *had* to make a practice room for ballet with a barre and a mirror, and she wanted to see lots of little girls in their exercise clothes doing pliés. The little girl at the front had to have red hair, like her. A ballet room seemed relatively simple. I could glue a little wooden rod to the cardboard wall – I could make do with a straightish stick if necessary. I didn't have a mirror, but I was sure Mrs Waverley would have one in her handbag. Maybe she would lend it to me. However, I didn't see how I could make lots of little ballet pupils. I was limited to peg dolls, and their legs would be too stiff for dancing.

I told Pauline, Petrova and Posy that it was *my* house and therefore *I* made the decisions. So they wandered off in a huff.

'See if I care,' I muttered, but my fingers had started to ache with all the cutting out and I had cramp in my legs from crouching. I decided to have a rest and read instead. I started the first few pages of *Ballet Shoes* but I knew it so well by now that the words appeared in my head even before my eyes got to them.

I tried *A Little Princess* instead, and was soon absorbed. I wished I looked like Sara Crewe, with her long black hair and beautiful green eyes. I hated my mousy bob and brown eyes. Maybe I could grow my hair here at Meadow Ridge. At home Mum carted me off to her hairdresser's to have an inch snipped off every six weeks.

There was nothing I could do about my boring brown eyes. They even had the wrong expression. 'Stop looking at me all wistful and pleading, like a bally dog,' Mum had said once.

I loved Mum more than anyone in the whole world and I missed her terribly, but I couldn't help thinking it was more peaceful here, without her nagging me all the time. Sara didn't seem to mind not having a mother. She loved her father so. And no wonder. He went to such lengths to buy her Emily, her wonderful doll. The description of Emily and all her amazing outfits was my favourite passage in the whole book.

I read slowly, savouring every detail, and enjoyed the bitter-sweet part where Sara has to say goodbye to her papa. I remembered saying goodbye to *my* dad. It wasn't quite the same. I was used to Dad going away. He travelled all over the south-east of England taking orders for his brushes. He was away the whole week, staying in cheap bed-and-breakfasts, or even working men's hostels if he hadn't made many sales.

He always brought fish and chips back with him, so I looked forward to Friday nights, but neither Mum nor I made a song and dance of seeing Dad himself. We weren't a family for big hugs and kisses. Dad would just pat my head and say, 'How are you, Tuppenny-Ha'penny?' – his silly name for me. I'd say I was 'champion', because I'd heard it on a radio show and it always made Dad laugh.

I suddenly longed to be back home, with Dad coming through the door and patting me and calling me Tuppenny-Ha'penny. Sara's papa never came home again. He hadn't gone away to war, he'd simply gone somewhere abroad and caught a fever. Dad might be fighting already, now that we were actually at war. He might be wounded. I saw him in a hospital bed, groaning softly, a large bandage around his head. He might even be dead.

'Stop it, stop it!' I said, slapping the side of my head. I wished I didn't imagine things so easily.

What if Dad never, ever came back?

I heard shouting downstairs and went to see what was going on. The front door was open and Kevin and Archie were capering excitedly in the drive as a huge truck drew up outside the house.

'It says *Army* on the side. It's soldiers! They're coming here!' Kevin yelled excitedly.

'*Bang, bang, bang!*' said Archie, shooting ferociously with two fingers.

Chubby stood in the doorway, telling them to calm down. 'It's not real army men, you pair of sillies, or navy men, either. It's the name of a department store in London. They'll have brought your camp beds at last. And about time too – they were ordered nearly a week ago,' she said, admonishing the delivery men who climbed out of the truck.

'Keep your hair on, missus. Don't you know there's a war on?' one man said.

'Oh, that's going to be your excuse for bad service from now on, is it?' said Chubby.

'Miss Hoity-Toity!' said the other.

They carried on joshing each other as the men took the beds and various other parcels through the door and up the stairs, Chubby at their heels like a terrier, telling them to watch the paint and look sharp. They were all insulting each other, and yet I could see by the way the men were looking at Chubby that they liked her, and she seemed to like them too. Her face flushed, her eyes sparkled, and there were dimples in her cheeks. She looked much younger and much prettier. I wondered why she had never got married and set herself up in her own house. I remembered the photograph of her dancing with the good-looking young man in white. Perhaps her sweetheart had died in the war.

That brought back all my fears about Dad, but I managed to blot them out in the bustle of unpacking the beds. They were good, sturdy ones made of metal and deep blue canvas, and we had blue down sleeping bags to match, with feather pillows. There were three different sizes: large, medium and small.

'Count yourself lucky we were able to bring you a large one, missus. The manufacturers are working night and day to keep the army supplied,' the men said.

They'd brought a length of pink rubber sheeting too. Chubby fitted it onto the small bed, tactfully waiting until the delivery men had gone.

'Though let's hope you won't need it, Archie,' she said. 'You're going to be a big boy now you've got your own lovely new bed, aren't you? Did you hear what those men said? These are soldiers' beds. You're a soldier now, and soldiers never, ever wet their beds, do they?'

'I *don't* wet the bed,' said Archie. 'And I won't wet this one, promise, promise, promise.'

He was so excited about his camp bed that he climbed into his sleeping bag and lay down, ready to go to sleep.

'Night-night,' he called, and shut his eyes.

'Bless him,' said Chubby. 'Come on, Archie, up you get. You haven't even had your dinner yet. Now, mind you all three say thank you to Mrs Mad. It was very kind of her to buy you three such lovely beds.'

Archie actually threw his arms around Mrs Waverley and gave her a big hug. I thanked her politely, wondering how I might make a miniature camp bed for my doll's house. Kevin said nothing at all until Chubby prompted him. Then he mumbled thank you in an expressionless voice.

He was very quiet all through dinner, and didn't even clear his plate. It was a delicious dinner too. I'd been dreading another rabbit pie, but it was a fish pie instead, with big chunks of cod, and mashed potato instead of pastry.

'I went chasing after the fish van specially yesterday,' said Chubby. 'Simply because some fussy little madam turns her nose up at my lovely r-a-b-b-i-t pie.'

'The fussy little madam is very grateful,' I said. 'This fish pie is scrumptious.'

'*Scrumptious*, is it?' said Chubby. 'Is that one of Mr Mitford's words? Did he make you spell it too? You *are* a brainbox!'

I felt lit up with happiness. Being thought clever was usually an embarrassment. Children mocked me and called me names. Grown-ups weren't much better. Even Mum had an edge to her voice when I showed her my marks at school. 'Well, it comes easy to you, doesn't it?' she'd say. 'Don't go thinking you're better than anyone else. And you might be a little boffin when it comes to English and Arithmetic, but I'd score you nought out of ten when it comes to common sense.'

We had pudding too – creamy rice with a big spoonful of raspberry jam.

'You make lovely meals, Chubby,' I said gratefully, finishing every scrap and wishing I could lick round my bowl.

'Doesn't she just,' said Mrs Waverley. 'I think we all need a nap now we're so full.'

'Yes, yes!' said Archie, desperate to get back in his camp bed.

'But aren't we going to the village? You promised we could!' I said.

'There's plenty of time, silly. Just have a little lie-down till two. Read a book if you like,' said Mrs Waverley.

282

For once in my life I couldn't settle to reading – I was in such a fever to get to the village and find Jessica. After I'd tried out my camp bed and read a page or two of *A Little Princess* I went downstairs and sat in the hall, watching the grandfather clock. I was all set to go and gather the boys when it struck two.

At five to two there was a loud rapping at the front door. I wondered if it might be more delivery men and went to see.

Mum was standing in the doorway.

MUM AND I STARED at each other.

'What's happened to your best skirt, Shirley?' she gasped. Then she shook her head and opened her arms and I flew into them.

'My little girl,' she said, hugging me tight, her chin pressing so hard on my head that it hurt.

I didn't care. I wanted to stay there for ever, breathing in Mum's familiar smell of Coty L'Aimant and washing powder and pear drops. The tight knot inside me unravelled and I started crying into her chest.

'There, there. Mummy's here. It's all right now. I've got you safe. Stop that crying now. You'll get stains on my art-silk blouse.' Mum held me away from her, felt for the hankie up her sleeve and started mopping my face. 'Don't you worry, Shirley. You're not staying here another minute,' she said.

'Am I coming back home then, Mum?'

'Of course not, especially now war's been declared. I'm not having my girl blown to bits or gassed senseless. No, I'm taking you somewhere else. Gerald says he's got family in the Cotswolds and he's sure they'll make room for a well-behaved, quiet little girl,' said Mum.

'Gerald?'

'Mr Pendleton. You know – Pendleton's Metals, though it's Pendleton's Munitions now. He's my boss, but first thing Monday morning he told me that there were to be no formalities in *his* office. He's Gerald and I'm Doris, and we're getting on like a house on fire, I must say,' Mum told me proudly.

My head was spinning. 'But why have I got to go to the Cotswolds?'

'Because you've been so badly treated here!' Mum said. 'I'll just say my piece to these two madwomen. How dare they starve you and lock you up in an empty room! The nerve of it, when they live in a great big house like this! And what's all this about *guns*?'

'They're not mad. Well, Chubby calls Mrs Waverley Mrs Mad, but she's not really. And Chubby's got a gun but it's only for rabbits, which is horrid, but she doesn't make me eat them now,' I gabbled.

'You're not making any sense whatsoever.' Mum took me by the hand and marched me inside.

She paused in the hall, peering at the sparkly crystal chandelier hanging from the ceiling and the grandfather clock and the paintings on the wall. 'It's like a bleeding stately home – and yet they give you bread and milk!' she said.

'No, it was just that first night. How do you *know* all this?'
I asked her.

'You wrote it all on your postcard, you ninny! I practically
dropped down dead with horror when I got it. I was in such a
state Gerald said I could have the day off even though I'd only
just started, but we had this massive order in, so I waited till
the weekend and then I came first thing. The journey! All the
stopping and starting and hanging about in tin-pot little
stations, and I paid a fortune for the ticket too. And then it
was such a business finding this place, and I've worn my heels
down to a frazzle climbing all the way up this bally hill. Talk
about the back of beyond! But I had to come and get my girl,'
Mum proclaimed. 'So where are these women, eh, Shirley? I'm
going to give them such a mouthful!'

'Oh, Mum, you mustn't! You've got it all wrong. They're
quite nice, really. Mrs Waverley even bought me new clothes,'
I said.

'How dare she! You're not *her* little girl. And you've got
lovely clothes – though that skirt's ruined now. I'll never be
able to iron the pleats back. And what in God's name are those
shoes you're wearing?' Mum peered at them as if they were a
pair of cowpats.

'I know, they're horrible, but actually my red shoes are a
bit small for me,' I said.

'Rubbish! They fitted perfectly and made your feet look
dainty. Now look at you. They've already turned you into a
country yokel!'

'What's a country yokel?' a voice piped up. It was Archie,
peering through the banisters on the landing.

'Who's that? Is it one of the rough boys?' Mum said, not lowering her voice. 'You come down here, you big bully. I'll teach you to say nasty things to my daughter!'

Archie wriggled his head free and obediently came down the stairs, sucking his thumb. He looked smaller and scrappier than ever walking down the big staircase, the new fluff on his head like a baby's.

Mum stared at him. '*He's* the bully?' she said incredulously.

'No, of course not.'

'So where's the other one?'

'I don't know. And he's not a bully, either, I never said that. He's my friend,' I said.

Then Kevin appeared at the top of the stairs. He looked quite grown up in his new long trousers. The sunlight through the landing window made his strange ears look alarmingly red. He was grinning.

'Yeah, I'm Shirley's boyfriend,' he said, swaggering down the stairs like a movie star, though he tripped over his own feet and nearly went flying.

'What? You're much too old to be my Shirley's boyfriend!' said Mum.

'He's not my boyfriend, Mum, he's just mucking about,' I said. 'And he's ten like me, truly. He's in my class.'

'A likely story,' she said, glaring at Kevin. She even included Archie in the glare. 'I'm not having you living with these boys, it's not suitable. Now where are these wretched women?'

'I'm here,' said Chubby, coming along the passageway from the kitchen. She'd taken off her sloppy slippers but her gumboots weren't really a suitable alternative. She'd kept her turban and her pinny on. She stood in front of Mum, arms folded.

'How do you do, Mrs Smith,' she said, though she didn't try to shake hands. 'I'm Miss Chubb, Mrs Waverley's housekeeper. We've been looking after your daughter.'

'Well, it depends on your definition of looking after,' said Mum. 'My Shirley here says she's been half starved and has to sleep on the floor.'

Chubby looked at me.

I hung my head guiltily. 'I didn't say that. Well, I might have put something silly in my postcard, but that was just because I didn't like it here at first. But now I do. I don't want to go to this Cotswolds place, Mum. I want to stay here,' I said.

Mum flinched.

'I mean, I'd much, much sooner come home with you, of course I would, but if you won't let me, then please let me stay in this house.'

'You're not staying here, not when they won't even give you a bed to sleep in,' said Mum. She looked at Chubby. 'Shame on you and this other woman, making little children sleep on the floor!'

Chubby got angry then. 'You can get the wrong end of the stick and treat me like dirt and I don't give a monkey's – but don't you go bad-mouthing Mrs Waverley. She ordered beds from the Army and Navy Stores for the children on Monday. They only arrived today, but that's not our fault. And she's kitted out all three kiddies with suitable clothing. We didn't ask for any evacuees, and we've ended up with one more than our quota, but we've just got on with it.'

'Don't you tell me Shirley hasn't got suitable clothing,' Mum blustered. 'I sent my daughter off into the wilds with clothing the little princesses would be proud of. Her red patent shoes cost sixteen and eleven, I'll have you know – more than you or I would pay for footwear.' She cast a scornful glance at Chubby's boots. 'And her skirt and bodice came from Derry and Toms children's department. It's practically brand-new, and yet now look at it – ruined! Why on earth did you wash it, you stupid bally woman?'

Mum had got carried away. I shrivelled on the spot. Kevin gawped. Archie snuffled and suddenly darted up to Chubby and butted his head into her tummy.

'You're not stupid!' he mumbled.

She patted his downy head. 'That's right, little chum.' She looked straight at Mum, her blue eyes very beady. 'Folk have called me a lot of names in my time and I daresay some of them have been deserved. But I'm not stupid. Far from it. And it's not nice to swear in front of the children, either,' she retorted.

We'd heard Chubby say far worse words than *bally*, especially when she scorched one of the sheets that constantly needed washing and ironing because of Archie's night-time troubles. But she made Mum go pink.

Mum seized my hand. 'Come on, Shirley. You're not stopping here a moment longer. Show me where your things are and we'll get you packed up this instant!' she said.

'But, Mum—'

'Don't you *but* me. Come *on*!'

So I had to take her upstairs and along the corridor to my bedroom. Mum saw the new bed and sleeping bag and fluffy pillow and seemed almost disappointed. But she looked around the rest of the room and sniffed.

'Imagine, putting a nicely brought-up little girl in a completely empty room. Where's the rest of the furniture then? I daresay this Mrs Whatsit is down on her luck and had to sell it off, for all she's throwing her weight around and treating you like a charity case. The sooner you're out of here the better.'

Mum sank to her knees and started packing up my things, practically throwing my books into Dad's sample case. She came across my blouse and tunic and shuddered. 'We'll leave them behind. Talk about hideous! The woman wants her brains tested, wasting her money on frightful stuff like that. Shirley Temple herself would look frightful in that get-up.'

'Lots of the children at my new school wear tunics,' I felt obliged to say.

'Country yokels. They don't know any better,' said Mum, cramming book after book into my suitcase. '*Why* did you bring all these books? And what's all this cardboard rubbish?'

I felt as if she'd kicked me. 'It's not rubbish,' I said, desperately hurt. 'It's my doll's house. Look, Mum, I've made all the kitchen stuff out of silver paper – it took ages, see?'

'Oh, for goodness' sake, Shirley, aren't you too old to play with bits of paper?' said Mum, slamming the case shut and straining to snap the locks.

'But what shall I put it in?'

'You're not putting it in anything. It would get all squashed anyway. Leave it here, for goodness' sake. And don't give me that look. You can make another one when you get to the

Cotswolds. Gerald – I suppose you'd better call him Uncle Gerald – is going to drive us there – isn't it kind of him?'

'He's not my uncle and I don't want to go to the Cotswolds, whatever they are!' I shouted in despair.

'Goodness, what's all this noise?' Mrs Waverley stood in the doorway.

She must have heard the rumpus, because she'd had time to pin up her hair and put on some lipstick. She looked very smart in her suit and her suede sandals, which made her seem stately. I realized she was several inches taller than Mum, and effortlessly grander.

Mum valiantly tried not to look overawed. 'I'm taking my daughter to a more suitable billet,' she said. I think she'd only seen the word written down, because she pronounced it affectedly, like ballet with an *i*.

'I'm sorry to hear that,' said Mrs Waverley. 'I've become rather fond of your daughter.'

'Yes, well, she's *my* daughter, not yours,' said Mum. '*I'm* the one who says what's what where she's concerned.'

'Of course you are,' said Mrs Waverley. 'I'm Madeleine, by the way.' She held out her hand, and Mum had no option but to shake it.

'I'm Mrs Smith – Doris,' said Mum. She blushed a little, because she hated her name. She'd tried calling herself Doretta once but people laughed at her.

'Now, I understand you have other plans for Shirley, but do you have to chase off immediately? There's not another train until five o'clock – the service isn't very good out here in the sticks. Why don't we all have a cup of tea and you

292

can recuperate after your long journey. Then, later on, I'll run you to the station in my car,' Mrs Waverley said smoothly.

Mum fidgeted, not wanting to give an inch, but was forced to be reasonable and accept the offer. She insisted on dragging my suitcase with us though. I craned round, looking at my cardboard creation.

Mrs Waverley looked too. 'Oh, Shirley, a doll's house! Did you make it all by yourself? It's lovely! And you've made little furniture! My goodness, even tiny knives and forks. Isn't she clever, Doris?'

'She's always messing about making funny stuff – when she hasn't got her head stuck in a book,' said Mum.

'That's why I was persuaded to take her on. I didn't think my home at all suitable for children, especially as I suffer from a nervous condition, but Shirley's personal library quite won me over,' said Mrs Waverley, leading the way down the stairs.

'Nervous condition?' Mum repeated. She sniffed, regaining ground. 'You mean mental problems?'

'Mum!' I said, agonized.

'I've just been a little melancholy since I was widowed,' said Mrs Waverley. She spoke lightly and calmly, but even Mum in her present mood didn't pursue the subject. Instead she nodded curtly and muttered that she was sorry.

We headed for Mrs Waverley's lovely sitting room. Chubby was hovering, arms akimbo.

'I daresay you've met Miss Chubb, my housekeeper and companion?' said Mrs Waverley. 'Chubby dear, do you think you could rustle up a pot of tea for Mrs Smith and me, and maybe some lemon barley water for the children?'

Chubby let out a long hissing sigh, but stomped off kitchenwards. Mrs Waverley insisted Mum take the best armchair. I sat on the sofa with Kevin and Archie. They were gawping at Mrs Waverley and Mum as if they were at the pictures. Mum was mostly silent now, but Mrs Waverley kept up her side of the conversation, talking about the village and the school.

'Apparently Shirley's doing really well. Top of the class,' she said.

'Really?' said Mum.

'Yeah, she's a clever dick,' said Kevin, giving me a friendly nudge.

'Are you in Shirley's class?' Mum asked faintly.

'We sit next to each other. On the blooming floor. They ain't got no desks for us,' said Kevin.

'I believe they're trying to remedy the problem,' said Mrs Waverley. 'It can't be easy for anyone, teachers or pupils. But I suppose we've all got to put up with a few inconveniences nowadays.'

'I don't sit on the floor, I mostly get to sit on *my* teacher's lap,' said Archie. 'She picks me up whenever I grizzle.'

'Do you cry a lot at school, Archie?' asked Chubby, returning with a loaded tray of drinks and a plate of custard creams arranged in a pattern. 'Who's picking on you, pet? You tell me and I'll have a word with them.'

'No one's picking on me. I just get bored and fancy a cuddle 'cos Miss Appleby's so lovely. *Much* better than Auntie,' said Archie.

'Oh, so she's your favourite now, is she?' said Chubby huffily, handing cups round rather carelessly so that tea spilled into saucers.

Archie wasn't daft. He gave Chubby the most beautiful smile. 'No, *you're* my favourite,' he said.

Chubby rewarded him with two custard creams, one for each hand. She only let Kevin and me have one.

'That's not fair!' Kevin protested.

'Archie's a growing boy, he needs a bit of extra grub. *You* don't need any. If you grow any more you'll be bumping your head on the ceiling,' said Chubby as she went out.

'That's another thing,' said Mum. 'My Shirley said in her postcard that she wasn't getting enough to eat, only bread and milk.'

I squirmed. 'That was only the first night, Mum,' I said quickly. 'We have lovely food. Chubby made us fish pie today and it was smashing. Even better than your steak and kidney.'

I meant that I liked fish and potatoes better than meat and pastry, but the moment I'd said it I realized that Mum would take it the wrong way.

'I'm sorry, I didn't mean—' I blurted.

'It's clear what you meant, young lady. But don't worry, I'm pretty certain they serve such things as fish pie in the Cotswolds,' said Mum sarkily.

Mrs Waverley laughed gently, as if Mum had made a joke. 'Of course, you know best where your daughter is concerned. And if you think she'd be happier elsewhere—'

'No I won't! I want to stay here!' I said.

For a moment Mum looked as if she might burst into tears.

'I think it's simply because Shirley desperately wants to be with her best friend,' Mrs Waverley said quickly.

'She hasn't got any best friends, not at Paradise Road,' said Mum in a choked voice. 'Not unless she means—' She looked at poor Kevin in horror.

'She means her friend Jessica,' said Mrs Waverley.

Jessica! Oh no, Mum arriving out of the blue had made me forget entirely. I was supposed to be meeting Jessica down in the village *now*.

'She hasn't got a friend called Jessica. She's been telling stories. She does that a lot,' said Mum.

'But I've met Jessica. She goes to St Agatha's Convent, and by a remarkable coincidence their school has been evacuated here too,' said Mrs Waverley. 'It was very touching seeing the girls meeting up in the village.'

'A convent girl?' said Mum.

'Yes, she's ever so posh, but lovely, and guess what, Mum, *her* mother is Imogen Starlight, truly! We're such friends. We've both read all the same books, and *Ballet Shoes* is her favourite too. If we go down to the village you can meet her. Oh please, she'll be waiting for me now,' I said eagerly.

'Imogen Starlight! Well, you're a little mug if you believe that! Imogen Starlight hasn't got any children. She's only in her twenties. As if she'd have a schoolgirl daughter! You're so gullible, Shirley. And how come you've never mentioned this Jessica before?' Mum demanded.

'Well, I met her on the train.'

'On the train coming here? That was only a week ago, you silly girl! How can you be bosom friends with some girl you met on a train?'

Kevin and Archie nudged each other because Mum had said the word *bosom*. She glared at them.

So did Mrs Waverley. 'Why don't you two boys go and play?' she suggested.

'I thought we was going down to the village,' said Kevin.

'We want to buy sweets!' Archie chirruped.

'I'm not sure I trust you two to go alone,' said Mrs Waverley.

'But I'm going too!' I said.

Mum stared at me.

'I mean, with you too, Mum. Then you can meet Jessica and see how lovely she is and she'll tell you all about her mother,' I said. 'Oh please, Mum. I promised I'd meet her and she'll think I can't be bothered if I don't turn up,' I said desperately.

'Shirley, I've come all this way on a nightmare journey, using up nearly all my housekeeping money on the train ticket, because I've been frantic ever since I got your postcard, and I've walked so far already I've worn down both my heels and I've got a blister on each foot, and yet you expect me to go trailing back to the village because you want to meet some silly girl.' Mum's voice got higher and higher, and suddenly tears were streaming down her face.

I stared at her, horrified. I hovered near her. 'Don't cry, Mum!' I tried to put my arm round her, but she shrugged it away violently.

Mrs Waverley patted me reassuringly, and gestured to the two boys. 'Don't sit there gawping. Run off and find Chubby.

If you want some sweets, perhaps she'll let you make toffee,' she said.

They ran off, whooping. I wished I could run away and make toffee too, but I had to sit there fidgeting while Mum went on weeping. I felt horribly guilty – I'd upset her so much. It had all gone wrong so quickly. I knew I should just be thinking of Mum, but I was getting more and more agitated about Jessica. She'd be waiting down in the village, going up and down the street, looking for me everywhere.

She'd think I simply couldn't be bothered to meet her. She'd be fed up with me and wouldn't want to be my friend any more. Maybe she'd even chum up with one of those awful convent girls, Goofy or Munchkin, and not give me a second thought.

I'd never, ever make another friend like Jessica. I didn't care if I'd only known her a week. It was as if I'd known her all my life. I didn't feel shy with her or worried that she'd tease me or think me peculiar. We seemed to be soulmates.

My throat went tight and I felt my eyes prickle. I started crying too.

'Oh dear,' said Mrs Waverley.

Mum scrabbled in her handbag, looking for her hankie. She dabbed at my face, she dabbed at her own. Her mascara had run and her lipstick was smudged. I was embarrassed to see how awful she looked. I'd always thought she looked pretty – I was sure she was much more stylish than anyone else's mum – after all, she took such care to be neat and tidy and keep up with the latest fashions – but somehow she looked sad compared with Mrs Waverley.

'I'm sorry,' Mum mumbled. 'I'm making an awful exhibition of myself. I don't know what's got into me.'

'Please, you mustn't worry about it. I'm the one who's often in tears. Dear God, I've been the laughing stock of the whole village. Here, I know what will help.' Mrs Waverley went to the sideboard and brought out a decanter and two glasses.

'I'm not really a drinker,' Mum protested.

'But a sip or two of brandy is purely medicinal,' said Mrs Waverley. 'Shirley, why don't you join the boys while your mother and I have a little talk?'

I was happy enough to get away. As I passed the front door I had a mad urge to charge down to the village, but I knew that would be unforgivable. Instead I went to the kitchen, and after a few minutes managed to get totally involved in toffee making, which proved glorious fun.

'Are you really going off with your mum, Shirl?' Kevin asked.

'I don't know,' I said.

'Don't go.'

'I'll have to if Mum says. You know what mums are like.'

Kevin shrugged. '*My* stepmum don't tell me what to do,' he said.

'I haven't even got a mum,' said Archie. 'I've just had aunties. And now I've got Chubby, haven't I?' He grinned up at her, golden syrup all round his mouth.

She smiled back fondly, wiping his face with a corner of tea towel. 'Yes, you've got me, sticky little mite,' she said.

When Mrs Waverley eventually called me back into the sitting room, Mum had stopped crying, and had put on fresh make-up too.

'Don't look so worried, dear,' she said to me.

I hung back a little shyly.

'Come here, poppet!'

I did as I was told. Mum pulled me right onto her lap, though I was really much too big now.

'There's my girl,' she said, rubbing her cheek against mine. I could feel myself getting all powdery. 'My little Shirley.'

I liked her babying me, but it was very embarrassing in front of Mrs Waverley.

'All better now?' Mum asked, as if *I'd* been the one doing all the crying.

I nodded anyway.

'Mrs Waverley and I have had a long talk. I can see you put a lot of silly things in that old postcard. You seem to have settled in well here. So for the moment I think you'd better stay where you are, if Mrs Waverley's kind enough to keep you,' said Mum.

Mrs Waverley nodded graciously.

'Say thank you then, Shirley,' said Mum.

I did so, awkwardly.

'Well, I'd better see what the boys are up to. I expect the kitchen is in chaos,' said Mrs Waverley. 'Please relax here in the sitting room. And later on I'll run you to the station, Doris.'

'That's very kind, Madeleine,' said Mum.

Then she was gone, and Mum and I were left clasped together.

Mum let out a long sigh. 'Well,' she said. 'What a kerfuffle!'

'Yes,' I said.

'You shouldn't have written all those things in that postcard. That's what got me all worked up.'

I hung my head.

'Still, I can see you're sorry now – because this is quite a nice house,' Mum said, looking around.

It was fifty times grander and fifty times bigger than our flat, but of course we both knew that.

'Mrs Waverley seems a nice enough lady. I suppose she couldn't help having a nervous breakdown,' said Mum.

'Did she talk about it to you?'

'Not really. Just said she went to pieces after her husband died in the last war. They'd only just got married. Tragic. Still, it happened to many thousands of others too,' said Mum.

'Dad's not going to die, is he?'

'No, no, of course not,' Mum said quickly. 'He wrote to say he's hoping to get some leave before they send him off abroad.'

'I do miss him, Mum.'

'Of course you do. So do I,' she said.

'And I miss you too. Awfully,' I told her.

'My girl,' said Mum, rocking me. But after a minute she gently pushed me off her lap. 'You're getting a bit of a lump now. I've got pins and needles in my legs!'

'Perhaps you need to walk a bit.' I swallowed. 'We could go down to the village. There's some good shops.'

'Oh, for pity's sake, Shirley! I know you just want to go and see this Jessica.'

'She'll have gone back to Lady Amersham's by now,' I said mournfully, though there was just a chance she might still be waiting for me. 'Shall we go and see?'

'No! I didn't come all the way here so you could rush off with some little girl you barely know,' said Mum. 'Now stop it.'

I stopped. I sat on the rug in front of her. She asked me more about school. I asked her about her new job, and that gave her a chance to go on and on about this Gerald chap. He sounded a bit of a creep to me, though it was clear that Mum thought he was the bee's knees.

'Imagine, offering to place you with his relatives! He's been such a pal to me – much more friendly than you'd ever expect from a boss,' Mum said proudly.

'How come he can be your friend after just a week working for him, when you say I can't possibly be proper friends with Jessica?' I asked.

'I've known him much longer than a week, silly. We met when he interviewed me. And, if you must know, I passed the time of day with him before. We met in a tea shop. It was crowded so we had to share a table. He was very gentlemanly – he insisted on paying for my tea, and my Bath bun,' said Mum.

She picked up her cup of tea now, but it had gone stone cold.

'I could ask Chubby to make another pot,' I offered.

'No thanks. Now, she's a rum one, isn't she? Very lippy. I don't know why Mrs Waverley doesn't get herself a proper servant,' said Mum. 'And does she always wear gumboots in the house?'

'She's all right,' I said, not liking Mum criticizing her.

I looked at the gold clock on Mrs Waverley's mantelpiece. We had another hour and a half to go. There didn't seem anything to do except talk, and after a while we ran out of topics of conversation.

'I could show you around the grounds if you like,' I suggested. 'There's a lake.'

'It all looks a bit of a wilderness, if you ask me,' said Mum. 'No thanks.'

In the end we were reduced to playing Snap with Mrs Waverley's playing cards. I couldn't help glancing at the clock several times – the game seemed to be lasting for ever.

'Don't say you've got bored of me being here already!' said Mum sharply.

'Oh, Mum. I want you to stay for ever,' I said, fibbing to save her feelings. Inside I was longing for her to go – she made me feel so uncomfortable.

Yet when she eventually left I clung to her like a baby and wept.

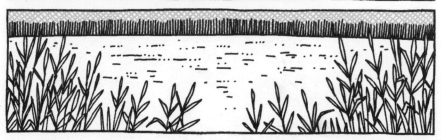

THAT NIGHT I COULDN'T sleep properly, even though my new camp bed was so comfortable, with the pillow cushioning my head. I wriggled round and round in my sleeping bag. When I heard the grandfather clock downstairs chiming twelve, I started telling myself the story of *Cinderella*, and then I tried to turn it into a ballet. Pauline played Cinderella. She wasn't the best dancer but she looked the part with her long blonde hair. Posy played a tiny Fairy Godmother and did a very complicated series of pirouettes before waving her magic wand. Petrova and I were the Ugly Sisters and worked out a comical routine.

But after a while it was too much effort to keep pretending. Worries about Jessica and Mum and Dad kept stopping the dancing. I curled into a tight ball, trying to ignore the twitch of my bladder. I knew I needed to go to the double-you-see but

I was afraid of going along the pitch-dark corridor. I started to wish Chubby had put a chamber pot in my room as well as Archie's.

Eventually it got so painful that I had to struggle out of my sleeping bag and feel my way out of my room and down the corridor. I got to the right room at last and opened the door – and then bumped straight into something big and cold and bony, just like a skeleton.

I screamed. It screamed too.

'*Kevin?*'

'Shut up! You'll wake everyone!' he hissed.

It was too late. Suddenly, outside, the light went on. Kevin and I blinked at each other. He was sitting on the toilet with his sleeping bag draped around him as if he were camping there. He was shivering, his face very pale, his eyes all peepy with tiredness.

'What on earth are you two playing at?' Chubby stood looking at us, arms folded, shaking her head. She wore an old coat as a dressing gown and her bare feet looked very pale and flat, like a pair of plaice.

'I needed to go to the toilet. I still do!' I said, hopping from one foot to the other in agony.

'Out you come then, Kevin,' said Chubby, grabbing hold of him and hauling him out into the corridor.

I charged in and slammed the door and then weed for a long time. I could hear Chubby scolding Kevin. When I came out at last he was hanging his head, his sleeping bag trailing on the floor, looking thinner and ganglier than ever in his old underpants.

'What were you playing at?' Chubby demanded. 'Were you hiding in there on purpose to give everyone a fright?'

'No, of course not. I needed the toilet. It's not a crime, is it?' Kevin said truculently.

'Well, there was no need to drag your brand-new sleeping bag in there too,' said Chubby. 'Now get back to bed, both of you.'

'I haven't been yet,' said Kevin. 'Chance would be a fine thing!'

'Well, go then, while I wiggle little Archie out of his bed and get him to tinkle into that pot. He's got a rubber sheet just in case, though he's got to get himself trained. He might look like a baby but he's a little lad, after all,' said Chubby.

I helped her ease Archie out of bed and hold him over the pot. He was still half asleep, all warm and limp.

'Come on, little soldier, do a wee for Chubby,' she said, rubbing her cheek against the top of his head. 'Bless him, Shirley, he's going to look like a baby duckling soon with all this fluff.'

Once he'd performed we tucked him into bed again. Chubby sent me back to bed too. I heard her berating Kevin, who was still in the double-you-see. He grumbled back at her through the door but had to come out eventually. I was pretty sure she wouldn't tuck *him* up tenderly.

I drifted off to sleep, feeling sorry for Kevin. I felt even sorrier in the morning. I woke to hear Chubby yelling at him again. She sounded really furious this time. I went and stood in the boys' bedroom doorway, gaping. Kevin's sleeping bag lay unzipped and spread out. It was sodden.

'It was *you* peeing the bed all the time!' she shouted, smacking Kevin about the head.

'I *said* it wasn't me,' said Archie.

'A great lummox of a lad like you!' Chubby was laying into Kevin again.

'I couldn't help it!' he cried, trying to dodge the blows. 'I tried to stay up so I wouldn't do it. You should have left me in the toilet. It's your fault, not mine. I can't help it!'

'Of course you can help it. You're just too bone idle to get yourself up when you need to go,' Chubby insisted. 'And I'm the poor soul who has to cope with all the washing. But it's not even that. It's the fact that you let poor little Archie take the blame!'

'I didn't say it was him,' Kevin said. 'You just guessed. I can't help it if you was wrong. It's not my *fault*!'

'It isn't his fault, Chubby,' I said, feeling sorry for him.

'You keep your nose out of it, miss,' she said.

Kevin went painfully red. He hadn't seen me peering in. 'Yes, clear off!' he said ungratefully.

So I did. I really *did* feel sorry for Kevin. It seemed awful that he should still do such a babyish thing as wetting the bed. He was so ashamed, he wouldn't even look at me at breakfast.

Archie was in his element though. Chubby made a great fuss of him because she'd given him so many tickings-off for the wet bed. 'My poor lamb,' she kept saying.

Archie put his head on one side and went 'Baaa'. It wasn't particularly amusing, especially when he kept on and on doing it, but Chubby roared with laughter and chucked him under the chin.

'You're a little card, Archie,' she said. 'You'll end up on the stage, you mark my words.'

'I might be on the stage one day,' I said.

Chubby looked at me. 'You're a bit plain for it, aren't you?' she said bluntly. 'Aren't actresses supposed to have blonde wavy hair and curvy figures?'

'I might get a curvy figure when I'm older. And I could dye my hair and have a perm, if I wanted. Only I don't actually want to be an actress, I want to be a ballet dancer,' I said loftily, trying not to show her she'd hurt my feelings. 'Dancers don't have to be pretty, just so long as they're graceful.'

'Graceful, eh? I wouldn't say you're that, either,' said Chubby.

I hadn't finished my breakfast but I went off in a huff. Kevin sloped off too. We met on the landing. He took hold of my wrist.

'Listen,' he said urgently. 'If you say anything about me doing you-know-what at school I'll flipping well kill you.'

'I won't say a word. Stop it – you're hurting me!'

'You promise?'

'*Yes*. Now shove off,' I said.

He slouched off, his hands in his pockets, trying to whistle as if he didn't have a care in the world. He wasn't very convincing.

I holed up in my bedroom and found all the dance illustrations in my copy of *Ballet Shoes*. I did my best to copy them. Then I tried inventing the *Cinderella* dance, taking all the parts. It was exhausting but exhilarating. '*Ex-haust-ing, ex-hil-erat-ing, Shir-ley's full of grace,*' I sang to that 'Immortal, Invisible' hymn tune as I pirouetted around the room.

I'd show Chubby. I didn't like her any more. I hated the way she shouted at Kevin and hit him. She was so unfair. I worried about her telling tales to Mrs Waverley. She was sleeping late, but eventually I heard her tapping her way down the stairs. I swept a deep curtsy to my imaginary audience, caught many invisible bouquets of flowers and then went down to the kitchen. Chubby had made Mrs Waverley a cup of tea and some toast. They were deep in a discussion about Kevin. Archie was standing on a stool playing with soap bubbles in the sink. He was chewing noisily on last night's toffee.

'. . . soaked through! And how am I going to get the damn thing dry by tonight? Even if the sun's out, this is Sussex, not the bally Sahara!' Chubby complained. 'And he hasn't even said sorry, the lazy great lump.'

'He didn't say sorry because he's too embarrassed,' I said. 'He didn't do it on purpose. He can't help it – can't you see that?'

'I'll thank you to hold your tongue, missy, and stop being so impertinent,' said Chubby, but she gave me two squares of toffee. I wanted to refuse them out of principle, but I couldn't resist popping them in my mouth.

'Shirley's right, I suppose,' said Mrs Waverley. 'Bedwetting is an illness. Enuresis. I suppose I'd better take young Kevin to the doctor's.'

'He won't go. He'd absolutely hate talking about it to anyone,' I said indistinctly, my teeth glued together with toffee.

'Well, we can't just ignore the problem,' Chubby snapped. 'My hands are getting rubbed raw with all this extra washing.

I don't know what we're going to do with the boy. He's a bag of nerves, forever blundering into things and biting his nails. He'd be far happier somewhere else. We've heard about this hostel for boys – I'm sure he'd love it.'

'No! Stop it! You don't really think that. You just want to get rid of him! You never wanted him in the first place,' I said furiously.

'Hold your tongue!' said Chubby, giving me a little shake. 'Of course we didn't. You were thrust on us, all three of you. One more kiddie than everyone else in the village. We've more than done our duty. *You've* settled down in spite of your faddy ways. Only yesterday you were begging your mum to stay here. And little Archie's no bother, bless him.'

Archie turned round at the mention of his name. He smiled at her and blew her a soap bubble. Chubby blew him a kiss back.

'But as for Kevin,' she continued, 'well, he doesn't fit, does he? He needs to go to this hostel place. It'll probably be the making of him.'

'Oh, Chubby,' said Mrs Waverley, looking at her directly. 'Do any of us fit?'

Chubby's face went as red as her sore hands. 'Off you go now, Shirley, and stop cluttering up my kitchen,' she said quickly.

'Yes, run along, Shirley,' said Mrs Waverley.

I didn't run, I dawdled, not knowing where to go. I considered creeping upstairs to get the key to the locked room. I longed to see that doll's house again, but knew it was too risky.

I went back to my room, though it suddenly seemed very empty, in spite of the camp bed and my neat pile of books and Dad's case. Pauline, Petrova and Posy had gone. Perhaps they hadn't liked my impromptu ballet. Maybe they'd simply faded away because I couldn't imagine them well enough. This happened all the time now. It was probably because I was getting older. It frightened me. I didn't know how to cope without imaginary friends, not when I didn't have any real ones.

I had Jessica of course – if she was still my friend now. And what about Kevin? He wanted us to be pals, but that wasn't really the same as proper *friends*.

Even so I looked for him, but he wasn't in his room. His bed was stripped back, his sleeping bag removed – in a public demonstration of his shame Archie's rubber sheeting was now folded at the bottom.

Archie himself didn't want to play. He was too happy being spoiled by Chubby, even when I suggested a paddling trip to the 'seaside'.

'Don't you dare suggest that, you silly girl!' Chubby protested. 'He half drowned himself before! Don't listen to her, little man. You stay away from that nasty water or Chubby will have your guts for garters.'

Archie chuckled at the expression and cosied up to her. 'Me stay with my Chubby,' he lisped in a sickening baby voice.

So I wandered off into the garden myself. I circled the henhouse and ragged vegetable patch. There were a couple of rabbits busily nibbling cabbages and I tried squatting beside them, asking them if they'd like to be my special pets. I promised them a cabbage each whenever they fancied, plus carrots, lettuce, and whatever else was a rabbit delicacy, but they whisked away hurriedly, showing me their white tails.

I wandered round to the front of the house and wondered about picking a bunch of late roses, but they were much too prickly. I went looking for the lake myself, which took quite a while because it was so easy to get lost – one clump of trees looked much like another.

I tried calling for Kevin, hoping he might be somewhere near, but no one answered. My voice sounded strange in the silence, and I pressed my lips together.

When at last I found the lake, I felt obliged to take off my shoes and socks and have a paddle. I even thought of going in for a proper dip – it was very warm and sunny – but the thought of swimming all by myself was a bit unnerving. I knew how to swim – I'd learned at the public baths near my old house, and had once managed a whole length breaststroke, though I was gasping by the time I got to the end. I wasn't sure how deep the lake was. Perhaps I'd panic halfway across, try to put my foot down and find I was way out of my depth. Besides, I didn't have a towel, and I didn't want to go back to the house dripping wet.

Instead I walked all the way around the lake, trying to appreciate the scenery, squinting up at the birds. I hoped I'd see a kingfisher again but all the birds were a dull uniform brown. I was getting very bored and decided I'd be better off reading.

I found my way back to the path and saw someone trudging along towards the house. Someone my own size, wearing purple uniform. A dark plait hung all the way down her back.

'Jessica!' I cried joyfully.

'*There* you are!' she said. 'I was just this minute willing you to appear and you have!' She rushed up and threw her arms round me. 'Where were you yesterday? I rushed down early and was outside that wretched sweetshop from half past two till half past three, when hateful Sister Josephine made us go back to the White House. What happened? You didn't forget, did you?'

'No, of course not! I wanted and wanted to come, but I couldn't because my mum came here,' I explained.

'Your mother!' Jessica seemed taken aback. 'Oh, Shirley, is she still here? Is she going to take you home again? Did she come because she was missing you? Oh, you lucky, lucky thing. How wonderful! I'm so happy for you!' She didn't look happy at all. Her face was very white and pinched and she was frowning.

'I think she just came because I wrote this postcard, see, saying I hated it here, and I didn't have a bed or any proper food – which was sort of true then, but actually now I've got a camp bed and Chubby gives us nice food, and she doesn't make rabbit pie any more and—'

'So what did your mother say? Was she very angry with you?' Jessica gripped my arm.

'Yes, a bit. Well, a lot,' I admitted. 'She shouted at Chubby too. It was ever so embarrassing.'

'You must tell me all about it in every detail,' said Jessica.

We were walking towards the house, but she veered away. 'We don't need to go in now I've found you. I don't want Mrs

314

Waverley phoning Lady Amersham or one of the nuns to tell tales on me.'

'So they don't know you're here?'

Jessica rolled her eyes. 'Of course not. I was at the back of the crocodile going to church and I just hung back and suddenly made a bolt for it in the other direction.'

'But won't you get into most the tremendous trouble?'

'Oh, I don't doubt it, but I'll make up some story. Who cares anyway? I simply *had* to see you.'

'Well, I was desperate to see you yesterday, and I kept begging Mum to come to the village with me, but she absolutely wouldn't. She just wanted it to be her and me together – you know what mums are like,' I said, sighing.

Jessica didn't look as if she knew at all. 'Tell me!' she said.

So we wandered arm in arm through the woods, and I told her everything, making it very dramatic, just to be entertaining. I had Mum banging on the door and screaming her head off and actually slapping Chubby.

Jessica listened attentively, frowning. 'She must care about you immensely,' she said. 'Imagine, missing you so much!'

Perhaps I wasn't being tactful. Jessica had made it plain that her mother wasn't bothered about her, though I hadn't quite believed that.

'She was just fussing, that's all. She always does. And she can't really be missing me – she won't let me come home with her. She wants me to go to the Cotswolds, wherever they are. There are some relatives there. Not *my* relatives. They belong to this Uncle Gerald, only he's not a real uncle. He's this man my mum knows,' I said in a rush.

Jessica's eyes opened wide. She gave an odd little smile. 'Oh, I *see*!' she said. 'So this Gerald's your mum's boyfriend?'

'What? No, of course not!' I was shocked. 'My mum's married to my dad!'

'As if that makes any difference,' said Jessica.

'Yes it does! Ladies don't have boyfriends, not if they're already married,' I insisted.

'Of course they do. My mother has boyfriends all the time, whether she's currently married or not,' Jessica said airily. 'You're such a baby, Shirley.'

'No I'm not. Your mum might be like that because she's an actress, but my mum's just an ordinary secretary and this Gerald is her new boss,' I said.

'Well, that's the most classic situation of all,' Jessica said.

'No it's not! Look, my mum would never do that. She loves my dad,' I said, but even as the words came out of my mouth I was starting to wonder. I was sure Mum *did* love Dad, but she was always nagging at him and wishing he would make something of himself. She was very bitter when we had to move to a cheaper flat. She'd cried when Dad went away to join the army, but she didn't seem to miss him the way I did.

'Perhaps she loves this Gerald now,' Jessica said relentlessly.

I tried to picture him. Perhaps he was big and powerful, the sort of man who wore a camel-hair coat and smoked cigars, the kind Mum would call 'a real gentleman'. I imagined her looking up at him admiringly, hanging on his arm, all girly and soppy. My stomach turned over.

'You shut up!' I said, and untangled my arm from Jessica's. I ran a few steps away from her but she chased after me.

'Oh, Shirley, I'm sorry. Don't go off in a huff! I didn't mean to upset you. I'll shut up about this Gerald now, I promise,' she cried.

Of course I made it up with her, and we wandered on till we got to the lake. Then we walked round and round it, arms linked again. We talked a bit more about Mum's possible boyfriend, calling him This Gerald, Jessica deftly turning him into a cad who had deliberately seduced my mother. She even gave him a moustache to twirl.

It wasn't so upsetting now she'd turned the situation into a joke. We acted it all out. I was Mum, all fluttery and squealing, and Jessica was This Gerald, pursuing me ardently, holding the end of her plait under her nose as a moustache.

When we got bored of that game we talked about *Ballet Shoes*. We wanted to act this out too.

'Who do you want to be? I think I'd like to be Pauline, even though she's blonde and I'm not, but I don't mind being Petrova because she's interesting and dark like me. I can't be Posy though because I can't dance for toffee,' said Jessica.

'I'll be Posy if you like. I can do ballet a bit,' I said modestly.

But it got rather confusing with Jessica swapping between Pauline and Petrova, so we acted out *A Little Princess* instead. Jessica was Sara. I made the best of being Becky, the little servant girl. I didn't exactly mind, but it felt strange. In all my solitary *Little Princess* games I'd always been Sara. For all Jessica fancied herself as an actress, I didn't feel she was doing it properly. She was too theatrical, striking poses and tossing her plait. I was sure that Sara was quieter and more

317

dignified, but I knew that Jessica would be hurt if I criticized her performance.

The sun was quite hot so we sat down on a tufty patch of grass and idly threw stones into the water. We slid out of our Sara Crewe game and pretended to be two glamorous ladies sunbathing. I enjoyed talking about my visit to a beauty parlour, and described my peek-a-boo hairstyle and coral nail varnish and lipstick that exactly matched my polka-dot swimsuit and red suede sandals, but Jessica got a bit fidgety.

'You're reminding me too much of my mother,' she said. 'I'm never, ever going to be like her. When I'm grown up I won't wear any make-up whatsoever, and I'll keep my hair in a plait so I'll never have to go to a beauty salon, and I won't bother about my clothes – I'll always wear black with an artist's smock, because I'll be a famous painter.'

I twitched a little, because Jessica had effortlessly trumped all my future ambitions.

'Perhaps I could be a writer,' I suggested timidly, 'as I like reading so much. And Mr Mitford says I have an excellent vocabulary. Sorry, that sounds like showing off, but he really did. Though of course your vocabulary is better than mine. You always sound ever so grown up. I bet you're top of the class too.'

Jessica shrugged. 'Who knows? Sister Josephine doesn't give proper marks because she thinks it will foster pride and envy. And she never praises me. She says I'm too bumptious already.'

'No you're not!' I said indignantly.

'Yes I am,' said Jessica, rolling nearer. She bumped against me with her bottom. *'Bump, bump, bump!'*

'Give over!' I said.

She bumped more, so I bumped back, and then we were wrestling. We were the same size but she was much stronger than me so she ended up on top, pinning me down.

'OK, you win!' I gasped.

'I always do,' said Jessica, very pleased with herself. 'And I always know best.'

We wriggled free of each other. I lay back, closing my eyes tight.

'Hey, you're not going to sleep, are you?' Jessica asked.

'No, I'm just thinking. Jessica, you don't *always* know best. Not about my mum and This Gerald. She wouldn't *really* have him as a boyfriend.'

'Oh, Shirley, you're so innocent. That's what grown-ups are like. Don't look so upset. It doesn't *matter*,' she said.

'Yes it does. I'm sure my mum *isn't* like that. And even if she is, *I'm* never going to be,' I declared. 'I shall fall in love and get married and stay true to my husband.'

'Oh, go on! What if you're mad enough to marry someone like . . . like that loopy boy with the sticky-out ears. Well, you'd get fed up after a bit, wouldn't you, so if some young guy looking like Cary Grant came moseying along and asked you out, you'd say yes, wouldn't you?'

'No! Well, maybe. I don't know. I wish I didn't have to grow up, it's too complicated,' I said. 'Perhaps I'll be like Mrs Waverley and live by myself with a Chubby to look after me.'

'Yes, but perhaps you'd *be* a Chubby. That wouldn't be such fun,' said Jessica.

'Actually, *you're* rich – I know you are – and if you get to be a famous artist you'll get even richer, so perhaps I could be *your* Chubby. I don't think I'd mind that,' I said, sucking a blade of grass.

'And when I wanted you I'd call you like this,' said Jessica, taking a blade of grass too and holding it against her lips. She blew into it and made a piercing whistle.

'Show me how to do that!'

I tried and tried but I just made the grass limp and soggy and no sound came out at all.

'Oh well, we'll just have to buy you a whistle instead,' said Jessica. 'And we'll live in a house together like sisters and take turns doing all the chores. I'll be an artist and you'll be a writer and we'll collaborate on books, you doing the story and me doing the illustrations. How would you like that?'

'It would be heavenly,' I said. I hummed the first line of 'Praise My Soul the King of Heaven', substituting the words, *To play that role would be blissful heaven!*

Jessica laughed, but it made her look at her watch. 'I'd better be getting back, worst luck. They'll be finished at church now.'

'What are you going to do? Just hope to tag along at the back of the crocodile going home?'

'Something like that.'

'I do hope you don't get into trouble,' I said anxiously.

'Well, it will be worth it. It's been blissful seeing you, Shirley, truly,' said Jessica.

I gave her a hug, loving her so much I felt I might burst. Then I walked her back to the path and all the way down the driveway.

'See you at two thirty at the sweetshop next Saturday?' Jessica said.

'Yes, I swear I'll be there this time,' I promised.

KEVIN CAME BACK FOR Sunday dinner, but he hardly said a word. He wouldn't even chat to Archie. He just bolted his food and then rushed out again.

'Never even asked to be excused!' said Chubby.

'Poor chap, he's still embarrassed,' said Mrs Waverley. 'Remind me to make an appointment for him at the doctor's tomorrow.'

'He's not sick! Not when he can chomp his way through pork with crackling and my apple pie and custard – a blooming great helping too. He can't stop his eating. Or his wee-wee.'

Archie burst out laughing. 'Um, Chubby! You said *wee-wee!*'

'Now, now, little 'un,' said Chubby, but she was laughing too.

'You're horrible!' I said.

'Uh-oh, Miss Prim's starting now.'

'Well, you *are* horrid, mocking poor Kevin,' I said angrily.

I stood up. 'Please may I leave the table!'

'No, you may not, Shirley. Not until you've apologized to Miss Chubb. I won't have you speaking to her like that,' said Mrs Waverley.

'I'm sorry,' I mumbled, though inside my head I shouted, *I'm not the slightest bit sorry, so there!*

'Come with me, Shirley,' said Mrs Waverley. 'Please excuse us, Chubby dear.'

She led me to her sitting room. I perched on a velvet chair, fidgeting, expecting a lecture.

'I know you're not really a rude little girl,' said Mrs Waverley. 'I can see that you're very concerned about Kevin. You always stick up for him so fiercely, bless you. You must be very fond of him. I do understand, Shirley.'

She didn't understand at all. I didn't really like Kevin. I found him just as silly and annoying as everyone else. I just felt sorry for him – after all, he couldn't help being so awkward.

'And I know you must be missing your mother dreadfully now,' Mrs Waverley went on.

I wasn't even doing that. It was dreadful, but I was actually relieved she'd gone. Now I could still be best friends with Jessica. She must really like me if she'd come all that way to find me, risking getting into terrible trouble. I felt a glow of such happiness I had to lower my head to stop Mrs Waverley seeing it reflected on my face.

'You poor dear,' she said, thinking I was trying not to cry. 'Do you know, I was very touched when you said you wanted to stay here. I know it's not the most conventional household, but you do seem to have settled in. Perhaps it's because we've actually got quite a lot in common. We both love books, don't we?' She looked across the room at her wall of books. 'Would you like to borrow any of my books while you're here? I've kept all my E. Nesbits – do you see, on the middle shelf? Have you read *The Railway Children*?' She smiled. 'It's a story about three children leaving London and going to live in the country. It might strike a chord with you.'

I picked out the fat brown Nesbit book reluctantly. I didn't want to be friendly with her and it didn't look a very promising book anyway as I wasn't interested in railways. But then I spotted a slim blue book on the shelf above with a much more beguiling title.

'*The Doll's House*,' I murmured.

'Ah, that's an Ibsen play, and probably a bit too grown up for you now. It's not really about a doll's house as such. I think you must have your own doll's house at home!'

'No, but I've always wanted one,' I said.

'Really?' said Mrs Waverley. 'Well, I'm very impressed by your little shoebox house, Shirley. You made it beautifully.'

'Yes, but it's not the same as a real doll's house,' I said.

Mrs Waverley looked at me. 'I'm going to tell you a secret, Shirley. I have a doll's house of my own.'

I did my best to look surprised. 'Can I see it?' I asked, my heart beating fast. She hesitated and then stood up. 'Come with me,' she said, holding out her hand.

She took me upstairs with her and fetched the key from the jewellery box in her bedroom. Then she led me next door, turned the key in the lock, and opened the door with a theatrical flourish.

It was easy enough to gasp convincingly because the splendour of the house overwhelmed me all over again.

'Oh!' I exclaimed. 'Oh! Oh!' My famous vocabulary had seemingly deserted me. I just went on saying one vowel, but it expressed everything I felt.

Mrs Waverley's eyes shone and her cheeks flushed. She looked much younger. 'Do you see which house it is?' she asked.

'*This* house!' I said.

'Yes, it's a perfect replica. I had the carpenter build three other houses before he got it exactly right. And then the fun began.' She undid the gold clasps and carefully opened out the front. I stared at the three floors – ground floor, bedroom floor and attics.

The man and the lady had been in the sitting room, cosily cuddled together on the chaise longue. They weren't there now. The woman was in the kitchen, stirring a pot on the cooker with a little wooden spoon. The man was upstairs in the bathroom, his jacket off, his braces hanging down. He was holding a tiny shaving brush in one hand and peering in the looking glass above the washbasin.

For a moment I actually thought they were real and had wandered around the house by themselves. Of course this was ridiculous. Someone had obviously moved them. The only possible person was Mrs Waverley. She must *play* with her doll's house!

I stared up at her. She was shaking her head fondly at the little dolls.

'They're a little behind today,' she said softly, as if she didn't want to disturb them. 'They had a lie-in this morning.'

She reached into the main bedroom and twitched the covers straight on the bed. 'He's still shaving, do you see? She's got dressed and run down to the kitchen to make Sunday lunch. I hope she's got a chicken in that oven, because the contents of that pot won't make a very sustaining meal for two. I don't think she looks very good at cooking, do you?'

'She needs to have a Chubby in the kitchen,' I said.

I thought Mrs Waverley would laugh, but she shook her head, frowning. 'No, she doesn't want Chubby or anyone else. She wants the house just for the two of them. She likes to do the cooking and all the chores herself,' she said firmly.

I thought that a bit rich coming from a woman who couldn't even be bothered to run her own bath, but I didn't say so.

'So they're husband and wife,' I said.

'Yes, they are.' Mrs Waverley stared at them intently.

'Shall we pretend they've had their Sunday dinner now and give them a little lie-down?' I suggested. 'My mum and dad always have a lie-down on Sunday afternoon.'

Mrs Waverley looked a little startled. 'Very well,' she said hesitantly. She took hold of the lady doll and laid her neatly on the bed. Her little arms and legs were bendy. Perhaps there were pipe cleaners under her soft, pinky-beige skin. Mrs Waverley arranged the doll's arms down by her sides, with her legs neatly together. She was wearing weeny sandals with heels but they were stitched onto her feet so she had to wear them, even in bed.

'Can I?' I asked, reaching for the little man doll.

Mrs Waverley breathed in, considering. 'If you're very careful and gentle,' she said.

I picked him up and eased his braces back over his shoulders, but didn't try to stuff his arms into his jacket sleeves as he was going for a lie-down too. I hung his jacket on a tiny peg in the main bedroom, and then made him walk over to his wife, moving his legs from side to side.

'Budge up, darling,' I said in a deep voice, making him snuggle down beside her.

'Let's have a lovely snooze, beloved,' I said in a high lady's voice.

Mrs Waverley shook her head. 'You're a very quaint child,' she murmured.

'There! Have forty winks now,' I said, putting a little shawl over them. 'I wonder what their names are.'

Of course I knew what the lady doll's name was. She was Madeleine. I stroked the soft dark-wool hair of the gentleman doll. He had a matching moustache.

'His name is William,' Mrs Waverley whispered.

'Go to sleep, William,' I said, but of course he couldn't close his embroidered eyes. They were very blue and piercing.

'And her name is . . . Maddy.' Mrs Waverley's voice was scarcely audible.

'And they live happily ever after in their house, Maddy and William,' I said.

'That's right.'

'And William never, ever dies,' I whispered.

Mrs Waverley swallowed. 'The real William died in the Battle of the Somme,' she said.

'Mr Waverley?'

'Yes. We'd only just married, in 1916, when he was home

on leave. I bought this house and started furnishing it for us, but then the telegram came. He died in July, but I didn't hear until the end of August. I think I went a little mad then. I can barely remember. I was in a nursing home for a while. And then, when I was well enough to come home, I couldn't see the point of finishing the house, not without William to share it with me,' she said. 'All these years later, and I still haven't got round to it. Perhaps I *am* a little mad.'

'No, I don't think you're a bit mad. It's just like a fairy tale, so sad and so romantic,' I said, sighing. 'So the dolls are living the life you and William should have had.'

'Yes, they are. Oh, Shirley, thank you so much for understanding. I hoped you would. But you won't tell anyone, will you? Especially not Kevin and Archie. They wouldn't understand at all. They're not sensitive little souls like you,' she said. 'The doll's house means so much to me.'

'I won't tell, I promise,' I said, and I put my arms round her waist and hugged her shyly.

I felt honoured to be taken into Mrs Waverley's confidence. Mum and Dad and Chubby and the teachers at school all treated me like a little girl, but she talked to me like a grown-up. I went round in a daze for the rest of the day, feeling so happy. I wondered if I might tell Jessica about Mrs Waverley's doll's house when I saw her next Saturday. I'd promised not to tell anyone, but I was sure she'd be sensitive too.

When I went downstairs Kevin was fooling around in the hall. He'd taken two walking sticks from the umbrella stand and was swinging himself along between them, up and down the worn Persian rug.

'Where have you been?' he asked.

'Where have *you* been?' I retorted.

'Just out.'

'Well, I've been just in.'

'No you haven't. You weren't in the kitchen or Lady Muck's sitting room. You weren't in your bedroom, either.'

'You stay out of my bedroom! It's private. And stop poking those sticks in the rug – it must be worth heaps.'

'This old thing? It's all faded and falling to bits,' said Kevin scornfully, but he looked down at it anxiously. There were two lines of little indentations.

'Look, you idiot!' I said.

'They'll smooth out,' said Kevin. He rubbed at them with his big new shoes and caught a thread.

'Watch *out*!' I pushed him away and did my best to sort it out, but there was a big pucker in the pattern now.

'It doesn't really show,' he said hopefully.

'It does. Oh, Kevin, what's the *matter* with you? How could you be so daft? You'll be in such trouble when Chubby sees it,' I said, sighing.

'So what? I'm in trouble already.' Kevin sighed too.

'Oh, Kev.' I lowered my voice. 'Why don't you get up when you want to wee in the night?'

'I don't wake up. I just do it,' he muttered. 'Then in the morning I'm all wet. I really thought it might be Archie, not me.'

'Truly?'

'Well, I *hoped* it was Archie.'

'You'd never wet the bed at home?'

'Never!' said Kevin. Then, 'Maybe once or twice. When I was younger.'

'And did your mum or dad take you to the doctor's?'

'No, my dad belted me,' said Kevin.

'What, really? He hit you with his actual belt?' I asked.

'Yeah.'

'How awful!' I tried to imagine my dad taking off his belt and hitting me. It was impossible.

'Nah, he's got to learn me, hasn't he?'

'But it hasn't worked – you're still doing it,' I argued.

'Well, I'm not any more so stop going on about it,' said Kevin.

That night he tried to take preventive measures. He didn't tell me, of course, but Archie saw and told me the next morning.

'He put this towel in his pants like a great big nappy! He looked ever so funny. And then it didn't work properly because he still ended up with a little bit of wet in the bed. He's scrubbed at it, and washed the towel in the sink, but Chubby found out,' Archie gabbled as I supervised his tooth-brushing.

He wasn't used to cleaning his teeth and was inclined to muck about pretending his toothbrush was a cigarette.

'Was she cross?'

'Yep,' said Archie.

'You won't say anything to all your little pals in the Infants, will you?' I said.

'Ain't got no pals. They all call me Baldy.'

'You'll make some friends soon, Archie. And you're not bald

any more. Your hair's growing nicely now.' I played with the fluff. 'I reckon you're going to be curly soon. Then all the girls will be after you.'

'I don't want any girls. I just want Chubby. I'm going to marry her,' said Archie. 'Give us a bit of that silver paper you've got in your room and I'll make her a ring. Well, you can help me.'

'Do you think she'll say yes?' I asked, humouring him.

'Of course she will. She says I'm her little lamb,' said Archie, smiling.

'Well, we'll all expect an invitation to the wedding,' I said. 'In fact, I'll be your bridesmaid and Kevin can be your best man.'

'And Mrs Waverley can be the fairy godmother,' said Archie, mixing up fairy tales with marriage.

'She's actually *like* a fairy godmother,' I said, picturing her in a long sparkly dress with her hair waving about her shoulders and a starry wand in her hand. Her magical house-within-a-house was far more impressive than any pumpkin coach.

I felt as if she'd waved a wand over me. I no longer felt so hideous in my tunic and clumpy shoes. For once the ribbon in my hair stood up in a neat bow instead of drooping. Even my hair seemed a longer. Perhaps I could try to encourage it to fall over one eye like Mrs Waverley's.

I set off for school with a spring in my step. Archie skipped along too, planning his wedding, deciding that we'd all have a wedding cake each and eat it for breakfast, dinner, tea and supper. Even Kevin cheered up, his damp bed a secret left back at the house.

He still glanced at me anxiously when we went into school and started mingling with the other Paradise Road children, though of course I didn't tell on him. He was worried about the big Meadow Ridge boys, but I didn't have anything to do with them. The Paradise Road kids and the Meadow Ridge children barely spoke to each other.

Well, there was one exception. The Meadow Ridge boys tried to chat up Marilyn Henderson. Mr Mitford paid her a lot of attention too, forever having little chats with her about monitor duties. He called me up to his desk once when he'd given a piece of my work ten out of ten, but he didn't smile at me. I didn't *want* him to, but all the same I wished I had Marilyn's power.

He watched her when we were playing with an old washing line in the school yard at dinnertime. He clapped when she managed ten skips in a row and marvelled when she sang out, '*All in together, girls, never mind the weather, girls, if you do you'll get the cane!*'

'Nicely sung, Marilyn,' he said. 'You've got a very sweet voice.'

When we'd had our dinner – fatty mince and lumpy mash – Mr Mitford said he'd had a good idea for the end of term.

I stared at him. *The end of term?* What was he talking about? We wouldn't still be here, would we? Everyone said the war would be over by Christmas. It hadn't really come to anything yet. The man on the wireless said there hadn't been any bombs at all. We all thought we'd be going home in a week or two.

What if we were staying longer? My head was in a whirl. I wanted to go home as soon as possible, didn't I? Or did I want to stay on at the Red House?

I shook my head guiltily but I couldn't stop my heart

thumping. I could play with Mrs Waverley's doll's house – and see Jessica!

'Why are you shaking your head, Shirley Smith? Don't you believe that I've had a good idea?' Mr Mitford called.

I jumped. 'No, sir. I mean, yes, sir, of course you have good ideas,' I stammered.

'Indeed I do – and this one's a cracker, even if I say so myself. I think you older ones can put on a Christmas concert for the Infants. In fact, I don't see why we shouldn't entertain the whole village. I'll endeavour to write a little play with a festive theme, and we'll have a few variety acts too. Marilyn, you've got a very sweet singing voice, dear. You must sing a couple of songs. I wonder who else has a special talent. Hands up anyone who'd like to audition for our concert!'

Two more girls said they could sing. A boy said he could do acrobatics. I was startled when Kevin said he could tell jokes. Suddenly everyone wanted to audition.

Mr Mitford looked at me, head on one side. 'What about you, Shirley? Are you any good at singing?' he asked. 'Don't be shy, dear.'

'She can't sing,' said Marilyn. 'Our teacher at Paradise Road said she had a voice like a foghorn.'

Everyone sniggered. And the worst of it was, it was true. Inside my head I could sing beautifully, but when I opened my mouth my voice couldn't find the right notes. Our old teacher taught us 'A Fairy Went A-Marketing' but said, 'I think *your* fairy had better stay at home, Shirley, utterly silent.' Then she added the voice-like-a-foghorn part. The other children had sniggered then too.

'Oh dear, Shirley,' said Mr Mitford, raising his eyebrows. 'So you can't sing?'

I shook my head. I saw Marilyn smile. 'I can't sing but I can dance, sir,' I said.

'You can dance?' Mr Mitford said encouragingly. 'What sort of dancing? Ballroom?'

'No, sir. Ballet!' I said.

'She can't do ballet,' said Marilyn, addressing the whole room. 'She's never done ballet. She's just making it up. I bet she's never had a ballet lesson in her life.'

'I've been doing ballet for nearly three years,' I said. It was true too. I'd been given *Ballet Shoes* for my eighth birthday and had been dancing privately ever since.

'You must audition for the concert then,' said Mr Mitford, writing my name on his list.

I swallowed. 'But I haven't got my ballet shoes with me, sir,' I said.

'Never mind. I'm sure you can dance in your socks.' He scanned his piece of paper. 'Well, we've certainly got a variety of acts listed. Let's hope you all live up to expectations. We'll have the audition on Friday. Practise hard!'

I took his advice seriously. Chubby had started making us cocoa after school, with a slice of bread pudding to keep us going until supper. I choked mine down so quickly that I got hiccups when I started practising in my room. I did a few warm-up exercises and then started my dance.

I'd decided to do the Fairy Godmother solo from my own version of *Cinderella*. It was short but quite difficult, with an arabesque that made me wobble, and lots of pirouettes. Sometimes I whirled around too wildly and fell over.

'Whatever are you doing up in your room, Shirley?' Chubby asked at supper. 'You've been thumping around like a herd of elephants above my head.'

'I'm rehearsing my Fairy Godmother ballet piece,' I said with as much dignity as I could muster.

Chubby snorted. 'Fairy Clodhopper, more like,' she said. 'Give it a rest, Anna Pavlova.'

'We've got to practise, haven't we, Kevin? Mr Mitford said.'

Kevin shrugged. He was very pale. That afternoon Mrs Waverley had taken him to the doctor, who had recommended a special bell-and-pad cure for his bedwetting. Kevin would have to sleep on this special pad. If he started to wee in his sleep the pad got wet and triggered the alarm. Then Kevin was meant to leap up and carry on weeing in the chamber pot.

The doctor had said it was a new miracle cure. Kevin was supposed to carry on until he'd been dry for fourteen consecutive nights.

I suppose he wasn't really in the right mood to rehearse a comic turn.

'But you do know lots of jokes?' I asked him anxiously.

'Course I do.'

'Tell us one then,' I said.

He told us a joke about a boy and a girl.

'You what?' said Archie, puzzled.

I wasn't sure I understood it, either. Chubby did though, and gave him a clump about the head.

'Go and wash your mouth out with soap, you dirty boy,' she said.

'I'm not being dirty. It's a *joke*. My dad told it me,' Kevin protested.

'Well, it doesn't say a lot for your dad then, telling a joke like that to a kiddie,' said Chubby.

'Don't you dare insult my dad,' said Kevin, and sloped off to practise his turn in private.

'Don't you think you'd better rehearse in front of me?' I suggested at bedtime.

'What, so you can laugh at me?'

'Aren't I *supposed* to laugh if it's a comic turn?' I said.

'Yes, but you might laugh in the wrong way. I don't want you putting me off,' said Kevin.

'All right then, but don't tell *rude* jokes. Mr Mitford would go bananas,' I warned.

'They're *not* blooming rude,' said Kevin. 'OK then, hadn't you better rehearse this ballet stuff in front of me? It might be rude too. You could be kicking up your legs and showing off your knickers for all I know.'

I gave him a shove and flounced off to my room. I wished I had a big mirror to check that I *wasn't* showing my knickers. I wondered how real ballet dancers got over this problem. Perhaps they didn't care. The male dancers certainly didn't seem to mind wearing astonishing revealing outfits.

On Friday morning I was feeling very nervous. I wore my jersey and pleated skirt because I would hardly look like a ballet dancer in my tunic. I tried putting on my red shoes again, but they hurt so much I could only hobble. In any case

Mr Mitford had told me to dance in my socks. I noticed that I had a hole in the toe of my left sock and wished I'd asked Chubby to darn it for me, but there wasn't time now.

The auditions started after dinner. We had to wait until the dinner ladies had cleared all the tables to make space for us in the hall. Mr Mitford asked Marilyn to go first. She sauntered to the front, tossing her ringlets.

'I'm going to sing "Blow the Wind Southerly",' she announced. She threw back her head and started singing. Her voice was sweet and clear, but she sang in a weird, showy-off way, emphasizing the words and making hand gestures. When she said the word *lover*, a lot of us had to smother our giggles, and whenever she said *wind*, a big Meadow Ridge boy made a very rude sound that made us clamp our lips together to stop laughing.

'Well done, Marilyn!' said Mr Mitford when she swept a curtsy. 'That was absolutely beautiful, dear. You should feel very proud.'

She looked proud too, marching offstage with pink cheeks and another toss of her ringlets. I wanted to seize a handful of those curls and pull hard.

We'd smothered our laughter when Marilyn performed. When Kevin started his joke routine, no one laughed at all. He had taken my advice and didn't tell rude jokes. He told ancient ones instead, many of them involving chickens, and at the end of each he did a chicken impression, clucking and flapping his arms like wings. It should have been funny but it wasn't at all.

Then he started on a long-winded joke about an Englishman, an Irishman, a Welshman and a Scotsman. He attempted the right accents but he couldn't do them properly. Then he kept losing the thread, mumbling, 'No, hang on a minute, I think I've got that bit wrong. I'll start again, shall I?'

'Please don't, Kevin. We've got the gist,' said Mr Mitford. 'I think you can sit down now and let someone else have a turn.'

Kevin had to slouch off back to his seat without finishing his act. I clapped loudly but no one else joined in. I didn't dare look at him.

I longed for my own audition to be over and done with, but I was the very last child to be picked. I took off my shoes and jumper so that I could dance in just my skirt and bodice. After all, it looked almost like a ballet dress now.

The Meadow Ridge boy who had made wind noises at Marilyn whistled when I took off my jumper. I felt my cheeks go hot and knew I must be scarlet.

'The next time I hear a stupid noise I will fetch my cane!' Mr Mitford threatened. 'Come along, Shirley. I'm looking forward to your ballet dance. Will you be able to manage without any music?'

'There isn't any music because I made my dance up myself,' I said.

'My, my!' said Mr Mitford, sounding impressed. 'Does your ballet have a title?'

'Yes, it's the Fairy Godmother solo from my ballet of *Cinderella*,' I announced.

'I think we're in for a treat, children,' said Mr Mitford.

I struck an attitude, copying one of the illustrations in *Ballet Shoes*. Then I began. I whirled around the stage, leading with my arms and turning on one foot. My legs had gone a bit trembly and I staggered. There were a few hastily smothered titters. I righted myself and whirled around again. Then I waved my imaginary wand. Some of the boys in the audience waved back, grinning.

I turned my back on them and tried my arabesque. I didn't wobble at all, but they were laughing out loud now, in spite of the threatened cane. I spun round and saw that even Mr Mitford was grinning. Did they think this was a comic ballet? Or did they simply think *I* was comic?

I felt all the strength drain out of my body. I couldn't even stand on tiptoe any more. I wanted to crawl away without finishing the dance but I forced myself to go through the motions. Pauline and Petrova and Posy danced around me protectively, urging me along. They told me that the audience were all fools – country bumpkins and cockney sparrows. They couldn't appreciate the finer points of a beautiful, historic way of dancing. I danced on, and then the bell rang abruptly for the end of school. I was teetering on one leg. I slipped, slid helplessly in my socks and fell heavily on my bottom.

The whole class erupted, shrieking with laughter. I sat where I was while they rushed whooping out of the hall.

'Oh dear, oh dear. Are you all right, Shirley?' said Mr Mitford weakly, mopping his brow. 'My, you were a sight for sore eyes! Whatever made you say you could dance, you little silly? You haven't had a ballet lesson in your life, have you?'

I didn't reply because I knew I'd start crying. I'd had lessons. I'd learned everything from *Ballet Shoes*. Pauline, Petrova and Posy had taught me. I knew all the dance moves, I'd copied every illustration. Of course I could dance!

Or had I just been kidding myself? Was it all pretend? Pauline, Petrova and Posy weren't real girls. I'd been making it all up. And I'd stumbled, I'd staggered, I'd fallen on my bottom. Of course I couldn't dance.

I hung my head.

'There now. It's not the end of the world,' said Mr Mitford, surprisingly gently. 'Run along home now.' I heard him march down the hall, his shoes squeaking on the polished floorboards. The doors at the back swung open and then closed behind him.

I thought I was on my own. It was safe to cry. Then someone bent down beside me and put their hand tentatively on my shoulder.

'I thought you did good,' said Kevin.

I cried harder.

He sat down cross-legged beside me. 'We'd better go and find Archie. He'll be waiting,' he said at last. He held out his hand and helped pull me upright. I wiped my wet face with the back of my hand.

'I liked your dance – *really*,' he persisted.

'I was rubbish,' I said. 'You know I was.'

We found Archie in the playground, kicking stones aimlessly.

'*There* you are!' he said. 'Come on. Chubby might drink all our cocoa herself!'

Miss Appleby was standing nearby, keeping an eye on him. She waved goodbye cheerfully and he waved back.

'I love Miss Appleby. I love her almost as much as Chubby,' said Archie, skipping. 'I love this school.'

'I hate it,' I said. 'I hate, hate, hate it and I'm never coming back.'

MEANT IT TOO. How could I possibly go back to school on Monday with my dance performance still fresh in everyone's mind. They'd all jeer and tease. Marilyn Henderson would do a cruel imitation of me and they'd all collapse with laughter again. I simply couldn't bear it.

I burned to tell Jessica. I knew she'd be understanding. I couldn't wait to see her.

All Saturday morning I was in a fever of impatience. While I was sitting by the lake going over all our conversations last Sunday, I heard a gunshot. My stomach heaved. I couldn't face rabbit pie again.

Much later I trailed back indoors, determined not to eat a mouthful of dinner. Chubby had indeed made a rabbit pie, but there was another smaller pie on the serving mat. It had a golden crust, little clouds of steam escaping from the fork holes in the middle.

'I found some early mushrooms so I made a special mushroom and bacon pie just for you, Miss Fussy Guts,' said Chubby.

It was so unexpectedly kind of her that I was lost for words. I'd thought she disliked me, but she must have liked me just a little bit to go to so much trouble.

'It's delicious, Chubby,' I said after I'd taken a big mouthful. 'Thank you ever so much.'

'*I* want my own pie too,' said Archie.

'You! Watch out or I'll chop you up and *bake* you in your pie,' said Chubby, miming chopping with her knife.

Archie squealed in delighted horror. He picked up his own knife to chop her back.

'Hey, hey, calm down, Archie. And you, Kevin, please try to close your mouth when you eat. Hasn't anyone ever taught you table manners?' asked Mrs Waverley.

I thought this a tactless question, but I smiled at her even so.

'We can go down to the village this afternoon, can't we?' I asked.

'I don't see why not. After you've all had a little nap to let your lovely lunch go down,' she said. 'But I'd better not give you a lift now that we're all being told to save petrol because of the war. You'll have to go by yourselves. Mind you behave! Don't be late for tea – I think Chubby's planning something special. And I shall be out tonight, dining with Dr and Mrs Marshall.'

Kevin's head jerked.

'It's not to discuss you, Kevin,' Mrs Waverley said gently. 'This is simply a social invitation. Dr Marshall and I are good friends.'

'He might be a good friend but I don't think he's a good doctor,' said Chubby, sniffing. 'All that bell-and-pad nonsense and there's still a wet bed every morning.'

Kevin blushed painfully. He looked very tired. He hadn't managed to get much sleep – and he hadn't had a dry night yet.

'We have to give the method time, Chubby. It doesn't work instant miracles,' said Mrs Waverley. 'Now, off you go for a little nap, children – just until two.'

Of course I didn't doze at all. I flicked through all but one of my books in turn, unable to settle. I couldn't bear to pick up *Ballet Shoes*.

I paced my room, listening for the sound of the clock downstairs. When it struck two I bolted along the landing and down the stairs. I didn't bother with chit-chat with Kevin and Archie on the way down to the village. I just thought, *Jessica-Jessica-Jessica,* chanting her name inside my head.

Mrs Waverley had given us tuppence each to spend on sweets. I hastily chose a Sherbet Fountain and stood outside the shop, sucking up the sherbet as I peered up and down the street.

Kevin and Archie took ages, and eventually decided on giant gobstoppers. They came out of the shop with grossly swollen cheeks. They kept taking their sweets out of their mouths to see if they'd started turning colour.

'Stop it, it looks revolting,' I snapped. 'Go off and play somewhere.'

'You come too,' said Kevin, licking slurp off his fingers.

'No fear! I'm waiting for Jessica,' I said.

'I don't know what you see in that stuck-up, lumpy girl,' he said. 'She's no fun.'

'You shut up. She's my best friend in all the world,' I said angrily.

'Well, here she is.' Kevin was pointing at a little parade of purple coming down the street.

Sister Josephine was sailing along at the front, her black skirts billowing. I saw Goofy and Munchkin and Freckle Face, but no Jessica. I waited tensely, forgetting my sherbet.

I hoped she'd simply be trailing along behind, but after ten minutes there was still no sign of her. I ran up and down the street in case she was looking in the windows or wandering down one of the little alleyways, but I couldn't see her. I rushed back to the sweetshop. Kevin and Archie were sitting on the step, comparing gobstoppers. The convent girls were having to step round them, holding their tunics clear of all the stickiness.

'Go away, little boys,' said Sister Josephine, glaring at them. 'You're not supposed to loiter on the step like this. You're getting in everyone's way.'

'Please, Sister Josephine, where's Jessica?' I asked.

'I beg your pardon? Who are you? How do you know my name?' She sounded outraged.

'I was on the train with you – don't you remember? I'm Shirley. I was the girl with the heavy suitcase,' I reminded her.

'Oh yes,' she said, sighing.

'And I'm Jessica's best friend,' I said. 'Do you know where she is?'

'Yes, I do. But it's none of your business,' said Sister Josephine. 'Now off you go, and take your brothers and their wretched bonbons with you.'

'They're not my brothers! And it's not my fault they chose gobstoppers. My mum doesn't allow *me* to have them. She says they're common,' I said.

'I agree with your mother,' said the nun. 'Now please go away.'

'But I'm waiting to see Jessica!'

'Then you'll be waiting a long time. She's not coming to the village today.'

'Why not?' I asked, agonized.

'Questions, questions! It's none of your business,' she said, her moustache bristling.

She clapped her hands to gather the St Agatha's girls together. 'Come along. Quick sharp. We're going back to Lady Amersham's now,' she called.

Goofy and Munchkin were last out of the shop, blowing bubbles of bright pink gum behind Sister Josephine's back.

'Excuse me,' I said quickly. 'Can you tell me why Jessica isn't here? Didn't she want to come?'

'Oh, look, it's Totty Toilet!' said Goofy, and they both laughed.

'Shut up! Tell me about Jessica. Is she sick?'

'Sick in the head, more like,' said Munchkin.

'What do you mean? *Tell me!*'

But they just looked at each other, smirking.

'Tell me, or – or I'll duff you up!' I said, doing my best to sound menacing.

They laughed so loudly that Sister Josephine came marching up. 'Girls, girls, I will not have you making a spectacle of yourselves in the street. Silence! Join the crocodile immediately,' she commanded.

Goofy and Munchkin sloped off, turning their heads furtively to pull faces at me. I felt as if I might burst with frustration.

'So she's not coming then?' said Kevin, lurking nearby.

'Yes she is,' I said fiercely.

'She's not. They said.'

'I don't care what they said. They're just mean and stupid,' I insisted.

'But that nun lady said she wasn't coming. Nuns aren't allowed to lie,' said Kevin.

'I bet Sister Josephine lies her head off,' I said. 'She might have said she wasn't coming, but Jessica wouldn't let me down. *You* see, she'll be here any minute.'

'You're nuts,' said Kevin. 'Come on, you can't just hang about outside the sweetshop. Come and play with Archie and me. There's a swing in that field over there.'

'I'm not the slightest bit interested in a little kids' swing,' I said. 'I'm waiting here.'

'Suit yourself.' Kevin took hold of Archie's wrist and steered him towards the field.

I waited and waited and waited. I played games where I shut my eyes and counted to a hundred, telling myself that Jessica would be standing in front of me by the time I'd finished. When this didn't work I tried counting to a thousand, but I kept getting muddled. I pretended Pauline, Petrova and

Posy were waiting with me, but that reminded me of my ballet fiasco. I shook my head violently to get the thoughts out of my head.

'Oh look, she's waggling her head about like she's in agony. Perhaps this is a new dance. Not the Dying Swan. More like the Dying Lumbering Elephant!' Marilyn Henderson and Mary were standing there, mocking me.

I started to feel like a freak show at a carnival. First Goofy and Munchkin and now Marilyn and Mary. I was terrified I might actually burst into tears so I turned my back on them. Long after they'd wandered off I stayed there, staring through the mottled glass window at the jars of sweets.

After a while the sweetshop man came to the window and made little shooing gestures with his hand.

I took no notice.

He came to the door. 'Oi, you! Buzz off!'

'I don't want to!' I said, trying not to cry.

'Oh, don't go all weepy on me. What's up? Haven't you got any pocket money left for your sweeties?'

I shook my head, but he didn't understand.

'Look, you can have two ounces on me. Too soft-hearted for my own good, that's what I am. What would you like? Wine gums? Aniseed balls? Fruit drops?' he offered.

'No thank you,' I sniffled.

'Well, you're a rum one and no mistake. Never once had a kiddy turn down free sweeties. You're one of the London lot, aren't you? Don't you get no sweeties at home?'

'Yes, sometimes. And I already bought a Sherbet Fountain off you – don't you remember?' I said.

'You evacuees all look the same to me. Pale, puny little things, the lot of you,' he said. 'Well, I'm about to shut up shop now. I'm putting the blinds down so you won't have anything to look at. You'd better run off home. Where've they billeted you?'

'I'm staying with Mrs Waverley and Miss Chubb at the Red House,' I said.

'Oh, them! Well, they're a strange pair. The tales I could tell!' he said.

'What tales?'

The sweetshop man rubbed his nose. 'Ah, that would be telling,' he said maddeningly. Then he went back into the shop. I heard him bolt the door, and within seconds he had let down the blinds.

I knew Jessica couldn't possibly be coming now so I wandered off to find Kevin and Archie.

'Where's your friend then?' Archie asked.

'She didn't come,' I said shortly.

'Doesn't she like you no more?'

'Yes, of course she does,' I said. I hoped I was right. Once again I wondered whether Jessica had made a *new* friend, someone as clever and grand as herself. Maybe they'd both been naughty and Sister Josephine had banned them from coming down to the village. They could this very minute be wandering the fancy rooms of the White House discussing their favourite books and inventing imaginary games.

I knew deep down that this was extremely unlikely, but I tortured myself with the thought all the way back to Mrs Waverley's. Chubby had our tea waiting for us. The treat was a special iced sponge cake with jam and buttercream. She cut three generous slices. Kevin and Archie gobbled theirs enthusiastically and begged for more. I just nibbled at the icing.

'Don't you like *cake*?' Chubby asked, astonished. 'What's wrong with it? I still make a feather-light sponge, even though I say so myself. Mrs Mad and I have got out of the habit of cakes, but now we're lumbered with you kiddies I thought I'd start baking again. But there's no point bothering if you turn your nose up at it, Miss Fusspot.'

'*We'll* eat her cake, Chubby!' said Archie, grabbing my slice from my plate.

'Don't mind her. She's just upset because her posh-nob friend didn't come to meet her,' said Kevin.

'Shut *up*,' I snapped.

'I'm just explaining, that's all,' he said, wounded.

'Well, don't.' I stalked off.

'Little madam!' I heard Chubby say. She'd go back to hating me again now.

I trudged up the stairs, sodden with self-pity. It felt as if everyone hated me now. Perhaps Jessica simply couldn't be bothered to come and see me – paying me back for standing her up last Saturday, though it hadn't been my fault. I hadn't known Mum would turn up on the doorstep. Everything had gone wrong with Mum too. She was angry with me because I wouldn't go to the Cotswolds. And Dad hadn't even bothered to write to see how I was doing in my new home. Only it wasn't a home.

Chubby said they'd been *lumbered* with us. She acted as if it was our fault we were stuck in this village in the back of beyond. We hadn't asked to be there. We didn't want to go to that horrible school with hateful Mr Mitford. And now even he didn't like me any more. When I'd made a fool of myself doing ballet, he'd laughed along with all the others.

Even though I was alone upstairs I could feel myself blushing. I went into my room and stared at my ramshackle cardboard house. I took the ballet-studio box and stamped on it until I'd completely flattened it.

Everything was spoiled now. I couldn't bear to be in my room any more. I wandered along the corridor, all the way to the end. Mrs Waverley had gone to dine with this doctor and his wife. She wouldn't be back for hours. I slipped into her bedroom. The pink silks and satins calmed me. I rubbed my flushed cheek on the slippery bedspread and then crept over to her jewellery box. I opened it carefully and felt among the pearls and bangles for the key to the room next door. I clasped it tight and then dropped it in my tunic pocket.

I heard a gasp and looked up. Kevin was standing in the doorway, staring at me with his mouth open.

'What are you doing, creeping after me? How dare you come spying on me!' I hissed.

'What are *you* doing?'

'Nothing,' I said.

'Don't give me that! I don't blooming believe it! You're nicking her jewellery!'

'No I'm not.'

'I saw you with my own eyes. You're a thief, Shirley Smith, for all your fancy talk and prissy airs!' Kevin shook his head and laughed.

'Shut up! Archie will come to see what you're laughing at!'

'No, he's downstairs with his precious Chubby-Wubby. I still can't credit it, Shirl!'

'Shir*ley*, not Shirl. And I'm absolutely not a thief. I haven't touched Mrs Waverley's jewellery.'

'Then what's that you've got in your pocket?' Kevin grabbed at me, sticking his long fingers into my pocket before I could stop him.

'Get out! Careful, you'll tear it. Stop it!' I protested, trying to fight him off, but he had the key in his hand now.

'What's this then?' he asked, puzzled.

'What does it look like? It's a key.'

'Yeah, but what's it for?'

'Are you that thick? It's obvious what it's for. To open a door,' I said.

'What door?' said Kevin – but then the penny dropped. 'The door to the next room? But how come you knew it was in her jewellery box?'

'She showed me. She took me into that room. It's a special secret between her and me,' I said, unable to resist showing off.

'And me now,' said Kevin. 'I'm opening it.'

'No, you mustn't! You can't. I'll get into terrible trouble if you see what's in there. You'll never be able to keep it a secret,' I said, really frightened now.

'I keep all sorts of secrets,' said Kevin, marching out of the bedroom purposefully.

'No, please! You mustn't,' I said, trying to snatch the key back. He held his arm high and I couldn't get anywhere near it, even though I jumped up in the air.

We scuffled in the corridor, but I couldn't stop him slotting the key into the lock and opening the door. Then he stood still, staring.

'OK, you've seen it. Now lock the door again and let's scarper,' I whispered.

But Kevin walked right into the room, marvelling. 'A little house!' he breathed.

'It's a great big house,' I said. 'Isn't it beautiful? Do you see what it is?'

'A house – I just said.'

'Yes, but it's a replica, isn't it?'

'You what? I don't get what you say half the time, you with your fancy vocabulary,' said Kevin, reaching out to touch the roof. He ran his fingers over each little bump and groove. 'It's like real tiles, but teeny-weeny ones.'

'Careful,' I said. 'You shouldn't touch it. It's ever so precious. Look, it's *this* house, see? Exactly the same roof, windows, even the knocker on the door.'

Kevin shivered. 'It's like a fairy tale or something. Maybe we're inside it, looking at another even tinier doll's house.'

I'd felt exactly the same way! I beamed at Kevin, pleased by his reaction. 'OK, let's open it!' I said.

Kevin touched the place where the doors met at the front, digging his fingers in to pull.

'No, not like that! See the clasps. Let me do it!' I unhooked them and carefully swung both sides open.

'Cor blimey!' Kevin breathed. 'Look at it! But there aren't any empty rooms. It's all fully furnished, like Mr and Mrs Doll have just had a mammoth delivery from Heal's fancy furniture store.' He reached in and picked up the two dolls.

'*Careful!* You mustn't touch,' I said.

'It's a toy, isn't it?'

'No, it's Mrs Waverley's special house. That little lady doll is her when she was young. And the man is Mr Waverley, before he got killed. Isn't it romantic? But it's so sad. It's Mrs Waverley's wish house – everything is the way she wanted it to be.'

'It's a bit weird. So she plays with it, does she?'

'I think she just looks at it really. She still misses him dreadfully. It must be so terrible for your husband to die.' I thought of Dad and wondered if Mum would want a similar house if he got killed in the war. It didn't seem likely.

'Would your mum miss your dad terribly if he died?' I asked Kevin.

'Nah! She cleared off with some other bloke when I was little,' he said.

I stared at him. 'Cleared off without you?' I tried to imagine Mum walking out on me. 'Don't *you* miss your mum?'

'Can't properly remember her. Dad don't, either. He's got this new lady now. Lil. I suppose she's my stepmum. She looks all glam but she ain't got no teeth. I've seen her early in the morning, all gummy. I had a right laugh,' said Kevin. He peered down at the lady doll. 'You got your own choppers inside your little head, missus?'

'Put her back! *I'm* the only one allowed to touch them. Mrs Waverley trusts me because I'm careful. You're dead clumsy,' I said.

Kevin dropped the little doll on the miniature Persian rug. The stitches were so small you had to squint to see them.

'There now, little Mrs Waverley. Come and sit on the sofa,' I said, picking her up carefully and trotting her along on her sandals. I settled her down comfortably, leaning back on a cushion, with one leg crossed over the other.

'Hey, you're good at it. It's like they're real. Make the little man work too,' said Kevin. 'He wants to go to the toilet. Go on, walk him to the bathroom.'

'Trust you to think of that. And it's not a toilet, it's a double-you-see,' I said grandly, but I walked the miniature Mr Waverley out of the room and up the flight of stairs to the bathroom.

'Now make him go,' said Kevin. 'Has he got little weeny fly buttons?'

'No, he hasn't,' I said, though I had a good look just in case.

'Well, he's going to wet his trousers then.'

'You'll know all about wetting,' I said unkindly, and then wished I hadn't when I saw him blush. 'Sorry, sorry. Look, he won't wet – he can take his trousers down.'

I unhooked his braces and pulled at his trousers so they slipped down past his hips. I perched him on the toilet and Kevin laughed.

'Here, you know Mrs Waverley's gone to have dinner with that horrible doctor? Do you think they're gassing about me? She'll tell him that awful bell thing ain't working. She won't really send me away to that hostel place, will she?' Kevin asked.

'No, of course she won't,' I said, though I wasn't at all sure.

'I'd top myself if I had to go there.'

'Don't be daft.'

'No, I would, really.' Kevin swallowed. 'Swear you won't tell, but I was sent to Parkways last year.'

'Where?' I said, wrinkling my nose.

'You know. Well, you obviously don't. It's this big school for boys up our way. *Approved* school. You know what that is, don't you?' he asked.

'A school for when you've done something really bad. What did you *do*, Kevin?' I was all agog.

'It wasn't *that* bad. And it wasn't my fault. These older lads made me. They were doing this factory, see, and they needed someone to climb over the wall, and I was the tallest. Anyway, I was supposed to let them in, only the night watchman came along and they all scarpered and I was the one who got arrested. I didn't snitch, so they thought I'd planned it all myself. So I was the one sent to Parkways for six months to learn me.'

'You poor thing. Were they very strict there?' I asked.

'Yeah, the screws were, but that wasn't the worst bit. It was the other boys, see. Especially the monitors. In the morning they'd do bed inspections, and if you'd had a bit of an accident, like, they put your sheets over your head and you'd have to do this ghost walk, and everyone would jeer and take a kick at you. Every time, again and again.' Kevin was shaking. I saw that he was holding the little china washbasin. It was very delicate, with tiny taps.

'Careful! Here, let me!' I took it from him and very carefully tucked it back into place against the bathroom wall. 'Well, I'm sure you won't be sent away. And it's weird here, I know, but at least Chubby doesn't make you put your bedclothes on your head.'

'I bet she'd like to,' said Kevin. He took several deep breaths, trying to calm himself down. 'Here, that little guy's been on the toilet ages. Has he got a tummy bug?' He made disgusting noises.

'Stop it! He was just having a rest. Come on, little man. Let's make you decent.' I stood him upright, and carefully pulled up his braces. 'There, that's better.'

'Thanks awfully,' I made him say in a deep, posh voice. 'I'm tickety-boo now.' I helped him to extend his hand so that he could shake mine. I waggled his little arm up and down while Kevin laughed hysterically.

The arm was stiff at first, but then it suddenly relaxed, as if it had become real. I gave it a little pull – and the arm slid right out of the shirt sleeve. I was left holding a glorified pipe cleaner with a tiny curved hand at the end of it.

'Oh crikey!' said Kevin. 'Look what you've gone and done!'

For a few seconds I couldn't take it in. It was Kevin who was the clumsy one. I had only just stopped him from dropping the little china basin. I was the careful girl, the one to be trusted. And yet I'd somehow pulled this doll's arm right off!

I tried thrusting it back up the man's shirt sleeve as if it might magically meld into his shoulder again, but it hung limply. When I tried standing him up, the arm fell right out onto the bathroom floor.

'What am I going to do?' I wailed.

'It's OK,' said Kevin, though it clearly wasn't. 'Look, put the man dolly back on the bed. The arm will stay in his sleeve then. Mrs Waverley won't notice.'

'But she'll pick him up!'

'No she won't. She's not going to *play* with them, is she?'

'I think she does sometimes.'

'Go on! She's an old lady. She might look a bit crackers, the way she drifts about, but she's not a total nutter. Put the doll down, Shirl.'

I was in such a state I didn't bother to correct him. I did as he suggested, putting the man doll back on the bed, carefully arranging his broken arm inside his sleeve.

'There, he looks as good as new. It doesn't show a bit,' said Kevin. 'Come on, let's get out of here.'

I shut up the doll's house and we hurried out of the room. I locked the door and returned the key to Mrs Waverley's jewellery box. Then we walked back along the corridor. Kevin reached out and squeezed my hand.

'There. No one will ever guess. It's all right,' he said, trying to be comforting.

THAT NIGHT I DREAMED about Dad. He came to visit me, looking smart in his uniform, but when he hugged me his arm suddenly slid out of his jacket and fell on the floor. I woke up sobbing, and then tossed and turned so restlessly I nearly capsized my camp bed.

When I got back to sleep I dreamed about Mum instead. She didn't seem to mind about poor Dad and his missing arm. She told me I was going to have a new dad now. Uncle Gerald was going to be a much better father, she insisted, and when the war was over we would live happily ever after in the Cotswolds, the three of us. I cried and said I was never going to the Cotswolds, especially not with Uncle Gerald, but Mum simply shrugged and said *she* was going, and I'd have to stay with Mrs Waverley for ever.

'You've made it plain that you'd prefer to stay with her anyway,' she said.

Then Mrs Waverley came into the dream and shook her head fiercely. 'She's not staying with me! I don't want that girl anywhere near me! Look what she's done to my husband!' she cried. She opened up the doll's house, and there, inside, was an enormous man doll taking up all the rooms, his head and torso and limbs pulled apart and spilling stuffing.

I ran to look for Jessica, rushing all the way down to the village, wondering if she might be waiting for me outside the sweetshop. I couldn't see her, but Goofy and Munchkin were there, and they started jeering and throwing sweets at me.

I woke up half smothered in my sleeping bag. It still seemed to be the middle of the night, but I couldn't go back to sleep. I wondered if Kevin was awake too, and wondered about pattering along the corridor to find out, but he might be dealing with a wet bed and I didn't want to embarrass him. Besides, we might wake Archie, and he couldn't be trusted to keep his voice down.

The rest of the night seemed endless. In the morning I was terrified of seeing Mrs Waverley. Chubby made me take a breakfast tray up to her. I couldn't stop my hands shaking so her cup of tea spilled onto the saucer. I felt sick when I passed the locked room. I stood for several minutes outside Mrs Waverley's bedroom before I could force myself to knock and go in.

I expected her to rise from her bed like an avenging angel, all set to cast me out of her house altogether for desecrating her beautiful doll's house, but she simply smiled sleepily at me.

'What a lovely surprise, Shirley,' she said, sitting up and stretching. 'Oh, and a boiled egg too. Bless those hens! I hope they laid enough for everyone.'

I mumbled something and made for the door.

'No, don't go!' She patted the side of her bed. 'Come and keep me company.'

I was forced to sit there as she chatted away as if we were great friends. She obviously hadn't looked at the doll's house when she came home last night. Maybe she'd look after she'd had her breakfast, or when she'd had her bath and got dressed – or perhaps she'd wait until this afternoon. Whenever it was, I was pretty sure she'd spot the poor broken gentleman doll immediately.

'Did you and Jessica have fun together yesterday afternoon?' she asked, smiling at me indulgently. 'It's marvellous that you've made a friend so quickly. When I was a little girl I didn't have the knack of making friends. I was always a bit of a misfit. I didn't know what to say to the village children and I didn't care for the girls my mother invited to tea. It was always such an ordeal. Perhaps we *should* ask Jessica to tea sometime. Would you like that, Shirley?'

'Well, yes, I would, ever so, but—'

'Then you may invite her next week. I'm sure Chubby will make one of her sponges – or perhaps little fairy cakes. I think we'd better give ourselves a few treats while we can. The newspapers are warning that food rationing will be introduced soon, and butter and sugar are bound to be on the list. We'll be fine for eggs, so long as our girls keep on laying. And Dr Marshall says several of the villagers have bought piglets to fatten up for pork and bacon if meat gets rationed. I'm not sure I could stomach rearing a pig – treating it like a pet and then killing it. Though I'm sure Chubby would be up to it.' Mrs Waverley raised her eyebrows at me in a conspiratorial manner. 'You mustn't mind Chubby, dear. She can be very direct at times, but there's no real malice in her. I don't know what I'd do without her now.' Her voice grew softer, almost as if she were talking to herself. 'Strange how things turn out. We've come through thick and thin together.'

I wriggled uncomfortably, wondering whether to tell her that Jessica hadn't turned up yesterday. Perhaps she'd wanted to come and meet me, and something had cropped up. Maybe she'd been kept in as a punishment.

Of course! It suddenly made sense. She had been rude or naughty in some way, and Sister Josephine had refused to let her go. That *must* be it. She still liked me – of *course* she did.

Last week, when I wasn't able to go down to the village myself, Jessica hadn't given up on *me*. On Sunday morning she'd walked all the way here to find me.

I'd do the same! I felt a surge of excitement. Yes, I'd find her! Mrs Waverley babbled on while I devised a plan of campaign, just like a soldier. I'd set off immediately, through the village to the church, where I'd lurk until I saw Sister Josephine and the girls. If Jessica was dawdling at the back of the line, I'd wave at her and she'd rush off to join me. If she *wasn't*, it meant she was still being punished. So then I'd go right up to the White House and break in somehow and jolly well find her.

Then we could run away together! I wasn't sure I wanted to go and live with this old nanny person. Perhaps we could find somewhere by ourselves. Jessica was rich and seemed very resourceful. Maybe we could rent a cottage . . .

I knew my ideas were galloping away with me – I was making things up like a storybook – but I couldn't help it. I was fizzing with excitement, and it was hard to keep still.

'So what are your plans for today, Shirley?' Mrs Waverley asked, nibbling her toast. 'Would you like to look at the doll's house with me?'

'No!' I blurted. I swallowed, knowing how it must have sounded. Mrs Waverley looked shocked and hurt. 'I mean, I'd love to, of course I would, but Kevin and Archie want me to play some silly boys' game with them, and if I don't they might come looking for me.'

'Oh, I see. Yes, of course. You're very sensible, Shirley. You'd better run off then.'

'I'm sorry, really sorry,' I said.

'Don't look so worried, dear. I understand. We'll wait till we're sure we can have a quiet moment together,' she said, and patted my hand.

I went downstairs feeling utterly dreadful. But I didn't have time to brood about it. I was on Mission Jessica.

I didn't go near the kitchen. I didn't want to talk to Kevin or Archie or Chubby. I struggled with the heavy bolt of the front door, twisting it slowly and carefully so it wouldn't make too much noise. Then I slipped outside, shut the door carefully behind me, and started running.

It was easy running downhill. I kept up the momentum all the way down to the gate, holding out my arms as if I were an aeroplane. I kept up a jog trot until I reached the village, speeding along in my clodhoppers. They might look dreadful but they made walking so much easier now that the new leather had softened.

I reached the school in fifteen minutes, though it took a full half-hour on weekdays. I heard the mocking laughter at my Fairy Godmother dance all over again, and spat at the school gate as I passed.

'You dirty little tyke,' said an old village lady. 'Don't they teach you better up London? I wish all you evacuees would beggar off home. We're sick of you here.'

'Well, *we're* sick of *you*,' I said, and ran past her.

'What kind of a mother must you have?' she called after me.

I burned then. How would Mum feel if she could see me now, spitting in the street and cheeking old ladies? She'd die of shame. But I wasn't her Shirley any more. I was a soldier and I was on a mission to find Jessica.

For a while I waited outside St John's church. Ladies in hats started arriving.

'Do you want to come in for the service, dear?' one of them asked. She smelled of Coty L'Aimant perfume and I suddenly wanted Mum badly.

'I'm waiting for the other girls,' I mumbled.

'Which girls, pet? The Sunday School service isn't until this afternoon,' she said.

'The girls in the purple uniform. The St Agatha's ones. They go in the morning, I'm sure they do,' I said.

'Oh, they're the convent children. They'll go to Our Lady Immaculate, the Roman Catholic church. That's down the lane at the end of the village,' she told me.

I thanked her and rushed off. There were more ladies in different hats bustling into Our Lady Immaculate. I wondered if the St Agatha's girls were inside already, but when I looked up the hill I saw a purple crocodile winding its way down, still so far away I couldn't make out who anyone was. I waited, hiding behind a tombstone. I picked away at the yellow lichen, muttering, 'Dear God, if you're here in the churchyard, please let me find Jessica.'

God seemed to be elsewhere. I scrutinized every girl in purple as she filed into church. I saw Goofy and Munchkin, older girls, girls my age, little girls . . . but none of them were Jessica. I saw Sister Josephine and three more nuns, all looking very busy and holy. There were several stout older ladies in shabby coats and funny hats, who were probably servants. And there was a very grand lady in a fur coat, though it was a warm, sunny day. I couldn't see her face properly because she wore a black hat with a veil, but it was clear that she was Lady Amersham herself.

Jessica must be back at the White House, all by herself. I had an hour, maybe an hour and a half, to dash up the other hill. I really did dash at first, but by the time I was a quarter of the way up I was gasping for breath and had to bend over to ease my stitch.

I didn't have enough puff to start running properly again, but I walked as fast as I could, muttering, *Jess-i-ca, Jess-i-ca, Jess-i-ca,* marching to the beat. The White House still seemed a long way away. I had another rest, sitting on a tree stump.

It was strange looking out over the village to the other hill and seeing the Red House there, as small as the doll's house in the locked room.

I narrowed my eyes to see if I could spot Kevin or Archie running around, but there was no sign of them. I started climbing again, running a few steps, then walking, on and on, and at last I came to the tall gates of Lady Amersham's house. They'd been left open for when the St Agatha's girls returned, so it was easy enough to slip inside.

The grounds were so different from Mrs Waverley's. It was like walking through a municipal park. The emerald-green grass looked as if it had been polished. I heard the distant rattle of a lawnmower, even though it was Sunday. That Worzel Gummidge gardener must work seven days a week.

There were flower beds in precise squares and circles and rectangles, with flowers making red and purple and white patterns. There was a large pond, but nothing like Mrs Waverley's exciting lake. This pond was edged with paving stones, and a pair of sedate ducks swam up and down. The water was so shallow, their webbed feet must nearly touch the bottom.

I decided that though this garden looked pretty, I preferred Mrs Waverley's. The house was much grander too, tall and very graceful, with white fluted pillars, and wide steps leading up to double doors with great brass handles. Those doors looked far too formidable to approach.

I went all the way around the house, ducking whenever I passed a window, though there didn't seem to be anyone about. It took several minutes' brisk walking to get round to the back, where there was another set of steps, much less grand.

I screwed up my courage and tiptoed up them. I tried the handle of the back door – and it turned. I opened the door slowly, holding my breath. There was a thick meaty smell of cooking and a damp basement whiff like old dishcloths. I wrinkled my nose and crept inside.

The kitchen door was open. It was hot and steamy and I heard someone clanking saucepans and swearing softly. I scurried past, treading as lightly as I could on the stone-flagged floor. I continued for a while, not daring to try any of the doors to the left and right of me. Then the passageway lightened and I came out into a huge hallway, brightly lit from large windows in the wall beside the great wooden staircase.

I peered up it, trembling, and then started creeping upwards, step after step, holding my breath at each creak of the old oak. I seemed to be climbing for ever. I kept imagining Lady Amersham coming down the stairs in a long gown, glittering with diamonds, though I'd seen her go into the church with my own eyes.

There were silk wall hangings upstairs, the tall ceiling was painted with garlands, and the crystal chandeliers were dazzling. Mrs Waverley's house was big and posh but it was nowhere near as grand as this one. A door upstairs was open a chink, so I peeped in. It was fully furnished with grand gilt furniture, and huge paintings hung on the walls. They were portraits of people in old-fashioned clothes, apart from one of a skinny girl in a tunic with a white face and untidy hair. I was staring at my own reflection in a mirror and backed away rapidly.

I wasn't going to find Jessica in these grand rooms. I wandered down the long corridor. Then a door suddenly opened and I came face to face with a small maid clutching armfuls of sheets. We both gasped.

'Oh my, miss, you gave me such a fright!' she said. 'Why aren't you at church with the others?'

'Oh, I – I was sent home in disgrace by Sister Josephine,' I gabbled quickly.

She tutted, looking at me suspiciously. 'Why aren't you in your uniform?'

'This *is* my uniform, my old one,' I said. 'I'm new here, so my mum – my mother – hasn't got me the proper uniform yet.'

'You're not like the other girls,' she said.

'I know. I'm a scholarship girl. I'm poor but I'm brainy,' I said.

She nodded. 'Oh well. Good for you. But you're in disgrace, eh? What did you do?'

'Oh, nothing much. Just mucking about. Anyway, Sister Josephine said I was to go and sit with Jessica. Do you know where she is?'

'What, the dark one with the plait?'

'Yes, that's her!'

'She's up at the end, in the box room. But I thought none of you other girls were allowed near her in case she infected you?'

Oh no, was Jessica ill? Did she have some dreadful contaminating disease? Well, I didn't care if she gave it to me. We were best friends.

'Sister Josephine *said*,' I insisted.

The maid shrugged, dropping several sheets. 'All right, all right,' she said, picking them up with difficulty. 'I'd better get this lot to the laundry room and then go and help Cook. It isn't half hard work looking after all you blooming girls. Why can't you wash your own sheets, eh?'

'I know, it's daft, isn't it?' I said soothingly, and walked along the corridor as if I knew exactly where I was going.

I heard her trailing off down a different set of stairs altogether, smaller and darker. It looked like there was one set for the posh folk and another for the servants. I was glad there was only one set of stairs at Mrs Waverley's. Chubby did all the housework and cooking but she was treated like an equal person. In fact, in many ways Chubby was boss there.

It was obvious that in *this* household Lady Amersham ruled the roost. Even the nuns probably had to hold out their habits and bob curtsies to her.

I tried the next room and saw lots of narrow iron beds in rows, but there was no sign of Jessica. I tried the next. It was locked, but the key was on the outside. I turned it and opened the door. It was a small box room with old chairs and suitcases and trunks piled up inside. There was a bed rammed against the wall – and Jessica was lying on it on her tummy, a book propped on her pillow.

'Jessica!'

She looked up, blinking hard behind her glasses, and then tumbled off her bed, squeezed round a washstand and ran to me.

'Shirley! Oh, how wonderful! I can't believe it!' She clasped me tightly and I gave her a huge hug back.

'I had to see you!' I said. 'I don't care if you're infectious! I'm not scared of germs.'

'What?' she said, and then she started snorting with laughter. 'I'm not *ill*, silly! I'm shut away here so I don't infect any of the other girls with my mind, not my germs!'

'Your *mind*?'

'Oh, Shirley, it's all so ridiculous. The other day I was dreadfully bored in lessons – the others are so slow and so ignorant, you can't imagine – so I started writing a story to amuse myself. It was in my own notebook and I'd completed the exercise donkey's years ago, so I had the perfect right to do so, didn't I? Well, I thought I did. But Sister Josephine – Adolf! – came frog-marching up and snatched my notebook, my own property, and confiscated it. And now she and all the other nuns say I'm a rotten influence on the other girls and they can't risk my being in their company, so I'm shut up in this room all day. They even bring my meals here – I have to eat them on a tray. I'm allowed out to go to the bathroom, but it's under supervision, would you believe. Sister Josephine takes me for a half-hour walk after tea, but I have to stay near her. She practically puts me on a lead like a little dog. And if I try to make a bolt for it she has that creepy gardener chap standing by, ready to catch me! You absolutely wouldn't believe it!'

'You poor thing! This is awful. How dare they treat you like this! Just for writing a story!' I said, quivering with outrage.

'Well, it wasn't any old story,' said Jessica, laughing again. 'What do you mean?'

'It was one of my more lurid efforts – all about Hollywood film stars and their affairs – about which I know a *lot*. It was a very sophisticated story, chock full of seductions. Sister Josephine practically had a heart attack when she read it. But it's her fault, isn't it? She shouldn't have read my private notebook. Now there's all this nonsense about my infecting the other girls with my disgusting thoughts when I wouldn't *dream* of sharing my story with any of them. I'd show you, of course, but I can't because the nuns still have it. Maybe they pass it around as bedtime reading.'

'But they can't keep you locked up like this! Can't you write to your mother? *I* could write to her if you like and say you're being treated abominably.'

'*They've* written to her. And she's outraged. She sent me the most beastly letter. She's such a flaming hypocrite. The story was mostly based on her and her horrible love life. She said she was ashamed to call me her daughter. I only wish I wasn't! I can't stand her. I don't care what she thinks of me,' said Jessica.

'Look, I've had the most marvellous idea!' I said, so excited I could hardly get the words out. 'We'll run away together, just like you wanted. We can go right this minute. I'm rescuing you! It'll be the best fun in the world, you and me together. We'll look after each other and play games, and we can scrump apples and beg bread and milk from farmhouses like tramps, and we'll sleep in haystacks . . .' My voice tailed away because Jessica was looking at me pityingly.

'Oh, Shirley, you're so sweet. But I don't need to run away. The nuns *want* me to go. I'm to be expelled. My mother's sending a chauffeur for me. He'll be arriving sometime this afternoon, and he's going to drive me all the way to Wales, to Nanny! Isn't it wonderful?'

I stared at her.

'Oh, please say you're happy for me! It's so bizarre, isn't it? This is meant to be the most terrible punishment, and yet it's what I wanted most in the world!' said Jessica.

'Well, I *am* happy for you, of course I am,' I said, struggling. 'But what about us?'

Jessica wriggled. 'I know, it's awful, isn't it, just as we've got to know each other! I'll miss you so much, Shirley.'

She didn't really look as if she thought it was awful. Her eyes were still shining, though she was pulling a pantomime face of woe.

'Wales is so far away,' I said.

'I know. Maybe I'll have to wear one of those funny black pointy hats and a red cloak! What larks!' Then she saw that I was near tears. 'Oh, Shirley, don't!'

'Can't I come too?' I begged her.

'But I'm going to Nanny's.'

'Yes, but you said we could both run away to your nanny's. You did, honest. Honest*ly*.'

'Did I? Well, that was sort of make-believe. That's what we do together, isn't it? Make things up.'

'It wasn't make-believe. You sounded as if you really meant it. Oh, Jessica, please mean it. Let me come and stay at your nanny's house. I'm so miserable here.' The tears were dripping down my cheeks now.

'I'd give anything for you to come, you know I would, but I don't think you *can*. Nanny lives in her sister's house. The sister has one bedroom and Nanny has the other, and I'm going to be squashing in with her. We might even have to share a bed at first. Actually I won't mind a bit – when I was little I was always getting up in the middle of the night and squeezing into Nanny's bed. But we can't possibly fit three in a bed.'

'I don't need a bed. I slept on the floor my first week here and it was all right,' I insisted stubbornly.

'Yes, but you see, Nanny and I are sort of family, and so the sister doesn't mind too much. But I don't think she'd like a stranger coming too. Besides, your mother probably wouldn't allow it,' said Jessica.

I cried harder. 'My mum wanted me to go to the Cotswolds and I didn't, and it was because I wouldn't leave you. I really upset her – but I didn't care, I put our friendship first. And now you don't care a jot about me – you're just eager to go rushing off to your nanny's and I'll be left and I'm in huge trouble at Mrs Waverley's and they're all laughing at me at school and my life's just totally unbearable!' I howled.

Jessica tried to put her arms round me but I fought her off.

'You're not a true friend,' I sobbed. 'Not a true best-ever friend, or you'd stay here because you want to be with me.'

'I *do* want to be with you, silly.'

'Stop calling me silly! I know I'm not as clever as you or anywhere near as rich or posh, but I still thought you liked me!' I cried.

'I *do* like you. I've never, ever found a friend like you. But I *can't* stay here. The nuns are chucking me out, I told you.'

'You could go to the village school with me. And come and live at Mrs Waverley's house. She likes you. She'd swap you for Kevin any day of the week. I could suggest it. She wants to get rid of him.' I felt bad as I said it, but I was just so desperate to keep Jessica.

'Shirley, it's all arranged. The chauffeur's coming. I'm to go to Nanny's. See, I'm all packed.' She pointed to the nearest suitcase and I saw her name on the label.

'And you were going without even saying goodbye to me?'

'I wanted and wanted to, but I was all locked up here, so how could I? I was going to write to you, of course I was. I so hoped you'd understand. I didn't mean to upset you so much. Do stop crying now. Let's make the most of the time we've got together,' said Jessica.

I did my best, but I'd given myself hiccups and I sat on the end of Jessica's bed making ugly noises, my fists clenched. She put her arm round me and patted me on the back as if I were a baby.

'Promise we're still best friends, even if we live so far apart?' I said.

'Yes, absolutely. And we'll write to each other heaps, of course we will.'

'Every week?'

'Every *day*. And look, I'll give you my favourite book as a special goodbye present.' Jessica leaped up, unsnapped her suitcase and took out *The Blue Fairy Book*. 'Here you are! I'll write in it too, to make it official.' She took a Parker fountain pen out of her blazer pocket and wrote *To my dearest friend Shirley, with all my love for ever from Jessica* on the inside page.

'Oh! How lovely! Then I must give you *Ballet Shoes.* I'll run all the way back to Mrs Waverley's and get it for you!' I said.

'Don't be a dope, there isn't anywhere near enough time,' said Jessica, consulting her wristwatch. 'They'll all be trooping back from church soon. It's OK, I've got a copy of *Ballet Shoes* at home somewhere.'

'But I must give you something! Oh, what have I got?' I put my hands in my tunic pockets but they were empty – apart from a sliver of silver paper left over from when I was making doll's-house cutlery. 'I know! I'll make you a ring!'

I fashioned it quickly, smoothing the silver paper and circling it round twice so that it wouldn't unravel. Then Jessica held out her hand and I slipped it on her ring finger.

'There! It's beautiful,' she breathed, as if it were sparkling with diamonds. 'I'll wear it always.'

We hugged again. I didn't think it was possible to feel so happy and so sad all at once. It was such a significant moment that it didn't seem appropriate to start playing a game or chat about ordinary things, so we just sat quietly together on the bed, hand in hand. I cried a little and I rather hoped Jessica would cry too. She looked very solemn, but her eyes stayed dry.

After a while I saw her looking at her watch. 'Is it time for me to go?' I asked.

'Oh dear, I think you really had better make a move,' she said. 'It would be awful if they caught you here with me.'

'If only Sister Josephine had let me come with you when we arrived at Meadow Ridge. Then I'd have written your story with you – though I don't know much about seductions and stuff, but you could write that bit. And then we'd both be being expelled and we could stay together,' I said miserably.

'No, because I'd still be sent to Nanny's and you'd be sent to your mother's,' said Jessica. I knew she was simply being logical, but it sounded a little hard-hearted.

'You will miss me, won't you?' I asked.

'Of course! I *said*, I'll write heaps, and I'll come back and visit sometime, you just wait and see,' she assured me.

'How will you visit if you're far away in Wales?'

'I'll find a way. Even if I have to go on the train by myself. I promise.' She licked her finger. *'See my finger wet, see my finger dry, cut my throat if I tell a lie.* There, that's the most solemn promise ever.'

We had one more hug, and then I had to go, clutching the precious fairy book to my chest. It was awful locking the door on her again. I scooted back down the corridor to the stairs, and then rushed down them so quickly I very nearly tripped, but I managed to save myself by clutching onto the banisters.

I didn't want to risk the front door in case the purple crocodile was coming, so I crept down the passage towards the back. The meaty smell was stronger now, and the air outside the open kitchen door was steamy. I heard the cook chuntering away inside, giving someone a ticking-off – maybe the poor maid. I didn't dare peep round to see.

I eased open the back-door latch and then was off like a shot. I didn't run directly down the driveway for fear of bumping into the returning churchgoers. I veered right, ploughing through the grass, going down a hooped alleyway festooned with climbing roses, though most of them were drooping now. The gardener was there, halfway up a ladder, snipping at the withered rose heads with sharp pruning shears.

He narrowed his eyes when he spotted me. They were vividly blue in his brown, wrinkled face. 'You!' he said, holding his shears aloft.

I tried to run back up the rose alley, but he leaped nimbly off his ladder and caught me. He hung onto my arm, the shears in his other hand horribly near my face. I hated his strong smell of earth and leaves and sweat.

'Let me go, you brute!' I said, struggling.

He laughed in my face, spraying me with spit. He had several missing teeth, which made him look feral. 'Oh, Miss Hoity-Toity. What you doing here, eh? *Eh?*' He actually shook me.

'Stop it! I'll tell Sister Josephine. I'm a pupil here,' I bluffed.

'No you're not. You ain't got that purple uniform. And you're not grand enough. You're a mucky little kid from the East End, up to no good. You've just nicked that book, haven't you?'

'No, I haven't! It's a gift. Look, I can prove it.' I opened the book and showed him my precious message.

He laughed scornfully, not even looking. I wondered if he could actually read. 'Can't fool me,' he said. 'I remember you. Trying to tag along, you was, with the young ladies and them nuns. So where did they billet you, eh? You been put in that special hostel with all the bad kids and the dopey ones?'

'No! I'm actually living with Mrs Waverley, if you must know. And she'll be very angry when she hears how rude you've been to me,' I said, hoping to quell him.

But he laughed even harder. 'Her? That poor mad cow?'

'Don't you dare call her that. She's a real lady. She just happens to be Lady Amersham's *sister*,' I said triumphantly. 'There!'

'Everyone knows that,' he said. 'I knows Mad Maddy. She was living here when I came to work in the gardens as a boy. There was a big team of us then. Including Will Waverley.' He nodded meaningfully.

I was startled. 'Mrs Waverley's husband William? You mean, he lived here too?' I asked, nodding my head at the White House behind us.

'Not in the big house, you little fool. He had a bunk in the sheds with the rest of us lads. He was one of us *then*. One of the village boys. Year or so older than me, and he didn't half lord it over me too. Oh, he thought he was the bee's knees, that Will. Everyone else thought the world of him too. Charm the birds from the trees, he could. Charmed *her* all right.'

'Her?'

'Miss Maddy. She fell for him hook, line and sinker. Along with half the village girls. But *they* didn't have anything to lose. *She* did, all right. It caused such a scandal! A posh young lady from the White House cavorting with a common gardener! They reckoned he was only after her money – and they were probably right. But she lost her inheritance when she went gadding off with Will. Silly cow.' He turned his head and spat. It sizzled on the ground, a horrible little spot of phlegm.

'Stop it! I don't believe a word of it. You're making it all up,' I said.

'Am I?' he said. 'You ask her then. She thought it was the love match of the century. Oh, he followed through and married her, but he'd never have stayed. He wasn't that sort. I doubt he'd ever have come back after the war, but he copped it anyway. So now she wanders around like a wet weekend, pining after her Will, when she didn't have a clue that he was always carrying on behind her back.' He chuckled and made his tongue flicker.

'You're horrible and vile and I won't listen a moment longer!' I shouted, and I wrenched myself away from him and started running.

I thought he'd come after me, shears in hand, but when I eventually turned round I saw that he was standing by his ladder, laughing. I hated the way he'd talked about Mrs Waverley. I didn't want to believe any of it. Her enduring love for Mr Waverley was pure and wonderful and tragic. But somehow the gardener's words seemed dreadfully convincing.

'**WHERE HAVE YOU BEEN** then?' Chubby asked when I came in the back door. 'I'm about ready to dish up my roast!'

'It's not rabbit, is it?' I asked anxiously.

'No, it's pork, but that blooming butcher is getting stingier than ever, starting up his own form of rationing *and* putting up his prices. It's plain foolishness forking out a fortune when we can have a nice tasty rabbit for free,' Chubby snapped. 'You're going to have to get over your fussiness, missy. You're living in the country now. We can't have any truck with faddy ways, not when we're poor as church mice.'

'Mrs Waverley's rich,' said Kevin. 'She lives in this great big house with all these gardens.'

'Oh, so you've had a look at her bank account, have you, Mr Clever?' Chubby sniffed, opening up the oven to check the meat. Her hair was damp with steam from the boiling vegetables on the hob. She was so irritated it wouldn't have surprised me if steam had risen straight from her bobbed head.

'You can tell she's rich,' Kevin persisted unwisely. 'She talks posh.'

'That don't signify. Mrs Mad's a lady and of course she's posh, but she lives on a pittance. You've no idea how generous she was being, kitting you out in all those new clothes, you kids. And giving you board and lodging. Turns out we're supposed to be paid, but I ain't seen a penny piece from any of your families.' Chubby prodded the whirling carrots with a fork. It looked as if she'd like to prod us into the bargain.

'My dad would fork out, but he don't even know where I am,' said Kevin sulkily.

'My dad would pay too, but he's in the army,' I said.

'I ain't got a dad but I bet he'd pay if I had,' said Archie.

'Oh, bless the little lamb,' said Chubby, leaving the range to give him a hug and a quick kiss on his fluffy head. He looked quite a different little boy, especially now that his cheeks were pinker and he'd lost the dark circles under his eyes.

'Right, the veggies are all done. Run and tell Mrs Mad I'm dishing up, Shirley,' said Chubby.

I went into her sitting room but she wasn't there. I trailed back to the kitchen. The savoury smell turned my stomach. 'I can't find her,' I mumbled.

'What?' Chubby was fidgeting the meat onto a serving plate, trying not to splash the fat.

'I said, I can't find her. She isn't in the sitting room,' I said.

'Well, look upstairs, gormless. In her bedroom,' Chubby commanded.

'I don't like to disturb her. She might be having a nap,' I said.

'Don't talk so daft – she won't be taking a nap *before* her dinner. Now go and fetch her down. Pronto! Or else!' Chubby took her big metal spoon and thumped it on her palm, indicating what she'd do to me if I didn't do as I was told.

So I walked up the stairs very slowly, feeling sicker than ever. *It will be all right, it will be all right, it will be all right*, I gabbled inside my head.

I paused outside the doll's-house room. The door wasn't locked. It was slightly ajar. My heart thumped. I stood there, holding my breath. I was conscious of very small sounds inside the room. I took one step forward and craned my neck. I could just see Mrs Waverley in profile. The skin was stretched tight across her cheeks, her eyes screwed up tightly as if she was in terrible pain.

I backed away as silently as I could but my shoe squeaked on the floorboards. Mrs Waverley looked up and saw me. She came to the door with something clasped in her hand.

'Shirley!' she said, sounding so disappointed I wanted to die. 'Shirley, why did you do it?'

I shook my head helplessly, not knowing what to say.

'Why didn't you tell me? It was so cowardly of you to hide him away. Did you seriously think I wouldn't notice?' Mrs Waverley held out her hand. The little gentleman doll lay helplessly on his back. She'd taken his tiny white shirt off. His arm was wrenched right off, the pink-silk skin fraying, the empty socket of his arm an ugly black hole.

'Can't you . . . Can't you sew it back on?' I whispered.

'But it won't work properly, even if I do. His arms were specially jointed so that they moved smoothly. Now it will just hang down, even if I can make the stitches hold,' she said.

'I'll save up all my pocket money to get you another one,' I said frantically.

'I can't get another one. These dolls come from a toymaker in Germany. How can I order one now we're at war? This one was perfect, an exact replica. And now he's spoiled.'

'I'm so sorry,' I said, starting to cry.

'I'm sorry too, Shirley. Sorry that you should be so careless when you knew how much these little dolls and their house meant to me. I thought I could trust you. I thought you were special. But you're just a clumsy, deceitful child like any other,' she said.

'No she's not!' It was Kevin, coming along the corridor towards us. 'It's not her fault. It was me.'

'What?' Mrs Waverley wheeled round. '*You?*'

'Shut up, Kev,' I said.

'You let *Kevin* into my doll's-house room?' she asked incredulously.

'She didn't mean to. I followed her. And I don't know why you're making such a huge great fuss. It's just a little doll. You're nuts, you are. Totally loopy,' said Kevin.

'How dare you!' Mrs Waverley's face went an ugly deep red. 'I've had enough of you, with your rough manners and crude ways. I've even put up with your enuresis, but I can't stand your hateful clumsiness. Or maybe you twisted the arm off deliberately, in a fit of malice. I wouldn't put it past a boy like you. Well, you can't stay here any longer. I won't have you under my roof. I'm going to pack you off to that hostel!'

Kevin stared at her and then darted back down the stairs. He ran to the front door, got the latch open and then was off, banging the door so hard that the sound echoed all around the great hallway. We went along to the landing and looked down.

'Well, good riddance,' said Mrs Waverley, but she put her hand over her mouth, sounding uncertain.

'He didn't pull the arm off your doll,' I said.

'Well, I know it was probably an accident,' she said. 'I didn't mean that. I was just saying that because I'm so cross. I lost my temper.'

'*I* did it. I didn't mean to, I promise it was an accident, but *I* did it. I was too scared to tell you because I knew you'd be terribly upset. And you are,' I said.

'Oh dear,' said Mrs Waverley. 'Oh God, what a mess.' She suddenly crumpled, sitting down on the top stair, holding the little doll to her chest.

'Whatever's going on?' Chubby called, hurrying along from the kitchen, Archie hanging on her skirt. 'Who was that slamming out the door? And whatever's up with you, Mrs Mad?'

'It's Kevin. Mrs Waverley said he was hateful,' I said, and I shivered at the memory of his shocked white face.

'I didn't – I said his hateful clumsiness,' said Mrs Waverley wretchedly. 'I thought he was the one who broke . . .' She held out the little man doll, and his torn-off arm fell to the floor.

'Oh Gawd,' said Chubby, and she came panting up the stairs and put her arm round Mrs Waverley. 'There now. Don't take on so.'

'Why's she crying?' Archie asked, coming upstairs too. He picked up the doll's arm. 'Oh, what's this?' He peered at Mrs Waverley's hand. 'It's come off your dolly! Why are you playing with dollies when you're a great big lady?'

'It's special to her,' I said. 'And I broke him, though I didn't mean to.'

'You blooming kids,' said Chubby. 'What did you have to come here for? We was managing fine. Mrs Mad hardly ever had one of her turns. Now look what's happened. And I've just dished up my lovely piece of pork too.'

'It's not their fault, it's mine,' Mrs Waverley wept. 'Kevin's right. I'm nuts, I'm loopy.'

'Dear goodness, he said that? The cheeky little whatsit! Wait till he comes back! I won't half give him what for,' said Chubby.

'He was just sticking up for me,' I said. 'And *she* said she was sending him off to that awful hostel.'

'It's the best place for him. Why should we have to cope with him? That pad-and-bell palaver is a waste of time. It's still wet bed, wet bed, wet bed every blooming morning, and I'm the poor mug has to wash his sleeping bag,' Chubby complained. 'And does he even say thank you? No, he doesn't!'

'It's because he's embarrassed,' I said. 'He doesn't *want* to wet the bed. It's awful for him. Imagine how you'd feel.'

'If any of us kids wet the bed when we was little, our mam would tan our backsides. That learned us!' said Chubby. 'Kids have it too soft nowadays.' She said it fiercely, but when Archie nestled close she gave him a cuddle.

'Am I going to this hostel too?' he whispered.

'No, you're not, my lamb. You're staying with your old Chubby,' she said, playing with his fluffy hair. 'Now come on, everyone, don't let's waste my pork. Downstairs, lickety-split,' she said.

'I think I need to go and have a lie-down,' Mrs Waverley muttered. She took the tiny broken arm from Archie and stumbled off towards her bedroom.

'Perhaps you can take a tray up to her later, Shirley,' said Chubby. 'You two come down and have your dinner anyway. And I daresay old Wet-the-Bed will be back soon wanting some too.'

'Don't call him that!' I said, appalled.

'You kids should learn to toughen up. The things I've been called in my time! But that old rhyme's right: *Sticks and stones may break my bones but words will never hurt me.*'

Words could hurt horribly, but it was a waste of time arguing. I could hardly eat any of my dinner. Archie just nibbled the crispy bits, eating them like biscuits. Even Chubby left half her plateful. We kept listening out for Kevin but he didn't come back.

Chubby sent me upstairs with a tray for Mrs Waverley, though I protested she wouldn't want me anywhere near her now. The door to the doll's-house room was still ajar but her bedroom door was shut. I knocked on it several times. She didn't answer, but eventually I went in anyway. She was lying on top of her bed, fully dressed, still clutching the doll.

I wasn't sure if she was awake. 'Mrs Waverley?' I whispered.

She didn't answer, but I saw her arm moving, her fingers curling tight around the doll.

389

'Mrs Waverley, I'm sorry to disturb you, but Chubby sent me. I've got your dinner here on a tray,' I said.

Mrs Waverley groaned.

'Shall I put it on your dressing table?' I said. I pushed her silver brush-and-comb set to one side and edged the tray into place. 'Perhaps you should try to eat it before it gets cold?' I suggested.

'Leave me alone,' she murmured, her head buried in the pillow.

So I crept away again. I went to my room and lay on my own bed, reading *The Blue Fairy Book*. I read until my eyes started blurring, and three bears blundered around my room and a wolf lurked in my bed and a wicked witch filled my mouth with toads.

I heard the clock downstairs chiming and ran down to see if Kevin had come back. Chubby and Archie were in the kitchen. She was teaching him how to write his name on a paper bag. He was concentrating so fiercely, his tongue sticking out of the corner of his mouth.

'Look, Shirley, I'm such a big boy I can write!' he announced proudly.

His letters were all over the place but he'd managed it, just about.

'Isn't he a clever boy, Shirley?' Chubby said proudly.

I nodded. 'Has Kevin come back yet?'

'Nope. Still skulking somewhere. Dratted lad.'

'I hope he's all right,' I said anxiously. 'He's very upset.'

'He'll turn up like a bad penny when it's teatime. He didn't have any dinner, don't forget,' said Chubby. 'And that boy's a walking stomach. Beats me how he stays so skinny.'

'Can't you stop him being sent away?' I asked. 'Look, *I'll* wash his sleeping bag if you like.'

'Don't be daft, girl. Look at your soft little white hands. You'd be useless at it,' said Chubby. 'Why do you care about Kevin? He's a waste of space.'

I tried to find the right answer. Kevin was so silly at times, and he looked silly too, with his gangly limbs and his goofy smile and his jug ears and his bitten nails. Perhaps I simply cared about him because no one else did.

'You don't think he's run away, do you?' I asked.

'Where would he run to?' said Chubby. 'He'll be back any minute now. Ah, talk of the devil!'

We heard footsteps coming along the passageway, but it was Mrs Waverley, not Kevin. She'd tied her hair back in a knot and put a slash of lipstick on her lips, but she still looked dreadful, her eyes swollen, her nose red.

'Did you eat your dinner?' Chubby asked.

She shook her head.

'What a waste,' said Chubby, but her voice was gentle. 'I'll pop the kettle on and we'll all have a flapjack. Archie helped me make them, didn't you, poppet?'

'I did, I did! I can cook *and* I can write now. I'm ever so clever,' said Archie. 'Aren't I, Chubby?'

'Yes, you are, my pet,' she said.

'Kevin ran off and he's not back yet,' I blurted out.

Mrs Waverley looked at me for the first time since she'd come into the kitchen. 'He often wanders off, doesn't he?' she said.

'But he was so upset.'

Chubby sighed. 'I'll go and have a look round the grounds after we've had a cuppa.'

She made the tea and poured us some milk and passed round the tin of flapjacks. I was too tense to be hungry, but I nibbled one end so that I could tell Archie it was delicious. He ate two flapjacks with relish and reached for a third.

'Hey, hey, Mr Greedy-Guts,' said Chubby.

'It's not for me, it's for Kevin,' said Archie. 'Why hasn't he come back yet?'

Chubby sighed again. 'I'll go and look for him. I bet he's lurking in one of the outbuildings. It's a bit nippy today. Won't be a tick.'

She was gone for a long time. When she came back she looked concerned.

'Did you see him anywhere?' I asked.

'No, he's obviously playing silly beggars, trying to worry us,' she said. 'Have another flapjack, kids – might as well eat them while they're fresh.'

She stood near Mrs Waverley, bending to whisper in her ear. I listened hard. I heard one word.

'What did you say? *Gun?*'

'Mind your own business, Miss Waggle-Ears,' Chubby snapped.

Mrs Waverley looked distraught.

'Chubby's gun?' I asked.

'My old shotgun – the one I keep for rabbits. I hide it in the chicken shed. And now I can't find the dratted thing.'

'Kevin?' Mrs Waverley whispered.

'He wouldn't have taken it. He wouldn't know where I hide it,' said Chubby quickly.

'He would. He's always in the chicken shed. He likes the chickens,' I told her.

'Oh Lord,' Mrs Waverley said. 'Perhaps I should call Constable James?'

'Now don't be silly. We're all jumping to daft conclusions. I've probably just mislaid the damn thing somewhere. And even if Kevin's got it, he's not going to do any harm. He's a poor silly sap, but he's not vicious. It's not like he's going to try to kill anyone,' said Chubby.

'But he might try to kill himself,' said Mrs Waverley, turning to leave the kitchen. 'I think I'd better make that phone call.'

'Kevin's got a gun!' Archie said, his eyes wide. He turned his hand into a fist, with his first two fingers pointed like a gun barrel. '*Bang! Bang! Bang!*'

I suddenly remembered Kevin and Archie playing cowboys up a tree.

Chubby went off to see if Mrs Waverley was phoning the policeman.

'You stay here,' I said fiercely to Archie. 'I'm going to find him.'

I went out of the back door, skirted the henhouse and started running. I left the path and ran down as far as the lake, and then tried to remember where the cowboy tree was. I was surrounded by hundreds of trees. Kevin could be hiding in any of them.

'Kevin? It's me, Shirley! Where are you?' I called. My voice sounded eerie in the silence. I wished I hadn't been reading the fairy-story book. Harm always came to children who wandered into woods. They always strayed from the path and got lost and couldn't find their way home. They were waylaid by wolves and eaten alive or trapped by witches and bundled into cages to be baked in a pie.

'Kevin?' My voice was just a whisper now.

'Shirley?'

I nearly jumped out of my skin. I looked up and saw him crouching precariously high up in the branches. He was holding the gun, pointing it at me.

'Don't shoot me!' I cried.

'I'm not going to shoot *you*, you banana!' said Kevin.

'So what are you doing, holding it like that? Stop it, you're scaring me!'

'That's the whole point. I've got it for protection, so they can't send me away to that hostel. They won't dare now,' said Kevin. 'They're just two old women anyway.'

'But it won't just be Chubby and Mrs Waverley. They're calling the police because they're so worried,' I said. 'Oh, do come down, Kevin.'

'Not flipping likely!' he said. 'I'm not going and that's that. Over my dead body!'

'Yes, well, that's what they're scared of. They think you're going to kill yourself,' I said.

'What?'

'I know, it's daft, but they're frightened. If you come down I'm sure they won't be cross with you, they'll just be relieved. Kevin, please climb down. It's hurting my neck craning up at you.'

'Not going to.'

'Then I'll bloody well have to come up!' I felt very bold and daring saying such a rude word. It gave me courage to start climbing. It was easy at first because the branches were evenly spaced. It was practically like climbing a stepladder. But then the branches grew spindly and wobbled when I clung onto them.

I wasn't sure I could get all the way up to Kevin now. Perhaps I'd better get down. I peered through the leafy branches, then leaned my head against the scratchy bark, clinging on for dear life.

'Shirl?' Kevin called.

'Shir*ley*,' I muttered.

'Come on up then,' he said.

'I can't. I'm stuck, you fool,' I hissed.

'What? Come on, it's easy-peasy.' He leaned right down so that he could nearly touch me. 'Just grab my hand and I'll pull you up.'

'No! We'll both fall if you start monkeying around,' I said, closing my eyes because everything had started whirling about me.

'Yeah, I'm a monkey – *jabber-jabber-jabber*,' said Kevin, and then swung himself down so that he was clinging beside me. The hard gun nudged my back.

'Careful! Watch that gun! You'll shoot me!' I cried.

'No I won't. You have to take aim and pull the trigger. As if I'd ever shoot you. We're mates.'

'Yes, but you know how clumsy you are!'

His face fell.

'Sorry. I didn't mean to be horrid, but you *are*.'

'That mean cow went on about my hateful clumsiness. And all that other stuff,' said Kevin.

'I know. She was horrible. She didn't mean it though. She cried after you ran off. She was just upset because her little doll got broken. But I told her it was my fault, honest. Honestly.'

'Why was she going on about it so?'

'It's her fantasy thing. He's like her little husband. In the doll's house the pair of them live the life that she longed for, only Mr Waverley got killed in the war – not this one, the last one. Do you see?'

'Clear as mud,' said Kevin. 'It still sounds pretty loopy, if you ask me. And she still hates me, doesn't she?'

'No, she doesn't, not really. She feels terrible now. I've never seen anyone look so worried,' I said.

'She'll still send me to that hostel place though, won't she?'

'Probably,' I said reluctantly.

'Well, she'll have to catch me first,' said Kevin, aiming the shotgun.

'Are you going to shoot her?'

'Well, I'm not going to kill her dead. I just want to hurt her a bit.' He started muttering, 'Bang! Ouch! Bang again. Ouch again!'

'It won't be like a silly cowboy film. She won't just lie down and then whisper that she forgives you. It'll be all bloody and she'll be in agony, even if you just shoot her in the arm or leg, and she'll have to be carted off to hospital, and my mum says they're full of germs and you can get gangrene and die, so you'll have killed her even though you didn't really mean to,' I said.

'That's rubbish,' said Kevin, but he didn't sound certain. 'Anyway, she deserves to be shot. She's been hateful to me. And nasty to you too.'

'But that's not a reason to *shoot* anyone. I won't let you!'

'Why are you sticking up for her anyway? You're meant to be on *my* side.'

'I am. Mostly. But I still quite like her. And I suppose I like you too, so that's why I don't want you to shoot her – because the policeman will come and arrest you, and if you've murdered her or even just wounded her a bit they'll put you in prison, and I bet it'll be worse than any boys' hostel. You know, with the bullying and that. Kevin, please let's both climb down. I'm starting to feel ever so dizzy.'

'It's OK, I've got you.' He wrapped a long spidery arm around me.

'Thanks, but I still don't feel safe. And we've got to get away. I worked out where to find you so maybe Archie will as well – he played the cowboy game too.'

I felt Kevin tense. 'No, he's too little. He's just a baby.'

'Yes, but he's not daft. He's as sharp as us. He'll remember.'

'But he won't tell. He's my little mate,' said Kevin.

'Chubby's his big mate. You know how he adores her. She'll winkle it out of him.'

'Well, all right, but it's OK, we'll just run off to another tree. There are thousands of flipping trees. We'll be able to hide for weeks,' said Kevin.

'No we *won't*. We've got to eat for a start. You didn't have your Sunday dinner so you must be starving already. And they'll search and search for us. The police will.' I'd once skip-read a copy of *Uncle Tom's Cabin* from the library, though I'd found it horribly upsetting. 'They'll bring tracker dogs. Bloodhounds. They'll sniff you out and attack you.' I wasn't sure if English police did this, but Kevin wasn't to know.

He took his hand away and started biting his nails. 'No they won't,' he said indistinctly.

'Yes they will. And they'll track me down too and bite me, because I'm your accomplice.'

'I won't let them!' said Kevin, but I could feel him shaking. 'So what are we going to *do*?'

The answer was suddenly obvious. 'We'll run away!' I said triumphantly.

'We've run away already.'

'No, I mean *really* run away. To London. Back home. I'll go back to my mum, though I'll have to try and stop her sending me to this Cotswolds place. And you can go back to your dad. You said how much he'd be missing you. He'll be thrilled to see you,' I said.

Kevin didn't look very sure.

'Oh, come on, Kevin, it'll be such an adventure!' I said. I'd show Jessica. I could run away without her.

Kevin perked up when I said the word *adventure*. 'OK then! Yeah, let's do it!'

'Now!'

'Now!' said Kevin.

'But you'll have to help me get down first,' I said.

'It's simple – just go down instead of up,' said Kevin. 'Go on!'

I'd got so scared of falling, my arms and legs had gone rigid. He had to prise them away from the tree trunk and then pull at them. I got to the ground somehow, and then my legs gave way altogether and I had to sit down for a moment.

Kevin jumped down beside me. 'Come on then! Before those dogs get us!' he said, brandishing the shotgun.

'Put that down! Look, you can't take it with us.'

'It's our protection! I can't leave it here.'

'But the moment someone sees two children with a blooming great gun they're going to guess we're runaways,' I said.

'I'll disguise it then.' Kevin took off his jacket and wrapped it around the gun. 'There!'

'Now you'll be cold,' I said. 'Please leave the gun here – it frightens me.'

'That's what it's for, to frighten people,' said Kevin.

I saw that the gun was not negotiable. I was already starting to go off the running-away idea. I wished we'd had time to plan things and prepare. What about all our possessions? I thought of my books. How could I leave *Ballet Shoes* behind, and my wonderful new *Blue Fairy Book* gift from Jessica? I wondered if I could possibly run back to the house and retrieve them without Mrs Waverley or Chubby seeing me. I didn't even have my gas mask on me. I needed my clothes too, and Timmy Ted, and I couldn't leave Dad's real-leather sample case behind – and if I was taking that, perhaps I could squeeze in all my other books too? And stuff in a change of clothes for Kevin, and his own gas mask, while I was at it. Then all I had to do was creep out again without them seeing me . . .

'You hang on here a minute while I nip back and fetch—' I started, but then I broke off.

'Kevin! Kevin, come here! I'm going to give you such a hiding when I find you!' Chubby called. She sounded far away but coming nearer. There was no time to fetch anything.

'Quick!' I said.

We started running. Kevin had much longer legs, but when he saw I was falling behind he grabbed my hand and pulled me along so fast my shoes barely skimmed the ground. It seemed as if we'd be flying any second.

We were still at full speed when we got to the gates, and had to brace ourselves to stop slamming straight into them. Kevin struggled to get them open, and then we were out, and rushing towards the village. I had a terrible stitch in my side now, and Kevin was wheezing horribly, but we didn't dare slow down in case Chubby caught up.

'Children! Children!' It was bossy Mrs Henshaw, the lady who'd taken charge of us when we arrived at Meadow Ridge.

'Run!' Kevin hissed, but she was already crossing the road, almost upon us.

'Hello, dears! Are you settling in all right? I'm making it my mission to check that all you evacuees are happy. You're the ones with Mrs Waverley and Miss Chubb, aren't you? Wasn't there another little one too?'

'That's Archie, but he's back at the house with Chubby. We're running a special errand for Mrs Waverley,' I said hurriedly.

'Really? And what's that?' Mrs Henshaw asked.

'Ah. Well. It's a private matter,' I said.

'And we're supposed to be quick about it, so you'd better let us go now,' said Kevin. He shifted his jacket from one hand to the other. The rifle was making it stick up at an odd angle. I suddenly felt terrified. He wasn't planning to gun down Mrs Henshaw, was he?

'You funny children! You're playing a game, aren't you?' she said. 'All right, run along now. Bye-bye!' She waggled her fingers at us.

I waved back politely. Then we hurried on, not quite running, but walking as quickly as possible.

'There, I frightened her off, didn't I?' said Kevin proudly.

'Sort of,' I said. 'But you were acting pretty weirdly.' I turned round. Mrs Henshaw was staring after us, her head on one side. 'She's still looking at us.'

'Nosy old bag,' said Kevin.

'Come on then, hurry.' My heart started thumping again. 'Where exactly are we going?'

'London, dopey.'

'Yes, but how?'

'We'll get a train.'

'We haven't any money.'

'It's easy enough to get on a blooming train. We can hide in the toilet if the ticket man comes,' said Kevin.

I thought about spending half the journey crammed into a smelly double-you-see with Kevin and felt depressed, but I couldn't come up with a better alternative. We walked smartly to the railway station. It had been only a couple of weeks since we arrived here, and yet it seemed more like years. It was hard remembering that London and all my old life was still going on at the end of that railway line.

Maybe it had already changed because of the war. I tried to imagine armies marching through the streets, sirens screaming through the nights, bombs raining down. No – Mrs Waverley listened to her wireless every day and assured us that there hadn't been any bombs yet. I hoped she was right.

We walked along the lane where the cows were.

'Remember how scared Archie was of them?' I said to Kevin.

'Funny little beggar. Still, I don't like leaving him behind. Wish we could have taken him with us,' he said.

'He loves being with Chubby.'

'Yes, I know, but he loves being with me too. He's a loyal little kid.' Kevin paused. 'He knew it wasn't him. You know, wetting the bed. But he never told on me.' His voice went all high and funny, as if he were going to cry.

'Come on, don't go all soft on me,' I said.

'Well, it's got so he's like my little brother,' said Kevin.

'Jessica's like my sister, my closest, best friend, but I'm not making a fuss about leaving her.' I wanted Kevin to see that I was making a wonderful sacrifice running away with him.

But it didn't look as if we *could* run away after all. When we reached the station the platforms were empty. The waiting room was empty too, and the ticket office. We eventually found the stationmaster in his garden next door, cutting Michaelmas daisies.

'Excuse me, but could you tell us when the next train to London leaves?' I asked.

'There isn't another one today,' he said. 'Here, would you like a flower in your hair?' He snipped a little purple daisy and stuck it into my slide. 'Pretty! How about you, young man? Fancy a flowery buttonhole?'

'No, ta,' said Kevin. 'What do you mean, there isn't a train?'

'Last one went half an hour ago, laddie.'

'But it's only five o'clock!' I said.

'Reduced service, see. Special war timetable. Only three a day at weekends.'

'So when's the next one?'

'Eight o'clock tomorrow. *If* it's running. There's so many cancellations now it's hard to keep track of them. It's not my fault, yet I'm the one who gets all the abuse. Now run along, kids. Come back tomorrow and try again.' He carried on snipping.

Kevin and I wandered off disconsolately.

'So what do we do now?' I said. 'Where are we going to go till eight o'clock tomorrow? The police will find us if we hole up in a shop doorway or somewhere. They'll probably be staking out the station by then anyway. We're done for.'

'No we're not,' said Kevin. 'I know what we'll do. We'll hitch.'

'What's hitching?'

'You'll see.'

WE STOOD TOGETHER BESIDE the crossroads a mile or so away from Meadow Ridge. We weren't entirely sure which road led to London as someone had taken down the signpost, but we knew it must be one of them. Every time a car or a lorry passed by we had to put our thumbs in the air. Most didn't even slow down. One car stopped and a lady wound down her window, but it was just to tell us off.

'Go home to your mothers, you silly children! Hitch-hiking is very dangerous!' she said.

'So couldn't you give us a lift, missus?' Kevin asked.

'No I jolly well couldn't. I'm not going to encourage you. Now go home at once,' she said.

We pretended to do as we were told, wandering back down the road towards the village. She watched us for a while, but then drove off.

'Mean thing,' said Kevin. 'I bet she was going to London.'

'Why do you think she said hitch-hiking was dangerous?' I asked. 'Because we might get run over?'

'I don't know,' said Kevin. He clutched his stomach. 'I'm starving. I wish we had something to eat. I didn't have my dinner, remember.'

'I didn't eat much of mine. Kevin, do you think this is really going to work? No one's stopping for us.'

'Maybe they think we're German spies or something.' He started goose-stepping up and down the scrubby grass, a finger sideways under his nose, playing at being Hitler.

'Don't act daft like that or they *certainly* won't stop.'

'I'm just trying to warm up a bit. And I'm dying for a wee. I'm going to have to go.' Kevin looked around desperately. 'I'll go behind that hedge over there. No peeping now!'

'You think I *want* to peep?' I said.

I stood at the side of the road by myself while he ran off. I didn't even have my thumb up, but bizarrely a lorry slowed right down and then stopped a little beyond me. I stood still, watching.

The driver stuck his head out of the window. 'Come on then, girly,' he called.

I blinked. 'Are you talking to me?'

'Of course I am, silly. You want a lift, don't you?'

'Well, yes, but—'

'Where is it you're going then? Making for London, are you?'

'Yes, I am!'

'Then let your Uncle Mick be your personal chauffeur, dear. Up you hop, into my cabin.'

He seemed friendly enough. He was rather red in the face and he had greasy hair, but he couldn't really help that. I walked up to the front of the lorry. He was a long way up, but he reached over and opened the passenger door. He held out a hand. 'There now. I'll pull you up,' he said.

I took hold of his hand and clambered up. I felt tremendously high. I nodded at him gratefully. He smiled back. He was fat, with a great roll hanging over the waistband of his trousers.

'Right! Off we go then,' he said, starting up the engine.

'No, wait! There's my friend! We can't go without him!' I said.

'Your friend?' he said, frowning.

'Kevin. He's just coming.' I peered out of the window. 'Yes, there he is. That tall boy. He's going to London as well.'

'Oh, he is, is he? We don't want him along too, do we?' said this Uncle Mick.

'Yes, he *has* to come too!' I was getting scared he might drive off without Kevin. I put my hand on the door handle so that I could jump out quick if necessary.

'Let the boy find his own lift,' said Uncle Mick.

'No! No, I'm not going without him,' I said.

He started up the engine and I tugged hard on the handle, struggling to get it open. I was crying now, in a panic.

'Hey, stop that! No need for tears. All right, all right, we'll take the other kid too.' He leaned over me and got the door open easily. I didn't like the way he smelled close up.

Kevin came running towards us eagerly, his gait awkward because of the gun under his jacket.

'You taking us to London, mister?' he yelled.

'Looks like it, don't it?' Uncle Mick let Kevin clamber up unaided. 'Gawd, you're a right daddy-longlegs,' he said.

'Suppose I am,' said Kevin. 'Can't stop growing. See these long trousers? Brand new and they fitted perfectly, but they're already on the short side. Give it another month and I'll be showing my ankles.'

Uncle Mick was busy getting the lorry into gear and starting to drive off. Looking at him again, I liked his red face even less.

'I'm not sure I want to go to London after all,' I said in a rush. 'Kevin, let's get out now. Come on.'

'Are you nuts?' he said.

'I don't like him!' I mouthed at him.

'He's all right,' Kevin said. It was supposed to be a whisper but it sounded too loud. I glanced anxiously at Uncle Mick. If I squinted he looked like one of the big ogres in Jessica's fairy book.

'I feel too high up,' I said, putting on a little-kid whine. 'I want to get out.'

'Don't be daft. It's great. I've been in lorries heaps of times,' said Kevin. 'My dad's got this mate who's a lorry driver. He gives me a lift sometimes. I think I'll be a lorry driver when I grow up. It must be smashing, having your own set of wheels and driving up and down the country delivering stuff. Driving all through the night! Best job in the world!' He grinned at Uncle Mick.

'I wouldn't go that far, mate. But it has its perks,' he said.

I wished Kevin was sitting next to Uncle Mick instead of me. I edged as far away from him as I possibly could, until I was squashed uncomfortably against bony Kevin.

'Budge up, Shirl,' said Kevin. He carried on chatting to Uncle Mick, going my-dad-this and my-dad's-mate-that. It was very boring, but Uncle Mick nodded now and then, even commenting occasionally. But then he started yawning elaborately, taking great noisy gulps of air and making a noise like a zoo animal.

'You all right, mate?' Kevin asked.

'Just a bit tired, that's all. Reckon I'd better take a bit of a break. I've been up since five this morning. I'll pull up at the next layby,' he said.

But when we came to a layby there was another lorry there, and Uncle Mick drove on.

'There was plenty of room for us too,' said Kevin.

'Yes, I know, but there's a better place a bit further on. You'll see,' he said.

He turned off the main road and stopped the lorry halfway up a lane with a dense canopy of trees overhead.

'This is better, isn't it? Proper countryside now,' said Uncle Mick. 'You kids hungry?'

'I'm absolutely starving,' said Kevin.

I supposed I was too, but I was too anxious to think about my stomach now.

'What about you, Princess? Cat got your tongue?' asked Uncle Mick. 'Here, you get stuck into this.'

He reached into a bag down by his side and brought out a big slab of something wrapped in greaseproof paper. It looked grey and very stodgy. I looked at it dubiously.

'The wife's bread pudding. Can't beat it! It'll put flesh on a skellybob's ribs. Go on, try it,' he said.

I felt a bit relieved at the mention of Uncle Mick's wife. It made him seem less scary.

Kevin took a big bite and munched appreciatively. 'It's great! It's much better than Chubby's, Shirl.'

'Shirley,' I said in a very small voice. I tried one bite. It tasted damp and soggy. 'Thank you very much, Uncle Mick,' I added politely.

'Oh, it's Miss Manners now,' he said. 'Have some more. And tell you what, I'll even share my Mars bar with you. In fact, you two can have it between you. I'd like to give you kiddies a bit of a treat.'

He took the Mars bar out of his carrier bag, unwrapped it and broke it in two.

'Oh, mister, you're a true gent,' said Kevin, cramming his half into his mouth.

I wanted to refuse mine, but Mars bars were a huge treat, my absolute favourite chocolate bar. 'Thank you very much,' I repeated, nibbling at my own half.

'You're welcome, Princess,' Uncle Mick said. 'Come here

then.' He reached out and took hold of my wrist.

'Let me go,' I said.

'Oi! Leave her be!' said Kevin.

'You mind your own business.'

'She *is* my business.' Kevin got the door open and grabbed my hand. 'Come on, Shirl, scarper!'

Uncle Mick tightened his grip on me.

'Let her go, mister!' Kevin shouted. 'Or else!' He poked the shotgun out of his jacket.

'Jesus Christ!' said Uncle Mick, and ducked down, hands over his head.

'Quick, Shirl!' said Kevin.

He jumped, pulling me with him. We tumbled down onto the ground and then ran for it as fast as we could down the lane.

We heard the lorry engine spark into action.

'He's coming after us!' I gasped. 'Quick, let's get off the road!'

We jumped over the ditch and started haring through the trees. It was getting dark so it was hard to see the twisty tree roots and the thick growth of nettles and brambles. We were stung and scratched and kept tripping, but somehow kept going.

At last, when we could hardly breathe, we sat leaning against a big oak, holding hands, listening for footsteps. We heard an owl hooting, and small rustles in the bushes – maybe rabbits or stoats or weasels – but nothing else.

'I think he must have driven off,' Kevin whispered.

'Oh, I hope so!' I breathed. I hung onto him. 'I couldn't

believe it when you threatened to shoot him!'

'I wouldn't have really done it. Well, I don't think so,' he said.

'Didn't it take him by surprise! His face! I wouldn't have got away otherwise, he had hold of me so fast. You were brilliant, Kev.'

'Kev*in*!' said Kevin – and then we both doubled up, laughing hysterically.

'Shh! He could be creeping up on us,' I said.

'Nah! He's not fit enough. He could never have run this far. Besides, he's scared of John Wayne here.' He patted his chest. 'He's my dad's hero. My dad's hard too. Tough as they come. He's famous in our road. You don't cross him. He ain't got a gun but he doesn't need one. Got a fist like iron,' Kevin said proudly.

I didn't like the sound of Kevin's dad at all.

Kevin felt me shiver. 'He'd never hit *you*,' he said quickly. 'He never hits girls. Muriel and Poppy can twist my dad round their little fingers.'

'Are they your sisters?' I asked, surprised. He'd never even mentioned them before.

'Not really,' he said.

'Well, that's a daft answer. Either they are or they aren't,' I said.

'Well, they're my dad's kids with *her*. The woman he lives with.' Kevin snorted contemptuously.

'Your stepmother?'

'She's not really anything to do with me,' said Kevin airily.

'She won't be stopping long, I'll bet. Then it'll just be my dad and me.'

It sounded as if she'd stopped quite a long time already if she had two little girls, but I could tell he didn't want to talk about her any more.

'Anyway, what are we going to do now? Do you think we're lost? Which way back is the road? I don't want to do hitch-hiking any more, it's too scary,' I said.

'We could try walking then,' Kevin suggested.

'We can't walk all the way to London!' I said. 'It would take days and days and days. And how would we get food? And where would we sleep at night?'

'We could eat apples off trees and pick blackberries. And beg bread and milk from farms. And sleep under hedges or up on haystacks,' said Kevin.

'Do you really think we could?' I asked.

'Of course we could,' said Kevin. 'Don't worry. I'll look after you.'

'Well, let's think about it,' I said. 'We'd better find our way out of the wood first. I don't like it being so dark!'

'We'll be all right. Come on, I'm sure it's this way.' Kevin took my hand. He sounded so confident, I was surprised to discover that he was trembling. Or was he simply shivering because it was so cold? Whether by sheer luck or actual judgement he soon steered us back to the lane.

We peered up it, looking for distant lorry lights, but it seemed completely empty. We trudged along and eventually found ourselves back on the main road.

'We'll stick to the edge of the road for a while, just so we know we're going the right way to London,' said Kevin. 'But we won't hitch any more. I'm not having you scared by any more weird old blokes.'

'Can we jump into the hedgerow whenever we hear a lorry coming anyway, just in case?' I asked.

'Good plan,' said Kevin.

There was hardly any traffic now, and it got darker and darker. There were no lights anywhere, not even when we passed houses.

'I don't like it,' I said. 'I know it's just because everyone's got black curtains up in case of bombers, but it's hard remembering there are families tucked cosily inside. It's as if we're the last people in the world.'

Then a car came along and shone its headlights on us. We both backed away, scared it was the police. But through the dazzle I could see a man and a lady and two children in the back.

'Are you two all right?' the lady called. She had a voice a bit like Mum's – trying to be posh but not quite managing. 'It's a bit dark for you to be out by yourselves, isn't it?'

'No, we're fine, missus,' said Kevin.

'You're not hitch-hiking, are you? Because it can be very dangerous,' said the man, winding down his window too.

'We're definitely not hitch-hiking,' I said.

'So what are you doing then?'

'Just . . . going for a walk,' I said lamely.

'And exactly where are you walking? I can tell from your

accent you're not local. You're from London, aren't you, dear?' said the woman.

I looked at Kevin. I thought we'd better run for it again.

'Evacuated, were you? Like our Tommy and Brenda?' She nodded at the two children in the back of the car.

I pulled at Kevin, but he was peering at their kids. He waved at the little girl and she waved back. 'Are you visiting them?' he asked.

'No fear! We're taking the poor little mites home. We just came down on a day trip, see,' said the lady. 'My George gets a special petrol allowance as he's a fire inspection officer. And we were shocked, weren't we, George? I don't think our two have had a square meal since they got here. And the couple were so strict with them too, I couldn't believe it. And they've only gone and cut off all Brenda's ringlets, her pride and joy. Had the cheek to say she had nits! I feel like suing them. It'll be years before her hair grows back, won't it, pet?'

I peered at Brenda in the back. She'd had her hair chopped off in a pudding-basin cut. It had gone a bit lopsided. I couldn't help wishing that Marilyn Henderson had been evacuated to the same household.

'So you're taking them back home now?' I asked, suddenly excited.

'Of course we are. The missus missed them like crazy anyway,' said the father. 'And there's been no bally bombing whatsoever. I think it was all propaganda. Our kids belong in their own homes.'

'So could you give us a lift back to *our* homes?' I asked.

415

'Don't tell, but we're running away from our foster-people. They were horrid to us too. They made us sleep on the floor and we just had bread and milk to eat and they're both a bit loopy, honest. Honestly. Our mum and dad are desperate to have us back but they haven't got a car so they can't fetch us.'

Kevin was staring at me, impressed. The couple looked at each other, murmuring so that we couldn't hear. Then the woman jumped out of the car and opened the rear passenger door.

'All right, I don't see why not. We Londoners have to stick together, haven't we? Hop in, then,' she said. 'Budge up, Tommy. Brenda, you'd better go on this little girl's lap.'

So we set off for London, the six of us. It was as easy as that. They chatted away to us at first. They were Mr and Mrs Baxter, and they asked us all sorts of questions. Kevin left most of the talking to me. He was preoccupied with hiding the gun under his jacket. I thought it better not to be too truthful, just in case, so I made up the first things that came into my head. I'd always been good at making things up. Kevin clucked his tongue softly.

He talked to Tommy about cowboys and I asked Brenda what books she liked, but she said she couldn't read properly yet. I thought she was a bit backward, but maybe she was just tall for her age, like Kevin. After a bit she nodded off, her shorn head resting on my shoulder. Then Tommy wriggled round and fell asleep too, noisily sucking his thumb.

I wasn't sure if Kevin was sleeping. I pretended, because I

was worn out with talking. After a bit Mr and Mrs Baxter started murmuring to each other. I listened to see if they were plotting to hand us over to a policeman once we got to London, but after a few 'Poor little kiddies' they chatted about boring things like when they'd start bringing in rationing and whether the vegetables they'd planted in their front garden would ever see the light of day.

I must have nodded off myself, because the next I knew the car was slowing down, and I was aware of big buildings all around us. I blinked, suddenly feeling sick.

'Wake up, dears. We're in London now. Whereabouts do you want to go? We live over Hackney way,' said Mrs Baxter.

'Are we anywhere near Petticoat Lane, do you think?' asked Kevin.

'You're spot-on, son. We've just passed Liverpool Street,' said Mr Baxter.

'Then can you let us out here? We're very near,' said Kevin. 'You awake, Shirl?'

'We can't just let you out by yourselves. It's so dark! You'll get lost,' said Mrs Baxter. 'We want to take you right to your front door.'

'But you can't – we're down an alley. It's all right, missus, I promise, we're less than five minutes away,' Kevin gabbled.

I couldn't tell whether he was fibbing or not. I hadn't lived in our new flat long enough to know the surroundings well. I hoped Kevin would take me home – otherwise I wouldn't have a clue where I was going. But I had to get out of the car

417

quickly in any case – I was scared I might throw up all over Brenda.

So we jumped out and thanked the Baxters and said goodnight, and they asked again and again if we were sure we'd be all right. Then at last they drove off and I could bend over in the gutter and be sick. It was awful having to do it in front of Kevin, but at least there wasn't much because I'd had so little to eat.

'You all right?' he asked anxiously, clutching the gun inside his jacket as if he were guarding me.

'Obviously not,' I said, spitting. I wished I had a hankie and my toothbrush and toothpaste.

'You poor thing,' said Kevin. 'I'm hardly ever sick. Well, I was that time I ate a cherry trifle when the custard had gone mouldy, and *then* I was sick about twenty times and you could see the cherries bobbing about in it.'

'Shut *up!*' I said sharply. I hoped I hadn't been sick down my tunic. I couldn't see in the dark. 'Do you really know where we are, Kevin?'

'Think so. It all looks different in the dark, don't it? But I think if we go up that road, past the shops, The Lamb should be on the corner,' he said.

'A lamb?' I asked, imagining some small fluffy white creature tied to a gatepost.

'It's a pub. My dad's local,' said Kevin. 'Then we live the first on the right, down Sycamore.'

'And do you know where I live? Whitebird Street?'

'Haven't got a clue. Sorry,' said Kevin.

'Oh no! So how am I ever going to find it?' I asked, panicking.

'It's OK, don't flap. We'll go to my home first. I know the way to school from there. And then *you'll* know the way from school to your house, OK?'

'Yes! You're a genius. At times,' I said.

We started walking in the darkness. It wasn't the terrifying total black of the countryside, though all the houses had their curtains pinned in place. It was a long street and I started to worry that Kevin had got muddled, but then he pointed eagerly.

'Can you make out that big building a bit like a castle? That's it, that's The Lamb.'

We drew nearer. When a man came out of the pub there was a sudden glare of light, a gust of warm, beery air and a trill of laughter.

He was tall and well built. He leaned against the wall, head bent as he lit a cigarette. We saw the tiny flare of flame outlining the shape of his trilby and his shadowy face. Kevin gave a little grunt.

'That's not your dad, is it?' I asked.

'No, but it's one of his mates,' said Kevin. He went up to him uncertainly.

'Hello, Mr Chambers,' he said. His voice sounded very young all of a sudden.

'Who are you then, kid?' He lit another match. 'Oh, you're Joe Moffat's boy. What you doing here? Going for a pint with your lady friend?' He guffawed at his silly joke.

'She's my pal Shirley,' said Kevin.

'How do you do,' said Mr Chambers, raising his hat to me in a mocking gesture. 'How come you're hanging around here, young Moffat? Thought you was sent off to the country with the other kids.'

'Yeah, well, I've come back now,' said Kevin.

'Does your dad know?'

'I'm just going home to tell him.'

'He's in the pub, son. He lost a pony in the two o'clock at Kempton yesterday and he's not got over it,' said Mr Chambers. 'Now he's already lost a tenner at cards trying to win it back.'

'Oh cripes,' said Kevin.

'You'd better get in there, see if you can bring him luck.' Mr Chambers laughed unpleasantly.

'I don't think—' Kevin started protesting, but Mr Chambers had him by the shoulders and was pushing him towards the door. 'Go on, kid.'

Kevin didn't have any choice. I followed him. The pub was so bright it made my eyes go squinty, and so smoky I started coughing. I'd never been in a pub before. I didn't think children were allowed. Mum would certainly never have allowed me. She didn't even allow Dad.

Mum said public houses were disgusting places where people got drunk and women acted shamelessly. I looked hopefully at the men leaning on the bar and sitting at the tables. Some were merry and some were morose, but none were falling-down drunk. I couldn't see any shameless women, either, though there were a couple of old ladies in squashed hats and old coats and mangy fox-fur tippets. They were laughing, showing gaps where their teeth were missing.

'Where's your dad then?' I asked.

'He'll be in the back room. That's where they play cards,' said Kevin. 'But maybe it's better to leave him alone. We could just stay in a corner here till we're sure that Chambers bloke has gone and then go out again.'

'Why? And what's this about a pony? How can he have lost it?' I asked, puzzled.

It turned out it was a cockney word for some money his dad had lost betting.

'Twenty-five *pounds*?' I repeated incredulously.

I'd thought Kevin came from a poor family, but they must surely be very rich to bear such a huge loss. I doubted my dad made that much money in a month of Sundays.

I had a clear picture of Mr Moffat now: a big man in one of those long camel-hair coats, with pinstripe trousers and shiny patent shoes. He'd wear a big black hat and puff away on a cigar, just like the gangsters Mum and I watched at the pictures. I'd always secretly rooted for them because they looked so glamorous.

'Oi, you kids! Hop it! Do you want to lose me my licence?' The landlady came bustling up. She certainly had a bust for bustling. It jiggled all over the place inside her tight lavender jumper. She jangled too, bracelets on both her plump wrists. She had blonde hair with a mauvish tint to match her outfit.

'I'm very sorry, but the gentleman outside, Mr Chambers, sent us in. We've to see Mr Moffat. This is Kevin, Mr Moffat's son,' I said, in my best grown-up voice.

'Joe Moffat's lad? Well, well,' said the landlady, shaking her head as she peered at Kevin. She raised an eyebrow as if she thought I might be fibbing.

'It's all right. I don't want to disturb my dad,' Kevin mumbled. 'Let's go, Shirley.'

'Kevin!' I couldn't understand him. He always went on and on about his dad. Why on earth didn't he want to see him now? 'He's supposed to wish his dad luck at cards,' I insisted.

'I think Joe's going to need more than one gawky lad to help him out of his troubles,' said the landlady, but she took us each by an elbow and steered us through the crowds to the back of the pub, where there was a door with a frosted-glass window. She tapped on it and then stuck her head inside. 'Visitors, lads,' she said, and pushed us through into the little room.

It was even smokier, and the men gathered round the table smelled of drink and sweat. I couldn't help wrinkling my nose. These weren't glamorous gangsters. They were mostly thin and whey-faced, with cloth caps and mufflers. One of the skinniest had red, sticky-out ears so I thought he had to be Kevin's dad – but it was the biggest man with a broken nose and mean eyes who looked up from the cards in his hand and let out a swear word. It was the rudest word ever. I'd never even heard it said aloud before.

Kevin clutched his jacket, swaying on his feet.

'What the flipping heck are *you* doing here?' said Mr Moffat. 'You're meant to be in the blooming country.' He didn't exactly use those words.

'Sorry, Dad,' Kevin said. 'I couldn't stick it. They was being mean to me so I did a runner.'

'Well, you'd better run right back because I'm not taking you. I've got enough troubles keeping one family going. Didn't

I make that plain? You've got two parents. Why don't you go and find your mother?'

'You know I don't know where she is,' Kevin mumbled.

'Have a heart, Joe,' said one of the card players. 'If the kid wasn't happy where he was billeted, then you can't blame him for wanting to come back.'

'I'll thank you not to stick your nose in,' said Kevin's dad. 'The kid's never happy, wherever he is. When his mum pushed off he was forever wailing for her and wetting the bed, the dirty little tyke. I'm not wishing that on my Lil, not now we've got the two girls. You go back to whoever's been looking after you.'

'I only came to wish you luck at poker, Dad,' said Kevin. His face was contorted because he was trying not to cry.

'*You* wish me luck? You jinxed me right from the day you was born!' said his father.

'Come on, Kev,' I said. I stared at Mr Moffat. 'You're the worst dad in the whole world!' I declared. 'Kevin should thank his lucky stars he doesn't live with you any more.'

There was a sudden shocked silence. Then some of the men started tittering uneasily.

Kevin grabbed me, looking at his father. 'Quick!' he said, and we both shot out of the frosted-glass door, through the pub and out the front.

We ran down the street. Kevin was making funny gulping sounds. After a while he had to slow down. He fumbled with his jacket and I saw the glint of the gun in the moonlight. He was taking aim, pretending to fire.

'Who are you shooting?' I panted. 'Your dad?'

'All of them,' Kevin cried.

'But not me,' I said.

'Of course not you.'

'But put the gun away just in case you do it by accident,' I said. 'You're a bit het up.'

'No I'm not,' said Kevin, but he sat down on the kerb and buried his face in his hands.

I took the gun, wrapped it back in the jacket and then sat down beside him. 'Now you're the one needing a hankie,' I said.

Kevin made a funny snorting sound.

'Don't, Kev!' I begged.

'I'm not crying, I'm laughing. You're the only person in the whole of London who's ever dared badmouth my dad – a little girl!'

'I'm not that little,' I said. 'And I hope you don't mind me saying this, Kevin, but he's *horrible.*'

'I know,' he said, sniffing.

'So why do you always go on about him as if he's so marvellous?'

'Well, because – because he's my dad. And everyone looks up to him,' said Kevin.

'So did you think he'd be pleased to see you?'

'Not really. But I sort of hoped . . . I had this thing in my head that he might have missed me. I kept thinking about him giving me a hug, saying, "Welcome back, son," and all that stuff. I knew he wouldn't, but I sort of made it up so hard I believed he might. I know it sounds mad,' said Kevin.

'No, it's not mad at all. I do that too. Like when I made myself believe I could do ballet,' I said.

'Yeah, you did make a bit of a fool of yourself,' said Kevin tactlessly. 'But I clapped, didn't I?'

'Yes, you did. You're a great pal.'

'And so are you, sticking up for me like that – to my dad, of all people. So what am I going to do now, eh?'

'Simple,' I said. 'Come home with me.'

WE WALKED TO OUR old school. I couldn't really see it properly in the dark, but I could sense it there, and almost smell the chalk and plimsolls and sour milk scenting the corridors. Then it was my turn to be the leader, trying to remember my way home.

All the while I prayed fervently in my head: *Please let Mum be happy to see me and please let her not mind Kevin too much.* The streets were mostly empty. London had become a ghost town. Nowhere seemed to be open. Whenever a lone man or a couple passed us we strode out purposefully, as if we'd been sent out on an important mission, so that nobody stopped us. When we turned into Whitebird Street we heard firm footsteps coming towards us and saw what looked like a very tall man with a strange head. Or was it a helmet?

'A copper!' Kevin whispered, and whisked me up an alleyway. We leaned against the cold brick wall, hands clasped tight, waiting until the footsteps had receded.

It felt extraordinary to have become the sort of person who had to hide from the police. I was on the run, a girl with a friend who had a real gun! I felt oddly light-headed and insubstantial in the dark, as if the real Shirley were tucked up safely in bed dreaming this adventure.

Kevin's hand was clammy in mine. 'Your mum won't mind me tagging along too, will she?' he whispered. 'Because I'll scarper if you like.'

'Oh, Kevin, don't be silly. Where would you go?'

'I've got friends – all sorts of mates,' he boasted. 'No need to worry about me. And I've got my old pal here to take care of me.' He patted the gun. It sounded suspiciously like a line out of a cowboy film.

'You're sticking with me,' I said. 'Come on.'

We crept back down the alleyway and peered out cautiously, worrying that the policeman might be lurking there to nab us. But he seemed to have carried on down the street. We walked on too. The houses all looked identical. I was scared I wouldn't find the right one. I couldn't see the house numbers at all. Ours had a little privet hedge at the front, and all the tenants had to take it in turns to trim it, though Mum said she didn't know what to do now that Dad had joined up.

I put out my hand, feeling along the brick walls, waiting for the springy touch and odd peppery smell of privet.

'Ah! Here we are!' I said.

Kevin was trying to peer at the house in the dark. 'It's ever so big!' he muttered.

'No it's not. We don't live in all of it, just the first floor,' I whispered. There was no light in our windows, but then it was hard to tell with the blackout curtains.

'Even so,' said Kevin. 'I knew you were posh, Shirley.'

'You tell my mum that and she'll be thrilled,' I said.

I walked up the five stone steps. I didn't have a key to the communal front door. I knocked tentatively, not wanting to make too much noise in the silent street. I wasn't sure how late it was, and neither Kevin nor I had a watch.

The door opened quite quickly, and I saw in the dim hallway light that it was Miss Jessop from the basement. She'd probably been squinting up at us through her curtains. Mum said she was a right old busybody, always wanting to know everyone's business, but I quite liked her because she always gave me a Blue Bird toffee when she saw me.

'Oh, my! It's little Shirley, isn't it?' she said. 'Have they sent you back already? And who's this with you?'

'This is my friend Kevin,' I said.

'Goodness gracious! Have you travelled all the way from the country by yourselves? You look exhausted! Come in with me and I'll find you both a toffee,' she said eagerly.

'Thank you, but I think we'd better go up to see Mum. I want to surprise her,' I said quickly.

Miss Jessop giggled. 'Of course, silly of me. And I think Mummy's got a little surprise for *you*!'

I didn't understand what she meant. I didn't care. I suddenly desperately wanted my mum. My legs had a will of their own. I bounded upstairs, with Kevin lumbering beside me and Miss Jessop peering up after us.

I didn't have a key to our flat, either, but we kept a spare under the *Welcome* doormat so it was simple to let myself in. It was very quiet and dark in the sitting room. The chairs were empty. Had Mum already gone to bed?

'Mum?' I called, and dashed along to the bedroom.

I heard someone stirring inside. 'Mum, oh, Mum!' I ran into the room. There was Mum in bed! I could just about make out her dark hair on the pillow. But there was Mum getting out of bed, hastily putting on her pyjamas. *Two* Mums? No, it wasn't another Mum. It was a man!

Jessica's voice echoed inside my head. Was this man *Uncle Gerald*?

'What are you doing here?' I shouted. 'Get out of my mum's bedroom!'

'Yes, scarper or else! I've got a gun!' Kevin shouted.

The man snapped on the bedside lamp. He stared open-mouthed at me, and at Kevin brandishing his shotgun. 'Oh my flaming aunt!' he said.

It wasn't Uncle Gerald.

'Dad! Oh, Dad!' I said, and I flew into his arms.

'Dear goodness, what on earth is going on?' said Mum, sitting up in bed, her hair all tousled. 'Boy, put that wretched gun down this minute! Don't you dare come brandishing that silly toy in my house, frightening the life out of us.'

'That's no toy, it's a proper shotgun,' said Dad. 'Give it here, son, quick.'

He set me aside gently and examined the gun, opening it up. 'It's loaded too! Where did you get hold of this? You didn't steal it, did you?'

'No, it's Chubby's gun – she kills rabbits with it – but, Dad, what are you doing here, have you left the army, oh, I'm so glad it's you, I thought—' Luckily I stopped my frantic gabble just in time.

'Calm down, sweetheart! I've got a forty-eight-hour pass before we get sent off to do our bit. I only got here yesterday. It was a shock discovering you'd been dispatched to the country! I was going to travel down to see you tomorrow – but now here you are!'

'And why *are* you here? You wouldn't blooming budge before when I trailed all the way to fetch you!' said Mum. 'And why on earth did you bring this wretched boy? Have you taken leave of your senses?'

Kevin blinked at her. Then his face crumpled. Tears poured down his cheeks and he made an awful wailing noise. 'No one wants me. No one in the whole world,' he sobbed.

'I want you, Kevin!' I said. 'You're my best-ever friend and we'll stick together, you and me!'

'Really?' he gasped.

'Good for you, Shirley!' said Dad. 'Come here, son. Dear, oh dear, it sounds as if you've been through more wars than a battalion of soldiers. Have a hug, matey.' He put his arms round Kevin and patted him on the back. Kevin clung to him, sniffling.

'Oh, my,' said Mum, putting on her dressing gown. 'I think we could all do with a cup of tea.'

We sat round the kitchen table, drinking our tea and eating Garibaldi biscuits.

'That's it, Kevin – there's nothing like a squashed-fly biscuit to cheer a man up when he's down,' said Dad.

Kevin had clearly never heard of the nickname because he laughed uproariously, even though tears were still dripping down his cheeks. He sat very close to Dad.

Mum reached out and pulled me onto her knee. 'How did you *get* here, Shirley? Who gave you the train fare?' she asked, rubbing her cheek against the top of my head.

I wriggled a little. I decided it might be better to fib. 'Mrs Waverley kept giving us pocket money so we used that,' I mumbled, hoping Kevin wouldn't be daft enough to contradict me.

'She's got more money than sense, that woman,' said Mum. 'Dear Lord, my heart's thumping at the thought of you travelling on a train all by yourself!'

If she knew about the uncle in the lorry, her heart would thump right out of her chest, I thought.

'So what are we going to do with you?' she said. 'Gerald's aunt in the Cotswolds has taken in another couple of kiddies, but perhaps he knows of someone else in the village.'

'For goodness' sake, Doris, we don't need this Gerald bloke interfering,' said Dad. He didn't sound keen on Uncle Gerald, either.

Mum didn't snap at him. She even patted his arm. 'So what do you suggest?' she asked, quite meekly for Mum.

'I suggest we all get a good night's sleep and decide what to do in the morning,' Dad said. 'Have you got a phone number for this Mrs Waverley where our Shirley's been staying? I'd better go down to the phone box at the end of the street and give her a tinkle. She'll be worried sick that the kiddies have vamoosed.'

I stared at Dad as he pulled on his trousers and jacket over his pyjamas and jingled his pockets looking for change for the telephone. He seemed different to the old Dad, even though he'd only been away for a short time. He seemed less vague and dithery, more in charge, somehow.

'Do you *have* to phone?' Kevin asked tremulously. 'They were going to send me away to this hostel. And now they've called the police. And when they find out I've got the gun they'll send me to prison, won't they?'

'Not if I can help it, lad,' said Dad. 'I don't think you've done anything so very dreadful. I'm sure you just borrowed the gun for protection. Damn silly thing to do, mind, but understandable in the circumstances. I'll speak up for you, don't you worry. If Shirley says you're her friend, then you're practically part of the family.'

He clapped Kevin on the shoulder and went out to make the call. Mum poured us another cup of tea. When Kevin made to take a sip I shook my head surreptitiously at him. I was terribly worried he might have an accident in the night. Mum seemed to be tolerating him now, but she wouldn't if he wet the old put-you-up sofa she was making up with a sheet and blanket.

Dad was all smiles when he came back. 'Those poor women were so relieved!' he said. 'They were going spare, especially when they realized you'd gone missing too, Shirley. That Mrs

433

Waverley was crying her eyes out on the other end of the phone.'

'That's because I broke her little doll,' I said.

'You broke her doll, Shirley?' Mum repeated, shocked.

'I didn't do it deliberately! It was a terrible accident.'

'She thought *I'd* done it. Don't blame her really. I'm usually the clumsy one,' said Kevin.

'You shouldn't be so down on yourself, lad,' said Dad. He put his hand gently under Kevin's drooping chin. 'Buck up, boy! That's the spirit!'

Dad seemed so genuinely taken with him that I took him to one side while Kevin was in the bathroom.

'Dad, can you keep this a secret? Especially don't tell Mum, but Kevin sometimes has a little problem at night,' I whispered.

'What kind of problem?' Dad asked.

'Well, it's a bit embarrassing, see. He doesn't always get to the toilet in time,' I said, feeling terrible for betraying Kevin even though I was doing it for the best of reasons.

'Oh, wets the bed, does he?' said Dad.

'Shut *up*, Shirley!' said Kevin, coming out of the bathroom and looking agonized.

'It's all right, it's a common enough problem,' said Dad. 'Sometimes it even affects grown men, especially when they're nervous like. There's a chap in my unit had the same problem but the army chaplain got him sorted.'

'How? Do you have to *pray* not to wet the bed?' I asked.

'No, it was a bit of practical advice. He told him to set his alarm clock to go off two hours after he went to bed, then to jump up and try to have a jimmy riddle in a bucket. Then he reset the alarm, and did it again two hours later. And again. You get the picture. He was knackered in the morning, but he kept his bed dry. I'll fetch a bucket and you give it a go,' said Dad.

'It won't work,' said Kevin. 'Chubby tried me with that bell-and-pad thing and it was hopeless. I was already soaking by the time the bell woke me up.'

'Well, you try the clock-and-bucket army way. But we'll pop my old mackintosh under your sheet just in case it doesn't work. Though it will – you'll see.'

'Promise?' said Kevin.

'Promise,' said Dad.

It was only my dad saying it. Dad was often wrong. Mum was always pointing out his mistakes. But Kevin looked at Dad as if he were Superman. He believed him – and he didn't wet the put-you-up.

I don't know if he set the alarm clock religiously and used the bucket. I think I heard the buzz of the alarm once, but it was very faint because I wasn't in the sitting room. I started off in my own room, but that felt so strange, as if I was on a visit with a friend. The bed with the faded pink eiderdown, and the wardrobe of limp dresses, and the chest with the wonky drawers where I kept my socks and knickers and hankies, and the little ottoman full of old comics and crayons and magic painting books and jigsaw puzzles – none of them really seemed to belong to me any more.

I fell asleep quickly, snuffling into the familiar smell of my old pillow, but woke in the middle of the night feeling scared. I slipped into Mum and Dad's bedroom and got into bed between them as if I were still very little. I thought they might be cross but they both cuddled me close.

'My little Shirley,' Mum murmured.

'The jam in our sandwich. Strawberry Shirley,' said Dad.

Then we all three went to sleep and didn't wake up until breakfast time. Mum made us all egg and bacon for a treat, with lots of toast.

'Thanks ever so much, missus,' said Kevin. 'That was smashing. I like it here. I wish I could stay here for ever.' He looked at Mum and Dad wistfully.

'You must come and visit us often when this pesky war is over,' said Dad. 'But until it is you both need to be somewhere safe. They're calling this a phoney war, but us army chaps know better. There's going to be bombing on a big scale, just you wait and see.' He squeezed Mum's hand. 'I wish you'd move out to the country for the duration, Doris.'

'I've got my job to do here,' said Mum. She looked up at the kitchen clock and tutted. 'I'm late already, but I daresay Gerald will understand. Now, you children need to go back. Your dad's taking you, Shirley. I'm still not that keen on those women at the Red House, but Meadow Ridge itself seems a nice enough place. Perhaps your dad can have a chat with the billeting officer and find you somewhere more normal like.'

'Can you find us another school too, Dad?' I asked, though I knew there was only one school in the village. I burned when I remembered them laughing at my ballet.

'You've gone all red, Shirley!' said Mum. 'What is it?'

'I just . . . don't want to leave here,' I said, which was true too.

436

It was awful saying goodbye to Mum all over again. I clung to her until Dad had to gently unclasp my arms. He was saying goodbye to Mum as well, planning to go straight back to his barracks after he'd left us in the country. He didn't give her his usual peck on the cheek. He gave her a real long film-star kiss right in front of us. Mum was quite pink when he eventually let her go, but she didn't seem to mind.

We caught the bus to the railway station as Dad was loaded down with his kitbag. He stowed Chubby's gun in it too, after taking the cartridges out. It felt so odd being back at the station again. The last time, the concourse had been crowded with hundreds and hundreds of children with little suitcases and labels on their coats. Now it seemed almost empty.

We queued to get our tickets and I felt bad when I saw just how much Dad had to pay.

'I'm sorry we've caused all this fuss, Dad,' I said as the train set off. 'As the tickets were so expensive, you don't need to give me a Christmas present.'

'Right you are,' said Dad. 'But Santa Claus might have other ideas.'

'Don't tell me you believe in Santa Claus!' said Kevin.

'Of course I do – and you'd better start believing in him too, matey, because I think he's made a special early trip to you. See what I've got here?' Dad fumbled in his kitbag and brought out a parcel wrapped in crumpled Christmas paper. I recognized the little robins and snowmen from last year. The parcel was a funny, roundish sort of shape.

'That's not for me!' said Kevin. 'It's for Shirley, isn't it?'

'Well, you're right, Shirley's got a present too,' said Dad, fishing around for it.

Mine was a bigger parcel. I knew that shape all right! 'It's a book!' I squealed.

'I popped into a newsagent's on the way home and they had a whole shelf of children's books. I know what you're like with your reading, Shirley! It's got heaps of stories in so they should keep you going for a while,' said Dad. 'Have a peep at it then.'

It was *The Bumper Book for Girls*. I wasn't always that keen on short stories, but I spotted one written by Noel Streatfeild, my *Ballet Shoes* lady.

'Thank you ever so much, Dad! It's fantastic!' I said, giving him a hug.

'Is mine a book too?' asked Kevin.

'Well, lad, it doesn't look like a book, does it? And does it sound like a book? Hold it up to your ear and see if you can hear any stories,' said Dad.

'That's daft,' said Kevin, but he held his package up all the same. His mouth opened. 'It *is* saying something. Well, it's ticking!'

'I hope Santa hasn't given you a bomb!' said Dad. 'Better have a quick look to see if we need to chuck it out the window.'

Kevin cautiously opened his parcel and drew out Mum and Dad's alarm clock – the round chrome one with little legs they'd been given as a wedding present. 'Your clock?' he whispered.

'I know, it's a bit of a daft present, my old clock, but I wasn't sure if you had one yourself. I thought it would be useful if you have to keep waking yourself up. It's got a good tick, that clock. It keeps you company if you wake up in the middle of the night.'

'It's the best present ever,' Kevin mumbled. He seemed overwhelmed. 'You don't mind giving me your clock?'

'Of course not,' said Dad heartily. I knew it was a present from my Auntie Mavis, his favourite sister, and he'd always treasured it. I loved that clock myself actually. For a second I wished Dad had given it to me instead, but when I looked at Kevin's face I knew he'd chosen right.

The first journey to Meadow Ridge had seemed endless, but somehow today it seemed more speedy. The train chugged steadily on its way, with no stopping and starting, and Dad kept us busy. First we played I-Spy, which passed the time, though I was painfully reminded of Jessica. I was the best at I-Spy. Then we played Famous People, and Dad was the best at that. And then we played I Went to Market, and Kevin was surprisingly good at remembering ridiculously long lists and won three times in a row.

'You're showing us up, Mr Memory Man,' said Dad, clapping him on the back.

Kevin went scarlet and grinned at him. I'd never seen him look so happy. But when the train drew into Meadow Ridge station and we started the long trudge through the village and up the hill he walked as if he were wearing lead boots.

'Step out, lad,' said Dad, shifting his kitbag to his other shoulder.

'I don't want to,' said Kevin. 'They're going to be angry with me.'

'The two ladies? Yes, I expect so. You've given them an awful fright. Plus you borrowed their shotgun. Though it seems a damn daft idea to me, leaving it lying around where any curious boy could find it.'

'Well, Chubby hid it actually. In the henhouse. But I found the hiding place. I'm always in the henhouse. I quite like them funny birds. I'll miss them when I'm sent away to this hostel,' said Kevin.

'Why's that exactly?'

'Because they thought I'd broken the lady's doll.'

'A grown woman fussing about a doll? And I believe it was our Shirley who did the deed, not you,' said Dad.

'They'll send me packing anyway,' said Kevin. He lowered his voice. 'Because I wet the bed.'

'But you don't any more.'

'And they don't like me. No one does,' said Kevin mournfully.

'That's just plain nonsense. There are two people right here who like you, lad. Shirley and me. And if you mind your p's and q's and make yourself useful about the house and tend those chickens, then those ladies will be glad to have a big strong lad like you around the house,' said Dad.

I loved it that Dad was trying to reassure Kevin, though I didn't quite believe him. I'm not sure Kevin did, either, but he stepped out more smartly, and insisted on taking a turn carrying Dad's kitbag. He could hardly lift it, but Dad tactfully let him stagger a few yards with it before claiming it back.

'Thanks so much, son. You've given me a nice rest. Very sporting of you,' he said.

Dad had to take several more rests before we got to the Red House driveway. He was tremendously impressed with the grounds.

'It's like a stately home!' he said. 'Your mum said it was big, Shirley, but this is massive! So what's the house like? Buckingham blooming Palace?'

'It's not like a palace,' I said, thinking of the towers and turrets pictured in Jessica's fairy-tale book. 'It's a *house* house – but big.'

'And empty,' said Kevin. 'Most of the rooms haven't got a stick of furniture.'

'Did this Mrs Waverley run out of money then?' asked Dad.

'No, she's tragic. She couldn't bear to finish it when Mr Waverley died in the last war. She's never been quite right since,' I said.

'She *was* in a state last night on the phone, but you had given her a fright. Still, if she's permanently a bit doolally I can see why your mum wants to move you somewhere else.' Dad took a deep breath. 'Oh dear, this is going to be embarrassing.'

He looked a bit sweaty now, and when we got to the front door he quickly mopped his face and adjusted his army cap before reaching for the door knocker. Almost immediately the door was flung open. Archie hurtled forward, arms outstretched.

'Kev!' he yelled, and he leaped up and clung to Kevin like a little monkey. 'Chubby was scared you'd gone and shot yourself dead but you've come back!'

'Yes, you gave us the fright of our lives, you little beggar,' said Chubby. She stood on tiptoe to give him a cuff, but then took hold of his chin and waggled his head. 'What are we going to do with you, eh, you great daft lummox? And as for you, missy!' She turned to me. 'First Kevin disappears, then you prance off too, and send us demented. Poor Mrs Mad! She blamed herself, poor soul.'

'I'm so sorry, both of you,' said Mrs Waverley, running across the hallway. In her good suit and suede shoes, with her hair tidied back in a roll, she looked relatively normal. But then she saw Dad standing on the doorstep with us, and she stopped dead. 'Oh!' she said. 'Oh my goodness!'

'Mad! Get a grip!' said Chubby sharply. 'It's Shirley's father. You knew he was bringing the kiddies.'

'Yes, but he looks—'

'It's just the uniform,' Chubby told her. 'Calm down now. Let's all go into your sitting room and I'll make us a cup of tea.'

'There's ginger man biscuits too!' said Archie. 'I gave them currant buttons, didn't I, Chubby? And there's a little boy ginger man just like me!'

'Yes, I'm so sorry. Do come in,' said Mrs Waverley, back to being a polite hostess, though she was very pale and shivering.

Dad was nervous too. After he'd taken off his cap he kept slicking back his hair, and he sat right on the edge of the sofa, as if he was scared of dirtying it. Kevin sat very close to him, and hardly said anything. When Chubby served the drinks and biscuits Kevin clutched his glass of lemon barley water, but managed to stick his little finger out every time he took a sip, trying to be genteel. I was on edge too, thinking of the miniature sitting room upstairs and wondering if the man doll was lying wounded on the chaise longue, his empty sleeve dangling. Even Chubby seemed tense, continuously glancing at Mrs Waverley.

Archie was the only one acting naturally, skipping around the sitting room with his gingerbread boy, giving a little running commentary each time he took a bite: 'Now I'm biting off his foot and he's going, *Oh, oh, that tickles – where's my foot gone?* and I say, *In my tummy and it's sooooo delicious*, and the foot in my tummy says, *I'm lonely all by myself,* so I'm biting off the other foot now, and my gingerbread boy says, *Oh, oh, that tickles and—*'

'Give it a rest, Archie!' said Chubby, shaking her head at him. But then she said proudly, 'He's very bright for his age, isn't he?'

'I can see you're doing a grand job looking after him,' said Dad. 'But I wonder . . . maybe the older two might be too much work for you. I know you've had a few problems with Kevin here, and my Shirley can be a bit of a madam at times, bless her. Perhaps I can find them another billet . . .'

'Oh dear!' Mrs Waverley looked stricken. 'I've so enjoyed having Shirley here. I hoped she could stay.'

My tummy turned over. I clutched my gingerbread man tightly. 'But you were so upset with us,' I said. 'Do you *really* want us back?'

'Of course I do,' she said. 'I've enjoyed having you here enormously. You're like a special little friend.'

'Then I'd love to stay with you!' I said, so relieved that she still liked me.

'She doesn't want me though,' Kevin muttered.

'*I* want you,' said Chubby. 'Gawd knows why, because you've been nothing but trouble, but you're a kind lad and I know you mean well. I felt awful when you took off, taking my gun. What have you done with it?'

'I've unloaded it and brought it back in my kitbag,' said Dad. 'I hope you'll keep it somewhere safer in future.'

'There's no need to tick me off about it! I've given myself a right telling-off. What if little Archie had got hold of it? He's been missing you something terrible, Kevin. You're like a big brother to him now,' said Chubby.

'So there won't be any more talk of sending the lad to this hostel?' said Dad.

'I think Kevin's home is with us,' said Mrs Waverley.

Kevin had gone chalk white but his mouth widened into a huge grin.

'Good. That's all settled then,' said Dad, visibly relieved. He looked at his watch. 'I'd better be going soon. I've got to catch the train back to London and then get another to my barracks. And then I'm off tomorrow.'

'Oh, Dad!' I said. 'I don't want you to go and fight!'

'I'm not sure I want to go, either, Shirley, but what can you do? There's a war on,' said Dad.

'You're a very brave man, Mr Smith. Please keep very safe. And rest assured, we'll be giving the children every care and attention,' said Mrs Waverley earnestly. She even took hold of his hand, repeating, 'Keep very, very safe.'

At the door I gave him a big hug and lots of kisses. Kevin gave Dad a hug too. We were both near tears.

'You two try to stay out of mischief,' said Dad. 'I'll come and see you my next leave.'

'Promise?' said Kevin. 'You'll come and see me too?'

Dad mimed, *See my finger wet, see my finger dry, cut my throat if I tell a lie.* Then he took the gun and cartridges out of his kitbag, handed them to Chubby, stood up straight and saluted us.

'I'll give you a lift to the station in my car,' said Mrs Waverley.

'Are you sure you're OK to drive, Mrs Mad?' asked Chubby.

'Of course I am.'

'I can easily walk to the station. I don't want to be any trouble,' said Dad.

'It's no trouble at all,' Mrs Waverley insisted.

It was horrible watching the car drive away. I waved and waved, even after the car had turned the corner and I couldn't see it any more. Chubby put her arm round my shoulders, surprising me.

'It's awful saying goodbye, isn't it?' she said. 'Especially when they're going off to war.'

'Especially for Mrs Waverley, when her husband didn't come back. She must have loved him so passionately,' I said.

Kevin and Archie trailed off to the kitchen, squirming at this mention of love and passion. Chubby called Archie, but he took no notice. She let him go, sighing. They were making silly kissing noises, egging each other on.

'Boys! Let's see if there's any tea left in the pot,' said Chubby, going back into the sitting room.

She poured the dregs into her cup.

'I love my dad,' I said. 'I'm scared he won't come back.'

'Now don't you worry. All our men will come back from this war, you'll see. And it'll be over soon. Your dad will be safe and sound. He's a grand man,' said Chubby. She was obviously much keener on my dad than my mum.

'Was Mr Waverley a grand man?' I asked.

'In some ways,' said Chubby, sounding rather odd. She reached for the silver cigarette box on Mrs Waverley's table, felt for a box of matches in her apron pocket and lit herself a cigarette, breathing in deeply.

'I didn't know you smoked!' I said.

'I don't,' said Chubby. She poured herself a sherry from the cut-glass decanter too. 'I don't drink, either. I just feel the need now and then.'

'It must have been dreadful for Mrs Waverley to lose her husband – she's still so sad about it now,' I said.

'Yes. It was dreadful,' said Chubby, drinking.

'And she gave up everything for him too,' I said without thinking.

'Who's been gossiping to you, eh? Why can't people mind their own business!'

'He must have been pretty wonderful if she was willing to go against her family and have everyone disapprove of her.'

'He wasn't wonderful,' said Chubby. 'But he had charm. And he was very good-looking too, which always turns a girl's head.' She finished her sherry in three gulps and then poured herself another.

'Did you know him then?' I asked.

446

'Course I did. Everyone knew Will Waverley. We went to the same school. Will was the golden boy even then. Fell on his feet when he got the junior gardening job at the White House. Then young Maddy took a fancy to him, same as all the girls in the village. He couldn't believe his luck!'

'Don't! Don't say it like that. Like he didn't really love her,' I protested.

'Oh, he loved her all right, in his way. But let's say it helped that she was an heiress. When they found she was intent on marrying Will, they stopped her allowance, but she had money from some great-aunt and they couldn't take that away from her. She bought this house built bang on the opposite hill, bold as brass, and started setting it up when he went to France. Then the telegram came. And she stopped. Everything stopped. It broke her heart. She's never been right since.' Chubby sniffed.

'Don't you feel desperately sorry for her?' I asked.

'Of course I do. But it's not as if she's the only one. Thousands of women lost their loved ones in that war,' said Chubby. She paused. 'I lost my sweetheart too.'

I thought of the photograph tucked inside her Bible. 'I'm sorry,' I said timidly. 'That must have been awful for you. But so much worse for poor Mrs Waverley. Her heart was broken.'

'Mine was too.' Chubby stubbed out her cigarette and poured a third drink. Her eyes were glittering, her voice a little thicker. 'It was worse for me. I was having his baby!'

'What?' I stared at her, shocked. 'You were having your sweetheart's baby?'

447

'I was having *Will's* baby,' said Chubby, sticking her chin in the air and staring back at me defiantly.

'Oh, Chubby, how could you!' I said.

'I didn't work for Mrs Mad then. I was a kitchen maid at the White House. And Will was mine long before *she* took a fancy to him. She knew we were sweethearts too,' said Chubby.

The room seemed to be whirling as I tried to take it all in.

'I hated her then. I daresay she hated me too. So I still saw Will – I couldn't resist him. So there I was, left high and dry, six months gone, in a village full of gossips. I was dismissed as soon as the people at the White House found out. My own folk wanted me to go away and give up the baby once it was born, but I wasn't having that. Then Mrs Mad came to see me. She'd heard about my situation. She said I could come and work for her, and she'd help me look after the baby.'

'That's amazing!'

'I think she just wanted to get her hands on Will's baby. She was the last woman in the world I wanted to work for. But I didn't have any place else, so off I toddled. I thought I'd wait till the baby was born and then leave when I'd got a bit saved for both of us.' Chubby's voice wavered. She bent her head. 'Only the baby came too soon. It was too little. It died after only a few hours. And you dare say I don't know about heartbreak?'

I shook my head helplessly. I wanted to keep on shaking it until I was free of all this new, terrifying information. It was all too grown up for me.

'So do you still hate Mrs Waverley now?' I whispered.

'Don't be daft. She let me stay on. She nursed me because I was poorly for weeks after the baby died. I'd have been lost without her. I care about her like a sister – and she cares for me too. We couldn't cope without each other. Two daft old biddies doddering along – until you three arrived on our doorstep and shook us all up.'

There was a distant crash from the kitchen, and boys' guilty laughter.

'What are they up to now? I'd better go and see to them. Mrs Mad will be back any minute,' said Chubby, standing up. She took the used ashtray and her sherry glass with her. 'Don't you dare say a word about this to her or I'll have your guts for garters.'

'I swear I won't,' I said.

'And you won't tell anyone else?'

'I promise.'

I kept the promise too. I didn't even feel tempted to tell Kevin. I didn't think he'd understand, and of course Archie was too little. And though I started to make friends with a few of the girls at school, I couldn't share a secret like that. Marilyn Henderson stayed a bitter enemy. She still executed a mocking pirouette whenever I came near her, but the others had stopped teasing me now.

I didn't confide in Jessica, though I knew she'd have been riveted. We wrote to each other frequently. She sounded so happy, back with her nanny. She didn't even have to go to school, the lucky thing. Her mother organized a governess for her instead. She wrote pages and pages about all the books she was reading. She said she'd always love *Ballet Shoes* but she was really into adult novels now as they were more interesting, full of romance and tragedy.

I felt I'd had enough real tales of romance and tragedy. I read *The Bumper Book for Girls* and Jessica's *Blue Fairy Book*. I read *A Little Princess* and *Black Beauty* and *Alice in Wonderland* and *Peter and Wendy*. I read *Orlando*. I read *The Squirrel, the Hare and the Little Grey Rabbit* again and again. It wasn't just because the pretty blue print was wonderfully easy to read. It was also wonderfully easy to understand. The only thing to worry about was Weasel, and he was bad because he caught and killed little animals. Little Grey Rabbit was good, even though she shoved Weasel into his own hot oven, because it served him right. It was such a relief knowing who was good and who was bad. None of the animals had love affairs or betrayed each other or went funny in the head with heartbreak.

Mrs Waverley continued to have good days and bad days, but she never turned on me again. She sometimes spoke about Mr Waverley.

'He was the most handsome man ever, Shirley, just like a prince. If *only* I had a photo of him!'

She obviously didn't know about the photograph in Chubby's Bible, which I now knew was of Will. I wondered about telling her, but thought better of it. It was Chubby's special secret, after all. And it would be painful for Mrs.Waverley, seeing her Will literally sweeping Chubby off her feet.

Mrs Waverley still invited me into the locked room to look at the doll's house with her. I didn't dare touch anything now, not even a chair or tiny candlestick, but I stared and stared.

She had fashioned a tiny sling for the man doll so he looked as though he really had a broken arm. The lady doll didn't seem to mind in the slightest.

I wished I hadn't smashed up my own shoebox doll's house. Mrs Waverley agreed it was a great shame. She suggested I do some dusting and tidying for the daughter at the draper's shop, and in return she found me *five* empty shoeboxes.

I turned four of them into a big house with a red roof (I coloured in the tiles with a red pen). I tried my hand at making clothes-peg dolls. I made a Mrs Waverley doll with grey wool hair and gave her a sitting room with a luxurious pink-silk chaise longue made from a torn scarf stuffed with cotton wool. I used a little peg for Chubby, and crayoned scruffy little slippers at the end of each prong. I turned the smallest peg into an Archie doll, sticking a curly yellow hen feather on his peg head because he had proper hair now.

I saved the longest peg for Kevin. I was going to stick big red ears on either side of his head, but decided not to in case it hurt his feelings. I gave my own doll brown-wool hair right down to her waist, even though my hair had still only grown a couple of inches.

I made the last shoebox into my flat at home in London. I begged more pegs from Chubby, though she was getting irritated by now and said that at this rate she wouldn't have any left to hang out the washing. I made a Mum doll with a perm and red pen lipstick and a Dad doll with army uniform made out of an old grey sock I found at school.

Sometimes the Shirley doll lived in the big house with the red roof. Sometimes she trekked across the floorboards to the little flat in London to live with Mum and Dad. And some-times she let the Kevin doll come to London with her. Archie stayed in the big house with Chubby and Mrs Waverley. That way I hoped everyone would be happy. After reading all those fairy tales I believed in happy endings. The war would be over soon. Although the little holiday was lasting longer than I'd expected.

Have you read Hetty Feather's five amazing adventures?

HETTY FEATHER

Victorian orphan Hetty is left as a baby at the Foundling Hospital – will she ever find a true home?

SAPPHIRE BATTERSEA

Hetty's time at the Foundling Hospital is at an end – will life by the sea bring the happiness she seeks?

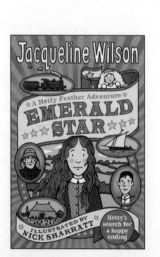

EMERALD STAR

Following a tragedy, Hetty sets off to find her father – might her sought-after home be with him?

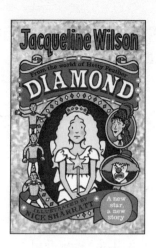

DIAMOND

Life at the circus is too much for Diamond to bear. Could her beloved Emerald hold the key to a brighter future?

LITTLE STARS

The bright lights of the music hall beckon – will Diamond and Hetty become real stars?

You might also like . . .

CLOVER MOON

Clover's chance meeting with an artist gives her an inspiring glimpse of another world – but will she have the courage to leave her family and find a place that really feels like home?

VISIT JACQUELINE'S FANTASTIC WEBSITE

There's a whole Jacqueline Wilson town to explore! You can generate your own special username, customize your online bedroom, test your knowledge of Jacqueline's books with fun quizzes and puzzles, and upload book reviews. There's lots of fun stuff to discover, including competitions, book trailers, and Jacqueline's scrapbook. And if you love writing, visit the special storytelling area!

Plus, you can hear the latest news from Jacqueline in her monthly diary, find out whether she's doing events near you, read her fan-mail replies, and chat to other fans on the message boards!

www.jacquelinewilson.co.uk

The No.1 Mag for JW fans!

The Official **Jacqueline Wilson** Mag™

You'll love it!

GIFTS FOR YOU!
✓ Notebook ✓ Fountain pen

The Official **Jacqueline Wilson** Mag

Jacky's Story Secrets — ONLY in JW Mag!

Write with me!

MAKE! Cutest sweet treats!

Yum!

I'll help you sketch!

HOW TO DRAW with

Spring things!

Let's shop!

BEST FRIEND FUN!
Puzzles ★ Quiz ★ Story

READ WRITE CREATE

VINTAGE NAIL ART!

You can do it!

Packed with lots of stuff to make, do, read and write!